UNTIL DEATH DO US PART

MARK BOUTROS

Cover designed by Bobby Birchall at Bobby&Co

Proofread by: David Price

Edited by Nicola Hodgson at Root and Branch Editing

Print ISBN: 978-1-9162974-6-3

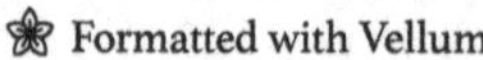 Formatted with Vellum

To Cinthia, who deserves more than a dedication, but in life we don't always get what we deserve.

CONTENTS

GET FREE BOOKS

To say thank you for buying this book, I'd like to invite you to join my exclusive *VIP Crew*, and give you some short stories for FREE.

Head on over to https://www.mark-boutros.com/freebie to claim yours.

As a member of the crew you'll get free content, updates, and no spam. I don't have the energy to spam.

If you enjoy this book, please leave a review. It helps indie authors with visibility. If you don't enjoy the book, let's just pretend you didn't read it and all move on.

PROLOGUE

THE RANK, freezing water invaded Rami's mouth as he clutched onto the corpse's ankles. He had wanted to sink the body in the river, but now it was his only hope of staying afloat.

He had always imagined he would have a family by thirty-eight, and when he had considered how he might die, he was convinced he would make it beyond seventy, with his loved ones by his side. He could understand dying young if there was a traffic accident or a sudden illness. Or maybe he could have died after rushing into a burning building to save a dog, but the dog then feeling threatened would maul him to death. This, however, was beyond miserable. Perhaps this was karma.

He coughed up more river as it assaulted his throat and nostrils. It had an earthy, musty taste, and definite notes of sewage.

The slow current dragged him and his human lilo into the night. He wanted to shout for help, but drowning seemed a better option than prison. It was hard to accurately weigh up the pros and cons while keeping his head above water.

His chest ached, the cold smothering his bones.

He had read that the Great Ouse was England's fifth most contaminated river, with chemicals ten times above safety levels.

Although this stretch, from Norfolk to the Wash, was apparently in good condition – whatever that meant. If he survived, he would probably end up with E. coli pneumonia.

He reached for the riverbank with his left leg, but it was too far. Why had he always made his mother write him notes to avoid swimming lessons at school? It was because he was ashamed of his twiggy body, and his fear of drowning. On reflection, both stupid reasons.

His survival was in the hands of the elements and the buoyancy of the corpse. He stared up at the night sky; his mouth, nose, and eyes desperately straining to stay out of the water.

The cold sapped what little strength he had. He hoped that, as the river curved, maybe they would edge closer to the bank.

His muscles spasmed, his heart raced, and he lost his grip on the corpse. Filthy water filled his mouth and jabbed his sinuses.

He fought as best he could, but a short lifetime of failure flashed before his eyes, with an array of disappointed faces staring back at him.

All Rami had ever wanted was to be loved and to inspire people to follow their dreams. Instead, he was an unlovable dream crusher.

As his body numbed and icy water consumed his head, two thoughts dominated. The first: that this was a really pathetic way to die. The second: that he wished he had never met his wife.

6 DAYS EARLIER

1
———

I DON'T LIKE THURSDAYS

Rami

Rami had read that 75 per cent of couples who did therapy were better off. However, the same article stated that 30 per cent had conflicting agendas, with one person wanting to save the marriage, and the other leaning out.

Was Mia leaning out? She was literally leaning on the rock-hard sofa arm, sat as far from him as she could. It wouldn't have surprised him if she jumped out of the window and onto Norwich city centre's colourful market tents to get further away.

The therapist had decorated her office to give the illusion of comfort, but it felt sterile. A luxury French teak lamp stood behind her, giving her and her armchair an authoritative glow. There was a small, rock water feature on the table next to her, suggesting peace, but coming across as pointless and cliché. Her certificates that could have been from anywhere covered the wall, and Rami hoped they translated into a skillset that could save his crumbling marriage.

Rami considered shuffling closer to Mia, but resisted. He

stared at the early-November frost on the window, wondering if Mia's energy had made the room colder.

If the therapist was taking note of how they sat as well as how they spoke, she had probably already marked them down as doomed.

Rami attributed meaning to everything. When the therapist sipped her water, was she blaming him or Mia? When she tapped her iPad, was she noting that they had hope, or was she bored and playing Candy Crush? When she shuffled in her armchair, was she thinking of solutions, or about how she could string them along for a few more weeks and put their money towards another luxury lamp?

He couldn't remember her name. Laura? Lou-something? No, that didn't ring any bells. He wished he could switch off his thoughts.

The therapist with an unmemorable name leaned forward, her eyes bouncing between Mia and Rami. 'So, I suggest you share more experiences,' she said in her soft Norfolk accent. It sounded more like an instruction than a suggestion.

Rami nodded and glanced at Mia, who hadn't so much as side-eyed him in thirty minutes. A flash of emotion would help him to understand whether she wanted to try. He may as well have been sat next to a bollard in a blazer.

Mia finally moved, leaning back on the sofa. 'We eat dinner together sometimes. Mostly haddock and spinach.'

Rami scratched his stubble. 'I can't eat yeast or refined sugars, and carbs before bed give me the night sweats.' It was out of necessity, not a lack of adventure.

He was sure Mia rolled her eyes, but she angled herself further away from him.

The therapist half-smiled. 'I mean get out, *together*. Try things outside of the daily routine. Drifting apart isn't uncommon – it's sadly a symptom of how our time is occupied by things that contribute to society, but don't necessarily feed the core of our relationships. You need to create new points of connection. Try a play, a trip, even something like axe throwing. Just anything, even if it's a walk.'

Mia shook her head. 'I have to prioritise work,' she said with the warmth of a dagger dipped in snow. 'One of us has to.'

Rami inhaled the jab, the negative energy likely finding a home deep in his body and doing some yet-unknown damage. Some people viewed a married couple as one entity; one being. If that was true, Mia probably saw herself as the functioning body and organs, while Rami was a case of incurable haemorrhoids.

The therapist's eyes shifted to him, expecting an answer.

'It's not exactly been easy to find work since I was blamed for Becca's death,' he said.

'I read about that,' the therapist, who may have been called Lorna, said.

Rami leaned forward. 'It doesn't matter that I was found innocent. Everyone's decided I'm as bad as the teacher from *Whiplash*, and now no university will touch me.'

The therapist gave nothing away. Another example of the accusation around Becca having more power than the evidence.

Mia remained still.

'I am tutoring, though,' Rami pointed out. 'Starting to rebuild my credibility.'

Mia's eyes shot towards him. 'Tell her the truth.'

'That is the truth,' he said.

Mia scoffed, then faced the therapist. 'He has one tutee. A pity hire from our busybody neighbour, Jenny.'

'It's not pity,' Rami said, hurt she was so quick to put him down. 'She's wanted me to help her with her screenplay for years, but I was always too busy with the course. And she's only the start. I've been putting ads around town and I'll have a website soon.'

The therapist placed the iPad on her lap and folded her

arms. Was her name Ronda? Likely not. 'Mia. Rami. Do you actually want to put the work in to improve your marriage?'

'Yes,' Rami replied without hesitation. Of course he did. Sure, it had been awful for a while, but this was part of the journey, right? It was normal to hit a wall, to go stale, to think your partner wanted a giant pigeon to fly beak-first into one of your eyeballs, piercing it and skewering your brain; but surely that was all temporary. Eight years together meant something, and he often thought back to their wedding day, six years ago, when Mia said her vows and his smile could've ripped through his cheeks.

Mia bit her lip then nodded.

An icy cold flooded Rami. It felt similar to when Mia had started bleeding thirty-one weeks into her pregnancy. That night, at 8.23 p.m. he was standing outside the locked bathroom as she wept and screamed, and he was helpless, numb from head to toe, only able to ask her what she needed. Now, he was helpless in a different way, scared to ask her why she hesitated because he feared the truth.

The therapist adjusted her shirt collar and smiled in a way that wasn't really a smile. 'Then take a break from routine. Together. And maybe introduce some variety to dinner. Obviously with your intolerances considered, Rami. This is going to take hard work and honesty, and not being hurtful. We need to find ways to express ourselves without demeaning each other.' She glanced at Mia. 'Next time we should discuss Becca's suicide, and understand how that made you feel as well.'

The therapist continued talking, but Rami couldn't focus. Why did Mia hesitate? She was leaning out.

~

The rice boiled and the chicken sizzled in its tomato sauce. The acidity from the tomatoes would definitely give Rami reflux, but he'd take it for the sake of their marriage.

He looked through his emails on his phone, trying to distract himself from Mia's hesitation and found one from the therapist with today's date: Thursday the 2nd of November. 'Samantha. That was her name.'

Mia offered a dismissive sound from the sofa on the opposite side of their open-plan kitchen and living room. She was sitting cross-legged and tapped away on her laptop. Her framed blue Mark Rothko print hung above her on the pastel green wall, adding a dull quality to the atmosphere.

Rami poured himself a glass of water and whistled the tune to the old gameshow, *Blockbusters*. He smiled, remembering their honeymoon in Istanbul, where it was the only show they managed to get on the hotel TV.

Did Mia relive any of their positive experiences? Or was she drowning in the misery of this slump? Maybe that was why she had hesitated? She wasn't as able to imagine the happiness yet to come. Rami missed them doing things together, but more than that he wanted a hug. They used to hug every day. He considered approaching her for one, but thought it was best to ask.

Mia huffed. 'Can you stop whistling, please?' she said without looking at him. At least she said "please."

Maybe he would ask for the hug later. He let the tune play in his mind, where it was safe. He wanted to ask her why she had hesitated, but right now the focus had to be on hope. The framed photos on the shelves below the TV offered him that: moments of joy from their wedding day and their holiday in Crete. He moved one, hoping it would draw her attention to them.

She remained focused on her laptop.

To her, they were probably reminders of failure.

He stared at one of the four ceiling spotlights that had been dead for months. They had planned to make so many changes to the house since he inherited it three years ago, to make it more "them". 'Do you still want to paint the walls Jasmine White?' Rami asked. 'Maybe we could do it this weekend, as a bonding thing?'

Mia tapped her laptop keys more forcefully. 'Nah, no point.'

Shut down. He would definitely tell Samantha in their next session. He grabbed the stepladder from the gap between the storage closet and the wall, then opened a drawer and found a spare spotlight.

He switched the room lights off.

'What are you doing?' Mia moaned.

'Sorting this. Won't be a second.' He set the stepladder up, climbed it and struggled to twist the spotlight out.

Water boiled over the sides of the pan. 'Shit.'

Mia tutted, rushed over to the stove and reduced the heat. 'You're meant to simmer it so it doesn't boil over.'

'I know... I know.' He changed the bulb and got down from the stepladder. 'Just got distracted.' He switched the lights on.

'For a change,' she said.

He would let her have that one.

Mia opened a drawer and took out a cloth embroidered with a Lebanese cedar tree. It was a wedding gift from Rami's nan.

'Don't use that,' he said.

Mia approached the spillage and wiped it. 'It's a cloth. It's for wiping, not decoration.'

He snatched it back, but it was soaked. 'Just use a different one, please.'

Rami knew it was weird, but this house, some paintings Mia had banished to the loft, and the cloth, were all he had left of his nan since her electric blanket had malfunctioned, reducing her and her holiday home in Canada to a charred shell. He took a breath.

Mia grabbed another cloth and wiped the overspill. 'If you

don't want people to use it, maybe stick it in a frame instead of in the drawer with the other cloths.'

She would never understand. There was something comforting, homely, about opening the drawer and seeing it in there.

The acidic smell of burning tomato sauce filled the room. 'Oh, balls.' He grabbed a wooden spoon and stirred the sauce.

'Did you follow the instructions?' Mia asked, knowing he obviously hadn't – otherwise they wouldn't be staring at ruined food.

'Yeah. I just got some bits wrong.'

Mia stared at him with the disdain normally reserved for traffic wardens. She was likely thinking of a self-esteem-deflating grenade to hurl at him. Thankfully, she just opened the freezer, removed a packet of haddock and plonked it on the kitchen counter.

Rami stared at the chicken shambles, destined to be fox food. 'At least I tried.'

'That should be your epitaph.'

And there it was.

They had been in the car for thirty-two minutes without a word. Rami hoped it was because Mia was concentrating on the moonlit roads to Great Yarmouth, but that was likely wishful thinking.

He cursed himself for screwing up dinner, but it was down to nerves. He needed to be relaxed to do things properly. Nervousness and tension created a chain reaction of useless outcomes.

He stared at the Rocky Balboa bobblehead on the dashboard. He hated the thing, but Mia had bought it and given no explanation to its significance. She didn't even like *Rocky*. Perhaps it was a sign that an underdog could overcome anything. In this case, love was the underdog trying to fight against the odds. Although, Rocky lost, so Rami stopped looking for meaning.

According to the map on Mia's phone, they would be at the pub in twelve more minutes, at 9.23 p.m. Then he would endure Mia's best friend Lyn's birthday party, and on the drive back he would ask Mia why she hesitated. He itched to ask now, but hoped that Mia might feel more optimistic if she had a good time.

Maybe he could start creating that positivity. 'I came across this interesting fact that Australia is actually wider than the moon.' The truth was he had asked ChatGPT for conversation starters and random facts.

She offered nothing, not even the cursory "I don't give a damn" sound of false interest.

He continued. 'The moon is 3,400 kilometres in diameter, while Australia, from east to west, is 4,000 kilometres.' He rubbed his hands together, as the faulty heater in their Toyota Corolla hybrid failed to battle the late autumn chill. 'Also, the idea of raising a toast comes from the Ancient Romans, who used to drop a piece of burnt bread into their wine for good health. The carbon would reduce the acidity of bad wine.'

She slowed down around a corner. 'Maybe you can share these fascinating facts when we're at the pub. I need to concentrate on the road.'

Rami swallowed his disappointment. Why had she invited him if she wasn't willing to try?

Mia's mobile phone rang. Lyn, requesting a video call. Mia pressed to connect.

How was that concentrating?

Lyn's overly made-up, grinning, silicone-filled face invaded the screen, as though she didn't want anything in the background to steal the spotlight.

Lyn beamed. 'Lyn for the win!' she chirped in a cockney accent.

Mia chuckled and replied less enthusiastically, 'Lyn for the win.'

'Lyn in the bin,' Rami muttered, unable to help himself.

Mia shot him a glance.

'Where are you, Mimi?' Lyn asked.

'Sorry, we got delayed. I'm just driving, so I need to go. But we'll be there soon.'

Lyn touched her tacky dolphin earrings. 'Notice anything different?' she asked. She was one of *those* people, the ones who aren't ever in a conversation with you, but just waiting for an opening to shift the topic to themselves. 'Dale got me these yesterday.'

'Already knows what floats your boat,' Mia said. 'Look, I can't really pull over to chat.' Mia slowed down, but the car behind them flashed its lights and beeped.

'I can't wait for you to meet him,' Lyn continued, completely disregarding Mia and Rami's safety. She held the phone away from her face to show Mia the function room. There was a 'Happy 35th Lyn Day' banner, and photos of Lyn through the ages, as different surgeries and materials gradually constructed the creation on the phone screen. 'Look what you're missing. Hurry up.'

'We'll be there soon, if you let me get back to driving,' Mia said.

Lyn moved the camera in close again. 'Me and Dale are already talking about moving in together.'

'You should probably pull over,' Rami told Mia, hoping she would opt for ending the call.

She huffed and pulled over, driving onto the grass. The car behind overtook them and beeped again. Moonlit fields stretched to the horizon.

'Are you sure about that, Lyn?' Mia asked.

Rami bit the skin around his thumb's nail. Their conversation was far less interesting than his fact about the Ancient Romans.

Lyn's voice grew louder. 'I know. I get this excited every time, and I get let down. Every. Single. Time. But I love him. He's too good to be true.'

Rami pulled at the hairs on his eyebrows.

Mia offered Lyn a half-smile. 'I can't wait to meet him.'

Lyn's grin revealed her chemically whitened teeth in all their blinding glory. She could use them to navigate through fog or to become a more sustainable version of Norwich's Christmas lights. 'We can go on double dates, go on wellness breaks—'

Rami hung up the call and felt nauseous. 'Enough.'

Mia glared at him. 'Don't touch my phone.'

Rami glared back at her. 'Why did you hesitate?'

2

SHEDDING DEAD SKIN

MIA

Mia took a breath, hoping Rami's stare would break. His pathetic, sad eyes, and his gloomy expression made it look as though he was endlessly receiving bad news.

How the hell did it get to this? She used to love his face. It used to have this wonderful shine, as though it was new. It always cheered her up, but now it sucked all of the colour out of a room. If he stared at a plant for too long it would probably wilt and die.

She turned the car engine off and rain started to tap against the windscreen. She waited for Rami to sigh as he did whenever the weather changed.

Right on cue.

She swallowed. 'Why do you think I hesitated, Rami?'

He undid his seatbelt and turned his body towards her. 'I'd rather you answer the question.'

Where would she even begin?

Mia's phone rang. Bloody Lyn. Mia rejected the call.

She had played through this moment in her mind an

exhausting number of times, hoping it would make the reality easier. In her version they were in the living room and Rami was in a good mood. It was obvious, however, that there was no ideal time. Whatever she said and whenever she said it, it would be like booting a dying dog. Not hard enough to end its suffering, but just enough to add to the pain by breaking a rib or two.

'It's been shit for ages, Rami. The real question is why were you so quick to say yes?' She leaned back against the car door, wishing she could get further away.

Lyn called again. 'Fuck off, Lyn!' Mia yanked her phone out of the holder and turned it off.

Rami exhaled, as though deflating. 'Part of me hopes we can get back to how we were.'

How they were? He was attached to a snapshot. Standalone events. 'You're a fantasist, Rami, scared to face the reality that us...' she pointed between them. 'It's dead.'

His eyes broke from hers. 'It is with that attitude.'

He had the emotional maturity of a toddler. 'We haven't slept in the same bed for a year and I work late because I'm sad at home. I'm sad around... this.'

His eyes met hers and he reached for her hand.

No chance.

His hand flopped onto the gear selector. 'What do you want to change? I'll do anything, but I need a little help here.'

Mia reached around to the back seat for her handbag, but couldn't grab it.

'Here.' Rami took it and passed it over, which almost made her not want it.

She dug around for her hip flask and took a big gulp of rum.

Rami stared at her.

'It's water,' she said. 'And look... we can change where we live, we can work on ourselves, and we can have all the shared experiences life has to offer. But the only thing I want to change right now is you.' The words unexpectedly energised her, although she did feel a touch harsh.

Rami's eyes welled up.

She stared at the hip flask. It was a wedding present, engraved with a quote from Westley in *The Princess Bride*: "Life is pain, highness. Anyone who says differently is selling something." Mia's cousin had bought her and Rami matching ones. Film, book, and TV references were probably the only good thing he had brought into her life, and annoyingly would remind her of him in future. Marriage had stained her with parts of his personality.

Rami stared ahead. 'I guess I won't be going to Lyn's party anymore. So, silver linings and all that.'

Mia chuckled. That's what things had come to, flickering moments of ease in an endless, gloomy abyss. It was like searching for a speck of gold dust in a bog of sloppy dog shit.

Rami cleared his throat. 'Why aren't you willing to try?'

'All we've done is try.' Mia took another swig, wishing he would accept her decision. 'Rami. When I see you I don't feel butterflies like I used to. I taste bile.'

He tapped his knuckles to his teeth and nodded. 'Well, bile aids digestion, so if anything I'm essential to you functioning.'

She shook her head. 'Something's gone, Rami, and it's not coming back. I'm sorry.'

He bit his lip. 'Are you sure this isn't just a symptom of... do you think if she hadn't, then we'd...' He hung his head.

The baby.

She took a big breath. 'I'm going to say the worst thing I've ever said in my life. I've never felt as much pain as the day we lost her, and it still kills me. But, sometimes, I think that loss was something's way of forcing me to see that we're done.'

'Wow,' he said. 'It's worth bringing that up with Samantha. Maybe—'

'We need to get a divorce.' Her heart raced.

He froze.

The power of that word was baffling. All other words and actions could be brutal, cutting, personal, draining, yet never terminal, but that word, "Divorce", was like yanking the plug out of the life support machine.

The rain drummed against the car.

Rami played with the zip on his coat. 'Just like that? One minute to obliterate eight years.'

Mia forced a sympathetic smile; the best she could do. 'It's been dead for a while, Rami. Let's stop trying to resurrect this and get on with our futures. Apart. We have a lot of life ahead of us.'

His lip trembled and he put his seatbelt back on. 'Take me home.'

A warmth filled her as though her soul had been fed and invigorated. This was it. She drank the last of her rum.

She switched the engine on and then the wipers. She turned on BBC Radio Norfolk to hopefully discourage Rami from speaking. Mariah Carey's 'All I Want for Christmas is You' came on, and she could see the funny side. There was no point changing stations: it would likely be some other Christmas song over a month too soon, probably about loneliness or loss like 'Last Christmas', or some glum self-pitying nonsense by Adele that Rami would read too much into.

Mia made an awkward U-turn on the Acle New Road and they headed back towards Norwich. 'I can stay at Lyn's if you want? While we get this stuff sorted,' she suggested.

Rami stared out of the window without a reply.

What a child. 'I'll do that then.'

Mia continued to drive, the music a glorious barrier to conversation. Petrol station lights shone through the rain on the Acle Roundabout.

'Stop in there,' Rami said. 'I need the toilet.'

'Can't you hold it until we get back?'

'I need to go now,' he demanded.

Mia huffed, pulled into the petrol station and parked by the screen wash machine.

Rami dragged himself out of the car and plodded towards the petrol station shop. When he was inside, Mia turned her phone back on. Five messages, all from Lyn. Her party must have been terrible.

Mia ignored them, turned the radio off, flicked through her recent calls and clicked on "Sally Work." The phone rang and Mia kept an eye out for Rami's return. She chuckled to herself, thinking *Rami's Return* sounded like the sequel to a horror film.

The call connected and a deep, comforting, heart-warming voice answered. 'Wilfred Throckmorton, delivering happiness the Throckmorton way.'

Mia smiled. 'Please tell me you do that for work calls, too.'

'Only a special few get the full Throckmorton intro, and you're still only on the middle-tier plan,' he said. 'How are you?'

'It's done.'

There was a long pause. 'You're going to have to be more specific,' he said.

Mia laughed, almost hysterical. She gripped the steering wheel with her spare hand. 'We're getting a divorce.'

Wilfred chuckled. The kind filled with relief. 'Well then, I guess I need to hold up my side of the bargain.'

Mia grinned. 'Yes, you do.'

'I'll tell her tomorrow,' Wilfred said.

Mia kept an eye on the petrol station, where Rami was scanning shelves.

'We're just at the Acle Roundabout, so I should be back around ten-twenty to drop him off, then I need to get to Lyn's to show my face for fifteen minutes. I'll aim to be with you around midnight.'

'Sure. I'll book us a room at the St. Giles,' he said.

Rami was at the counter, paying for whatever he had bought.

'Sod Norwich. Book something further afield,' Mia said.

'I should probably still be in Norwich for any fallout with the kids, but we can venture further afield soon enough – maybe Stowbridge. Recreate one of our weekends away.'

'Absolutely,' she said. 'And can you pop by the office and grab me some clothes? I've been taking bags of stuff in over the last few days, and I don't want to go inside the house to get anything.'

'It would be my pleasure,' he said. 'Is Throcky with you?'

Mia smiled at the Rocky Balboa bobblehead. 'Sure is.'

'Go on,' he encouraged.

'I'm not kissing it,' she said.

'He's brought us all this luck; you owe him.'

'He's done fuck all.' She chuckled. 'Rami's coming back. I love you.' It felt amazing to say that and to really, truly mean it.

'Love you too. This is actually happening,' he said.

'It's actually happening.' Mia's life could finally begin.

3

TO NEW ADVENTURES

RAMI

Rami heaved a handful of salted peanuts into his mouth and chomped as loudly as he could. It didn't matter anymore if Mia hated the sound of him eating. If anything, the thought of annoying her brought him joy. If any peanut crumbs fell on the seat, even better. He guessed she would probably keep the car – she was the one paying the lease for it.

He breathed slowly to fight the tears. He had let them flow in the service station toilet, but was in danger of another wave.

Mia sped down the dark, empty country roads, further obscured by the heavy rain. She looked completely unbothered, as though she had flicked on her "I-no-longer-give-a-shit" switch.

Questions flooded Rami's mind. This needed further discussion, processing and understanding. Anger, sadness, regret, and confusion all took turns punching his heart.

The dark fields and trees blurred past his window. 'Can you please pull over?' he asked.

She released a frustrated breath. 'You just went to the toilet.'

Rami faced her. 'We need to talk more. There are questions forming and I haven't said everything I need to say.'

She kept her eyes on the road. 'There's nothing left to say, Rami. I'll stay at Lyn's and then I'll get a mediator to do the rest.'

Rami stared at her, hoping she would realise how cold she sounded. They were both part of this failure and their feelings needed equal consideration.

She huffed. 'What's talking going to achieve?'

How did he ever fall for this inconsiderate demon? 'Pull over. I'd like to say some things with you looking at me instead of the road.'

'Fine. You can say what you want to say, but when we get back to the house, for a few minutes, before I head to Lyn's.'

'A few minutes? This is bigger than deciding what to have for dinner,' he argued.

'Rami, I'm not going to change my mind, so what are you hoping to gain?' she said. 'You might not think it, but it's best we start putting distance between ourselves. So, it's a few minutes or nothing at all.'

It was always her way. He had spent years letting her have her way, in the hope it would make her value his supportive nature.

He took slow breaths, trying to push the anger down, but every muscle in him tensed.

It was time for his way.

He grabbed the steering wheel and yanked it left. 'Pull over!'

She pulled it back to the right, driving into the wrong lane. 'Stop it!'

They fought over the steering wheel. The car swerved one way, then the other. 'Just stop the car!' Rami demanded, but the speed increased.

They barrelled towards an oncoming car, which swerved and avoided them by what must have been an inch. The driver beeped them.

'Prick!' Mia flung her left arm out and whacked Rami on the nose. He released the steering wheel and the car veered off the road and onto a grassy field. Mia slammed the brakes, but something smacked against the windscreen, cracking it, before the car skidded slowly into a tree by a large bush.

Rami groaned and pinched his stinging nose. There were drops of blood on his fingers. 'Must've been a deer. You alright?' he asked out of habit.

Mia finally faced him. 'You fucking idiot!'

Blood ran over Rami's top lip and he wiped it on his sleeve. 'I'm fine, thanks for asking.'

She ignored him.

Blood streaked the cracked windscreen. Rami hoped the deer was okay. He unbuckled his seatbelt, opened the door and stepped out into the field, the rain jabbing him. He dreaded the thought of having to finish the job. Growing up, his uncle had told him the most humane way would be shooting an injured deer in the brain, but this wasn't America, so he couldn't exactly pop to the nearest service station and buy a bazooka. It was unlikely he would find something sharp enough to slit its throat with either.

He considered looking for a rock to cave its head in. He felt sick.

Mia opened her door, took an umbrella from her bag, opened it, and groaned at the car damage.

It looked as though a T-rex had head-butted the right-hand side of the bonnet and bumper, and the headlight was smashed.

Mia picked up broken pieces of car and tossed them onto the back seat. 'As soon as we get this sorted I never want to speak to you again.' Mia shook her head at Rami. 'Fucking clown.'

'Fine by me,' he muttered before adding, 'Heartless witch.'

She glared at him, but he shrugged and stepped towards the large bush, his nose stinging. Maybe he shouldn't have called her a witch.

Suddenly, he wondered if he was in a nightmare. Everything spun and his body numbed. 'No...'

Rami's hands trembled as he pulled his phone out of his pocket, fumbling to turn the torch on.

The light shone against the broken twigs, illuminating a man, likely in his mid-thirties, blood running from the right side of his bald head. He had a ginger hipster moustache, a scar on his left cheek, and his left forearm was bent at an unnatural angle in his leather jacket. His leather trousers and yellow boxer shorts were bunched around his ankles over his boots, exposing his hairy legs and broken left shin.

Rami retched.

It seemed the man had wanted to relieve himself by the side of the road. His motorcycle was parked around the other side of the tree, his helmet on top of its seat.

Mia came over and placed her hand to her mouth. 'Is he?'

'No, no. He can't be,' Rami said, his chest aching. He edged closer and crouched by the body. He pressed his fingers to the side of the man's neck, under his jaw and beside his windpipe, the way they did in films and TV shows. Nothing. Rami stuck his fingers under the man's nostrils. 'Please, please, please...'

Again, nothing.

'What?' Mia asked.

Rami placed his hands on the man's chest, hoping for a heartbeat. He turned to Mia and shook his head.

She closed her eyes.

Rami pressed 999 on his phone. 'I'll call an ambulance.'

Mia rushed over and placed her hand on Rami's phone. 'Wait.'

'Wait? For what? Maybe they can resuscitate him.'

She stared down at the grass. 'We're fucked if you do that.'

Her callousness was no surprise. 'We've just mowed him down. We need to take responsibility, and maybe there's a chance for him.'

Her eyes met his. 'I've had more rum tonight than is legal over the course of a week.'

He had noticed her increased drinking recently, but to lie about what was in her hip flask and drive drunk was a new level of awful. 'That sounds like a you problem.' Rami pressed the call button.

Mia snatched his phone and hung up.

'Give it back! Every second matters.' Rami held his hand out.

'Rami. Please. This guy is dead. It's a tragedy. But, we can't bring him back, so why bury ourselves next to him?' For the first time in an age Mia looked like she needed him.

Rami stepped towards her for his phone. 'We have to let someone know.'

She stepped back. 'It was an accident, Rami, but the police won't care. We'll both end up in jail.'

'But it's the right thing to do.'

Mia gripped Rami's phone tighter. 'Yeah, but that doesn't mean it's the best thing. Jobs. Friendships. Futures. Everything will be gone if you call an ambulance, all because of a very unfortunate, sad mistake. Please, Rami... if we go to prison, by the time we get out we'll both be past our sell-by dates and it'll be near impossible to start new lives. Us suffering won't bring him back.'

She was thinking of herself, her precious career, and prob-ably having a family with whoever was her next victim. But, annoyingly, she was right, their lives would be over and it would be harder for him to see hope on the horizon from a prison cell. Rami paused for what felt like a week as the rain hammered him. If they called the police, they would be questioned, Mia would be breathalysed, and he would be screwed for his part in this. If they called an ambulance and drove away before it arrived, they would be found and questioned, and after some kind of investigation, also screwed. Their lives would be over. The tabloids had already slaughtered him over Becca's death.

They would paint him as some kind of sadistic killer with this one.

Rami hung his head. 'This is all so wrong. And when someone finds him won't they be able to check CCTV close to here and see our mangled car driving back?'

Headlights filled the darkness up on the A47.

Mia hid behind their car, and Rami ducked into the bush next to the dead man.

The headlights continued past.

'We're still not calling an ambulance,' Mia said, emerging from behind the car. 'Stop letting the fear get to you.'

'So, what? We leave him here and just wait to get caught? Whether it's a day, a week, a month from now, it's going to happen.' Rami crawled out of the bush.

Mia stared at him, a terrifying blankness in her eyes.

'No,' he said. 'We can't.'

'It's the only option that allows us to go free,' she said.

A hot sadness pulsated in Rami's chest. 'He's someone's son. Maybe a husband.'

Mia closed her umbrella and tossed it towards the car. 'Don't you dare start characterising him. Help me get him in the boot.' She pulled the dead man's right arm and struggled to drag him out of the bush.

Rami fought the tears. 'Mia...'

She glared at him. 'It's. The. Only. Way.' She strained and dragged the man further. 'You either help, or you make it more likely we get caught.'

Rami hesitated. Maybe getting caught was for the best. Although, if he helped, then maybe Mia would see his worth again. It would keep her in his life a little longer. He swallowed his frustration and gripped the man's thighs, careful around his broken left shin. He weighed a tonne. 'Lift him from under the armpits,' Rami told Mia. 'We don't want him all limp.'

'He's dead!'

'I mean to carry,' Rami said. 'It's easier to carry him from under the arms.'

She huffed and grabbed the man under the armpits.

The duo carried him over to the boot and dropped him by the rear bumper.

Mia opened the boot. They lifted the man and placed him inside it.

Rami checked the man's pockets. A phone and a wallet. He ran his thumb over the wallet.

'Don't,' Mia said. 'Don't let him exist.'

Rami turned the man's phone off and tossed the wallet next to him. He closed the boot and took a moment to sit against it, wondering whether this was worth it.

Mia stared at him. 'Is this a bad idea?'

'The worst.' He shivered.

'Is there another option that isn't jail?' she asked.

He shook his head.

They stood in silence for a moment, then Mia cleared her throat. She pointed to the motorcycle and helmet. 'And that?'

Rami wiped his face against his sleeve. 'I guess one of us should ride it away. That way if there's any CCTV it looks like he was still going somewhere. And it makes it less obvious our car was involved. I think. I don't really know.'

Mia opened the driver door to the car. 'Great; you take it and I'll drive.'

'Why don't you get your fingerprints all over it instead?' Rami asked.

Mia folded her arms. 'Because you're the only one of us who can ride a motorbike, genius. And, if there is any CCTV, they may wonder why he's suddenly shrunk half a foot. In fact, you should probably wear his clothes.'

Rami shuddered. He opened the boot, wishing he didn't have to look at the life they had wiped out. He stared at the man's motorcycle boots. He removed them, placing them next to the body, and felt a rush of nausea.

He struggled to pull the man's leather trousers off. He stared at Mia. 'Any help?'

She picked up the umbrella, opened it and stayed standing by the open car door. 'You'll be fine.'

Rami grumbled. He pulled the trousers harder, feeling the man's broken shin shuffle. He winced at every shift of bone, eventually getting the trousers off.

Rami removed his trainers and tried to pull the man's leather trousers over his jeans. They were too tight. 'Shit!' He removed his drenched jeans, tossed them into the boot and forced the leather trousers over his bare legs. The man's sweat, blood, and skin were now one with his. Rami's thighs itched and he felt dizzy.

Rami pulled the rest of the man's clothes over his. Whenever he glanced at Mia she was looking away. He could tell she was crying from the way her shoulders shook.

He pulled on the motorcycle boots. A damp heat surrounded his wet feet. He tossed his trainers into the car boot.

Rami stumbled towards the motorcycle, where leather gloves rested on the tail box. He dabbed his bleeding nose with a tissue, then tore bits off and jammed them up his nostrils. The last time he rode a motorcycle was four years ago in Crete, when he and Mia explored the island. When she seemed to like him.

He placed the helmet over his head and grimaced, feeling the sweat from its previous wearer. A strong whiff of cologne abused his nostrils and the helmet squeezed his head. Rami wished it would crush his skull and end this misery.

He approached Mia. 'Are you sure we shouldn't chance it with the police? Maybe they'll understand.'

Mia glared at him, her eyes pained. 'We're doing this. I'm not risking my freedom because you're an idiot who couldn't accept it's over.'

'Fine.' He checked his phone map, his hand shaking. 'I'll find somewhere along the River Bure we can meet to get rid of him and the motorbike.' He hated himself.

'Someone from the boats will see us,' she complained.

'It's too cold and barely anyone will be out on the water. Let's wait a bit for more people to be asleep, then I'll go ahead and look at the CCTV situation and call you.'

Mia huffed, closed the umbrella, chucked it in the back of the car, then got into the driver's seat and shut the door.

Rami heard the locks click, shutting him out.

He paced in the rain and waited, every moment increasing his fear. He wished he could go back in time like Doc Brown and Marty McFly in *Back to the Future*, only he would make sure his parents didn't get together so he wouldn't have to experience the misery of living.

He questioned himself constantly, and thought he and Mia could have used this time to discuss their marriage, but doubted Mia would be receptive.

He checked his phone. It was 10.47 p.m. He approached the car and tapped on the passenger window. Mia wound it down a crack.

He sighed. 'I'll turn right, and you head left and take a longer route around.'

She stared ahead. 'Try not to crash,' she said, without a hint of care.

4

WASH THE PAIN AWAY

MIA

Mia drove slowly with the one working headlight dimmed. She pulled the screen wash lever to wipe the man's blood off the cracked windscreen. The rain had helped to remove most of it, but some had settled in the cracks. Maybe she was imagining it, unable to shake blood from her mind.

How had it come to this? Maybe they could turn back and take their punishment.

No. It was an accident.

She would not let Rami ruin her chance at a better life. This was his fault. If anyone should be punished it should be him. She wished she had asked for a divorce sooner, and not while on the road.

The lack of streetlamps and cameras was welcome. As was the poor visibility. It was fortunate that the council didn't care about road safety.

Throcky still stood strong on the dashboard. Maybe she should have kissed him for luck.

Hopefully there would be no police on the drive. She

punched the steering wheel. Her rom-com with Wilfred had become a low-budget crime thriller.

If she and Rami were caught, she could claim he had forced her into it, playing the gender card. Although, he was such a drip nobody would believe him capable.

She turned down the dark roads and into Belaugh village, which was silent, as one would expect from somewhere with no pubs or shops. If only it also had no Rami.

Apparently, he had found a quiet path to the river. Mia drove slowly down the narrow road and turned the working headlight off, passing the boatyard. To her left, bushes covered the grassy riverbank. A house was further along, but the lights were off.

The idiot waved, stood by the motorcycle and a bush.

Mia's neck tensed as she drove towards him. Part of her wanted to drive straight through him. Instead, she waited as late as she could before turning past him and pulling into a lay-by.

Rami walked the motorcycle through the bush and onto the grassy riverbank.

Mia turned the engine off and her phone pinged, a text alert from Wilfred. She opened it:

At the St. Giles. Booked us both a pre-work massage tomorrow morning. Love, the Throck xx

Her anger towards Rami overrode every other emotion, but she typed a quick reply:

Can't wait xxx

Determined, she got out of the car and marched towards Rami.

They would dump the body, then she could get to Wilfred. 'Great. You've managed to pick somewhere with an audience.' She pointed to a houseboat, moored on the opposite bank.

Rami removed the dead man's helmet and placed it on the grass. He pulled the tissue out of his bloody nose. 'It'll be fine.'

Mia's phone vibrated. Lyn again.

Rami's eyes widened. 'Turn it off.'

Mia switched her phone to airplane mode and put it in her pocket. 'Calm down.'

He ignored her and unlocked the motorcycle tail box, which contained a first aid kit and a McDonald's burger wrapper. 'Maybe we could've used the first aid kit to help him.' He stared at it.

'Just get on with it,' Mia said.

Rami closed the tail box, locked it, and wheeled the motorcycle towards the water.

Mia stealthily took her phone out again and snapped several photos of Rami disposing of the motorcycle. They probably showed nothing without the flash, but maybe they would be helpful at some point.

A light splash and the motorcycle sank. The houseboat and the house ahead remained quiet. Mia, shaking, watched for any movement. She edged back to the car. 'Let's get this done,' she whispered and stared at the boot.

Rami followed and shook his head. 'I can't. What if he's come back to life?'

His stupidity baffled her. 'How?'

Rami grimaced. 'I don't know, like a second wind. It's not impossible.'

'I think it is unless he's a fucking White Walker.' She opened the boot and muttered, 'cretin,' under her breath. 'Oh look, he's still dead.'

Rami sighed. 'Well, I read about a woman in Ecuador who came back to life during her own funeral, so it's not completely against the odds.'

'Just grab his legs and shut up.' Mia grabbed the man under

the arms, avoiding his broken forearm. She closed her eyes to push the discomfort away.

Rami took the man's thighs.

They shuffled him to the edge of the boot and Mia stared at the body, not letting the guilt shift her focus. 'Right, we'll roll him into the water. We don't want a massive splash.'

Rami stopped.

'Hey, pay attention?' Mia said.

Rami put his finger to his lips.

'Don't shush me,' she said.

He raised a finger to indicate listening.

Mia heard it too. The boisterous shouting suggested a party, and likely a bunch of drunks. The outline of a boat formed in the distance under the moonlight. 'Quick, let's get him in the water.'

'No. We have to go.' Rami pushed the man's lower half towards the back of the boot.

'We can do this,' Mia said, still holding the man under his arms.

Rami shook his head. 'It's too risky.'

'Shit!' Mia nudged the man's top half away from the edge of the boot and closed it. She crouched by a bush, watching the boat, which very slowly headed in their direction. 'Is there another part of the river we can use? Or, shall we wait for them to pass?'

'The noise of the boat might wake other folks up,' Rami said.

Fuck.

Rami picked up the helmet and walked around to the car's passenger door. 'As much as I don't want to, we need to take the body home and make a plan. It might even work in our favour to... dispose... of him further away.'

Mia wanted to scream, but he had a point. She didn't want to risk her future with Wilfred – it was all that mattered.

She stood and opened the driver's door. 'Fine. Let's get you and the car home, then I'll call you from Lyn's tomorrow to work out a plan.'

Rami folded his arms. 'You're not leaving him with me and running off to stay at Lyn's. No chance.'

Mia huffed. 'We're getting a divorce, Rami. I don't want to be near you.'

Rami scoffed. 'Until this is over, you're not going anywhere. Otherwise I might get the urge to invite the police over for a cup of tea.'

Fuck. Fuck. Fuck.

Mia reversed the car into the cramped garage. The electric shutter stuttered to a close and she turned the engine off. 'Get out,' she commanded.

'My pleasure.' Rami exited the car, placed the helmet on top of a pile of boxes in the corner and stomped inside the house.

Mia waited a moment, then checked her phone. A missed call from Wilfred and several voice notes and calls from Lyn. Mia phoned Wilfred, but he requested a video call. She checked herself in the rear-view mirror and took a breath. She accepted the call.

Wilfred's wonderful, grinning face filled the frame. 'Wilfred Throckmorton, ready to Throck your world.' He held the camera out, revealing himself sat in a bubble bath, a glass of champagne in his free hand, and wearing one of Mia's silk scarves. He always found silly ways to entertain her, and his gentle face was a tiny flicker of joy in this ordeal.

She laughed. 'Thanks for picking up my clothes, but there's been a problem.' She looked down, not wanting to see any shift in his happiness.

Wilfred scooped up some bubbles. 'Nothing a bubble bath can't fix. But hurry up, they're going down, and my skin's getting uncomfortably wrinkly.' He blew the bubbles off his hand.

She flashed a smile then swallowed. 'Rami threatened to kill himself.'

Wilfred's face dropped. She couldn't tell whether it was concern or disappointment. 'Are you certain he's not manipulating you?'

She shook her head. 'I can't leave him like this. I'd never be able to forgive myself if he went too far, and it would affect us.'

Wilfred downed some champagne. 'I get it. Hey, at least he knows it's over. I guess he just needs to come to terms with the initial hit. If I were losing the Mia magic, I'd probably feel the same.'

Mia's body relaxed. He was so easy to talk to. 'Let's chat tomorrow. I love you.'

Wilfred smiled reassuringly. 'I love you too.'

Mia hung up and stifled the screams that wanted to leave her mouth. Freedom had been so close.

Her phone rang again. Lyn. Mia rejected the call and sat in the car staring at the garage bricks for a moment. She grabbed Throcky, ripped it off the dashboard and whacked it against the steering wheel.

When she entered the house, Rami was showered and sat on the living room floor in only his old blue pants, ripped around the elastic. He bashed the man's mobile phone with a hammer as his clothes spun in the washing machine.

Rami looked up at her. 'Just to be sure. I don't know how all that Find My stuff works.'

Mia dumped Throcky in the bin and then walked towards the stairs.

'Mia?' Rami called out.

She stopped and turned around.

He brushed the mobile phone pieces into a dustpan. 'Look,

um... I don't want to sleep on my own. The silence is making me replay everything and the study is so lonely.'

Mia nodded. 'Then put on some music.' She walked upstairs towards the bedroom and cursed the day she met Rami. Her friends had dragged her to a bar in West Hampstead in London, because she had been moping about her ex. There, in an overly slow bar queue, Rami awkwardly offered to buy her a drink. If she could turn back time, instead of allowing her vulnerability to accept, she would glass him.

5

AN UNWANTED GUEST

RAMI

Rami lay on the sofa with an ice pack on his nose, staring at the ceiling.

The morning light peeked under the curtains and he hadn't slept at all. He had spent the night washing the dead man's clothes repeatedly on 60 degrees while replaying the moment in the field. He must have typed 999 into his phone a dozen times, his thumb hovering over the call button.

He was relieved to hear the dustbin truck outside. He rushed over to the front door and looked through the peephole. A binman grabbed the bin bag packed with the dead man's clothes and the pieces of his mobile phone.

Rami had double-bagged it, worried it might split.

The binman tossed the bag into the back of the truck.

Rami returned to the sofa, his relief drowned out by guilt.

That poor man had been simply going about his evening. Now he was dead in a car boot wearing nothing but yellow boxer shorts.

Rami's private browsing on accidental killings confirmed

that if he and Mia had called the police or an ambulance, eventually they would have been jailed. Some cases were approached with sympathy, but those were when the fault was more on the dead person's side.

Rami's hands trembled. His skin felt slimy, as though the man's sweat had seeped into his pores through his clothes and helmet. Rami scratched himself, trying to scrape off the guilt and regret, leaving marks all over his chest and arms.

The stairs creaked under Mia's footsteps and she emerged wearing a suit and heels. The bags under her eyes suggested that she hadn't slept much, either.

She trudged over to the fridge, took out a bottle of white wine, unscrewed the top and drank straight from it.

Rami placed the ice pack on a sofa cushion, sat up and leaned forward. 'I've been researching.'

Mia took a slice of sourdough bread and ate it without any spread. She wouldn't look at him.

Rami scratched his nose. 'It turns out that the Walter White method in *Breaking Bad* of dissolving a body in the bath isn't that accurate, and we don't exactly have access to lots of hydrofluoric acid. Another idea could be sodium hydroxide which is in loads of drain unblockers, but it feels so undignified. It strips the hydrogen atoms, which—'

'We're dumping the body in the river, close to the sea.' She heaved more bread into her mouth.

He didn't like the word "dump"; it suggested discarding rubbish. 'But, there's a chance it resurfaces. After a few days micro-organisms in the digestive system eat body tissues. That releases gas that makes the torso and limbs bloat, basically turning him into a float.' It was all so horrifically casual. 'I have a list of options.'

She huffed and still wouldn't face him. 'River.'

Rami stared at the back of her head, hoping she could feel his anger burrow through her skull. 'There's burial,' Rami said.

'If we bury him ten feet down, then at six feet bury a dead animal, it'll be near impossible for any dogs to sniff his body out.' His stomach turned. Yesterday, he was sticking adverts for his tutoring around town, now this.

Mia turned the tap on and washed her hands. 'I need you to get the body out of the car, take the car to get fixed, then find a good spot along the river.' She grabbed her laptop bag and walked towards the front door.

'And what are you going to be doing!?'

She faced him. 'Working. Moving on.'

'Nobody's going to care about your spreadsheets in prison. We need to do this together.'

She pointed at him. 'This is your fault! So do something useful.' Her phone rang and she looked at it. 'Go away, Lyn!' She rejected the call.

Rami pulled the joke cushion of Nicolas Cage's face he had bought her as a gift into his chest. He wanted to hurl it at her.

'What?' she said.

'It's your ability to work as part of a team that I'll miss most.'

She turned and left, slamming the door.

Rami had stared at the closed car boot for over ten minutes. He took a deep breath again. The garage was so tight, it felt like everything was closing in.

He shuffled his feet on the bin liners he had placed on the concrete floor. He planned to lay the man's body on them, then cover him with a blanket so he didn't have to look at him.

Rami wasn't sure where to put the body afterwards. Should he leave him covered in the garage, so close to the street? The open-plan kitchen and living room was connected to the garden, so too exposed. The downstairs toilet was too small. Upstairs there was the study which was now Rami's bedroom, and he had no interest in having the body rotting in there. It would be too difficult to get the man into the loft on his own. He could leave him in Mia's home office. She barely used it these days. Or, he could leave him in the bathtub in the ensuite to what was now Mia's room, or better yet, in Mia's bed.

Rami sighed, he barely had the strength to stand, let alone carry the body upstairs. He would just cover it well down here.

His hand touched the boot handle. He gritted his teeth, opened it, closed his eyes and turned away. His breathing quickened and he clenched everything.

He opened his eyes, turned around, and under the garage's bright lights the man's pasty body and facial features burned into his mind. His dead, brown eyes gazed at nothing. Dried blood stained his face, the pattern reminding Rami of the marks residual coffee grounds would leave in his mum's mug. She and her Lebanese friends would read their fortunes in the marks. The last time she read Rami's fortune, she said he would have a long life. She didn't specify whether a lot of it would be spent in prison.

Rami spotted the man's wallet. He couldn't help himself. The man had a Nectar card, several twenty pound notes, and a loyalty card from Littlehaven Coffee Co. near Norwich City College. He was one stamp away from a free one. He had several receipts, and, on seeing the man's HSBC bank card and name, Rami burst into tears and closed the wallet, resisting any further investigation.

The man was someone's son. Maybe someone's sibling. He may have had children of his own. Maybe a wife or husband, although there was no wedding ring on his finger. Until yesterday, this man had been a part of the world. He probably enjoyed going for coffee with his loved ones and telling them about his plans. Maybe he wanted to be a painter, or to run his own interior design business or brand consultancy. Maybe he struggled

for work but didn't let it get him down, because he was optimistic and always grateful for what he had.

Rami stopped himself. He had to get this done, for whatever
the future was. He reached into the boot to pull the man out, but
recoiled and fell back against the wall, slumping to the floor. He
buried his head into his knees and let the tears flow. 'I'm so
sorry.'

The internal garage door opened.

Mia looked down at Rami with a shred of what could have
been sympathy, but was more likely disappointment. 'I've called
in sick.'

It was the least she could do, but it was also huge. Rami
wiped his tears against the back of his right hand. 'I just started
seeing his whole life. Maybe he has a kid who's now going to be
fatherless like me.'

Mia grabbed some Marigolds from a plastic box on a shelf.
'Please tell me you didn't look in his wallet.'

'He has a name.'

'I don't want—'

'D. B. Ragnor.'

'Fucking hell!' Mia groaned. 'He can't have an identity.' She
grabbed the motorcycle helmet and placed it over D. B. Ragnor's
head and pulled the visor down. 'Go and get dressed. We'll take
the car to a garage, and as soon as it's fixed we'll get rid of him.'

Rami nodded. He rose to his feet and stumbled upstairs to
the tiny study. He wanted his lucky blue polo shirt. He had
owned it for thirteen years, despite Mia's efforts to throw it away.
He wore it to his interview to teach at the University of East
Anglia, and he had got the job. He was wearing it on holiday
when Mia received a call promoting her to product director at
her telehealth start-up. Maybe now it would bring them some
much-needed luck.

He searched the drawers, but it wasn't there. It was probably
among Mia's clothes in her wardrobe. He was meant to move all

of his things to the study, but he deliberately hadn't, hoping they would be sharing a bed again at some point. It had been a year to the day now. He remembered the exact date – the 3rd of November – six months after they had lost their baby and three months after Becca's death.

He entered Mia's bedroom. He hated thinking of it as that. It was their bedroom. He opened the fitted wardrobe's sliding door. His polo shirt hung on its own. All of Mia's clothes were gone.

6

DEER IN THE HEADLIGHTS

Mia

Mia watched the garage shutter close in the rear-view mirror. She wanted to get the car sorted, get rid of the body, and get on with her life.

No amount of make-up could distract from the heaviness in her eyes. She had wondered if they had made the right choice, but of course they had. It was the only choice that didn't involve a prison cell. Anyone else would have done the same, and if they said otherwise they were full of shit.

Rami, more fidgety than usual, turned to her. 'I read that since 2020 there have been over 5,300 long-term missing people in this country. If we find the right place, we could be okay. Even if we don't deserve to be, the odds are in our favour.'

She gazed out at the cul-de-sac, worried someone might look into the garage and spot the body. It was under a blanket and behind a wall of boxes, and there was no way anyone would see it, but it was hard to think rationally.

Rami stared ahead, seemingly lost in whatever pointless thoughts he was having.

The shutter finally closed, but the relief was short-lived.

Jenny, their busybody neighbour, holding her high-visibility police support volunteer jacket under her arm and wearing a bumbag, waved enthusiastically and limped over. Her pregnant wife, Iris, who clearly had confidence issues to be married to Jenny, followed, with their irritating jumpy, yappy Papillon, Ballula, on a leash.

'For fuck's sake,' Mia muttered.

Rami smiled at Jenny and lowered his window.

Jenny waved her finger between the car bumper, smashed headlight, and cracked windscreen. 'Bit of a nasty knock, that,' she said in her thick Norfolk accent. 'But looks like you came out worse.' She nodded at Rami's nose and chuckled. 'You okay?'

Her hoody had a large image of an oddly shaped dice and the words: "DnD, this is how I roll," written on it. Mia had no idea what that meant, only that it clearly wasn't meant for a woman in her early forties.

'Cool hoody,' Rami said.

Losers.

'You play Dungeons and Dragons?' Jenny asked enthusiastically.

'No, but lots of my students... *former* students do.'

Mia was tempted to drive away to avoid this meaningless chitchat.

Jenny pointed at Rami's nose. 'So?'

Rami shrugged. 'I was getting a box of old books down from a shelf and it fell straight onto my face.'

Iris winced. 'Get an e-reader instead.' She chuckled and picked up Ballula, who barked at Mia. The dumb thing was always barking, and she always stared at Mia expecting affection. Mia wondered how far she could kick her.

Rami smiled. 'It's fine, Iris. The box is now ripped to shreds and having some good old-fashioned thinking time in the recycling bin.'

Iris and Jenny chuckled.

'That'll teach the shithead,' Jenny said, then held her hand to her mouth. 'Sorry!'

'Jenny!' Iris complained.

'It's okay, we're all grown-ups here,' Rami said. 'Mia says worse to me.'

She certainly would as soon as this ordeal was over.

Iris shook her head. 'Jenny's not allowed to swear until the baby is at least eight. She's got a rotten mouth.'

Jenny rolled her eyes. 'Doesn't stop you kissing it.'

Rami laughed.

Ballula stared at Mia and growled, as though she knew what Mia and Rami had done.

Mia leaned towards Rami's window, trying to avoid any part of her touching him. 'Anyway. It's great to see you both, but we should really get going.'

Jenny pointed to the car bumper and windscreen. 'And what happened there?'

Mia and Rami answered at the same time. He said, 'Deer,' while Mia said, 'A tree.'

Jenny raised an eyebrow.

Rami scratched his cheek, 'We hit a deer, then ended up bumping a tree in the chaos.'

Iris rubbed Jenny's back. 'Yeah, deer damage is common this time of year.'

Jenny nodded. 'October to November is normally rutting season, when they've only got one thing on their minds.' Jenny and Iris exchanged a suggestive look. 'You're lucky it didn't give your motor more of a bashing.'

'Maybe it was on a diet,' Rami joked.

Mia gripped the steering wheel and half-smiled at Jenny. 'Anyway, thanks for the info. We really should be going, though.'

Jenny leaned on the window frame, her head now inside the car. 'Have you reported it?' Her eggy breath filled the space.

Mia's neck tensed.

Ballula barked at Mia. Iris stroked her. 'Ballula, behave.' Iris shook her head towards Mia. 'Sorry, she's normally quite mellow.'

Mia stared at Ballula, but the awful creature stared right back at her, judging her.

Rami took his phone out of his pocket. 'Were we meant to report it?'

Jenny bobbed her head. 'Legally you don't have to, but it's the decent thing to do. I can do it for you.' She took her phone out of her bumbag.

Mia waved her hand. 'You don't have to do that, Jenny. It was on the side of the road so won't get in anyone's way. Probably already been cleared.'

Jenny tutted. 'Would you leave a dead human without reporting them?'

Mia's throat tightened.

Rami coughed. 'No. I guess we wouldn't.' His voice cracked.

Jenny listed with her fingers. 'Cats, badgers, foxes and rabbits. Along with deer, you don't have to report them, but you should. Dogs, goats, horses, cattle, donkeys, mules, sheep and pigs, you're legally obliged to.'

Rami nodded. 'The authorities not cat people, then?'

Jenny laughed. 'Maybe they decided deer and cats are dreadful. Anyway, I can put in a call to some of my old mates at the police station. Where did you mow the poor bugger down?'

Mia gritted her teeth. Jenny loved to pretend she was connected to the police. She thought being a police support volunteer meant she could go door to door – her stupid dog in tow – to see how people were doing. She was the self-appointed leader of the cul-de-sac. 'It was on the A140 to Cromer,' Mia lied. 'But please, let us do it. As you said, it's the decent thing to do.'

Mia flicked the indicator switch up to signal right.

'Okay, sure,' Jenny said.

Finally. 'Great, have a good day.' Mia took her foot off the brake.

'Oh, before you go...'

Mia broke again and let her obvious frustration out in a huff.

'Is Sunday good to chat about my story?' Jenny asked Rami.

'Of course,' Rami replied. 'Looking forward to it.'

Jenny beamed. 'Amazing. Have a good 'un.'

'You too,' Rami said.

The annoyances walked on. Ballula kept turning around to look at Mia. Mia stuck her middle finger up at the dog and then turned to Rami. 'You're going to have to cancel.'

'The tutoring? No way,' he said. 'If anything, we need to keep things looking normal, right?'

Mia drove. 'Well, until we're in the clear, keep any small talk to a minimum. Who knows what you might accidentally say.'

'I was only being polite.' He shook his head.

'She's annoying.'

'She's lovely,' Rami replied.

'Don't dogs develop personalities similar to their owners? Tells you everything you need to know,' Mia argued.

'What's Ballula got to do with anything? She's just a little dog.'

Mia tutted. 'She's a rubbish dog. Every time I go for a run and pass their house she barks, and she always pisses on the lamppost outside ours, like she's making a statement.'

Rami shrugged. 'Almost as bad as killing someone.'

'Just be rude next time.'

Rami folded his arms. 'It doesn't come as naturally to most of us.'

She scoffed. 'You make it easy.'

~

The mechanic at the counter wrapped an oily hand around a can of Sprite. 'I can get the windscreen, headlight and bonnet done this afternoon, but the bumper's going to take two, likely three days.' He sipped his drink.

'Any chance it can be done faster?' Mia asked.

The mechanic shook his head. 'Gotta order a new bumper.'

Rami tapped the counter. 'Okay, thanks.' He turned to leave but Mia stopped him.

She knew how to negotiate. It was why she could get people at the office to work harder, and why she was great at earning pay rises. 'What if we pay you a bit extra? Couldn't you get it here faster? Or...' She pointed to another Toyota Corolla hybrid, 'What if you give us their bumper and tell them there's a delay fixing their car?'

The mechanic's face dropped. 'Three days. I'll call you when it's ready.'

Rami shook his head.

They left the garage and walked towards Dereham Road.

'It's probably for the best anyway,' Rami said. 'Means we're doing it on a Monday night when nobody's out.'

He annoyingly had a point, but she couldn't stomach the idea that she would have to be around him for another three days.

Rami stopped to blow his nose and winced, scrunching his face to make a point of his injury. Mia walked on.

'Wait,' he said. 'There's something I want to ask you.'

'What?'

He hesitated. 'Any chance we can go for a coffee and talk?'

Mia huffed. 'No. If you want to ask me something, do it here and now.'

He rubbed his thumbs and forefingers together and stared at the floor, as though he were charging himself up to speak.

He said nothing.

She nodded. 'Okay. Well, I may have called in sick, but that doesn't mean I want to spend the day with you.'

'Great. I'll go and hang out with our new friend alone. Maybe we can watch daytime TV together, something like *Murder She Wrote*.'

'You'll be fine. Maybe research good places along the river to dump him.' She rushed away before he could reply.

~

Mia and Wilfred lay naked next to each other on top of the duvet. They were so excited to see each other that they didn't even bother to get under the covers.

It was incredible to be with him. She would happily live out of a hotel room for the rest of her life if it meant they were together.

She rubbed her foot against his. 'Do you ever worry that things will change between us? You know, when this is proper? When it includes all the boring stuff like buying insurance?'

Wilfred grinned. 'I can't wait for the boring stuff.'

Mia grimaced. 'Really?'

He leaned on his elbow. 'I rushed into a marriage in a panic. And I've tricked myself all these years that I could do it. That I could be married to someone I just really like, you know, for the sake of the kids, not hurting her, blah blah blah, and the rest. But it means everything has this whiff of regret to it.' He held Mia's hand. 'For me, the boring stuff is going to be amazing, because it's building a life with the most incredible woman I've ever met.'

Mia smiled. 'You're talking about me, right?'

He laughed. 'For now.' He placed his hand on her waist. 'Have you ever been to Thailand?'

'Bit random?'

'Well, people say Bangkok is really nice, but I know of a

much better place. You know what it's called?' He pulled her on top of him.

'Please don't say it.' Mia covered his mouth. 'I beg.'

He pulled her hands away. 'BangThrock,' he blurted out before she could cover his mouth again.

Mia cracked up and placed a hand over her face. 'I've never wanted to have sex with you less. That's the worst one yet.'

'Oh, there are worse. I just self-edit.'

Her phone rang. She looked over at it. 'It's just Lyn.' She cancelled the call. 'If I answer it she'll want to talk for hours about her party and have a go at me for not being there. She's left me about eight voice notes I'll have to sit through.'

'I can't wait to meet her,' Wilfred said.

'She'll love you,' Mia replied. 'Everyone will.'

Wilfred shuffled up the bed and sat against the headboard. 'I've booked this room for another week, but I'm planning to go home tonight to tell Samira the truth.'

Mia sat up next to him.

'So, it'd be good if you joined me here, and we could start looking at flats.'

Mia winced. 'I just need three more days.'

The joyous light in Wilfred's eyes dwindled behind sadness. 'That's oddly specific.'

She took his hands in hers. 'I told him I'd hang around for three days. To help him just by being there, but more importantly, to set a deadline for him. So he knows he needs to face reality.'

'He's not your responsibility anymore,' Wilfred said.

'It's just three days. And in some ways, he is. I've broken him.'

Wilfred stroked her hand. 'What happens at the end of three days if he does something stupid? He's manipulating you.'

Mia held Wilfred's hand to her chest. 'I won't let it go beyond that.'

Wilfred nodded and swallowed. 'Last week, Cindy said, "Daddy, why don't you and Mummy hug like other mummies and daddies?" It broke my heart. Her little innocent face with this broken image of love already. I can't lie anymore, Mia. It's hurting people. I want to be able to tell the truth and start repairing the damage, then she can – eventually, one day when she hates me less – see what love is really like.'

Mia kissed his hand. 'Just three more days. We're so close.'

Wilfred shook his head. 'I'm sorry, Mia. Last night, my hopes were so high before they got crushed. Then you gave me hope again, saying today was the day. I'm starting to worry that as this becomes less of a secret, dangerous, adrenaline-fuelled thing, that you're getting itchy feet.'

'I'm not. My feet are itch-free. I promise. I love you,' she said. 'He's just so sensitive. This morning he got teary when we passed a cafe, because we'd never go to one together again.'

Wilfred let go of her hand. 'I'm sorry, Mia. Tonight, if you're not here to stay, then we need to rethink this.'

Mia dug her nails into her palms, terrified by the ultimatum.

7

BURY THE PAST, PRESENT AND FUTURE

RAMI

Rami placed two shovels on a dusty table in the garage, next to two pairs of gloves, two pairs of wellies, a petrol can, an ice box, and a folded-up tent.

He was tired of feeling worthless. Had Mia been cheating on him? He wanted to ask, but what would that do? If she said yes, it would break him, and if she said no, would he believe her? Had she already made up her mind before they started therapy? Was she just going through the motions? He rubbed his face and tried to focus.

Instead of researching places along the river, he had done more research into burials. There was a great wood at the back of Dersingham Bog, near Norfolk's northwest coast.

Rami rested his head against the wall. Even if they succeeded, his future was over. He could be on a countryside walk with a new partner, at home making a salad, or laughing at an Instagram video of a dog befriending a turtle, then whack, he would remember he was a murderer. Any day from now until death it could catch up with him.

The front door slammed, followed by heels clacking on the wooden floor. Mia poked her grumpy face into the garage. 'We're doing this tonight.' She left and marched towards the kitchen.

'No, we're not.' He followed her to the kitchen counter.

Her expression was more flustered, on the verge of panic. 'I can't let this linger. I need him gone.'

'What do you plan to do, shove him in a suitcase and get a taxi to drop us in the middle of nowhere?'

She folded her arms. 'I borrowed Mum's car.'

'Oh...' She had to be desperate to go and talk to that dragon. He placed a hand on her shoulder, then quickly removed it. 'Look, it's too soon, and it's Friday, so people will be out and about. Plus, we don't have a proper plan.'

'Well, if we're not going to do it tonight, then I'm staying at Lyn's until we can.' Mia bit her lip.

Rami shook his head. 'No. Until we get rid of our new house-mate, neither of us is leaving. It's unfair.'

'I can't be near it anymore. It's driving me crazy! There's got to be a way, and we'll be careful. But, I just...' She sat on the sofa and buried her head in her hands. 'Every minute it's here it's worse, and soon he'll be reported missing. We need to get him away from us before anyone's looking...'

Rami didn't want to pity her, but she had a point, and the rescuer in him wanted to step up and prove his value. 'Okay, tonight then.'

She let out a long breath and looked at him. 'So, did you find somewhere along the river?'

'No. Burial is best, although there are some issues.' He walked to the freezer and opened it.

'But we agreed the river. We said river.'

'*You* said river, Mia.' Rami removed packets of frozen meat and placed them in a carrier bag. 'If you had been willing to have a discussion about it, I would've told you it's too risky. It's out of our control. At least with a burial we know exactly where he is, and... it's more respectful.'

'Respect!? Who gives a shit about respect?'

'Clearly just me,' he replied. 'If you want to do it tonight, we're doing it my way. Otherwise I'm not moving.' He closed the freezer.

The scornful look she would greet door-to-door charity fundraisers with flashed across her face. 'Fine. Burial.'

'Burial gives us a really good chance.' Rami said. 'We won't be able to dig a hole as deep as ten feet, as that can take a day and we're not exactly professionals. But, we could probably get four or five feet done in six hours or so.'

Mia stared at him. 'Okay...'

Rami nodded. 'They obviously have things like sniffer dogs. And I read about ground-penetrating radar, and machines that can detect how strongly a material opposes the flow of an electric current. But, they take ages to use, covering only small areas. Dersingham Bog alone is 393 acres, and they won't even know to look there.'

'I've agreed to it, Rami,' Mia pointed out.

He held out the bag full of packets of frozen meat towards her.

'What?'

'Get these in the ice box.'

She scrunched her eyebrows at him, confused.

'I wasn't going to get a dead pet, was I? So this should do for throwing dogs off the body's scent. It's worth a try.'

Mia shook her head.

Rami and Mia stood inside what must have been a four-foot-deep grave. It wasn't so much the seven hours of digging that destroyed Rami's arms, but having to fling the dirt and rocks away. The only mercy was that the hole gave them slight relief from the chilly wind.

Mia seemed less fazed and had done most of the digging. She appeared to be fuelled by anger, and oddly, her determination reminded him of one of the reasons he admired her. This was the most effectively they had worked together in years, probably because it was mostly done in silence.

The sycamore trees towered over the grave, making everything more claustrophobic.

Soon, they would be done with this nightmare twenty-four hours, and each other. His emotions exhausted him. He would glance at her and feel love and warmth, allowing memories to entertain hope of a reconciliation, but then she would look at him in a way that somehow was more like swearing, and his love would fade under flashes of a pure, poisonous hatred. She would make a great actress, as she could communicate so much resentment with the slightest movement.

He wished he could stay angry, but he blamed himself for so much of her sadness. Maybe acknowledging it would help to create some positivity. 'Mia,' he said through laboured breaths. 'I know we're over. But I wanted to say thanks.'

She continued digging.

'I wouldn't be managing my gambling addiction if you didn't take me to Gamblers Anonymous and show me so much love. And when you gave up your job in London so we could move here. That was massive.'

She stopped digging for a moment, but then carried on.

He dug up more dirt and tossed it out of the hole. He would never forget her eyes shining when he became a full-time employee on the University of East Anglia's Creative Writing course, nor the way she held him when he told her he had lost twenty thousand pounds of their savings in a combination of casino trips and online poker. He had expected her to leave, but she stayed, even when everyone blamed him for Becca's suicide. It must have all taken its toll.

He stopped digging. 'You stood by me through some pretty rough stuff. So yeah, if tonight is the last time I spend proper time with you, then thanks.'

She turned to him, but it was too dark to read her expression.

'You're welcome,' she said flatly. 'Let's get on with it.'

Rami swallowed his hurt. What was he expecting?

He checked his Fitbit: 4.03 a.m. He tossed his shovel out of the grave, his arms throbbing.

He used his remaining strength to push himself up and out of the hole. He knelt and reached a hand out to help Mia, but she tossed her shovel out of the hole and pulled herself up.

Rami took a moment to catch his breath. Mia slapped the dirt off her clothes and marched to the car, next to the tent, which was set up about thirty feet away in the clearing. Rami followed.

Mia opened the boot, revealing the dead man in his yellow boxer shorts and helmet. His body was stiff, rigor mortis having taken hold. The man's wallet was next to him. Somehow, even in the dark night, the man's face shone ominously. If Rami hadn't been so obsessed with why Mia had hesitated in therapy, none of this would have happened.

Rami reached into the tent. He pulled out the bunched-up three-by-four-metre tarpaulin sheet. He lay it down. 'Let's wrap him in this.'

Rami grabbed the man under his arms and pulled him outside of the boot enough for Mia to take his legs.

He wished he could reset the man's shin and forearm. It was bad enough he was dead, but something about looking at broken limbs made everything feel a lot more sinister. He looked like a figure in a horror film, limbs jagged and unnerving.

They placed him down at one end of the tarp.

It was nearly over. They rolled him as though they were making a Swiss roll – Rami wished he had a robust enough gut to eat one – then they carried the heavy corpse to the grave, placing him down at its edge.

Rami knelt by the man, breathing heavily. 'What do you think he did for a living?'

Mia knelt next to him. 'Just stop it.'

'It's how I cope. Rather than pretending we've done nothing wrong.'

'Well, cope in your head. Come on.' She placed her hands on the tarp.

A wave of regret hit Rami. They had already gone too far, but there was no turning back from this.

Mia huffed. 'Goodbye to an unfortunate mistake.' She looked up at Rami and held her gaze a moment too long.

It was as though a boiling hand gripped Rami's heart. He stood up.

Mia ran her hands through her hair. 'Don't get stroppy.'

'No.'

'No?'

'Do it yourself.' His head pounded.

Her eyes widened. 'Don't be a prick.'

He gritted his teeth. 'I don't care if we get caught. We deserve to get caught. We killed someone.'

'It was an accident,' Mia corrected.

Every sinew in him tightened, stretched to ripping. 'We're chucking a life into the ground as though it never breathed, never spoke to anyone. For what? So we can carry on with our empty lives?'

'We spoke about this, Rami,' she calmly said.

'It's not too late,' he pleaded. 'We can call the police, admit to what we've done, and take our punishment. I'll even say it was mostly my fault, and they'll never know you were drunk. But this... everything we do is just adding to the crime.'

'We're not calling the police. Stop being a scared little shit and push with me. You owe me.'

Using the times she was a good wife as credit was pretty low. Rami shook his head and walked away into the trees. A chill consumed the heat within him.

For so long he had hoped they could return to being a team, who worked together, for love and a future.

'You're a cunt!' she shouted, and then the shouting stopped.

He wiped his tears on his filthy sleeves and continued walking into the darkness.

8
____

SHOVEL TO THE HEAD

Mia rolled the tarp containing the stiff, dead man into the grave, but the tarp unravelled, revealing him in his yellow boxer shorts and motorcycle helmet.

She groaned, picked up a shovel, scooped some soil up and chucked it over the corpse. The dirt splatted against his torso and helmet.

She pushed and kicked soil into the hole. This was going to be a slog.

Half an hour passed and she had barely covered his legs.

She dragged her aching limbs to the car and jammed the shovel into the soil next to the rear right tyre. She retrieved a petrol can from the boot, returned to the grave, unscrewed the can cap and poured petrol all over the corpse.

She tossed the empty can towards the tent and approached the car's driver door to check her handbag. She took out a small pill box and removed a box of matches, leaving the Rizla papers and weed.

She closed the car door and noticed a tiny light in the distance. The useless clown probably had got scared of the dark.

But one light became two, and they moved quickly.

Mountain bikes.

Mia rushed over to the grave. There was no way to pull the man's body out before they got to her.

She pocketed the matches, then sprinted towards the mountain bikes to put more distance between them and the corpse.

The bikes slowed near her. She glanced back, the car and tent about twenty feet away, with the pile of soil barely visible another thirty feet behind them. She took slow breaths.

A boy and a girl, in their late teens, got off the bikes and leaned them against a tree.

'You okay, miss?' the girl asked, stepping closer. Her facial piercings became visible.

Mia smiled, wiping the back of her hand over her forehead. 'Yeah, just, you know, camping under the stars. Don't mind me,' Mia said. 'Love your eyebrow barbell.'

'Cheers. But, we have to mind you,' she said. 'My uncle saw your car drive in hours ago. He asked us to come and see what was happening, so thanks for dragging us out in this.'

'Sorry,' Mia said.

The boy ran his hand through his hair. He lacked piercings or anything that would make a teen stand out. 'You're not allowed to camp here between October and February.'

'Really?' Mia asked.

'Yeah,' the girl said. 'Surprised you'd want to in this cold. You can park in lay-bys and walk into the grounds, but no cars. It's a nature reserve.'

Mia nodded. 'Oh, I'm so sorry. I didn't know. I'll pack up and leave.'

'Cool,' the girl said. 'If you're looking for a place to stay, my uncle owns a bed and breakfast about a mile north. It's called The Happy Hen. But I'd skip the breakfast part.'

'Yeah.' The boy chuckled. 'He can barely make toast.'

Mia smiled. 'Thanks for the tip. I'll definitely do that. Have a good night.'

The boy got back on his mountain bike, but the girl shone her phone torch beyond Mia. 'You digging?'

'What?' Mia turned around spotting the shovel stuck in the ground by the car.

'You can't dig here.' The girl walked past Mia towards the car.

A wave of nausea engulfed Mia. She rushed in front of the girl and blocked her path. 'It's... erm... I was making a fire. Wanted to do it in a pit so it doesn't endanger the trees or disturb the... night animals.'

The girl shone her phone beyond the car and spotted the pile of soil. 'Christ. Must be a massive pit.' She tried to walk past.

Mia's heart pounded and she stepped in her way. 'Well, I'd rather just pack up and go. Now that I know I was mistaken.'

The boy placed his mountain bike back against the tree and marched over, his face sterner. 'Let us pass or we'll call her uncle.'

'There's nothing to see, but fine.' Mia walked ahead of them, towards the car, trying to figure out what to do. 'Not sure what you're hoping to find.' She stopped at the car boot, her hand shaking towards the shovel handle. The hole was thirty feet away.

The teenagers stood by the tent. The girl shone her phone torch on it, while the boy stepped towards the pile of dirt.

Mia yanked the shovel out of the ground and drew it back, but Rami, topless, sprung out of the darkness from behind the pile of soil. 'Stop! Please!' he pleaded.

The boy recoiled. 'Help!' He scurried behind the girl and they shuffled backwards, beyond the car bonnet.

The girl took a corkscrew out of her pocket and pointed it at Rami. 'Get yourself back or I'll stab you!'

'Sorry,' Rami said. 'I'm so sorry!' He raised his arms, surrendering. 'We were in the middle of a role play and you've ruined it.'

Mia tossed the shovel away.

The boy grimaced. 'Damn weirdos.'

The girl shook her head, appalled. 'Go role play in a bloody Travelodge!'

Rami walked towards Mia. 'She's always had this fantasy of making love within the earth, you know, to be connected to Mother Nature.'

Mia nodded. 'There's just something so raw and... pure about it,' she added unconvincingly.

Rami picked up some dirt and pressed it to his chest. 'Did you know that the bacterium in soil can boost resistance against stress and reduce inflammation?'

The teens looked confused.

Rami rubbed a clump of soil against his face. 'We've worked it into the scenario. She's so stressed in our capitalist society that she's been dreaming of escape, and she happens across this bog where she sees me, a bog demon. I represent freedom, so she watches me, fantasising and—'

The girl waved her hands to stop him. 'Just get out of here! And you're banned from my uncle's BnB.'

The boy tutted. 'If you want to get freaky, go to the River Babingley. That's where the doggers and deviants head to.'

The girl looked at him, surprised.

He shrugged. 'What? Cousin Kenny knows this stuff.'

They returned to their mountain bikes. The girl muttered, 'Nutters everywhere.' They cycled away.

Mia turned to Rami, who shivered in the cold air. 'Thanks.'

He wiped his nose and walked behind the pile of soil to gather his clothes. He pulled his jumper back on. 'Can't exactly bury him here now, can we?'

Mia shook her head. 'I want him out of my life.'

'A few more days,' Rami said.

~

Mia and Rami, covered in filth, sat on the car bonnet in the empty service station car park and ate their McDonald's. The 6 a.m. sun crept over the distant fields and was oddly calming.

Mia was so numb from trying to dispose of the body that she barely felt the cold. It was a far less enjoyable form of a beer or wine jacket.

She stared at the sky. 'Fuck, fuck, fuck, fuck, fuck, fuck, fuck, fuck, fuck.' What if they never got rid of the body? What if she had to stay with Rami for months as it slowly rotted? She had to free herself from this and get to Wilfred.

'Think you're a couple of fucks short there.' Rami chomped into a Big Mac, then removed the top bun and poured a salt sachet onto the beef patty.

Mia dipped a chicken nugget into some barbecue sauce. 'You sure you should be eating that? I don't want your arse leaking on the drive back.'

Rami chuckled. 'I don't care anymore. And these chips, even with all the silicone and rubbish inside them, are delicious.' He heaved a handful into his mouth and released a joyous groan. 'Plus, if there's a chance I'm going to prison, then I'm going to eat anything I want.' He took another bite of his burger.

Mia let out a long breath. 'You know, it crossed my mind to smash those kids' heads in with the shovel.'

Rami spoke with his mouth full. 'Don't be too hard on yourself. I was thinking all sorts of weird stuff earlier that made me sick.' He stuffed more of the burger into his mouth.

As much as Mia disliked him, she needed a distraction. 'What kind of weird stuff?'

Rami shrugged. 'While researching ways to dispose of him, I thought it might be easier to chop him into little pieces and remove him bit by bit. Bin a thigh somewhere. Chuck his ear into a well. Blend a hand and pour the mixture down the sink.'

'Wow! You're the one who wanted to keep it respectful.'

Rami scratched his ear. 'My mind is going to weird places. Like, it made me think about East 17.'

'Sorry, what? East 17? The band?'

'Yep. I've always wondered how a band with such perfect individual component parts breaks up? You know, Tony's song writing, Brian's singing, John and Terry's backing vocals. It was like alchemy. Other, inferior groups have split, but then became friends again and got together for a money-grabbing tour. Maybe East 17 accidentally killed someone, and the weight of the secret got so much that they could no longer work together. While the other three handled it, sort of, it killed Brian inside.' Rami scrunched up his burger wrapper into a ball. 'What else could drive a man's mind to go from singing those songs to YouTube rants? Secret murder.'

'Or mental illness,' Mia said. 'And stop calling it murder. It was an accident. We're not murderers.'

Rami lay back on the bonnet and they let the silence hang.

'I was going to set fire to him,' Mia said, then started laughing uncomfortably.

Rami joined in. 'We've got a dead guy in the boot.'

They both laughed harder.

Mia pressed her palms to her forehead. 'And he's covered in petrol, dirt, and probably our DNA.'

Rami groaned. 'We're going to have to wash him, thoroughly. I suppose at least it means we'll be making use of the bath.' He sighed.

They had installed the bathtub when Mia was pregnant. She remembered them choosing it and how she would imagine them washing their little girl together. Her body tensed to squeeze the thought away. 'I don't think I have the strength to lug him up the stairs after digging that hole and getting him back out of it. He's so heavy.'

'That's just the weight of the guilt.' Rami sat up. 'Heard it adds ten kilos.'

Mia swallowed. 'I keep thinking I'm imagining it.'

'I wish we were.'

Mia picked some dirt out of her fingernails. 'I've learned a valuable lesson, though.'

'Yeah?'

'Don't divorce and drive.' She chuckled.

Rami smiled and hopped off the bonnet holding his stomach. 'Turns out the burger was a bad idea.' He hurried towards the service station.

Mia took her mobile phone from her handbag and called Wilfred. His gentle voice was a soothing serum against the poisonous gloom.

'You're through to the New York Throck Exchange, what can I do for you?' he said.

'Hey...' she said with little energy.

His voice hardened, detecting it. 'I take it you're not on your way?'

'Something unexpected happened,' she said, her eyes welling up.

His tone softened. 'Look, Mia. I'm sorry I put pressure on you, but whatever it is, just tell me and we can get through it. That's one of the things I love about us, the horseshit-free, lay-it-all-out-there honesty. Like when you told me my pitch for that diabetes chatbot name was terrible.'

Mia chuckled. 'Diabot. More like diabolical.'

Wilfred laughed. 'It would have tanked on the Throckmarket.'

Mia wished she could tell him. He would probably understand, but it would change things. 'It's Rami's mother. She's got lung cancer.'

Wilfred cleared his throat. 'Are you sure he's not making this up?'

'I can't leave him like this.'

'I get it,' he said flatly.

'This is going to happen, Wilfred. Just a few more days.' She wanted to bash her head in with the phone. 'I just... please.'

He coughed, letting the silence hang a moment. 'You should go and be there for your husband, Mia.' He hung up.

~

Mia, showered and wearing her pyjamas, sat on the closed toilet as Rami, still covered in dirt, sat on the edge of the bathtub and scrubbed the petrol off the dead man's stiff, naked body. His skin had a purple and blue hue to it.

The man's motorcycle helmet was on a towel and his yellow boxer shorts were downstairs in the washing machine.

Mia remembered her first kiss with Wilfred. After a conference with their London team, everyone went to sing karaoke at Lucky Voice in Soho. Not them. They got drunk at The Green Man pub and negotiated with a rickshaw driver to take them to all the tourist spots for one hundred and three pounds.

Craig David's 'Seven Days' had blasted from the rickshaw speaker while they stood outside Buckingham Palace, and they got into a debate about time and what it meant, realising they were wasting theirs with their current situations. They ended up making their excuses to their partners and staying in London until morning.

Mia vowed to herself, as soon as this body was dealt with, no more time would be wasted.

'Mia? Mia?' Rami repeated.

She looked at him. 'Sorry. Drifted off. Knackered.'

'I have an idea.' He squirted more Tea Tree shower gel onto

the dead man's body and wiped it with the sponge. 'To help with the guilt, we give him a horrible back story.'

Mia put her head in her hands.

'He was an abusive father, who would steal local cats and blend them.'

Mia grimaced. 'Suppose I've got no qualms with us accidentally running over that type of man.'

Rami nodded. 'It's a public service.' Then his face fell. 'I'm washing a dead guy.'

Mia let out a long breath. 'We'll get through it.'

Rami turned the water off and grabbed a towel from the rail. 'We don't have the best track record of getting through stuff.' He dried the man's head, grimacing.

Mia stared at the stiff body. 'The cats he blended. Maybe he sold them to people as smoothies and they were none the wiser. He called them Smeowthies.'

Rami smirked and dried the man's body and legs. 'Can I ask you something?'

Mia didn't care about anything anymore. 'Go on.'

Rami wrapped a bandage around the man's broken shin and forearm. 'Were you cheating on me?'

A cold tension gripped Mia's neck. What did Rami know? Had he seen her phone? Or had he seen her with Wilfred? She looked him in the eyes. 'No. Of course not.'

Rami lifted the man under his arms. 'It's just. Earlier, I was looking for a polo shirt. I thought it was in our... your room. But when I opened the wardrobe all your clothes were gone.'

Mia's neck relaxed. She grabbed the man's thighs, uncomfortably close to his dead genitals, and they carried him out of the bathroom. 'I took my clothes to the office over the last few days. Kind of saw things coming. Just wasn't ready to pull the plug.'

Rami half-smiled. 'Bit rubbish, isn't it? We've lived in the same house for years, but for at least two it's felt like we've been nowhere near each other. Why do you think people grow apart? Can't just be because we don't go to enough plays or axe throwing?'

Mia shrugged and led them down the stairs. 'Ask East 17?'

Rami nodded.

The doorbell rang, startling them before they reached the bottom step.

Mia whispered, 'Do you think someone's seen something?'

Rami shrugged. 'Only if they've got X-ray vision. It's eight in the morning, probably a delivery.'

Someone banged on the door. 'Mia! It's Lyn!'

Mia's eyes met Rami's.

The doorbell sounded again. And again.

Rami's face dropped. 'We need to get him in the garage.'

The banging continued. 'I know you're in there. Open the door!' The letterbox creaked open. 'Mia!'

Mia wanted to die. 'Coming!' She whispered to Rami. 'Get him back upstairs and I'll keep her busy.'

Rami's eyes widened and he lowered his voice. 'What!?'

'She's staring through the letterbox.' Mia placed the man's legs gently on the stairs. 'Hold on, hun!' Mia gave Rami a matter-of-fact shrug.

Rami struggled to drag the body back up to the landing, stumbling a couple of times, but once he made it out of sight, Mia slapped on her fakest smile, approached the door and opened it. 'Lyn for the win! Sorry I haven't—'

Lyn's face was stained with tears and smudged mascara. 'You're a dogshit friend, Mimi.'

This wasn't an unfamiliar outburst. 'Are you okay? I wanted to call, but it's been crazy, and I didn't have time to listen to all the voice notes—'

'He didn't turn up, did he?' Lyn threw her arms around Mia.

'Who?' Mia asked.

'Dale.' Her tears soaked through Mia's pyjamas. 'You didn't turn up, and when he wasn't there by ten I packed the party in.'

Mia stroked Lyn's hair. 'He doesn't deserve you.'

'It's not that. I've heard nothing since last night and none of my messages have gone through.'

A knot formed in Mia's stomach.

Lyn wept into Mia's shoulder. 'Last message he sent was before he got on his motorbike to head over. I know it sounds silly, but Dale wouldn't just disappear. I know him. I really know him.'

The knot twisted and a sharp pain squeezed Mia's insides. She stopped stroking Lyn's hair.

9

ROOM AT THE INN

Rami

Rami stared down at the corpse as he dragged it back towards the study. The acid rose in his throat.

D. B. Ragnor.

Dale Ragnor. Rami had imagined the D was for Dennis, or, given the man's hipster energy, something like Denton, or Determination. Dale's corpse was thirteen steps, some plasterboard, insulation, and a carpet away from his lover, whose cries rang through the house.

Dale. His name was Dale. Rami saw a fuller life. Maybe he had people who depended on him? Maybe he had a pet, waiting to be fed? There could be a cute puppy sat at the man's front door right now, wagging its little tail, unaware that Dale would never give it another treat.

Rami left the body next to his single bed. Living in the cramped study made him feel like he was back in university halls of residence – a virgin with nothing but his screenwriting books for company.

He removed his filthy clothes, sprayed enough deodorant to neutralise a festival toilet, then put on a T-shirt and tracksuit bottoms.

He remembered the helmet. He rushed into the bathroom and grabbed it, his eyes catching the fluid stains on the inner padding. He retched, then washed his face with cold water, scrubbing the dry mud from his forehead and cheeks.

The boxer shorts. They were currently spinning around in the washing machine.

He waited for his heart rate to slow to normal, but normal no longer existed. He returned to the study, placed the helmet in the wardrobe, then dragged himself downstairs and into the kitchen.

Mia was sitting on the sofa with Lyn's head buried in her lap. Rami wished he could turn her crying down or, ideally, turn back time and not kill her boyfriend.

Thankfully, Lyn's view of the washing machine was obstructed by the kitchen island. It wasn't like she would connect the yellow boxers to Dale, but everything was driven by paranoia.

Mia mechanically stroked Lyn's hair and stared ahead, empty, as though somebody had disconnected her brain.

Lyn slammed her palm on the sofa cushion. 'The police are doing bugger all! They said that 'cos of his age and 'cos he's not a vulnerable person, that he's low risk, which means less people looking into it! I need them to get helicopters and whatever they can get their hands on. If he is okay, why isn't he phoning me back?'

The washing machine finished its cycle. Rami opened the fridge and poured himself a glass of water from the filter jug. 'Maybe he's fine and just lost his phone. Or had to deal with a family emergency and can't call.'

Lyn sat up from Mia's lap. 'What kind of family emergency?' she asked pointedly.

Rami wasn't expecting a follow-up for specifics. 'I, erm...'

'He has no family. I'm his family!' Lyn turned to Mia. 'They said with men who go missing it's usually them getting lashed-up or in financial trouble, or having a breakdown, but it's none of those things. I know Dale. They won't listen to me. One of the tossers even said maybe Dale just had enough and has done a runner.'

Believable, if he wasn't currently upstairs.

Lyn pressed her knees to her chest. 'I just...' she choked up and groaned. 'The longer it goes on the more I think something bad has happened. I've left over a thousand messages.'

Also believable.

Mia put her arm around Lyn. 'I'm sure he's fine and will call soon.' She cleared her throat and bit her lip.

Lyn buried her face into Mia's shoulder. 'I can't imagine anyone would want to hurt him. He's such a pure soul. He works at a dog's home, and he was in the middle of getting funding for his loneliness charity. We've been making so many plans. We were going to get a puppy.'

Rami coughed, the guilt scratching his throat. 'Does he have any pets we should go and check on?'

Lyn shook her head. 'No. He loved being around them but this was going to be his first.'

Relief flowed through Rami, but only a little. He had still killed the man.

Lyn groaned. 'Finally, a proper relationship, but...'

Mia burst into tears, as though everything she was pushing down had finally exploded out of her.

Lyn's crying managed to grow louder and she held Mia's hand. 'No, Mimi! If you're crying then it means you think something nasty's happened too!'

Mia's sad eyes met Rami's, as though she wanted to tell Lyn the truth. She squeezed Lyn. 'I'm just sad that you're sad. Because I know how much you love him.'

When they had lost their baby girl, Mia had this vacant, zombie-like look on her face. This wasn't as awful, but not far off.

Rami opened a drawer and took a plastic bag. He stealthily opened the washing machine and placed the yellow boxer shorts inside the bag, then dropped it in the bin. 'You can't be sure something bad has happened,' he said, trying to cut through the cries. 'Give the police time. They're short-staffed and struggling. Best thing you can do is keep calling him and contact his friends. And maybe wait at home, in case he turns up.'

Lyn pointed at Rami. 'You've given me an idea.'

Hopefully related to the going home part.

Lyn took her phone out of her handbag. 'If the police are too under it, I'm going to start my own search. Set my Insta Lynstas on it.'

Rami had spent the last day imagining all the different ways this could get worse. Maybe Dale would come back to life, or maybe someone did see them discarding the motorcycle. Lyn being wrapped into this was worse than everything.

Mia placed her hand over Lyn's phone. 'It could cause more trouble than help. What if it interferes with the police?'

Lyn tapped her fingers against her surgically reduced chin, thinking, or maybe she was imagining a handbag dancing. 'Interfere with them doing nothing?'

Mia took Lyn's phone from her. 'Give the police time. They're trained for this.'

Rami sipped from his glass, an idea forming. 'I take back my sympathy for the police. Screw them.'

Mia glared at him through her teary, red eyes.

Lyn tilted her head at Rami.

Rami leaned forwards. 'You have the influence to lead this investigation. We'll help.'

Lyn smirked and reached out for her phone.

Mia's look softened, seemingly understanding Rami. 'That could also work.' She handed the phone back to Lyn.

Lyn started typing. 'Let's find my Dale. But, I don't want to be alone, Mimi. Can I stay here with you?'

Rami furiously scratched at his chest. 'You sure you shouldn't wait at yours, in case he turns up?'

Lyn shook her head. 'I can't be in spaces he's occupied right now. The energy's too much. I need my Mimi.' Lyn hugged Mia, who stared at Rami as more tears ran down her face.

'Sure,' Mia said. 'You can stay in the room with me, and Rami will sleep in the study.'

Rami nodded, surprised Mia hadn't told Lyn the ins and outs of their disastrous marriage.

Rami placed boxes at the foot of the bed, so that if anyone opened the door they wouldn't be able to see Dale under it. He desperately wanted to sleep, but had to pretend everything was normal. Maybe he could sneak an hour.

He sat on the bed and stared out of the window. He could feel Dale's cold presence. He moved the facial muscles around his sore nose.

A dog's home and a loneliness charity. Dale was a saint. Dating Lyn could also be classed as a form of charity work.

Making inappropriate jokes didn't lessen the misery of the situation. He had a good, honest, dead man under his bed, all because he couldn't let go of his marriage and was terrified to be alone.

Rami lay down and got under the duvet. One hour would be fine. He set his alarm for 9.30 a.m.

Something shuffled, and Rami worried Dale was coming back to life, but it was his toenail scratching against the covers.

His head stung, and he imagined the body twitching under

his bed. What if when Rami woke up Dale's ghost was stood above him? What if insects attracted to Dale's rotting corpse crawled all over Rami and went in his ears and up his nose as he slept?

Rami squeezed his eyes shut and took long, slow breaths.

10

PARASITES

MIA

Mia placed Lyn's breakfast plate on the kitchen counter. A boiled egg on a bed of spinach with a drizzle of olive oil. Lyn had eaten the same thing for breakfast ever since university. She was almost as boring as Rami with his celery sticks and hummus. Almost. At least she had olive oil.

'Thanks,' Lyn said, her eyes on her mobile phone. 'Look. More than three thousand people have retweeted it, and it's on everyone's Insta stories already.' She smiled, determined.

Mia, her hands trembling, poured herself a glass of water, struggling to look at her friend and to stay awake. She adjusted her thin cardigan over her vest and T-shirt. Wilfred had most of her winter clothes, so she had to dig into her summer wardrobe.

'Why haven't you shared my post, Mimi?' Lyn asked.

'Sorry, I will now.' She'd been avoiding her phone, often leaving it face down. She had texted Wilfred multiple times and he hadn't replied, so she wanted to ignore her phone for as long as possible in the hope that when she checked it there would be a message from him. It was like being a teenager again.

75

She checked her phone. No messages.

Mia opened Lyn's post. A series of images of her and Dale, the man she could have potentially had a happy life with, had Mia not driven through him.

There was a selfie of Dale and Lyn in bed. There was the obligatory photo of them in a fancy restaurant holding the dinner plate up to their faces. A third image of the two of them on a train going somewhere inconsequential stared back at Mia. She couldn't look at the other photos, as Lyn's beaming smile crushed her.

The message read:

INSTA LYNSTAS ASSEMBLE!

My Dale's been missing since Thursday night (my birthday FYI). He was riding his bike from his home in Bungay along the A143 to Great Yarmouth. If you've seen the beautiful man in these photos please DM. Police being totally useless and shit.

Love,
xLxYxNx

#missing #fuckthepolice #999 #searchforlove #Dale

A143? They had hit Dale on the A47 between Norwich and Great Yarmouth. 'You didn't need to call the police useless,' Mia said.

Lyn shrugged. 'When it comes to people I love, you're with me or you're on the prick list.'

Mia grabbed her mum's car keys from the kitchen counter. 'Well, text me if there's any news.'

'Where are you going?' Lyn asked, annoyed.

Rami dragged his feet into the kitchen, his eyes puffed up.

Mia felt a pang of sympathy that he had to share a room with a corpse, but just a pang. She placed a hand on Lyn's shoulder. 'I've got to take the car back to my mum's.' Plus she wanted to pull over somewhere and have a nap.

Lyn jammed her fork into the boiled egg, and the metal clanged against the china plate. 'I want to drive the route he took. Some of my Insta Lynstas are keen to help. Thought you'd come.'

Rami took a tub of hummus from the fridge, opened it and sniffed it, grimaced, then scooped the contents into the food bin.

Mia gestured towards him. 'Rami will go with you.'

'What?' he said, half-groggy.

'I'll join you both once I'm done,' Mia said. 'I'm just going to drop the keys and run. I don't want to have to hear about which of her friends died, or why I look terrible.' Mia hurried out, struggling to look at her friend's face.

Mia had been sat on her mother, Andrea's, sofa for over an hour, sipping on a disgusting homemade kombucha that left a layer of fuzz on the roof of her mouth.

'Did you hear about Tony? You remember my friend Tony?' Andrea asked in a thick Italian accent. She adjusted her dress, far too formal for a Saturday of nothing, and shuffled on her armchair, which she sat on as though she were a queen on a throne. The rosary beads and crucifixes dotted around the room seemed more prominent than usual, making Andrea's judgemental aura more powerful.

'Yeah.' Mia had no idea who Tony was, but if she said as much, Andrea would insist that she definitely did.

'He died. Such a shame. And Eva has colon cancer.' Andrea sipped her kombucha.

Mia played Bad Vibes Bingo whenever she would visit. There was who had died, who was dying, who Andrea wished was dead, who was having an affair, whose children were a disgrace, or which service provider she was arguing with.

Andrea tutted. 'Yet somehow that cow Dorothy never even gets a cold.'

Tick.

Andrea continued. 'And I had to spend three hours on the phone to BT.'

Mia zoned out and sent Wilfred another WhatsApp message:

I love you. I know things have been off, but I promise, next week we can start our lives. I can't wait to do the boring things with you x

She needed to get something positive from this. Her stomach twisted and she held in the tears.

Andrea droned on. 'And I shouted at them to get me the manager. The problem is when you call customer service you're put through to someone in a completely different country.'

'I'm divorcing Rami,' Mia blurted out.

Andrea's face hardened. 'No, you are not.'

Mia stood up. 'I am, and I've told Rami. I want to be happy.'

Andrea cackled. 'Happy? You're a stupid little girl.'

'Right. Bye, Mum. Tell someone to call me if you have a fall or get a serious illness.' Mia strode towards the front door and fumbled with her phone to order a taxi to the train station.

Andrea hobbled as quickly as her arthritis would allow her. 'Happiness is not something you are, it's something that happens to you, sometimes, if you're lucky.'

Mia turned around. 'Yeah, and I'd like it to happen more than never.' She opened the door to the Japanese garden styled driveway that was larger than most flats.

Andrea stopped in the doorway. 'Our family doesn't divorce, Mia.' She looked around, likely checking for neighbours.

Mia didn't care who saw. 'And how did that work out for Dad?'

Andrea gripped the door handle. 'Come in and talk,' she said sternly.

Mia stayed where she was. 'Instead of telling him you were unfaithful, or divorcing him, you made him suffer. That's what killed him. Wondering why his wife didn't care about him.'

Andrea glared at her.

Mia shook her head. 'He often asked me if you were okay, because you were always so tense and irritable around him. And I didn't have the guts to tell him the truth about you.'

Andrea folded her arms. 'You're making a scene.'

'Fuck off. And he didn't have the strength to leave you because you're both from stupid families who think divorce is worse than living in eternal gloom, because you're worried about what some hag like Dorothy might say.'

Andrea shook her head. 'The world isn't as simple as you think, stupid child. I wish we'd never raised you in this country. It's stained your values.'

'My values are perfect compared to yours.'

'When you've calmed down, I expect an apology.' She retreated inside and slammed the door.

Mia took slow breaths and walked into the middle of the fancy Cambridge road, not caring. She stared at Andrea's front windows, wishing her angry thoughts were powerful enough to shatter the glass, or at least smear shit all over them.

She spotted a car coming and a couple of passing pedestrians. 'My mum used to cheat on my dad!' she yelled. 'With pretty much anyone. And I caught her shagging her best friend's son on my bed! Had to change the sheets myself, because she was too pissed. Don't let all the biblical stuff in her house fool you! When she kneels it's not to pray!'

As a car beeped her, she knew there was only one way to

avoid turning out like her mother. No secrets. She had to tell Wilfred.

Mia waited, sitting on a bench by the lake at the University of East Anglia. She watched the ducks swim around, carefree and stupid. They watched her, too, probably expecting food.

'Piss off.' Her breath floated away on the cold air.

She had left Wilfred a voice message, saying she would be at their bench. She wanted to talk and would be there for an hour.

This was where they had sat until the sun came up when they had to leave an Erasure gig at the university's concert venue. They had been gutted to miss most of the performance, but Mia had spotted a friend of Rami's and needed to avoid being seen. They had made the best out of a bad situation though, and spoke about their lives instead of fuelling their affair with alcohol. It was that night, vulnerable, and with no barriers or booze to hide behind, that she realised that Wilfred was what the word "home" meant.

It had been fifty-three minutes since she had left the message.

Andrea had phoned but Mia ignored her, knowing she would try to make her feel guilty, and certain she would succeed, because Mia blamed herself for her parents' terrible marriage. Her father had often talked about how he and Andrea once had a great relationship. They inspired and challenged each other. Once, they had learned how to make pottery together and sold their pieces to a small crafts shop in Great Yarmouth. Then, in their early thirties, they obtained licences to metal detect on south-coast beaches. Her father had always wanted to learn Greek, so Andrea went to classes with him for the fun of it, and there was the time they did paddle-boarding on the Norfolk

Broads, even though Andrea was scared of the water and hated the cold. Mia's father probably never realised that everything he said implied that they had lived a wonderful life, before Mia.

She gazed back at the Brutalist architecture of the university accommodation, hoping to see Wilfred interrupt the view.

A man walked his dog, while crows pecked around at the frosty grass.

Mia buried her head in her hands, remembering Lyn's smile as she spoke about moving in with Dale. It was a different smile to Lyn's usual ones. It was proper, like the one Mia felt that night with Wilfred.

She turned back to the ducks and the air drained out of her. This secret, this deed, this accidental murder, it had burrowed into her chest. It was a parasite, gnawing on her heart. It weighed on her every movement and thought. The only way to heal would be to yank it out and share it, lightening the load.

Would Wilfred be able to handle it? He was understanding, rational, and would see it wasn't deliberate. He knew her. She wasn't a murderer. They could support each other through it.

First, he needed to turn up.

Ten more minutes passed. Mia stood up, defeated, and dragged her feet back towards campus. She had wrecked everything.

'Mia!' a voice yelled from behind her.

Wilfred carefully tip-toe-ran on the grass, trying not to slip in his poor choice of brown loafers. He hoisted his suit trousers up around his ankles and his scarf blew all over his face.

The little energy Mia had drove her into his arms. She squeezed him, the warmth flooding through her.

He pulled away, holding her hands. 'I was on my way when my phone died and I went to the wrong bench. Sorry. You meant the Erasure night bench and not the...' He raised an eyebrow.

'The sex bench?' Mia laughed.

'Correct.' He stroked her hands. 'Look, I'm so sorry.'

She shook her head. 'No, you were right. And I—'

'No. It was unfair of me to put those demands on you,' he said. 'Divorcing him doesn't mean instant change, and the fact you've asked for one is such a gigantic step. I know it'll be bumpy, so take all the time you need.'

A huge grin formed on her face. Her entire body grinned. She released his hands and looked into his eyes. His sweet, caring eyes. She wanted to tell him. The words were there, the sentence ready for release. They would be a true team, capable of facing anything. 'I have to tell you—'

'I've done it.' His eyes lit up. His usual happy glow radiated brighter. 'I told Samira. Hence the...' He pointed to a cut above his eyebrow that Mia hadn't noticed. 'And, I've rented a little flat near here, just on Bluebell Road. This is it.' He smiled. 'Even though she's going to drag me through hell with the kids, I have this light energy, like I'm free. We're free, because I don't have the chains of secrecy yanking me down. I didn't realise how heavy it all was. But now it's out in the air and I feel like I could fly!' He turned to the campus. 'I love this woman!'

Mia's grin downgraded itself to a smile. He was amazing. She wished she had met him before she had settled for Rami, then everything would have been different. Better.

Wilfred released a relieved breath. 'I'm thinking, when things are done, we have a little festival weekend, three nights, three countries in Europe we've never been to, with a bespoke playlist for each one. Know what we can call it?' He smirked.

Mia's lip quivered. 'WoodThrock?'

Wilfred laughed. 'I was thinking Throck Till You Drop, Europe Edition, but I love WoodThrock.'

Mia stared at him and her body ached. The parasite chewed on her heart with more ferocity.

The joy Wilfred had at being free from secrets had made her

love him more. Telling him the truth would put him back in a cage, but this time forever.

'I'm sorry, Wilfred.' The parasite buried its teeth deeper into her heart and ripped chunks off it, but it was better it fed off her and left Wilfred free. 'We can't do this anymore.'

11

NEIGHBOURHOOD WATCHER

RAMI

Rami sat in the passenger seat of Lyn's fancy electric Lexus SUV, as she sped down the A143 from Bungay to Great Yarmouth, following what she believed was Dale's route. She hadn't stopped crying since they left, and the droning noise reminded Rami of when he would work from home and the neighbour would use their leaf blower for two hours straight.

Her abundance of jewellery didn't help either, rattling with every movement. Why would someone wear so much jewellery? Perhaps it was to drown out every sound and pull focus to her, or it was nature's way of giving people enough warning to flee from the approaching predator.

Lyn's perfume had formed a suffocating cloud of zesty toxicity that burned Rami's throat – or was that the guilt choking him from the inside?

Her attire was far too glamorous for a day trudging around a cold field. Other than wellies, her low-cut top and leggings suggested she was planning on going clubbing afterwards. If she complained about the cold, there was no way he was giving her his jacket. Maybe he should, though, considering he had murdered her boyfriend.

He opened the window a crack, hoping it would release the smell and liberate his nostrils, but the icy wind strengthened it and added more cold.

Maybe Rami and Mia's luck was in; if you could call it luck. This route was about a forty-minute drive from where they had hit Dale, and a further twenty to where the motorcycle was. If the search was focused here, they could bury the body somewhere far away.

Lyn sniffed back tears. 'What if we never find him?'

Rami hated that he hoped for that scenario. 'We will.'

Lyn nodded. 'But what if we don't?'

Rami wondered if he should take the realistic approach to ease her hurt, or give her hope. Both seemed equally cruel. 'You can't think that way, Lyn. You have to believe there is a positive outcome here, otherwise you'll struggle to do anything.'

Lyn reached for a tissue and wiped her tears. 'Thanks. I need him back. This is going to be the first Christmas where I have a boyfriend.'

It would not be. Rami swallowed. 'You know, I read that around 85 per cent of missing adults are found within two days, and only 5 per cent will be missing more than a week. Factor in your involvement, and I think we'll find him by tonight.' He decided not to share the more morbid statistics.

'Cheers, Rami.'

'You've got to let hope do its thing.' Rami gazed out of the window at the fields. Why was he sat here instead of Mia? Why did he have to face the pain they had caused alone?

Lyn huffed. 'Still no messages from Mia. How long does it take to drop a car off?'

'You know how her mum can be. She'll be here.' Rami got annoyed at himself for defending her.

Lyn held out her phone to Rami.

He stared at it, unsure of what to do.

'Check my Insta DMs for messages from Gyaldem Official. She'll have info on where to stop. Password's 9461.'

He opened Lyn's Instagram app onto a page of her videos: an endless stream of electric guitar covers with the same framing – Lyn, sat on a plush sofa, wearing a revealing thigh-split dress, with one leg crossed over the other showing off her snake tattoo that went from her right ankle all the way up her skirt. She held a guitar, and the glass windows behind her looked out onto a stunning garden. She had one hundred and three thousand followers for playing the electric guitar in a dress.

Rami checked her inbox and found the message. 'She says, "Hey, bitch tits."' Rami cleared his throat and continued uncomfortably. '"As you get near Haddiscoe, you'll see the muffmobile parked on the right by a dull-as-arse field. We're all here."' Rami sighed, hoping he never had to say "muffmobile" ever again in his life.

Lyn sped up. 'Message her back: Thanks babe. There soon. And put a kiss, L, kiss, Y, kiss, N, kiss.' Rami typed out the message. He thought being a soon-to-be divorced secret murderer was bad enough. Now he was Lyn's secretary.

He sent the message and closed the inbox, catching a flash of posts containing Dale. He locked the phone, handed it back to Lyn, and stared out of the window, trying to shake Dale's image from his mind.

They pulled up to the field fence and parked behind a pink Porsche with the licence plate MiN G3. Rami shook his head and gazed at the horizon on both sides: fields and fields.

The scale of the search needed to be within a mile of Dale's motorbike, never mind Dale himself, filled Rami with a guilty hope. Maybe he could leave the country to somewhere with no extradition laws. He could go to Lebanon to learn about his ancestry from his mother's side. Maybe he could visit Saint Charbel's tomb and pray for a miracle to get him out of this.

He shuddered. He had always championed those who were wronged, and now he was the wronger. There was nuance to it, he kept telling himself. An accident happened and they made a bad choice, but it was the best bad choice.

And the most selfish one.

They exited the car. Rami took a moment to fill his lungs with non-perfume-filled air. They approached a group, about eighty strong, of mostly young women, but also some out of place much older men.

Someone as glammed up as Lyn handed out wellies to people and posed for photos. On noticing Lyn, she dropped the bag of wellies and ran up to her, pulling her into a tight hug.

'Lyn for the win,' her friend said in a sympathetic tone.

Lyn closed her eyes and squeezed her friend. 'Gyal Pal, I love you.'

'We'll find that gorgeous ride,' she said.

Lyn smiled and her friend released their hug, then eyed Rami up and down suspiciously. Or that could have just been the way her face was set in the mould.

Lyn gestured at him. 'This is Rami, my best mate Mia's husband.'

Ex-husband. Discarded former husband. No-longer required life partner, unless it was to babysit devastated friends.

'Nice to meet you, Rami. I'm Gyal Pal,' she said.

'Nice to meet you, too,' he replied, knowing full well that Gyal Pal was not her real name, and that he would never say it out loud.

Gyal Pal and Lyn walked towards the starstruck crowd.

Rami followed, maintaining a healthy distance.

Lyn faced the crowd as her friend took her phone out to video the moment, which seemed insensitive.

Lyn clasped her hands together and took a deep breath. 'It means the world to see so many Lynstas assemble for my Dale. Thank you. We—'

'Can I get a photo? I love you,' a young woman pleaded.

'Course, hun.' Lyn waved her over, battling her tears. She smiled for the selfie.

The young woman looked like she had won the lottery. 'I loved your cover of "Enter Sandman", and "Nothing Compares to You" – amazing.'

'Thanks,' Lyn said. 'I appreciate that. Okay, everyone, the plan is—'

'Can I get one, too?' a creepy older man asked. 'I love all your covers.'

Lyn bit her lip and waved him over. He put his arm around her waist, inappropriately close to her arse, and took the selfie.

Rami grimaced, and more people demanded selfies while Gyal Pal continued filming.

It was a circus. Lyn's grief was nothing more than content to them. While it reassured Rami that with these idiots, Lyn had no hope of finding Dale, he wanted to keep up the charade and win her trust. 'Hey! Give her some space. We have a mission, and there'll be plenty of time for photos later.'

Lyn smiled.

Gyal Pal pointed her camera at Rami.

He tried his best to ignore it and approached the group. 'We need to split up and search these fields. Then, later, you can have all the selfies you want. If you find anything useful for the search, take a photo of it and DM it to Lyn or...' He gestured to Gyal Pal.

'Gyal Pal or Gyaldem Official,' she said.

'Yep. That,' Rami said.

Another creepy man approached Lyn, his phone ready to take a selfie.

'Later,' Rami sternly commanded.

The man sheepishly retreated.

～

Three painful hours that felt like months. Rami's teeth wouldn't stop chattering, he was exhausted, and he couldn't feel his fingers. This was like a reverse hell. Rather than walking through fire and feeling the heat of his sins, he was having them frozen into his bones.

How was Lyn not cold? Did being made of ninety percent synthetic materials keep her insulated?

Their group had reduced from a line of thirty-five, to seven, including Rami and Lyn. They had barely covered two fields.

Even though he knew they wouldn't find anything, any time Lyn's phone pinged with a photo message, or they saw a random item like a hat or a glove, he would get a tension headache.

Lyn stopped. 'This is hopeless.'

Rami stayed with her as others continued searching. 'You okay?'

Lyn's shoulders slumped. 'I give people so much content, yet they can barely give me a minute.'

Rami thought about putting a hand on her shoulder to comfort her, but he didn't want to touch her or suggest affection. 'People turned up. That's great. And you've already covered more ground than the police.'

She gazed around the field. 'What if we find him chopped up?'

'I think he's going to turn up fully alive soon, and there'll be a perfectly reasonable explanation about what happened.' He looked down, wishing mud would shoot into his mouth and nostrils, choking him to death.

One of Lyn's female minions whistled and waved them over to a ditch. 'Something here.'

'Oh God,' Lyn said.

'I'll check first,' Rami said.

'No, no, I've got it.' Lyn marched towards the ditch then stopped. 'No, I don't. You look.'

Rami approached. Even though he knew there would be

nothing Dale-related, his heart raced and breathing quickened. He closed his eyes to steady himself, and when he opened them, there was just a pair of muddy trainers at the bottom of the slope by the water's edge. 'It's a pair of trainers,' he told Lyn, his heart pounding.

'Are they Converse?' she asked.

'Hard to tell; they're caked in mud.'

The minion pointed. 'If there's trainers, maybe there's a body nearby?'

Rami glared at the minion disapprovingly.

'What?' the minion asked, unaware of their insensitivity.

Lyn joined Rami and looked at the muddy footwear.

'Has anyone checked if anything's in the water?' Rami asked.

They all shook their heads, and nobody seemed eager to volunteer.

Lyn turned to Rami. 'It's a great idea. Could you?'

No, but he couldn't exactly say that. 'Of course, Lyn.' He carefully stepped down the slippery slope, cursing the uselessness of Lyn's minions.

He slipped and stumbled, unable to halt his momentum and crashed into the freezing shallow water. 'Shit!'

'Are you okay?' Lyn yelled from the top of the slope.

He wiped the filthy, muddy water out of his eyes, and stuck his thumb up. Some of Lyn's fans filmed him, while Lyn remained focused.

'Do you feel anything?' Lyn asked.

'Only regret,' he replied, more concerned by what he couldn't feel thanks to the low temperatures. He was going to drag Mia to this field and chuck her in the ditch.

He waded around, but there was nothing. He grabbed the trainers and wiped mud off the logo. 'Not Converse.'

Lyn shook her head. 'He only wore Converse and his motor-bike boots.'

Rami, fuming, struggled to climb the slope, and Lyn's idiots were no help. When he made it, she threw her arms around him. 'Thank you for looking.'

For someone who cared so much about her appearance, she didn't seem bothered that her clothes and skin were now covered in sloppy filth.

Rami's arms remained by his sides as he shivered. Mia had a lot to answer for.

~

Lyn and Rami approached his front door. He took his key out of his pocket, desperate to get inside and out of the muddy clothes, but his hands were so cold he couldn't put the key in the keyhole.

Lyn sympathetically took his key from him and unlocked the door. 'Honestly, Rami, even though Mia's a massive flap for not turning up, never stop appreciating her. You never know when someone's gonna vanish.'

Rami chuckled. 'Well, that ship has sailed and hit an iceberg.'

Lyn frowned. 'What do you mean?'

'The reason she didn't take your calls for the last couple of days is because we had an argument on the way to your party and she asked for a divorce.' He pushed the door open and entered.

'What?' Her face scrunched as much as one pumped full of Botox could.

'You must've had some idea this was coming?' he said.

Lyn shook her head. 'Mia's not the biggest sharer. She said things were bad, but...'

Rami sighed. 'Well, yeah. As bad as they can get, it seems. But, let's not dwell on it, you've got enough going on.'

'Sorry, Rami,' she said, almost sounding genuine.

He removed his ruined trainers. What state would Dale's

body be in? 'Are you sure you wouldn't rather go back to yours, in case he turns up?'

Lyn shook her head and followed him in. 'I need people around me.'

'I get it,' he said, turning to close the front door.

'Hey, neighbour!' Jenny limped up to them, walking Ballula and carrying a little bag of dog poo. She smiled at Rami and pointed the hand holding the bag of poo at Lyn. 'You're much fitter than Mia.' She laughed at her comment and put the dog poo bag in the same hand as the leash, extending her now free hand to Lyn. 'I'm Jenny.'

Rami smiled.

Lyn reluctantly shook Jenny's hand. 'I'm Lyn, I'm...' She burst into tears. 'Sorry.' She dragged herself into the kitchen area, leaving Rami and Jenny at the front door.

Jenny winced at Rami. 'Was my joke that bad?' She returned the dog poo bag to her free hand.

Rami shrugged. 'Not your worst, but she's having a rough couple of days.'

'Rough!?' Lyn shouted from the kitchen area and stomped back to the door. 'Rough!? The love of my life is missing and the police are fiddling with their bits! That's more than rough!'

Rami raised his hands apologetically. 'The roughest. And they are looking.'

'Not hard enough,' Lyn pointed out.

Jenny opened her arms offering Lyn a hug. 'I'm sorry, love.'

Lyn threw herself into Jenny's arms and released more tears.

Jenny rubbed Lyn's back, the bag of dog poo shuffling against it, as Ballula sniffed Lyn's ankles. 'Police are in a tough spot, but I've seen how useless they can be first-hand when I spent time around them. A few bad apples in that bushel.'

'You worked for the police?' Lyn asked, releasing the hug.

Rami bit his lip.

'Yeah, but in more of a voluntary support capacity. I still do.

I've made loads of contacts in and around Norfolk and know an investigator. If you want, I can chat with him and we can see what we can do to help you find your fella?'

'One hundred per cent yes.' Lyn smiled and nodded. 'Bless you, Jenny.'

Rami gripped the door frame.

12

MANAGING THE ODDS

Mia

Mia pulled a stool in front of a slot machine at Anglia Fun Casino. She had never entered a casino before, but it called to her. A place where she knew nobody, and she could drink peacefully under the lifeless lighting.

She knew why Rami had fallen into addiction, and wanted to feel the power of intermittent reinforcement for herself. Rather than rewarding someone every time they pressed a button, occasional rewards got them hooked on hope and the odd success.

She caught a glimpse of her exhausted, tear-battered face in the slot machine's reflection. She put a pound in and pressed the button to start it. The reels span.

No matches.

Her phone buzzed. Wilfred. She ignored him again. Twenty-three missed calls. She didn't dare listen to the messages. His voice would pull her back to him.

She downed her vodka and coke. Maybe it was worth turning herself in. She could never be with anyone now, because the secret would be part of her forever. The only person she could share this disaster with was Rami, but that was a prison. At least HMP Norwich would have a more varied menu and likely more interesting conversations.

She won five pounds. The combination of the positive sound with the reels matching gave her a jolt of joy. She put a pound back in.

Was Rami still attached to her because of intermittent reinforcement? She hadn't shown him any positive outcomes recently.

What was she meant to do with her life? She rubbed her chest, trying to massage the parasite out of it. She wished she could talk to Lyn about it, but she could barely look at her. She checked her phone, all of the missed voice notes from Lyn. She pressed play on one of them, from 10.15 p.m. on the night they had accidentally hit Dale:

'Mia, you dickhead, where are you? He hasn't shown up. No call. No reply to my messages. Nothing. Have I misjudged it again? If he's another knob I'll rip his fucking eyes out. Where are you, Mimi?'

Mia couldn't listen to any more. She had caused this.

A grizzly man passed, eyeing her up. She furrowed her brow to make it clear that he shouldn't look again.

She walked to the bar, ordered another vodka and coke, then found another machine where she lost four more pounds.

Maybe she could focus on her work and make a ton of money. She was already doing brilliantly as a product director, but she could perhaps move into consulting, or go to a bigger, more established company. There was no way she could keep working at HealthWorld and face Wilfred daily. Even with remote work options, seeing his face on Zoom calls as a little thumbnail would crush her.

She won another ten pounds. She put another pound in. Then another.

She could have toy boys. Maybe that was it. Travel, experience luxuries, work from anywhere, and have emotionless, substance-fuelled sex whenever she felt frisky. Or, there was always celibacy. If she couldn't have Wilfred, then she didn't want anyone.

She lost another ten pounds.

She realised she could never win enough on the slots to want to stop. That was gambling's power. The more she played, the more she would think she knew what she was doing, and she would convince herself she had the upper hand and that a big payday was coming. But, it was that arrogance that would see her leave with nothing but a head full of regret and shame.

She put another pound in.

Mia stumbled through the front door, two hundred pounds down, and having drunk so much vodka that the house actually looked interesting.

She swayed into the kitchen, where Rami hoovered while wearing a jacket and beanie, the smell of haddock still in the air.

On spotting her, he turned the hoover off and stared at her.

'Smells exciting,' she said.

He shook his head. He looked like he was going to say something, but he didn't. He pulled the sofa out to hoover behind it.

'Don't shake your head at me,' she bit.

He leaned the hoover against the wall. 'You're an absolute disgrace, Mia.'

She stepped forward and steadied herself on the kitchen counter. 'Listen—'

He raised his right hand, cutting her off. 'No. I know it's hard to see your best friend like that, but I've spent the whole day babysitting her, getting caked in freezing, muddy water and whatever plagues that may bring. My nose hasn't stopped running for about five hours, and I've only just regained feeling in my fingers. To top it off, I've got a rotting body under my bed and Lyn's now over at Jenny's talking about hiring a private investigator.'

Mia's chest tensed. 'What?'

He walked across the kitchen and took an empty glass from the dish rack. 'Yeah. So you need to get your head screwed back on, and we need to make a proper plan of how we're going to deal with this... thing.' He took the filter jug and filled the glass.

Mia wanted to say something harsh to him, to put him back in his place, but he was right. Whatever future she pictured, she couldn't make it happen without sorting this out first.

He handed her the glass of water. 'I've got some ideas, if you're willing to listen.'

13

CLINGING ON

RAMI

Rami and Mia, both sat on the sofa, looked at a map of East Anglia on Rami's laptop. Mia seemed to pay attention, but she could simply have been asleep with her eyes open.

Rami pointed to the A143 between Bungay and Great Yarmouth, just outside of Haddiscoe. 'That's where we searched fields today. Lyn will want to check every inch of that area, because she thinks that's the route he took to her party.'

He wiped his still-running nose on the back of his hand and it stung, still wounded from when Mia whacked him. He pointed to the A47, just west of Acle. 'Our thing, happened here, roughly, which is about 16 miles from the search area.'

Mia nodded and made an odd, throaty noise.

Rami pointed northwest of Acle. 'His motorcycle is in the River Bure around this part of Belaugh. Another 12 miles away.' He leaned forward, grabbed Mia's glass of water from the coffee table and handed it to her. 'Are you following?'

She tutted at him. 'Yes. Belaugh,' she slurred. She downed her water, spilling some down her top.

What a disgrace. 'Well, I think we should avoid the east coast, because they might think that's worth checking if he was headed to Great Yarmouth. So we go inland, west. Somewhere around King's Lynn, over an hour away. It's quiet, and we can bury him there.'

Mia shook her head and groaned. 'Stop with the burying bollocks.'

'Burial is best,' he defended. 'Because we'll know where he is.'

Mia waved her hand around dismissively. 'Your thing about the meat distracting dogs is a myth for fools. Are you a fool?'

He swallowed. 'We'll bury him without the meat and nobody will ever find him, because they'll never even look in the area.' He scratched his neck and mentally told himself off for being so cold about it.

Mia tried to lean forward but fell back onto the sofa cushion. 'Let's get a boat, sail out to sea and dump him in the ocean. Done.'

'That would involve us hiring a boat, then getting him on that boat without being seen. It's too risky.'

Mia hiccupped. 'You talked about chopping him up before.' She pointed to the handmade Japanese knives on the magnetic rack above the toaster. Rami had bought them for her three years ago. They had barely used them. 'We could put him in bags to sneak him on the boat. Make it look like Waitrose shopping for the trip.'

Rami put his face in his hands, his mind invaded by the image of him standing over Dale's body, ready to chop him up. 'I think we'd need something sharper, and no.' He hated how much darker his thoughts had become. It was as though every second spent in this awful decision stripped away more of his humanity. 'Please curb your drinking until this is over.'

Mia offered a non-committal shrug. 'What about the river?'

'Less control. Burial is it. This is the way,' he said.

'Alright, Mandalorian,' she replied.

He shook his head at her childishness. 'The car's not ready until Monday, so we can use tomorrow to plan. Unless you want to borrow your mum's—'

Mia shook her head. 'Not going back to that hag for a while.'

Her expression turned sour. Her mother had a unique ability to make her feel utterly worthless. Rami wanted to ask if she was okay, but he was too hurt to show sympathy. It was tragic that caring was now something negative. He sighed.

Mia's phone rang. She silenced it and placed it face down. 'We need to see what's going on in the area as well. Avoid any busy nights. Stowbridge isn't too far from King's Lynn. Bit quieter.'

'Great idea,' Rami said.

Mia scoffed. 'Don't patronise me.'

'I wasn't. It is a good idea.'

'I know it is. I don't have bad ideas.'

He could think of several, but kept them to himself and closed his laptop. 'First thing, though. We're getting that body out of my room, now.'

Mia shook her head.

Rami stood. 'He's a foot away from me, Mia. Blood has started pooling on the carpet around him. In a day or so, gases from his broken-down organs may start to come out of his openings. *All* his openings.' His hands trembled. 'And when that endless reek starts pumping out of him, it'll be a beacon to all the insects. It's bad enough we killed him. But being in that room is like sharing the bloody coffin.'

'*Accidentally* killed him,' she pointed out.

As always, focused on the thing bothering her. 'Please. Jenny told Lyn she'd need her for a couple of hours. It's only been twenty minutes.'

Mia stood up and held on to the sofa arm to steady herself. 'Fine.'

Rami held Dale by his stiffened thighs and Mia took his arms to avoid an eyeline to his undercarriage. They placed his now more purple corpse on the wooden hallway floor.

It had taken a lot of effort to get Dale this far, mostly because Mia had forgotten the basics of standing and moving.

Mia unlocked and opened the garage door.

Rami paused. 'I've got an idea.'

'Is this the time for ideas?' Mia asked.

Rami dragged Dale's body into the kitchen and next to the coffee table. 'Trust me. Get the cling film.' Dale's body left a thin streak of bloody fluid along the hallway wood and kitchen tiles.

'No,' Mia said, leaning against the wall and glancing at the streak.

'I was researching ways to preserve a body,' he said. 'The elastic can handle the expansion caused by the decomposition changes. It can also hold all the rank liquids that are going to leak out of him.' Rami pointed to the drawer with the cling film in it. 'Come on.'

Mia staggered to the drawer, grabbed the cling film box and tossed it at him.

'Mature,' he said. 'We don't want him to start leaking and gassing in the garage. That smell might seep out into the street.' Rami crouched down and forced Dale's stiff arms by his sides, although his broken forearm was slightly wonky. Rami wrapped cling film around Dale's waist and genitals, the last things he wanted leaking. 'Clean that, please.' He pointed to the streak.

Mia closed her eyes and took a breath. She grabbed a mop and got to work.

Rami took a couple of dish cloths and wedged them underneath Dale's body, hoping no more rank liquid would trickle out of him. He wrapped cling film around Dale's feet and up to the bandage on his broken shin. He wanted to do his face last. He felt like he would be suffocating him, killing him again.

Mia opened the French doors to the garden and tossed the contents of the mop bucket into the weeds. She took the hose and sprayed the mop and bucket, then left them outside.

She re-entered, shaking her head at Rami.

'Thanks,' he said, ignoring her contempt.

She knelt by the body and helped Rami to wrap.

'Be careful not to overstretch,' Rami told her. 'Don't want any gaps.'

Mia glared at him.

'What?' he asked.

'I have the ability to understand what I need to do,' she said.

Rami held his arms up as a peace offering. 'Sorry.'

They wrapped cling film over the bandage on Dale's broken shin.

'How many metres of cling film do you think it takes to wrap a six-foot tall, average built man?' Rami asked.

Mia frustratedly tangled with some cling film. 'I don't know, Rami. I thought it would've been something useless you'd know, like how much cling film it would take to wrap the Eiffel Tower.'

Maybe he would check that later. A wave of guilt washed over him. 'This is horrible.'

Mia nodded, tears forming in her eyes. 'At least he's not *your* best friend's lover.'

Rami held Dale's legs up so Mia could wrap cling film around his knees. She had zoned out.

Rami stared down at Dale's stiff body. 'If there's an afterlife, I hope he's not watching us turn him into a bloody sausage roll.'

Mia's face was pained, then she retched. She ran to the toilet and closed the door behind her.

'Shambles,' Rami muttered. He continued wrapping up to Dale's stomach, going over his genitals again to be extra safe.

Mia's retching and throwing up added a haunting sound-track to the miserable experience.

Rami sweated through the T-shirt under his jumper and jacket. He felt light-headed as he tried to manoeuvre the cling film around Dale's chest. His hands shook, imagining Dale screaming "No!" and unable to do anything.

The toilet door opened and Mia stumbled back in. 'Sorry.' She rejoined the effort, which in her world meant sitting on the tiles, her back against the kitchen counter, and breathing heavily while staring at Dale.

'Do you want me to order you a kebab while you watch?' Rami asked.

Mia nodded, her eyes half shut. 'But hold the chilli sauce.' She grimaced.

Rami let himself smile as he pulled the cling film around Dale's shoulders. 'Remember when you made us hike three miles because you had a craving for a kebab and a walk at two in the morning?'

She smiled. 'Cravings are cravings.'

'Challenging the owner and the drunk students to a kebab-eating contest takes cravings to a new level.' He chuckled.

She nodded, proud. 'They were amateurs. You never eat the oily lamb doner first. The fat slows you down. It's chicken doner, then the shish, then onto the lamb. Simplicity.'

'We should see if your photo is still behind the counter.' He finished wrapping Dale's shoulders.

Mia's smile fell away. 'I'll get my own kebab.'

The doorbell rang.

Mia's eyes widened at Rami. 'A couple of hours?'

'That's what she said,' he whispered.

Mia struggled to her feet. 'I'll take her up to my room so she can whinge at me for not being around. Then you sneak him into the garage.' She pointed at him. 'Don't you dare mess this up.'

'I wasn't planning to.' Wounded his plan had been interrupted, he dragged Dale next to the sofa, out of view of the entrance.

Mia stumbled towards the front door, closing the garage door on her way.

Rami stood out of view, listening for Mia and Lyn to head upstairs.

'Hello,' Mia said in a shocked tone.

The voice that replied wasn't Lyn's, but was a deep male Norfolk accent. 'Good evening. I'm Detective Inspector Amini, and this is my colleague Detective Sergeant Opoku. We're here to see Lyn Fisher.'

The pressure squeezed at Rami's skull and a chill flooded his body.

14

NO REST FOR THE WRETCHED

Mɪᴀ

Mia leaned on the kitchen counter, repeatedly drinking water and refilling her glass. She stared at the uniformed officers who sat on the sofa: DI Amini, who looked straight out of a catalogue for middle-aged alpha males you wanted to avoid, and DS Opoku, a young, nerdy woman whose progressive ideas were likely listened to for show, then never implemented.

Underneath them, and only a cushion and a cheap wooden frame away, was the dead, mostly cling-film-smothered corpse. His empty eyes stared at Mia, and she would never be able to unsee his squashed genitals.

Rami, on the armchair facing the officers, tried to keep their attention on him. He clasped his hands and kept fidgeting. 'Been busy?' he asked DI Amini.

Mia wanted to throw the glass at Rami's head, or maybe wrap a roll of cling film around his face and squeeze the life out of him.

DI Amini blew his nose. 'Yeah. It's relentless. There's nothing dumber than the news folks broadcasting about budget cuts.' His eyes scanned the room a few times.

DS Opoku nodded and tapped her pen against her notepad. 'Might as well tell the criminals to fill their boots.'

Rami nodded. 'A bit like *The Purge*.'

'The what?' DI Amini asked.

'The film, where everything's decriminalised for twelve hours,' Rami said.

DI Amini chuckled. 'Not a cinema man, myself. But, yeah, not far off.' He pointed to DS Opoku's notepad. 'Look at that for a lack of resources. Should be iPads by now.'

DS Opoku nodded. 'Even have to buy my own pens.'

Rami chuckled, a little too loudly.

DI Amini glanced at Mia. She smiled and tried not to sway.

He smirked. 'It's okay,' he said. 'We're not going to arrest you for having a few shandies on your Saturday evening.'

Mia raised her arms in mock arrest. 'You got me. It feels odd, though. You're the police, so I feel like I've misbehaved.'

DI Amini nodded. 'I understand, but you've nothing to worry about. Unless you're hiding something?'

'Me?' Mia chuckled. 'I'm not exciting enough to hide anything. No skeletons in this closet.' She glanced at the corpse under the sofa. What if Rami was wrong and it started giving off gases now?

'If anything, she's too honest,' Rami said, a hint of bitterness in his voice.

Mia drank more water, willing Lyn to hurry up and arrive. 'It's been a long week,' she said.

'I know the feeling.' DI Amini held his gaze on Mia a fraction too long.

Rami played with his wedding ring. 'You sure you don't want a coffee or anything?'

'No, no. You're fine,' DI Amini replied. 'I love the stuff, but it's a killer on my rhinitis.'

'Really?' Rami asked.

'Supposedly. Some online hippy said it triggers histamine. Been off it two weeks, and already seeing results.' He blew his nose again.

Rami gestured to DS Opoku. 'And for you?'

'I'm okay, thanks. Had my fill for the day.'

The doorbell rang followed by knocking. Mia wished Lyn would understand she could do either, rather than both at the same time. 'That'll be her.'

Mia concentrated hard to walk in a straight line.

'Careful,' DI Amini joked.

She forced a laugh, her elevated heart rate reminding her she was one wrong action or word away from arrest. If she had to, she would show the police the photos of Rami dumping the motorcycle in the river. Maybe that would be enough.

Mia opened the door. 'Hey, Lyn—'

Lyn barged past her, rushing into the kitchen.

Mia undid a blouse button and followed Lyn.

'Finally taking it seriously?' Lyn asked, stood above the police duo.

DI Amini and DS Opoku stood up. DI Amini offered Lyn his hand to shake. 'Of course we are. I'm Detective Inspector Ali Amini, and this is my colleague, Detective Sergeant Georgia Opoku.'

Lyn reluctantly shook DI Amini's hand, then DS Opoku's. She pulled a stool up opposite them, the chances of seeing Dale significantly higher than Mia was comfortable with. The officers sat back down.

Rami hurriedly stood up. 'You sit here, Lyn. Much more comfy.' He moved the armchair at an angle that reduced Lyn's chances of seeing Dale. He joined Mia at the kitchen counter.

'You found him yet?' Lyn asked as she sat.

DI Amini shook his head. 'I'm sorry for the lack of care that appears to have been shown to you. But, I promise that finding Dale is our top priority.'

Lyn scoffed.

DI Amini scanned Mia's loosened top. Good. Eyes and mind occupied. She offered him a half-smile.

He took his hat off and placed it on his lap, probably covering his boner.

DS Opoku leaned towards Lyn. 'I'm sorry you're going through this, but I can assure you we've been following procedure.'

'Well, your procedure's shit,' she spat.

DS Opoku bit her lip.

DI Amini raised an apologetic hand. 'I know it may seem that way, but it's not. We've upgraded the risk level to medium. And—'

'He's *missing*! What about being missing is low risk to start with?' Lyn slumped in the armchair. 'And why's it only medium now!?'

She needed to be sat up. Mia walked over to Lyn and stood behind the chair. She stroked Lyn's hair. 'Lyn,' Mia said softly, rubbing Lyn's shoulder to encourage her to sit up. 'They're here to help.'

Lyn placed her hand on Mia's. 'Ain't very good at it,' she mumbled.

DI Amini swallowed his irritation. 'Our procedure gives us the best chance of reuniting you with Dale.'

Lyn shook her head.

'We've checked in with local hospitals. He's not been to any,' DS Opoku added.

Mia wished Rami would stop staring under the sofa. He was a walking clue. She coughed, clearing her throat of nothing to divert his attention. He snapped out of his stare.

DI Amini blew his nose. 'Our next step is to check which phone mast last picked up his signal. We've put the news on our website, and we've ordered CCTV from Bungay to Yarmouth. If you have a computer or device of his, we—'

'I don't,' Lyn said.

CCTV from Bungay to Yarmouth wouldn't be hugely helpful to the police. But, if phone masts pointed them closer to the A47, they might be in trouble.

DI Amini tapped his feet. 'Okay, well. If it goes beyond seventy-two hours, we'll be telling the Missing Persons Unit at the National Crime Agency, and then they'll lend their support, but hopefully it won't come to that.'

Lyn squeezed Mia's hand.

DS Opoku leaned forward. 'We have a couple of questions that can help the investigation. They might be uncomfortable, but at this stage we're looking for leads that may assist us in pinpointing Dale's whereabouts.'

Lyn nodded. 'Ask away. Anything to find him.'

DS Opoku prepared to take notes. 'Does Dale have any enemies or people in his life you think might want to hurt him?'

Lyn welled up and shook her head. 'He's the kindest man I've ever met. An angel.'

Mia's head throbbed.

DI Amini offered Lyn a tissue. The gap between her hand and his appeared as a chasm, and if the tissue fell into it, Mia and Rami were done.

Mia eyed up the Japanese knives, then caught herself.

DS Opoku tapped her pen. 'What about work colleagues? Family members? Any you think may have fallen out with Dale?'

Lyn took the tissue and wiped her eyes. 'No. He works alone on his charity, 'cos it's still new, and his family are all dead. He's excited about us starting a family together.'

DS Opoku put her pen down on the notepad. 'What's the charity called?'

Lyn sniffed. 'Band Together. 'Cos he wants everyone to

band together to fight loneliness, but also he uses music 'cos he was in a band. It's how we met. He saw my guitar videos.'

DS Opoku nodded. 'Do you know his bandmates?'

'No. He hasn't played with them for a while.'

DI Amini hung his head before looking up at Lyn, again casting a glance at Mia. 'I'm sorry to ask this, but are you aware of any ex-partners he may have upset, or if he has any other partners?'

Lyn's body stiffened under Mia's hand. '*I* am his only partner. He said before me he hadn't had a shag for three years.'

DS Opoku cleared her throat. 'And he didn't mention any other partners from before then?'

'No,' Lyn said bluntly.

A silence hung. Rami turned the tap on to wash his hands for no reason other than to find the most awkward thing he could do in this moment.

DS Opoku turned the page on her notebook. 'And do you have his address in Bungay? We may need to search his premises,' DI Amini asked.

She shook her head. 'We've only been together three months and he only ever stays at mine. Said he wanted to make things easier for me, 'cos all my recording equipment is there. He was... is thoughtful like that.' Lyn broke down.

'Don't worry. We can find it through other means,' DS Opoku said.

Mia stroked Lyn's head and glanced at the officers. 'Let's just give her a moment. Rami, water.'

Rami poured some water from the filter jug and brought it over to Lyn.

'Thanks, Rami,' Lyn said.

He nodded, then moved back to the counter, topping up the jug.

DS Opoku clicked her pen and placed it on her notebook.

'Sorry that this is so difficult.' Her pen rolled off her notebook and onto the floor.

Time slowed as Lyn reached down to pick up the rolling pen, her head a few feet away from Dale. Mia's pulse thundered. She considered yanking Lyn back by her hair.

Rami's eyes widened and Mia's legs trembled.

Mia stomped on the pen, breaking it.

Lyn and DS Opoku stared at it, shocked. Their eyes followed Mia as she picked it up and handed it to DS Opoku.

'Sorry,' Mia said. 'We have a spare in the drawer.'

'Yeah, especially as you have to buy your own,' Rami added.

DS Opoku forced a chuckle. 'It's fine. Honestly.' She stared at her broken pen.

Mia shuffled back behind the armchair and gripped the backrest, worried she would pass out. She took slow breaths.

DI Amini stood up. 'Well, you've given us a few things to check.' He turned to DS Opoku. 'Anything else?'

'Do you have any of his possessions? For a DNA sample?' she asked.

Lyn stood. 'He left stuff at mine. Would a toothbrush do?'

DS Opoku nodded. 'Perfect. Can we send someone over tomorrow?'

'Yeah,' Lyn replied.

'If we have more questions or information we'll be in touch,' DI Amini said, casting one last glance at Mia. He turned back to Lyn. 'And, look. We've been getting lots of abusive messages to the station because of your posts. It may help the investigation if you reduced social media activity around this particular topic.'

Lyn scoffed. 'Is that the real reason you came?'

DI Amini raised his palms. 'Of course not. We're asking you to reduce activity in case something sinister has happened, and the perpetrator's watching.'

Lyn shook her head. 'Give over. My posts will put the shitters up them, which you're failing to do.'

DI Amini frowned. 'We're on your side, Lyn. But, your actions could be interpreted as interfering with a police investigation, which is a crime in itself.'

Lyn smirked, annoyed. 'The only crime here is that you ain't found anything.'

DI Amini played with his hat. 'It's hard to phrase this, so apologies if it comes off insensitive. With a lot of missing person cases, often the perpetrator is someone close to home.'

Lyn's eyes widened. 'I know exactly what you're getting it.'

DS Opoku nodded. 'Until we have more details, you are technically not ruled out as a suspect.'

'Do one!' Lyn seethed.

'Lyn...' Mia pulled her into a hug and Lyn burst into tears. 'It's okay, honey. You didn't do it, so that won't be a problem. But maybe stop drawing attention to yourself. And also stop screaming at the people trying to help.'

DI Amini nodded his appreciation. 'We obviously don't think you did it. We just have to go through the—'

'Procedure,' Lyn mocked. 'Don't I bloody know it.'

Rami glanced around the room. He didn't seem to know what to do with himself.

'I'll show you out,' Mia said.

'We'll find him, Lyn,' DS Opoku added.

DI Amini and DS Opoku walked towards the front door. Mia opened it, while Lyn stood nearby.

'We'll be in touch,' DI Amini said to Mia. 'And look, to speed things up, if you need to update us, you can call me.' He took a card out of his pocket, with his phone number hand-written on it. He gave it to Mia.

'Thanks,' she said.

The police left, and Mia watched them from the door.

Lyn approached. 'I'm going to Jenny's to finish giving her details. Sod waiting on those muppets.'

'Are you sure?' Mia asked. 'After what they just said?'

'They can suspect me all day. I'm sorting this my way.' Lyn left, making a point of walking past the police car.

Mia closed the door, let out a huge breath and returned to Rami, who was sat on the sofa, his head in his hands. Useless.

Mia poured herself some wine and leaned on the kitchen counter. 'The body has to go back in your room.' She placed DI Amini's card in a drawer with flyers for takeaways and tree surgeons.

'What?'

'There's too much...' She waved her hand around. 'Movement down here. And it'll only be for a couple of days.'

Rami's eyes welled up.

Mia walked over to the door and looked through the peep hole. 'If your cling film idea isn't another myth, then you'll be fine.' She stared until the police drove away, but another car caught Mia's eye as it sped out of the cul-de-sac. A red Tesla Roadster with a glass roof. She didn't know many people with that kind of car, apart from Wilfred.

15

BUNGAY BUNGAY PARTY

Rami

Rami, every one of his limbs weak, knelt by Dale's naked body on the study carpet and wrapped the last of the cling film around his neck. Dale's face remained exposed. Of course it did. Rami considered putting multiple pillowcases over it.

The floorboards outside his room creaked under footsteps, followed by a light knock at the door. 'Rami?' Lyn's voice said.

Rami stared at the door, wishing it had a lock, but thankful for the box he had pushed up against it.

'Yeah?' he replied.

'Can I have a word, please?' she asked.

He got up and stood by the door. 'I'm, erm... I'm just... meditating. Are you alright?'

'I just wanted to say thanks again for today,' she said, loud enough for it to be a jab at Mia.

'You're welcome. And, erm... I'm sorry you're going through this.'

'Yeah, me too. Goodnight.' Her footsteps moved away from the door.

Rami pushed Dale's body under the bed. He squirted hand sanitiser on his left palm and furiously rubbed his hands together. His body itched, so he removed his layers and rubbed sanitiser all over himself.

He wanted to shower, to scrub as much of Dale off him as he could, but he couldn't risk leaving the room unguarded. He was a prisoner, sharing a cell with a corpse he had shanked.

He pulled his pyjamas on and got into bed. He stared at the ceiling.

Rami deserved this. Not only for killing Dale, but for thinking there was any way back for him and Mia. He had been living in a state of delusion, believing in a narrative that didn't exist. He had hoped the last couple of days would bring them closer, and that she might see value in him. Fanciful nonsense.

He was convinced that if you had ever loved someone, then a flicker of that feeling would remain, no matter how small. Mia's counter theory seemed to be that if you had ever loved someone, then you could find unique depths of hatred.

Every sentence he uttered to her must have sounded like failure.

What was the turning point in their relationship? The miscarriage? Was it the gambling? Becca's suicide? Was it one big let-down? Was it that he never booked anything for them to do and was happy for her to lead? Or, worst of all, was it that she had settled and then realised she could do better?

Lyn's fight for Dale showed Rami what love was.

Rami took his mobile phone from the bedside table and researched the location of phone masts. The nearest one to where they killed Dale was in Norwich, so they had hope.

He exhaled his relief, then sniffed. A whiff akin to cabbage and rotten eggs invaded his nostrils. Maybe he imagined it. He sniffed again and gagged. He had hoped that the small mercy of having a battered nose would be that he couldn't smell that well, but no such luck. If anything, his airways were clearer than ever, as though Mia had reset his nose to where it should have been.

He got up and opened the window, allowing the freezing night air in. Frustrated, he opened the wardrobe and grabbed a hat Mia had bought him for a trip to Estonia, thick socks she gave him on their third Christmas, and a Mercedes-branded fleece from a day they had out at Formula One, thanks to one of Mia's colleagues.

A dusty plastic box of photo albums hid itself in the corner of the wardrobe. Rami thought it would be romantic to get photos printed and placed in albums, the traditional way. He resisted the urge to look inside and torture himself.

That was what this long chapter of his life would become – a memory, stored away among others like his first love, passing his driving test, and the operation he had on his undescended testicle when he was four.

He had read that the most common duration for a marriage was eight years, although another article said it was eleven. Either way, they were below average.

He swallowed, closed the wardrobe and grabbed a can of deodorant, spraying the entirety of it towards Dale.

He lit some lemongrass incense sticks and placed them next to Dale. He wrapped a Norwich City F.C. scarf around his neck, got into bed, pulled the duvet over his face and cried.

Rami, his body beaten by exhaustion, stood in Bungay town centre handing out missing person posters. The wind whacked him from all directions, and he hoped it would carry him away and drop him into the North Sea.

The missing person poster featured a huge photo of Dale, obviously with Lyn in it as well, to make sure everyone knew exactly who owned him.

Most of the Sunday morning walkers ignored Rami's posters, preferring to head to the market stalls selling fruit, veg, and hotdogs by the domed structure known as the Buttercross.

Lyn and Mia handed out posters across the road. Lyn wore so much jewellery that it sounded like someone was carrying a sack of pennies up and down the street.

Rami handed one missing Dale poster out, then, when Lyn wasn't looking, he put one in the recycling bin.

Another passer-by ignored Rami's offer.

'I'm not trying to sign you up for a charity,' he said, but remained ignored.

Lyn had banged on Rami's door at 7 a.m. thinking she was waking him up, but he had been awake for hours.

He needed to take his mind off the stinking corpse under his bed, so took in the town. He had never been, but one of his former students was from the area and once punched another student who said Bungay was crap.

She would often explain that the town was by a loop of the River Waveney, which marked the boundary between Norfolk and Suffolk. You had to choose a side: you couldn't love both. She had made that clear.

Rami never quite understood the pride of being from somewhere. It wasn't like it was a choice. It was a piece of land you were born on. Maybe he struggled to understand because he was caught between three countries. His mum was Lebanese and his dad was Egyptian, but he was born in London. His lack of Lebanese and Egyptian cultural knowledge meant they rejected him, and English people eternally made him feel foreign. As a teenager he would show people at school his British passport to try to fit in, but Billy Ellis pointed out, "Just because a dog's born in a stable, doesn't make it a horse." Rami sighed, but he appreciated the humour behind the rejection.

Another person ignored Rami's poster, but with a hand gesture that infuriated him. He hoped they would fall over as they walked towards the Buttercross. The place used to be a prison, and the statue atop it, of a woman holding a sword and scales of justice, raised Rami's anxiety levels.

Everything in his daily life suggested prison. It could be overt, like the Buttercross, or the way a light flickered, making him imagine the strip light you might find in a prison canteen. Even the gap between his toilet and their bathroom wall made him wonder what it would be like to have a toilet two feet from his bed in a cell.

Mia and Lyn argued as Lyn taped a poster to a newsagent's window.

Rami needed to escape the cold. He pushed the door open to the Saint Henriette Hospice charity shop. The bell rang.

An old woman with an air of peace about her sorted through donation bags, chuckling as she removed a taxidermy pigeon.

'Morning,' Rami said.

'A lovely one, too,' she replied.

'If you love strong winds and a runny nose, absolutely.' He closed the door behind him.

She smiled. 'You've got no meat on you, that's why.'

Rami chuckled politely.

'You after anything in particular or just browsing?' she asked.

He showed her the handful of missing person posters. 'Was actually wondering if I could put one of these up in the window? A missing local.'

She walked over and took a poster, studying it. 'Such a shame. So fresh-faced.'

'You know him?'

'Never seen him. But lived here through the second world war, too many government changes, and six husbands, so if anyone has, I'll likely hear about it.' She handed the poster back. 'Give me some to keep on the counter, too.'

'That's incredibly kind.' Rami handed her several. He suddenly felt guilty for being in a charity shop and not buying anything. He scanned the shelves and grabbed a 1,000-piece puzzle of a meadow. 'I'll take this, too.' He loved puzzles and hadn't done one in years, as Mia found them pointless. He couldn't understand how anyone could dislike puzzles. Maybe she was a sociopath.

He followed the woman to the counter and paid. 'Thanks for the help.'

'You're very welcome,' she said. 'I hope your friend turns up.'

'Oh, he's not my...' Rami caught himself. 'Thanks.'

He left as she stuck the poster up on the inside of the window, next to an advert for grief counselling at the local community centre.

Rami swallowed. He was grieving for Dale and for his dead marriage. Guilt and failure took turns pummelling him. Would he ever stop grieving? Or would it eventually build up for one big hit that shut his body down?

Mia stomped towards him. What was she going to tell him off for now? Maybe he wasn't handing out posters with enough flamboyance?

'Why the fuck did you tell her we're getting divorced?' She folded her arms.

Rami took a breath and ignored her, offering another passer-by a poster.

Mia snatched it to divert his focus. 'It's not your place to tell my friend.'

Rami looked into her hate-filled eyes. 'It's not your place to leave me with your friend for a day while you get hammered.'

Mia shook her head and walked away. 'Prick.'

'Abandoning your friend again?' he said.

'Fuck off!' she shouted.

Rami wanted to shout something back at her, but what good would it do? Instead, he nodded at passers-by who had shifted their attention to the scene.

Rami turned back to Lyn who was weeping.

The up-its-arse cafe was packed full of people who must've been coming to the ends of their lives, and most of their eyes were on Lyn. It could've been because she was wearing skin-revealing summer clothes in autumn, or because her crying was so loud and screechy it sounded like an air-raid siren and likely triggered memories of the war.

'Why's she being such a flap?' Lyn asked.

Rami finished chewing his mushrooms, the next best thing, as the owner had found his request for celery and hummus offensive. He could stick the boot into Mia, but they still had a mission. 'She's not good at handling this kind of thing,' he said. 'And I know it's not about her, but she struggles to see people she cares about in pain. She feels it, and instead of sharing to deal with it, she backs off. In a selfish way, being around the grieving person reminds her of her own losses.'

Lyn wiped her tears. 'Not a very helpful way to be.'

Rami handed her a napkin. 'I know. Growing up, she had a best mate, Chayanika. Inseparable, but then Chayanika moved back to India, and this was before the internet, so contact just died. Went from phone calls on those expensive cards that cost about five pounds a minute and letters every so often, to nothing. Mia still tried to keep contact up, but Chayanika pulled away. Mia never really got over it.'

Lyn placed some wilted spinach on her fork. 'Yeah, well she needs to see a therapist.'

Rami nodded. 'Maybe several.'

Lyn chewed the spinach. 'I need her. I need to be able to put my trust in people who feel as strongly as I do.'

'She does feel strongly. She just has a terrible way of showing it.' Rami pictured Dale's lifeless face and shuddered. 'You're doing amazing, Lyn. You've got the police panicking to the point of doing actual work. You've got a private investigator on it, half of Bungay, and an army of Instagrammers, some currently searching fields in the cold. Maybe for all future problems people won't bother with the police, they'll just call you.'

Lyn chuckled, then laughed hysterically, which turned into more tears. 'I miss him so much. Just, his face has this energy about it, you know?'

He knew.

Lyn put her fork down and rubbed her head. 'Even when I'd have a crap day, or get inappropriate comments on Instagram, I'd take a look at him and then that stuff mattered less. Was like when I had a dog growing up.' She wiped her eyes. 'One look from Madonna's big, stupid happy face made everything seem...' She shrugged.

'I get it.' Rami bit his lip. He had shredded her life.

He ate another mushroom. The soft texture made him think of Dale's rotting organs. He forced the mushroom down.

Lyn checked her phone then put it on the table and looked at Rami. 'Someone's saying they've found a jacket that might be Dale's and attached an image.' She stared at the phone.

Impossible, unless they had rummaged through a landfill. 'It's okay, open it,' Rami said, studying her expression and what it might give away.

She picked up her phone, then her face fell. She buried her head in her hands.

'What? Is it his?' Rami asked.

'It's another dick pic.'

Rami grimaced.

'What is wrong with people?' she said.

'I'm sorry, Lyn.'

'Why? You didn't fucking send it.'

'I'm just sorry you have to deal with that.'

She shrugged. 'I know my videos will get a certain kind of attention. I'm playing music in proper sexy outfits, so sure. And it has helped my profile grow. But, creeps can just knock one out in the privacy of their rooms. I don't need to see... that. My work isn't an invitation for that.'

Rami nodded, no idea what to say.

Lyn scoffed. 'I've performed with Ed bloody Sheeran. I'm not some gimp. And, I post so much about sustainability, the clothes I wear are all second-hand, and I do loads for charity, but no. I could write something about famine and they'd probably still only think about my tits.' She exhaled.

Rami refilled Lyn's glass of water. 'You should make a collage of all the dicks and post it. Get your followers to spot their own bits.'

Lyn shook her head. 'I just don't get what their end game is. Especially when I'm looking for my missing boyfriend.'

Rami shrugged. 'Yeah, what is the best-case scenario? That you reply saying, "Hey, great willy, let's hang out and forget about Dale."'

Lyn groaned. 'Bunch of pricks.'

'Literally.' Rami put more salt on his mushrooms.

'Please tell me you've never sent a photo like that,' Lyn said.

Rami shook his head. 'No chance. In my Tinder days, around Christmas things got a little flirty once and there was some... activity on Snapchat, but I bottled it. She said if I sent her mine she'd send me her—' He gestured to his chest.

'Tits,' Lyn said. 'You can say tits, you won't get locked up. Tits!' she repeated.

An old couple glanced over from their table.

Lyn nodded at them. 'You've got a cracking pair, love.'

The old woman smiled.

Rami swallowed and whispered. 'She said she'd send me a photo of her breasts. But, I started to capture the photo of, erm... mini Rami, but it looked awful. It's just an unattractive veiny, purple bollard.'

Lyn raised an eyebrow. 'Bollard?'

Rami waved his hand dismissively. 'No, no. Mine's so thin I

can pick locks with it. Just couldn't think of another comparison.'

Lyn laughed.

'I tried several angles, and it could've been the harsh lighting, but I just felt hollow. I even used the edit tool to draw a little Santa hat and jacket on it, but I was too ashamed. So, I sent her a photo of the cover of my favourite book, and she replied with a photo of her middle finger, and I never heard from her again.'

'Maybe she hated the book,' Lyn said.

'It was *Misery* by Stephen King. Nobody could hate that book.'

'That's a classic!' Lyn's expression turned. 'What if Dale's getting Annie Wilkesed?'

'He won't be. Let's just keep looking.' He didn't want to feel sorry for her, as she had always looked at him as though he wasn't good enough for Mia, but the guilt had smashed through his anti-Lyn shield.

Lyn placed her hand on Rami's. 'Thank you, Rami. I know we've never really been best mates, but, thank you for caring.'

Rami nodded. 'Dale is lucky to have someone who'd fight so tirelessly for him.' He hadn't just killed Dale; he had ruined the lives of anyone who knew him or would have been positively impacted by him in future.

Rami burst into tears.

Lyn handed him a napkin. 'Bless you, Rami. You've got a heart of gold.'

16

I GOT NINETY-NINE PROBLEMS AND RAMI IS ALL OF THEM

MIA

Wilfred had requested that Mia join him at the Waffle House, where they had regularly met during their affair, under the guise of work brunches.

Mia looked down at the table to avoid the hurt in Wilfred's eyes. She fiddled with the Sunday specials menu, although she had no intention of ordering. 'You have to stop following me,' she said.

'What do you expect?' he replied. 'You call me on Thursday night, and things are up here.' He stretched his hand up. 'Ultimate happiness. Dreams. Finally free to be together. Then within twenty-four hours, bang!' He smacked the table, startling diners and drawing Mia's gaze. 'Something has happened, and you're not telling me. I know you.'

He did. He knew all of her, apart from this one thing. She could handle him hating her for breaking his heart – he would be able to move on one day. But, she couldn't stomach him hating her for taking a life, and for putting that secret on him. It would weigh everything down and trap him.

She sipped her coffee. 'You can't hover outside my house, and you definitely can't follow me to Bungay.'

Wilfred shifted in his seat. 'Are you scared your husband will find out?'

Mia scoffed. 'Ex-husband. I don't care about that idiot.'

'Then what changed with us? It doesn't make any sense.' His usual confidence was replaced by desperate confusion.

There was nothing she could say that would satisfy him. 'I just... I feel I need to be alone for a while. Rather than jumping from an eight-year disaster into more intensity.'

'I don't believe you,' he said. 'I know I sound like an obsessive loon right now, but there's something.'

Mia huffed. 'Please, just accept my decision.'

Wilfred stared at her. 'What did the police want? Is he abusing you?'

Mia laughed. 'I could kick the life out of him. They were there for Lyn. Her boyfriend's missing. That's who we were handing out posters for.'

Wilfred reached his hand across the table. 'Can I help?' Mia didn't want to touch it, but she couldn't help herself. A comfort filled her body, like a hug welcoming her home after a long, pointless business trip.

He was never going to stop trying. In some ways, she was glad he loved her so much. In other ways, it made the torture worse. She had been a thirty-minute drive away from having something truly special.

She pushed his hand back towards his side of the table and withdrew hers. 'You can help by respecting my decision. I'm sorry.'

Mia looked away, but caught a flicker of anger behind Wilfred's sadness. She hated herself more than she thought possible.

∼

Mia knocked on Rami's study door. 'Can we talk?' She waited for a response, hoping he wouldn't be in a sulk.

After some shuffling, the door opened, and she was greeted by a waft that was a mix of rotten eggs, cabbage, and a bin full of old fish. She retched.

Rami's irritated, exhausted face glared at her. 'I know.' He waved her in.

She rushed to the window, stepping around the dead man's naked, cling-film-wrapped body, which was surrounded by bags of ice. The smell of sandalwood incense sticks fought against the bodily rot, but lost.

Rami closed the door and blocked the bottom of it with a towel, then dragged a box in front of it. 'I've tried every incense stick scent, essential oils, and even covered the cling film in Vicks VapoRub. Still reeks and all I got was a headache.' He sat at the desk and cut the dead man's cards into pieces.

Mia coughed and spat out of the window. 'God, it reminds me of when I wanted to make you birthday breakfast in bed, but cracked the egg open and it was rotten.' The thought triggered her gag reflex.

'What birthday was that?' Rami asked.

'Not a recent one.' She shrugged.

Rami glanced down at the chopped-up pieces of the dead man's life.

Mia swallowed. 'I'm sorry.'

He rubbed his nose. 'Me too.'

Mia heaved. 'I want to talk, but it smells like a bunch of necrophiliacs have had an orgy.'

'Try sleeping in it.' He sighed.

'Kitchen?'

'Please.' He brushed the chopped-up cards into a small bin and tied the bag to throw away.

They relocated to the kitchen and Mia poured herself a glass of white wine, while Rami drank some water. She sat on the armchair, him on the sofa.

'Are you sure you should?' Rami pointed to the wine.

'It's the only thing that isn't terrible,' she replied.

Rami nodded his acceptance.

Mia gulped some wine down. 'Sorry you have to sleep in Chernobyl.'

Rami lay on the sofa and put his feet on the armrest. 'I don't know what anything is anymore.'

Mia sipped more wine. 'For us to get this done, I need to stop snapping at you, I know that. And the plan you mentioned sounds great.'

'Thanks,' Rami said, staring at the ceiling.

Mia put her glass of wine down and leaned forward. 'I've expanded on it. Not changed it. If Lyn asks, we're going to the Knights Hill Hotel and Spa, where we had a past date, to see if we can work through the divorce. To see if maybe we were too hasty. But instead we'll head to Stowbridge.'

'Sounds good,' Rami said.

'I found a place for the body on the riverbank,' she said.

Rami sat up, but Mia raised a hand to stop him protesting. 'For the burial.'

He lay back down.

'There are plenty of places with good tree cover along the River Great Ouse.' She showed him her phone, with a screenshot of a map. 'I spent ages on Google Maps. If we look around this stretch, we should be okay. 'There are some houses here and there, and then there's just a cattery around a mile away, and one pub on the other side of the river where there's a quiz on a Monday.'

'Okay,' Rami said.

Mia poured herself more wine. 'Tomorrow.'

Rami let out a big breath and sat up. 'Tomorrow.'

Mia sat on the sofa next to him. 'I don't want this to go wrong. So...' She held out her phone. 'I took this when we dumped his bike.' She showed him the dark, poor-quality photos she had taken of Rami pushing the motorcycle into the river.

His face fell.

She deleted the photos.

He stared at her, and the glum expression remained.

'I was angry. I still am,' she said.

He exhaled a long breath. 'What about the Cloud. Will they not...?'

'Don't worry. I don't have it synced.' She had turned that off a long time ago to avoid any photos of her and Wilfred finding their way onto her laptop, in case Rami snooped.

Rami shuffled. 'Well, thanks for deleting them.'

She looked into his eyes. 'There were things you wanted to say. In the car...'

Rami seemed surprised. He rubbed his eyes. 'No. I'm not interested in doing this so that you can feel better when you bugger off into your new life.'

She tensed. 'I'm not doing this to feel better. I want you to feel better, so that you don't fuck tomorrow up.'

'There she is,' Rami said.

Mia stood up. 'Yep, awful idea.' She walked out of the room.

'Wait!' Rami called out.

She didn't want to stop, but she had promised herself she would sit through this, and she had felt guilty for denying him a chance to talk before. She turned around.

Rami gestured to the sofa. 'Let's do it.'

She returned, sat, and drank more wine.

Rami leaned forward. 'Okay. Erm, obviously, the divorce is your decision.'

Because it was necessary and she was the only one with the

courage to push the button. Mia pinched the stem of her wine glass.

Rami continued. 'But, I need to know when you started to feel that way.'

Another broken-hearted man with a question she had no answer for. She considered her words. 'There's no specific moment, Rami. I know you want to be able to blame the gambling, the mess around Becca's death, or our loss, but we've just grown in different directions. My feelings have changed.'

'Yeah, but we can get back on the same path and grow together. It just takes effort and communication,' he appealed.

She huffed, trying to maintain a sympathetic facial expression. 'We're not a plant you tie to a support so it grows how you want it to. This can't be fixed, Rami. And I know it's hard to accept that, because you're a good person who is dedicated and likes to fix things. That's really wonderful. But, it's like with Roberto, before I met you, he just ended it saying, "I don't love you anymore." It's the hardest thing to be on the receiving end of, and I'm sorry.' She'd finished the bottle of wine so got up and opened the fridge to get another.

'What happened to "for better or worse"?' Rami asked.

Mia returned with the bottle and sat next to him. 'They're just words that are hundreds of years old, from when people died younger so they didn't have a chance to get sick of each other.' She stared at his gloomy face. 'And, I'm sorry I said that when I see you I taste bile; that was harsh. And sorry for what I said about losing Sarah. I'm just desperately trying to find something positive in that.'

He nodded. 'You said her name.'

Mia let herself smile, the hole in her soul still gigantic. 'It's about time I did.' She placed a hand on Rami's. 'Just think about things. Would you rather move on and maybe find something more special, or would you like to stay in something hollow?'

Rami shrugged. 'Hollowness can be filled.' He raised an apologetic hand.

She glared at him and took her hand away. 'Do you seriously think this is worth continuing to fight for?'

He hesitated. 'I just... I'm a believer in being able to work through problems. And I don't believe this low point is forever.' He downed his water.

'And that's admirable, but the only way we fix this is to decide we're fine settling for something that deep down isn't right.' She topped up her glass. 'Life's too short, and I don't want to look back on it thinking I spent years settling.'

'You know you've not been perfect in all this, right?' he said.

'Of course I know. I have a go at you too easily, I'm not trying to reconnect and I make you feel awful. But, I know that's because I feel stuck in something that's wrong for me. This isn't a version of me I like.'

Rami tapped his fingers against his glass and looked down. 'How do you know there could be something better out there?'

Wilfred.

'I don't. But there's something wonderful about trying to find it, even if I fail. And, you're always going to have questions. I still have some about Roberto. The main thing is to move forward so that you no longer care about the answers.'

Rami stared ahead, silent.

'Tomorrow,' Mia said, hoping the conversation would move on to more pressing matters.

Rami exhaled. 'You need to stop being terrible to Lyn. She's not my friend, and I don't want to be the one dealing with her.'

Mia's neck tensed. Lyn's name, her face, anything about her, sent shockwaves through Mia's body.

'You okay?' Rami asked.

Mia slumped against the sofa cushion. 'I can't be near her. I've wrecked her. The first proper love of her life, I shagged at uni. Now this one, I've...'

'Yeah, I know,' Rami said.

Mia buried her head in her hands.

Rami placed a hand on her shoulder. 'It's going to be okay. And thanks for the talk.'

Mia let him leave his hand there. She hoped he was right.

17

***

NORMAL IS AS NORMAL DOES

Rami

Rami knocked on Jenny's door and took a deep breath. This was it: acting normal, being normal, moving forward. Tomorrow, once they had buried Dale, normality could become more common, despite the guilt that would follow him around forever.

He glanced around at the cul-de-sac, peaceful under the night sky. *Normal.*

The door clicked open. The normal sound of a door.

'Rami Salami!' Jenny said with a huge grin on her face, welcoming him into her immaculate corridor that connected to the living room, kitchen, stairs to the first floor, and door to a basement.

He chuckled at the normality of banter. 'Never been called that.' He entered and took his shoes off.

'Yeah, not sure it'll stick, right?' she said. 'Not many words rhyme with Rami. There was tsunami, but wasn't sure if that was appropriate. What about calling you Rim Ram?'

He cringed. 'Well, I've never done any rimming, and my marriage is without ramming, so...'

Jenny laughed.

He nudged his shoes neatly next to the others. 'Umami rhymes with Rami, or origami. There's also a Lebanese word, *harami*, which means thief.'

Jenny grinned. 'Rami Harami. That's the one.' She nodded at him. 'Nose looks better.'

'Yeah, takes more than a box of books to keep me down.' He noticed the smell of red wine on her breath. 'Pre-lesson nerves?'

Jenny smiled.

Rami raised his palms. 'I'm not judging. For some writers it's part of the process. F. Scott Fitzgerald said drinking helped him to infuse more feeling into his work.'

'I'm shit...' She caught herself. 'I'm not very good with names. Which one's he?' Jenny asked.

'*The Great Gatsby*, among others,' Rami replied.

'So, you're saying if I want to be a great writer I need to get totally slammed?' She nodded, interested.

Rami smirked. 'No, it's more that I'm being polite. Fitzgerald was actually hospitalised for alcoholism many times, and most writers have serious substance abuse issues, which should tell you that writing is an utterly miserable experience.' He gave a thumbs up. 'You ready?'

She laughed, patted him on the back and limped along the hallway. 'We could all use a little more misery in our lives.'

Rami strongly disagreed behind his smile. He closed the door and Ballula leapt up at him, her tongue hanging out. He stroked her. 'Hello, Ballula.' He gazed into the cosy and warm living room, where Iris watched *MasterChef* from the sofa while rubbing her pregnant belly.

'Hi, Rami,' she said, a huge smile on her face.

'Evening, Iris.' He took a small hedgehog plushie from his

inside pocket and approached her. 'Got this for when...' He gestured to her stomach.

'She,' Iris said, beaming.

'For when she's with us.' Rami handed Iris the plushie and her eyes lit up. Rami felt a pang of sadness, remembering Mia with that same joyous look in her eyes when he would buy gifts in preparation for Sarah's arrival.

'How sweet.' Iris shifted her gaze to Jenny. 'Portabella's first gift! Thanks so much, Rami.'

Jenny leaned on the door frame. 'We will not be naming our daughter Portabella, but thank you, Rami.'

Ballula jumped up next to Iris and wedged herself between Iris' arm and pregnant stomach. Iris stroked her.

Rami reached into his side pocket and took a small pineapple chew toy. 'I can't buy one child a gift and neglect the other.' He dropped it next to Ballula and stroked her head. She immediately tore into the toy.

Jenny patted him on the shoulder. 'She's your friend for life now.'

The contrast with Rami's house was embarrassing. This was a home full of love, togetherness, and warmth. Rami lived in an icy shell that was as welcoming as the booby-trapped house in *Saw* 2.

'Come on,' Jenny said, heading towards the basement door. 'Iris, if you need anything, just bang the floor and I'll come up.'

Rami followed. 'What's your rhyming name for Iris?' he asked.

Jenny chuckled. 'With her mood swings I prefer to just go with King Kong.'

'You're sleeping in the shed tonight!' Iris yelled playfully from the living room.

'Love you,' Jenny replied.

They descended the carpeted stairs into the basement, which was a teenager's paradise, but without the coating of dust and stale air. In one corner was a gaming set-up, with a PlayStation 5, Nintendo Switch, big-screen TV, and a sofa you could easily live out your days on. In another corner, a rowing machine and fridge. In the centre of the room, underneath a strip light, was a table with a Warhammer game set up and an army of delicately painted figurines. The paints were fastidiously organised on a table.

Everything shone. It was welcoming.

'This is where I come to when... I pretty much live here.' Jenny said.

'Can I move in?' Rami replied.

Jenny laughed. 'The baby will destroy it soon.' She pointed to the writing corner, the most impressive part. An oak desk surrounded by framed film posters, including *The Goonies*, *The Piano*, *Thelma and Louise*, *Goodfellas*, *Ghost*, *The Lord of the Rings*, and *Along With the Gods: The Two Worlds*. Rami was glad there was no poster of *Weekend at Bernie's*.

Jenny pointed to a poster of *The Princess Bride*. 'Got that signed by Mandy Patinkin himself.'

'No way!' Rami said and went into an impression. 'Hello, my name is Inigo Montoya. You killed my father—'

Jenny joined him in finishing the line, '... prepare to die!'

They laughed, and then Rami swallowed his sadness, as he remembered the moment in the story when Westley seemed dead, but was only mostly dead. What if Dale had been mostly dead and they could have saved him by calling an ambulance?

Jenny, sitting at her desk, scribbled on a piece of card. 'Don't protect your main character,' she said and stuck the card on the wall with other pieces of advice.

'Yes,' Rami answered, pacing. 'Best advice I ever received. And, you've got to have her make tough choices. But, those decisions need to be truthful to her, how she's feeling, and what motivates her. Not for the sake of plot.'

'I get it,' she said. 'And, not simple choices like: should I cook or just heat up some pre-made chicken nuggets?'

'Yeah. Although in the dramatic context of a date, that could be interesting if your character is panicked.'

'Whatever the context, the answer is always chicken nuggets,' Jenny said.

Rami smiled. 'Not when you have intolerances. But, yeah, choices that have consequences to what she's trying to achieve, internally and externally. What's she going to do when she's faced with a big dilemma, and more importantly, why?'

'Lily will always do what's right for the people she's helping,' Jenny said.

'Okay, so why will Lily always do what's right? Where does that sense of duty, kindness, and desire to do right come from? Always ask *why*, like a toddler. Why? Why? Why?'

Jenny wrote "why?" in massive letters on a card and stuck it on the wall. 'Hadn't thought about that. Just wanted her to be good. If I'm being honest, she's kind of based on me.'

Rami shrugged. 'Well, let's dig in. What made you want to be a support volunteer?'

'I actually wanted to be an investigator, but the buggers rejected me.'

'Really?' Rami asked.

She looked down at her leg. 'Times were different. One look at the limp and it was on your bike, if you could physically ride one.' She smirked.

'I'm sorry, Jenny.' He sat on the sofa next to the desk.

She shrugged. 'Don't be.' She laughed, reminiscing. 'Thought I could blag the bleep test but I fell over immediately.'

Rami smiled.

Jenny stood and limped over to the fridge. 'So, I want my character to be hung up on that rejection, so she'll always give her best for people, to prove herself, and to prove to the prats who doubt her that she's capable.' She took a can of gin and tonic. 'Want one?'

'No, thanks. So, kind of like what you're doing with Lyn.'

'Exactly.' Jenny limped back to the desk. 'She's fierce, that Lyn. Sadly, I reckon this Dale fella is either dead or he's done a runner. Just need to confirm that before I say anything to her.'

'Yeah, she's in a fragile place.' Rami clasped his hands.

Jenny opened the can. 'It's actually been really hard finding anything out about him. My mate looked him up, but he's a ghost.'

'Well, don't put yourself in a difficult position looking. The police are on it.' Rami leaned forward.

'No, no. That Amini is every flavour of useless. Just coasting through his days doing as little as possible until he can retire.' She drank from the can.

'Really? He seemed quite on top of things.'

'All for show. He'll do the bare minimum to close something up and move on. There was a woman accused of robbing a delivery to the Nike store by the Riverside. She claimed she was forced to by a violent drug dealer. Amini didn't bother investigating the claim. She was held in custody for two months, before someone else looked into it and the claim was matched.'

'Wow. Does he not care or something?'

Jenny shook her head. 'Just bitter he's not been promoted, and hates women if they're not tapping his trousers. He was even investigated by the IOPC about his conduct, but you know, friends in high places.'

'Poor Lyn,' Rami said.

Jenny massaged her left shoulder. 'I heard he's so lazy that he still takes his washing to his mum's, and she's well into her nineties.'

Rami had never been so relieved at humanity's hopelessness.

'Maybe be wary of how much you tell Lyn about him. She might go and strangle him.'

Jenny laughed. 'I've got Lyn covered. I'll find her fella whether it's a happy reunion or one at the morgue. Show those idiots up, and hopefully they'll move DI Dickhead... sorry, DI Dipstick on. He's as rotten as they come.'

'You're a good person.' Rami smiled, wishing she wasn't.

His phone alert sounded. A WhatsApp message from Mia with a video of Lyn. She was on BBC News.

18

NOTHING. IS. GOING. TO. GO. WRONG

Mɪᴀ

Mia, dressed in layers of summer clothes to fight the autumn chill, and Rami, dressed to survive a night on Mount Everest, walked along the grass by the tarmac of Stow Road, heading towards the village of Saddle Bow from Stowbridge.

Today was the day. Monday the 1st of Fuck Off Corpse and Rami.

In the half-hour walk since midday, they had seen a couple of other walkers, forty-three cars – Rami was counting – and a dozen or so areas of potential activity, including houses, farms, and a solar energy equipment supplier.

They wanted somewhere with the fewest houses, the most trees, and no junctions, so they could trust that cars would pass by at speed.

Rami sipped from his flask of coffee, which he held with mittens. 'Who the heck's booked Lyn for *The One Show*?'

'Seems her story's getting her plastered all over the country.' Mia exhaled, glad they were getting rid of the body tonight.

'What about the police telling her not to interfere?' Rami asked.

'Lyn does what she wants. Being big on Instagram puts her above the law. Maybe we can tell the police, as concerned friends, that she's hired an investigator. Might stop Jenny blowing smoke up her arse.'

Rami drank more coffee. 'I don't know. Jenny knowing keeps us close to it. She's very open, and she seems to trust me.' He pushed his beanie up his head.

People did tend to trust those of low status. 'Okay, let's see how that goes and we can press the button should we need to.'

Rami took a packet of salted peanuts from his pocket, but struggled to open them because of his mittens. 'I guess it's a good thing. Broadcasting her loss to the nation will busy her with false leads, annoy the police, and keep the focus firmly on the wrong side of Norfolk.' He continued to wrestle with the packet of peanuts.

'You could take the mittens off,' Mia said.

He gave up and took her advice.

Mia struggled to understand why he always had to be doing something. Whether it was eating or fidgeting, he had an issue with just being. 'I'm not sure it's good she's everywhere,' Mia said. 'With the guy's face all over the country, someone who saw him closer to where we accidentally hit him might pipe up.'

Rami scratched his nose. 'All the more reason to get this done tonight.' He offered her some peanuts.

'I'm fine.' She bit her lip, then forced herself to find politeness. 'Thanks.'

They passed a ploughed field. Rami nodded to it. 'Getting ready for next year's harvest. Means they'll be sowing winter wheat.' He put his mittens back on.

Mia nodded. 'So let's get some distance between us and here.'

They crossed the road over to the fields by the River Great

Ouse. Mia stopped to tie her boot laces. 'Why would *The One Show* even have her? Are they that short on guests? Just get a magician, or one of the million desperate celebs crying to stay relevant.'

Rami chuckled. 'I saw an article about a chicken in Diss that laid a giant egg. They could get that on. Or, do an item on a bench that turned one hundred.'

Mia laughed. 'There was that couple who got married in the shark tank at Great Yarmouth Sea Life, remember?'

'All more interesting than Lyn's story,' Rami said.

They walked towards the riverbank, passing the hedge lining of a small cottage. A rusted, weed-covered relic of a jeep that wouldn't look out of place in a dystopian film was parked outside the door. They came to a grassy path with trees to their left and the river to the right. It was the thickest concentration of trees they had come across so far.

'This is the place,' Mia said.

'What about the little cottage?' Rami questioned, looking around.

'It's completely on the other side of the trees. They'll never see through them. And the house across the road is unsighted too.' She gestured across the river. 'And absolutely nothing over there. It's perfect.' She smiled.

Rami stared at the grass, tapping it with his foot. He nodded. 'There might be something better if we walk on.'

Mia shook her head. 'Look around. These are the only trees like this for ages. This is exactly what we need. We just dig far enough to avoid the roots.'

She was right.

He took a breath. 'Okay then.'

Mia pulled her phone from her pocket, her hands slightly numbed by the cold. She ignored the eight missed calls from Wilfred. 'So, what will we need to bring with us? Shovels. Wellies.' She typed her list.

'The tarp, tent so it looks like we're camping, and a mattock would be handy,' Rami added.

'We've got all that bar the mattock. So when I get the car from the garage, you go and pick anything else up.'

Rami nodded. 'I'll get a rake too, to tidy. Make it look less like someone's been digging.'

'Perfect.'

They walked further, then looped back on themselves.

Rami studied the area again and dragged himself towards the river.

Mia checked her WhatsApp messages. Fifty-six from Wilfred. She scanned them:

I love you, please talk to me x

We can get through everything and anything xx

You can't treat me like this

You're a cold-hearted bitch

I'm sorry, I'm just so confused xx

I love you xxxxxxxxxx

What the hell has happened to you? X

You're the most exceptional woman I've ever met. You make the world shine x

Please, let's just talk x

And the last message:

She fought back tears. She had created desperation in him, and it was horrible to witness, but the anger was a new side to him that scared her. She put her phone away as Rami returned.

He wiped his nose on his mittens. 'What if—'

'Don't,' she said.

'What?'

'I know you're going to say, "What if this happens?" "What if that happens?" Nothing is going wrong. Look at it.' She gestured to the surroundings.

'I know, but—'

'Nothing. Is. Going. To. Go. Wrong. Look to tomorrow. Think about your freedom. Focus on something else, like, what will you do when this is over?'

'Will it ever be over?' Rami walked towards the small cottage they passed.

'You can be a right mood hoover,' she said.

'It's true, though. Yeah, he'll be hidden. But he's not gone. He's not un-murdered.' Rami watched the cottage windows.

'Accidentally killed.'

'He'll still be here, waiting to be discovered. If I live forty more years, that's 14,600 days he needs to go undiscovered. And I'll probably live longer. What if the council decides to build a cafe or soft play here one day and they dig him up?'

'Just find a positive,' she said. 'Try. You love your stats. There are more than 170,000 missing person cases every year. Some proper, some nonsense. And you know which ones nobody gives a shit about? Missing young men, unless they're mental. Kids, women; all over it. Men...' She shook her head. 'They'll assume he ran off and changed his identity, especially now they've met Lyn.' She sighed, swallowing the guilt. Being mean about Lyn helped, but only momentarily.

Rami looked at Mia and bit his lip.

She held her palms out. 'What was it you said? Since 2020 there are over 5,500—'

'Over 5,300, but I guess that still works.' He caught himself and raised an apologetic hand.

Mia let it go. 'Over 5,300 long-term missing people in this country. We have the advantage. So, I'll ask you again. What are you going to do when this is over?'

Rami swallowed and ran his mittens over his beanie. 'I just want to experience something simple. Like on holiday, when you sit by the pool and the sun hits you. When you really feel it. Not like in the UK, where it's like a tickle, but when it gives you energy and everything else you have to do falls away for at least a moment. And I want to have a cold glass of lemonade in that moment, you know? Packed with ice. That says freedom to me. You?'

Boring. He couldn't even swim. What was the point of being by a pool?

She remembered when she used to find his boring simplicity attractive. Now it was annoyingly unambitious. A sign of a lack of growth. She had a plan, but it wasn't one for sharing. 'Not sure yet. Maybe rethink my job. Maybe punch my mum.'

'Not like you to not have a plan,' he said.

She shrugged.

An old man, who must have been in his eighties, emerged from the cottage using a walking stick. He tried to water a plant in a vase next to his door, but his aim was off and most of the water ended up on the stones.

Mia turned to Rami. 'I don't think he's going to be a problem.'

Mia and Rami carried the cling-film-wrapped corpse, with the motorcycle helmet on his head, over the adhesive floor covers and into the garage. They placed him in the open car boot. It was 10 p.m. and time to bury this body along with the last eight years.

Mia retched as the corpse's smell seeped through the cling film.

Rami coughed and took several packets of pine air fresheners, tipped them into the boot, and then poured the entire contents of a Hugo Boss aftershave bottle onto the body. Mia had bought it for Rami on their third anniversary and he had never opened it. A fitting use.

Rami stared at the dead body.

'Hey,' Mia said, knowing he'd be playing out a guilt-creating scenario. 'Don't do it.'

He nodded and swallowed. 'Sorry.' He retreated into the house and Mia heard the adhesive floor covers being pulled up.

Mia loaded the items into the boot then placed the tarp over the body.

Rami returned and sighed. 'What if there's—'

'No.' Mia raised a hand. 'What do you think could possibly happen?'

'I don't know: teenagers on mountain bikes, farmers, boats, extreme ramblers who only go walking at night, drunks looking for a quickie in a bush. Who knows, maybe an arguing couple will accidentally veer off the road. That sort of thing.' He was shaking.

Mia waved a dismissive hand in the air. 'This plan will not fail. We've seen the place. We've seen the nearest human is a corpse that walks. We've even got the only day this week with no rain, but it's also so cold that everyone will be indoors. There's no reason for anyone to be in those fields unless there are others trying to cover up a murd... an *accident*. I have considered everything you've mentioned and I *promise* you, we are covered for every potential issue, because there aren't going to be any.'

Rami shrugged. 'Your promises aren't really worth much.'

'Don't be petty,' she said. 'Not tonight.' She shut the boot and entered the car. Rami slowly followed.

They sat in silence. Mia turned the key in the ignition. 'You ready?'

'No,' he replied.

'Same.' She pressed the remote button to open the garage and watched the shutter rise. It froze halfway up, but after some more button presses opened fully. Mia drove the car onto the driveway, but a taxi screeched to a halt in front of them, with Lisa Stansfield's 'Been Around the World' blasting out.

Mia's heart raced. Lyn stumbled out of the taxi, drunk, falling out of her dress, screeching the lyrics at the top of her voice.

She had likely woken up the rest of the cul-de-sac and acted as a mating beacon to foxes.

'Lyn for the win!' she screamed.

'Lyn on the gin,' Rami muttered.

This was all Mia's fault.

Lyn staggered towards the taxi driver's door. 'Big up, Raheem! Five stars and a fat tip coming your way. Legend!'

Raheem smiled politely, turned his car around and swiftly left, the music fading into the night with his vehicle.

Rami turned to Mia. 'Just drive around her and go.'

Lyn stumbled up to the car and fell against Mia's window. Mia opened it and Lyn stuck her face inside, her amaretto breath filling the vehicle.

Lyn hiccupped. 'I know you're doing some divorce, bonding, rediscovery thing, but I'm coming with you.'

Lyn stumbled towards the back door.

'Wait,' Mia said. 'We're—'

'I don't care!' Lyn shouted.

The upstairs lights in Jenny's house came on and her silhouette appeared at the window.

Lyn banged the top of the car. 'You've been a shit friend. I've already booked a room for myself in the same place, the Knights whatever. I'm coming. I've had so much attention from that *The One Show*, most of it shit, that I just... I need you.' She got in.

Rami turned to Mia. '*Every* potential issue?'

Mia closed her eyes.

~

The first half an hour of the journey was filled with Lyn's crying.

She repeated her story multiple times. 'Like, it's great that loads of people are on it now. But, it's all starting to feel a bit real, I can just sense that something horrid has happened.'

Her wails squeezed at Mia. 'Don't let those thoughts eat at you, Lyn.' She glanced at Rami who was frantically trying to book a room at the Knights Hill Hotel and Spa.

Lyn sniffed. 'I know, but I can't help it!'

Mia bit her lip. 'Let's try to talk about something else.' This was as much for her own benefit as Lyn's.

'Good idea,' Lyn said. 'And sorry to get in the way of your bonding. I just think it's better to be out in case I see him, instead of sat at home waiting for news to come to me. I know it's stupid, but it's how I think. And I need to be around you.'

Rami turned to her. 'I'd be exactly the same.' He glared at Mia as he turned back.

Mia offered Lyn a reassuring smile in the rear-view mirror.

Lyn retched. 'Why does this car stink of death?'

Mia cleared her throat and inhaled. She picked up hints of the hellish smell emerging from the boot and through the back seats. 'There's no smell. Do you smell something, Rami?'

Rami took the hint to play along. 'No. Maybe it's the country roads? Could be rotting manure, but I can't smell it.' He opened his window and sniffed. 'No.'

Mia swallowed the horrific smell of rotten meat and sewage. She opened her window. 'I'm with Rami. I smell nothing. What if it's psychological?' The freezing air blew the death rot around the car.

Lyn's tears returned. 'What if you're right? What if, because I keep worrying he's dead, I'm starting to smell death everywhere? Maybe my brain's broken.'

Mia hated lying to her friend, and now she was gaslighting her too. 'You wanted to talk about something else; let's do that. Rami?'

He stared at her, his eyes scrambling for a solution. 'Oh, how about some facts?'

Mia huffed. 'I don't think Lyn—'

'Go on.' Lyn leaned forward, her face between the front seats, and her amaretto breath offering an almond note to accompany the death waft.

Mia focused on the dark roads.

Rami raised a finger. 'Did you know, the idea of raising a toast came from the Ancient Romans, who used to drop a piece of toast into their wine for good health?'

Not that boring rubbish again.

Lyn's mouth fell open. 'That's amazing, Rami. Isn't it, Mia?'

'Mmm hmm.' She gripped the steering wheel tighter.

Rami grinned as though someone had touched his cock for the first time.

He waved a finger. 'Apparently, it mitigates the taste of bad wine, the carbon reducing the acidity.'

'Nice knowledge. What else you got?' Lyn asked.

Rami turned his body as much as he could to face Lyn. 'Australia is actually wider than the moon?'

Mia rolled her eyes. Two facts. That's all he had. Two boring facts he recycled from person to person.

Lyn's eyes widened. 'You're shitting me, Rami.'

He shook his head. 'I am doing no shitting. The moon is 3,400 kilometres in diameter, while Australia, from east to west is 4,000 kilometres.'

'Another one,' Lyn demanded.

Rami obliged. 'You know The Backstreet Boys?'

'Do I?' Lyn burst into the chorus from 'I Want it That Way'.

'Yep, them,' Rami continued. 'Howie D has a condition where he has a permanent erection.'

'Piss off,' Lyn said playfully.

'It's true. They have to tape it down, and it's why for a lot of their live performances they're on stools, to do that half-standing, half-sitting thing. Look at any dance routines, and there's rarely any bending or difficult manoeuvres. You'll also notice he's often shot from the stomach up in videos.'

Mia was tempted to jump out of the car.

'Wow. Mind mangled.' Lyn took out her phone. 'I need to text that to Gyal Pal.' She sent the message.

Rami smirked. 'I should tell you, that was a massive lie.'

Lyn smacked his arm. 'You tosser!' She laughed, which became hysterical, which turned into tears. 'I'll probably never see Dale's erection again.'

Mia shot an annoyed glance at Rami.

He hung his head.

Mia drove the car into the Knights Hill Hotel and Spa car park and switched the engine off. The place was already riding the Christmas wave and it was only the 6th of November. An inflatable snowman, reindeer, and Christmas lights illuminated the entrance, and various Christmas ornaments were dotted around the car park.

Mia caught Lyn's eyes in the rear-view mirror. 'Lyn, we're going to check in, then we planned on having a picnic.'

'In this wank weather?' she said.

'We want to be out under the stars with no distractions. It might help us rekindle something.' She placed a hand on Rami's knee.

He looked at her hand. If he was thinking there was any hope, she would shut that down as soon as Lyn was gone.

'I'll come,' Lyn said.

Mia couldn't find the words to reject her. She looked to Rami for help.

Rami turned to Lyn. 'We love your company, Lyn, but we'd quite like this moment to ourselves. You know?'

Lyn nodded. 'You need me with you. I'm good at this sort of thing. Trust.'

Mia got out of the car and opened Lyn's door. 'It's fine. We appreciate it, but I'll get you checked in, then we'll see you for breakfast.' She grabbed Lyn's arm.

Lyn shook her off. 'I ain't going nowhere.'

'Lyn, please, we just want time alone,' Mia pleaded.

Lyn shook her head. 'Nope. You're a pair of stiffs and you need me to get through this. So, we can carry on arguing, or get on with it. I'll only need an hour with the two of you to lube this up, then I'll bugger off.' She folded her arms.

Mia entered the car and refused to look at Rami.

19

THE BEST KIND OF ANIMAL

Rami

Rami, Mia and Lyn sat in a triangle on the cold riverbank grass. The car was parked about six feet away, Dale's body still in the boot.

Three shopping bags of picnic supplies were between the trio, and the only source of light was the cloud-covered moon.

Rami wished Lyn would disappear or disintegrate. He could see the outline of the trees where they were going to bury Dale, just a couple of hundred feet away.

One hour, she had said. It had been three and it was 1.30 a.m. 'Do you want some more gin?' Rami asked, handing Lyn the bottle, hoping she would drink herself unconscious. Between bouts of her crying and repeating the same story, they had discussed what they were struggling with in their day-to-day lives, what they had hoped to have achieved by now that they hadn't, and they had each mentioned a good thing that had happened to them in the last year.

Mia swigged from a bottle of white wine. Rami kept

throwing her looks to give her a hint to do something, but there was a vacant nothingness about her.

Lyn gulped a stream of the gin down. 'What kind of bloody Co-op doesn't sell marshmallows? It ain't camping without marshmallows.'

'It's a picnic,' Mia pointed out numbly.

Lyn shrugged. 'Same thing. Both outside, both wank.'

Rami took a packet of ready salted crisps from one of the shopping bags. There was no way they were going back home with Dale in their boot. He couldn't spend another night with him in the house, never mind under his bed. He tried to open the packet, but his gloved hands were so cold he couldn't get any grip. He used his teeth.

'So, go on,' Lyn said. 'Now we've loosened up, say one nice thing about each other. Something you really appreciate and value?'

Mia huffed, unenthusiastic. 'Haven't we done enough?'

'I think it's a great idea,' Rami countered, hoping that enthusiasm would help Lyn to see her work was done. 'I can start.' He faced Mia, and despite the long list of awful characteristics she had recently shown, he found the answer easily. 'I admire your drive, Mia. When you're in, you're all in. No fear.' He sniffled. 'Obviously, that also makes me sad, because I know you're not all in with me anymore. But, I often remember when you were all in. And I love how you always want more. To get everything out of life. You're inspiring.' He choked up, realising his words pointed to how little he offered.

Mia stared at him with what may have been a flash of sympathy. It was hard to tell.

Lyn smiled. 'What a cracking answer, Rami. Mimi?'

Mia drank some more wine and paused for longer than was comfortable.

'Hard to pick just one from such a long list, right?' Rami nervously joked.

Mia rubbed her nose and stood up, walking towards the car. 'Your dedication. You're loyal, like a dog.' She leaned on the boot.

Lyn's mouth fell open. 'That all you got, Mimi? Like a dog? Or do you mean like how when you see a dog everything is okay, because their faces are magic?'

Mia shook her head. 'No. Loyal. Dogs are loyal.'

Rami nodded. 'And excitable, easily satisfied, something you need to pick up after.'

Mia stepped forward. 'I mean it in a nice way.'

Lyn scrunched her face. 'Might as well have said you like that he can dress himself.'

'But only if you give me a treat,' Rami added.

Mia folded her arms. 'Both of you piss off. I mean it as in, I know you'd never be unfaithful. You're not built that way. So, loyal, like a dog.'

'No need to repeat it,' Rami said. She was definitely a sociopath.

Lyn pulled on her dolphin earrings. 'I kind of get it, but you're rubbish, Mimi. He's also always there when you need him, smart, good-humoured, and cares about you.'

Rami hoped some of those words would sink into Mia's miserable brain.

Lyn pointed at Mia. 'I remember you gushing down the phone when he bought you that Women in Business Leadership course that you'd been banging on about for years.'

Rami ate a crisp. 'I did it to stop her going on about it.'

Lyn laughed. 'Oh, bloody hell, she did, didn't she? And there was your wedding day.'

'You've made your point, Lyn,' Mia said.

Rami swallowed and his body tensed. What about their wedding day?

Lyn drank more gin and faced Rami. 'When Mia had a

wobble, you were still there, all smiles, even though she was an hour late.'

'Wobble? You told me you were late because you had a bad stomach.'

Mia gave him a reassuring look. 'She's exaggerating.' Mia walked over to Lyn and reached out her hand. 'Let's go for a walk.'

Lyn drank more gin. 'Nah, I'm chilled here.' She leaned back on her elbows.

Rami shivered.

Mia drove her hand out more forcefully. 'For fuck's sake, Lyn! None of your shit is helping!' The fury in Mia's eyes could've lit the night. 'You're just getting in the way!'

Lyn's face fell into a sulk.

Mia stood in place, shaking. Her anger faded into shame. 'I'm sorry, I—'

Lyn put the bottle of gin down, stumbled to her feet, fell forward and swayed away.

'Lyn!' Mia called out.

'Leave me alone!' she screamed into the night air. 'Cow!'

Rami stood up. 'You had a wobble?'

'Let's not dwell on things that don't matter anymore,' Mia said, taking a deep breath. 'I'll go after her and keep her busy. You deal with this.' She pointed to the boot.

'What!?'

'What's the alternative?' she asked.

'It's a two-person job and we're behind.' He looked around at the nothingness, a car's headlights passed on the road on the horizon, far away.

Mia stomped over to the boot. 'You'll be fine. Pick your spot and keep your phone on. I'll message you if anything happens. Honestly, if there was another way where we could do this together, I would. We have to divide and conquer.'

She opened the boot and hurried away.

'Wait.' Rami got up and rushed towards the boot, shutting it, still paranoid. 'I need you.'

'And I'm doing what's needed.' Mia left.

20

ROUND ONE

Mia

Mia, the bottle of white wine in her hand, paced after Lyn, who leaned on a tree and cried. Mia glanced back towards Rami, so far away in the darkness that there was no way Lyn would spot him.

Mia had to keep Lyn here, or better yet, get her as far away as possible. She gulped some wine as she neared. 'I'm sorry, Lyn. I'm so sorry,' Mia said, imagining she was apologising for accidentally killing Lyn's boyfriend.

Lyn stared at Mia. 'Where have you been, Mimi? You've abandoned me.'

'I don't know what to say,' Mia replied.

'I get it. You have problems with loss and shit, but I'm dying. I'm actually dying, and my best mate is treating me like I'm a pest.' She folded her arms.

Mia looked away, struggling to absorb the pain on Lyn's face. 'I can't make any excuses, Lyn. I can't. I'm just... so sorry.'

'Do you value me?' Lyn slurred.

'What sort of question is that?' Mia swallowed.

Lyn blew her nose. 'Well, this all feels one-way.'

'I'll be around more—'

'This isn't a new thing. I'm the one always inviting you out on the razz. I'm the one always calling, always sharing stuff. I even moved to this part of the country to be closer to you. You've just... you've shut the door.'

Mia placed the bottle of wine on the grass between them. 'Of course I value you! You're the best person I know and the first person I call when anything happens. The break-up with Roberto, I called you. The promotion at work, you. The miscarriage, I messaged you while Rami was outside the toilet wondering what was happening.'

'Why not tell me about the divorce or that things were so bad?' Lyn asked.

It was because of Wilfred. One thing she wasn't ready to talk about. 'I was hoping it wouldn't get as bad as it did, and I guess I've been ashamed. I should have talked to you. Then maybe I would've dealt with it better.' She picked up the bottle of wine and offered it to Lyn.

Lyn waved it away.

Mia reached for Lyn's hand, which remained limply by her side. 'Remember that prick at uni. What was his name? The guy so confident he had a mullet in the early 2000s?'

'David Bunce,' Lyn said, a hint of a smile showing.

'Yes!' Mia replied. 'David Bunce, the pervy dunce.' She laughed.

Lyn half-smiled. 'Love how he explained everything to us without us asking. And didn't he wear a suit to lectures? Muppet.' She shook her head.

'We knew more than him and every other idiot in that room,' Mia said. 'It was when he sat next to you and smiled, but you tutted as loudly as you could, then got up and moved to sit next to me that I knew we'd be friends for life. Look what we've achieved since.' Mia took Lyn's hand and squeezed it. 'I'm one of the top people at my company, and you *are* your own damn company.'

Lyn smiled. 'It's bloody knackering.'

Mia nodded. 'We've only made it this far because we have each other. Whenever I'm struggling, I think about you and it lifts me. I'm sorry if I've not appreciated you.'

'You really haven't,' Lyn replied.

Mia swallowed. 'I'm sorry *that* I haven't appreciated you. That I've not been there during this shit time. Yes, I'm going through some crap, but it doesn't matter. This is bigger.'

Lyn gestured for the wine and Mia handed it over. 'Don't diminish what you're going through. I'm just saying stop treating me like wank.' Lyn drank.

Mia placed her hand on her heart. 'Please forgive me. I love you. Hurting you is the worst feeling in the world.' One of.

Lyn wiped her eyes and nodded. 'Okay. I forgive you.' She hugged Mia.

'Lyn for the win,' Mia said.

'Lyn for the fucking win,' she replied.

Mia pulled away from the hug and took Lyn's hand, reaching her other out for the wine, which Lyn handed over. 'It's been a while. What about we walk back to the hotel?'

'It's about a month's walk away!' Lyn chuckled.

'It's only a few hours. We could use the time to catch up,' Mia said.

'What about Rami?' Lyn asked.

Mia shrugged. 'I'll text him. He can take the car and do whatever.' She walked on, hoping Lyn would follow.

'But the whole point is you two bonding.' Lyn didn't move.

Mia turned around. 'It's fine. There's no hope for us. I'll text him as we walk. Come on.'

Lyn's face fell. 'You selfish twat.'

'Lyn, it's fine. This whole trip was a long shot anyway.'

'Wow,' Lyn said. 'This is what you do. Use people when you

need them, then when you don't, chuck them away like a used tampon.'

Mia exhaled, trying to push the anger down. 'I told you I'd message him. I'm not just going without giving him information.'

Lyn pointed back into the night, towards where Rami was. 'He's waiting, probably thinking there's some hope, and you're fobbing him off. We're going back and doing things as a trio.' She stumbled towards where they had left Rami.

'Lyn, wait!' Mia shouted. She chased Lyn, her body tense. She grabbed Lyn's left arm.

Lyn tried to pull free, but Mia gripped her arm tight and yanked it, hard. She gritted her teeth. 'I said, wait!'

Lyn stared at her imprisoned arm. 'Let go of me, Mimi.' She tried to shake free.

Mia's grip tightened. 'Let me handle my dreadful marriage my way. Now come on.'

Lyn stared at Mia. Anger washed over her face. She swung her right fist at Mia's head.

Everything faded as Mia's body flopped onto the grass.

21

THIS IS THE WAY

Rami

Rami stabbed the shovel into the soil again, having managed to dig a hole barely big enough to bury a pigeon.

He had wrapped Dale's rotting body in the tarp and dragged it a few hundred feet to where he and Mia had scouted. Dale's motorcycle-helmet-covered head poked out of it.

The trees loomed over them. It was just Rami, Dale, and Dale's stench, which the wind refused to carry away.

Rami's arms ached and he seethed. A wobble? He understood people got nervous, but a wobble suggested Mia had considered calling the whole thing off. He had been anxious, but never wobbly. The fact she had hidden it showed she wasn't all in.

The shovel pierced more soil, and he stepped on the blade to push it deeper. It was 2 a.m. He couldn't go any faster. He heaved more soil away and cursed himself.

He had stood in that church ready to work for a future, for a life. How many times over the years had she questioned her choice? Maybe if she had not turned up everything would have been better. He was certain he wouldn't be burying someone.

Dale had been a moving, thinking human, enjoying the newness of love. Maybe it would have turned sour with Lyn. From what Mia had told him, Lyn had at least three boyfriends a year and none lasted more than three months, but her and Dale were denied the chance to buck that trend.

'I'm sorry,' Rami said towards the tarp. More tears fell.

Rami still had moments of wanting to turn himself in, but perhaps knowing he would think about Dale every day was enough of a punishment. Dale was part of his DNA now.

Rami gazed at the trees, the river, and then into the empty distance, his paranoia taking hold. He thought he heard voices on the wind. What if a boat came along the river? What if the old man in the cottage was actually a hardcore marathon runner who trained under moonlight? What if a star gazer looked through a telescope, accidentally knocked it and caught a glimpse of him?

He wiped the back of his freezing, gloved hand over his runny nose and continued digging. Maybe one day someone would invent gloves that actually worked. Was prison warm? Or did they turn the heating off during the winter to be extra cruel?

'Rami!' he heard faintly in the distance.

Lyn.

'Rami!' Her yelling would wake up the whole of Norfolk.

He looked towards the sound, trying to make out how far away she was.

'Rami! It's Lyn!'

His heart pounded and every sound from the shuffling of his jacket to his breathing boomed in his mind.

He checked his phone. No message from Mia.

He had to think fast. He could drag the body into the bushes, hide, and wait for her to go away.

'Rami! Where are you?' she slurred. 'Rami!'

If recent experience had taught him anything, it was that Lyn was as persistent as a mosquito, and he needed to stop her shouting.

Lyn's phone torch flickered in the distance. Rami's phone rang.

It was her. He hung up and put his phone on silent.

'Rami! RAMI!'

It wouldn't be long before she could make out his silhouette.

He tossed the shovel into the bushes and rolled Dale's body out of the tarp. He scrunched up the tarp and shoved it next to the shovel. He tried to drag Dale by his ankles, but needed to be faster. He sat Dale up, placed his head under one of Dale's armpits, wrapped his arms around Dale's waist and lifted with everything he had.

He carried Dale towards the top of the slope by the riverbank and dropped him. He knelt, breathing heavily. 'I'm so sorry.'

And then Rami pushed him.

Lyn's silhouette formed on the horizon, her phone torch light growing closer.

The cling film smothering Dale unravelled as his broken body slid slowly towards the river. Rami willed Dale to slide faster, having expected it to be like pushing a sled, but the motorcycle helmet didn't help.

Dale's body stopped where the riverbank met the water. His right leg entered the river, nudged by the current.

Shit.

Rami didn't have time to get down and back before Lyn could see him. He rushed towards her and noticed her tears. 'Lyn! Hey. Are you alright?'

She hugged him and wept into his chest. 'She's such a bitch!'

He spun, manoeuvring Lyn to face away from where Dale's body was. 'What's she done?'

Lyn released the hug. 'She's so disgustingly selfish. I can't stand it anymore. And I... why are you crying?'

Rami took a breath. 'I don't see a way back for me and Mia.'

Lyn nodded. 'She doesn't deserve you anyway. You're a lovely guy, Rami. And I'm sorry I thought you were a bit of a stiff. It was all based on Mia and what she said. She's poison.'

'It's fine,' Rami said. 'I am a stiff, but that's me, so...' He shrugged. 'Where is she?'

'I decked the cow and it felt magical.' She smiled.

Rami's eyes widened. 'I need to check if she's okay.'

Lyn shook her head. 'No. You can't let her own you anymore, Rami.'

Rami took out his phone to call her. 'I appreciate that, Lyn. But she might need medical attention.'

Lyn grabbed his phone and threw it into the river.

'What are you doing!?'

'I'll get you a new one. But tonight, you don't let her in your head. Sit.' Lyn sat and patted the grass next to her.

'What if she's seriously hurt?'

Lyn waved her hand dismissively. 'The connection wasn't that true; she'll be up and about by now.'

Rami couldn't leave Lyn here, about thirty feet from Dale. He reluctantly sat, casting a glance over Lyn's shoulder and to the riverbank. Dale's body remained as it was. The slow current teased pulling him in, but only brushed his leg.

'That's better,' Lyn said. 'Now take a breath.' She hiccupped.

Rami followed her instructions, wishing he could exhale a powerful gust of wind and blow her to the moon.

'And again,' Lyn said.

Rami repeated and nodded.

Lyn smiled. 'When I find Dale, and when things settle down, I'm going to set you up with my mate Sashy. Runs an animal rescue in Kent. Heart of solid gold and glitter. Do you want to see her Insta and TikTok?' Lyn took out her phone.

Rami raised a palm. 'That's very kind of you, Lyn, but my head is all over the place. I kind of just want to be alone tonight to process everything.'

Lyn put her hand on his. 'I get it. But, I can't leave you, Rami. You're going through something rotten, and the last thing you need is to be alone in the wild. Trust me, I've been there.' Sadness flickered in her eyes. 'We don't even have to chat. I'm just here if you want to.'

'I promise I won't do anything that would worry you, Lyn.'

Lyn smiled sympathetically. 'I'm making sure of that. Plus, I find other peoples' energy is what pulls you out of the pits, so my energy is all yours.'

This was hell. He pulled his hand away from hers and looked into her eyes, needing to push her energy away. 'It's not only that, Lyn. It's just, you've been really nice to me. So lovely.'

She smiled. 'You've been great to me, too.'

'Well, with my brain being flung around in this tornado of emotions, I'm not used to someone being so wonderful. And, I know it comes from feeling rejected, and it's irrational, desperate clawing, but I worry I'm starting to have feelings for you. Like, strong ones. And I don't like that, because you're going through something awful and my issues are the last thing you need. So, yeah, I'd feel much better if you went.'

Lyn paused and nodded. Hopefully preparing to leave.

She looked down at the grass. 'Well, bloody hell.' Her eyes returned to Rami. 'Thanks for telling me, Rami. I know how vulnerability can make you feel all weird. I reckon the best thing is for us to talk about it, so you realise you're just sort of grieving and we can get you through it.'

No. Go away. Go away. Go away.

Lyn leaned back on her elbows, seeming completely relaxed. 'I reckon you're reaching for someone the opposite of Mia. It's like at uni, I went out with Alex Freedman, a massive boxer, proper dickhead. Never returned my calls, only got in touch when drunk, made me feel utterly worthless. Just sex, sex, sex. Don't think he gave a speck of shit about my interests. After him, I went for the nerdiest bloke I could find. He turned out to be too needy, then Mia shagged him anyway.' She frowned.

'You should've hit her twice,' Rami said, annoyed Mia had screwed up her one task.

Lyn took a hairband out of her handbag and tied her hair up and leaned forward, placing a hand on Rami's knee. 'What about me is making you fancy me? Saying it out loud will make you realise it's nothing.'

Rami gazed at the full moon, wondering if in a world of billions of people there was an incredibly awkward murder cover-up going on somewhere else at this exact moment. 'Well, you've obviously been very nice, which shows you have a kind heart.'

She nodded, as though waiting for more.

He scratched around his brain. 'You're very dedicated to your... art, and you're smart. Also... attractive.' Maybe he could walk into the freezing river and let it take him away.

'Thank you, Rami.' She smiled as though he was a best friend who was trying to leave the friend zone, but needed to be placed firmly back in it. 'Is there anything else? Get it all out.'

He couldn't take it anymore. He leaned in and kissed her on the lips, then pulled back, taking in her shocked expression. 'I'm so sorry, Lyn.' He buried his head in his hands. 'Please, you have to go. I'm so messed up!'

Lyn, confused, stood up. 'Please don't feel bad, Rami. Your head's scrambled and everything is going to be fine.'

'I know. I think. I'm so sorry.'

Lyn played with the zip on her jacket. 'Please don't feel ashamed. This is all coming from her screwing with you.'

'Thanks.' He kept his head in his hands.

'You promise me you'll be alright?'

He looked at her. 'Yes. I promise.' There was so much kindness in her eyes.

'We'll chat soon,' she said. 'And I'll get that new phone to
you.' Lyn stumbled the way she came. Rami watched her,
relieved she didn't glance back.

Finally.

Rami wiped his lips on his jacket sleeve, removing the taste
of gin, amaretto, and apple lip gloss. He returned to the riverbank and Dale's body. He could drag him back up and continue
digging, but it would take forever and he had already lost so
much of the night. 'If there's a heaven, Dale, I hope you've ended
up there. Given the circumstances, should I die soon, I don't
think we'll be meeting.' Rami put his foot against Dale's shoulders and pushed him into the water.

Dale's broken body floated away, face down, along the
current. Rami willed it to sink, but it didn't, as though the
helmet was keeping him up. Rami sprinted along the riverbank
and reached out for Dale, but he was too far.

He looked to the heavens, wondering what else could go
wrong.

He rushed into the freezing water and reached for Dale's left
ankle, but the cold shock hit him and he stumbled too far, too
deep. His body chilled to the bone and it hurt to breathe. He
grabbed Dale's ankle and tried to paddle back to the riverbank,
but his inability to swim meant the current won.

The rank river invaded Rami's mouth as he clutched onto
Dale, his only hope of staying afloat.

He coughed up water as more bashed his throat and nostrils.
The musty, shitty taste was what he deserved. His throat felt like
it was being frozen shut.

He kicked his legs out, hoping they would hit a part of the
riverbank where he could steady himself, but it was meaningless. The cold sapped what little strength he had left, and
mentally he was running on empty.

His saviour was a bloated corpse, but he couldn't hold on any more. Icy water squeezed Rami's face and his muscles spasmed. His grip loosened, his heart raced, and two thoughts dominated. The first: that this was a really pathetic way to die. The second: He wished he had never met his wife.

He closed his eyes.

22

FIRSTS AND LASTS

MIA

'Kick!' Mia shouted, using everything she had to yank Rami's head above water as the current dragged them.

The icy river attacked her, but she pulled his arm over her shoulder and kicked to stay afloat. She prodded his face as she tried to swim to the riverbank.

'Wake up!'

He stirred, but remained a limp sack of uselessness, dragging her down, reminiscent of their marriage.

She slapped him. He sputtered water and coughed.

'Kick!' she demanded and felt him move.

They neared the riverbank and she found her footing, dragging Rami onto the grass.

He crawled out of the water and lay on his back, coughing.

Mia, shivering and furious, rushed down the riverbank and reached for the corpse. She pulled him onto the grass and removed his helmet.

She pushed him back into the water and dunked his head. She was numb to everything.

As the body started to sink she pushed it away and sat back on the riverbank.

Rami crawled over to her, every limb of his shaking. He stared at the cut on the side of her head.

'Don't,' she said.

Rami held the man's helmet as heavy rain fell. He sighed.

They watched the river consume the corpse.

Mia stepped out of the fancy hotel shower enclosure and dried herself, relieved her body temperature was back to normal.

The adrenaline of being rid of the corpse pumped through her veins. Sure, his helmet was still in their car boot, but tonight was a success. It was 3 a.m. and she had never felt so awake.

She twisted a towel around her wet hair and put the robe on. The grapefruit smell of the hotel soap and shampoo was an invigorating relief. She had no interest in fields anymore – not that she had been keen on them before, and she never wanted to see a river again.

She gathered her wet trousers, top, knickers and bra from the shower floor where she had washed the river filth out of them.

She exited the bathroom into the lush suite fit for newly-weds with its four-poster bed. Rami had said it was the only room available. He was sitting, covered in a towel, shivering in the armchair by the mini bar. The hairdryer rested on the desk and was turned on, aimed at him. He tossed a packet of plasters into the air and caught it while eating from a bowl of room service chips. His soaked clothes were in a pile on the carpet.

They hadn't said a word to each other since they had succeeded, yet it was eerily comfortable.

Mia approached him and held her hand out for the plasters.

'The water pressure's amazing,' she said, desperate for some normality to counter the image of dunking the corpse.

He nodded and handed her the packet. He turned the hairdryer off.

Mia ate a chip and winced at the amount of salt. 'Christ!'

'What? Not enough salt?' he flatly said.

Mia chuckled. 'It's like when a kid licks their food so nobody else will eat from their plate.'

He smiled. 'Works, right? I know you won't be stealing any while I'm in the shower.' He picked up his wet clothes and dragged his feet towards the bathroom then turned to face her. 'Thanks for saving me.'

She had no idea why she had. Instinct took over. 'You would've done the same.'

He nodded. 'Though, we're not completely out of it. I read that the River Great Ouse is England's fifth most contaminated river, with chemicals ten times above safety levels.'

'Please don't—'

'Although the stretch we were in, between Norfolk and the Wash is apparently in good condition, whatever good means. But still, we're probably going to get E. coli pneumonia.'

Mia huffed and stared at him.

'Yeah.' Rami bit his lip and entered the bathroom.

Mia hung her wet trousers and knickers on the radiator. She hung her wet top and bra on hangers in the wardrobe, next to her coat.

She opened the packet of plasters and stuck one over the cut. In less than a week she had lost a marriage, a best friend, the love of her life, and had accidentally killed someone. She took her hip flask from her handbag and drained the rum, warming her body.

She removed the towel from her head and opened the mini bar, which had two miniature bottles of wine, three cans of gin and tonic, a couple of bottles of beer, and five shot bottles of spirits: a mix of vodka and gin. She grabbed all of the alcohol and sat on the bed. She downed the bottles of wine and three of the shots while drying her hair.

She checked her phone, but she had no messages. Nothing from Wilfred. And nothing from Lyn apologising or forgiving her. Not even a message from her mother trying to manipulate her into making peace.

Mia drank another shot.

Rami, wrapped in a towel, re-entered. 'You're right; the water pressure's immense,' he said numbly, then did a double-take, noticing the bottles around Mia, but not saying anything.

She offered him a can of gin and tonic, but he shook his head.

'Thanks, but I don't think I can emotionally handle any hangovers.' He noticed the radiator was occupied, so grabbed his soaked jacket from the carpet and hung it in the wardrobe, then placed his hat on the windowsill. He took the rest of his clothes into the bathroom. 'Wim Hof is a liar,' he said. 'There is no benefit to be gained from cold exposure.' He re-emerged with his scrunched-up, damp boxer shorts.

He aimed for the bin, threw and missed, then trudged over to pick them up and put them in.

Mia offered a polite smile.

Rami sat in the armchair. 'She really nailed you.' He ate some more chips, opened a bottle of water and drank.

Mia rubbed her head, over the plaster. 'Her fist was dripping in more jewellery than a bazaar,' she slurred.

'Thanks again,' Rami said, more colour returning to his face.

'We did it,' she said.

'Yeah,' Rami said with no enthusiasm.

She stared at him, and her body tingled. 'We did it. We improvised and dealt with an obstacle worse than the police.'

Rami drank more water. 'Why are you friends with Lyn when you have so little respect for her?'

He had a point, and Mia realised Lyn was right. Mia didn't value her. She was friends with Lyn, because it worked for her, because it was on her terms. 'Don't think that's an issue anymore. But I don't care.' She wondered whether Lyn had made it back to the hotel, and how? 'Anyway, start dreaming of that lemonade in the sun.'

Rami exhaled.

'Thanks for the help,' she said.

'You too,' he replied.

'I know it can't have been easy, with everything.' She gestured to the air. 'And it's been a rotten few days, but sharing the rottenness with you helped.' She downed another miniature bottle of vodka.

Before they had accidentally killed the man, she couldn't wait to get away from Rami. She would never have to look into his pathetic eyes, listen to his voice that could make even good news sound depressing, or listen to another damn fact. Now that it was becoming reality, she was sad. Maybe it was the alcohol, but it was easy to be nice knowing she wouldn't have to see him again. 'I hope one day I can look back on our marriage and miss you in a nice way, wondering how you are, hoping things are good, and thinking of the better memories.'

Rami smiled. 'Hard to think of them with the last few days.'

'Yeah,' she said. 'But they're there, just buried.' She tutted. 'Sorry, shit choice of words.'

Rami shrugged. 'At least you didn't say drowned.'

Mia stood up and pulled the duvet cover off the bed, offering Rami the thick duvet underneath. 'You have it.'

'It's fine,' he said.

'At least take the sheet then,' she said.

He shook his head. 'I've been exposed to the cold so long that my body no longer acknowledges warmth.' He took one of the pillows, placed it on the carpet and lay down.

'Okay, but if your teeth start chattering, I'm ignoring you.'

Mia got into bed. She stayed still until the room stopped swaying. She pulled the duvet and sheet over herself and turned the lamp off. The body was gone. Sure, but it wasn't gone, gone. But it was no longer in her possession, and she was going to enjoy every minute of it being out of her life. No more wasting days. She felt taller, stronger.

Rami laughed. 'I kissed Lyn.'

'What?' Mia chuckled, shuffled to the side of the bed and looked down at him.

'I bloody kissed Lyn.' He shook his head. 'I couldn't get rid of her. After she Mike Tysoned you, she found me and wouldn't leave. She wanted us to talk through my sadness, and Dale was about thirty feet away.'

Mia laughed. 'I'm so sorry. She's persistent, isn't she?' she slurred.

'I tried so many things. Then I thought, what repels all the women? Worked wonderfully.'

Mia snorted. 'Be careful, she'll probably fall in love with you now.'

Rami groaned. 'Worse is she thinks I fancy her. I've got to live with that.'

Mia smiled. 'That is true dedication to the cause.'

'Well, I am loyal like a dog,' he said.

Mia frowned. 'There's obviously lots I appreciate in you, Rami. Before I met you I had no confidence, but you helped me to grow—'

'To the point you outgrew me.'

Mia swallowed. 'Maybe. But I also have so much respect for how you keep the gambling addiction down, how passionate you are about your work, and how you're always keen to engage. You've never once made me feel insecure.' She felt the guilt of probably having made him feel endlessly insufficient. 'It's just been hard to admire those things when... you know?'

'Yeah.' He took a breath and shuffled on the carpet. 'What now then?'

Mia tapped her fingers on the side of her head. 'I guess we'll start the divorce process. I doubt I'll be staying at Lyn's, so I'll start looking for somewhere.'

Rami cleared his throat. 'You don't have to rush out of the house. And we should stay in touch about updates on Lyn, Jenny, and the thing.'

'Yeah.' It made sense, but hopefully would only be short-term. 'Thanks. Maybe it will be a good idea to move once I know what my next steps are.'

'Good. And stay as long as you need.'

She huffed. It was odd to find his affection and attempts at connection frustrating. All she had ever wanted was someone dedicated and faithful. Then she met Wilfred and realised she could have that plus more. But was that where it would have ended? What was to stop her wanting more than Wilfred? Maybe that was the path her life was on, always wanting more, and then eventually dying, having never felt complete. Why was she so desperate to keep levelling up?

Rami shuffled on the floor. 'You know, the saddest thing for me is thinking about firsts and lasts.'

'How do you mean?'

'At some point, it's going to be the last day we share a house. Then it's going to be the last time a delivery comes to the door for you. Then there'll be a first, like the first date with someone new, if ever. Or the first time you're not the person I call or message when I have to share something. Then there's when your smell fades from the house and I forget what it was like. Bit shit, really.'

Mia swallowed. It was a bit sad. 'But, there'll also be the first time we look back fondly and think this marriage helped us to get to wherever we go next.'

He didn't reply for a moment. 'Night, Mia, for almost the last time.'

She was very far from falling asleep, so thought about more firsts and lasts. One day she would message him and not get an instant response. Had she taken his dedication and attentiveness for granted? Just because certain things had become normal or habitual, it didn't mean they were less special.

She shuffled around in the bed, agitated. 'Do you want to sleep in the bed?' she asked, surprised at herself. 'It seems a bit cruel for you to be down there.'

Rami swallowed. 'You're fine. I've been through worse recently.'

'Come on,' she said. 'Don't be a hero.' She felt like she could run a marathon.

'Yeah, this carpet is actually incredibly uncomfortable. Feels like rope and I can only imagine how many weird mites are crawling around.' He stood and walked around the bed, getting in on the other side, staying close to the edge. 'I appreciate it.' He turned away from her, facing the window. 'Good night.'

'Night,' she replied and turned her back to his.

She shouldn't. She couldn't.

She bit her lip.

Rami cleared his throat.

The darkness and the emptiness gnawed at Mia, as though the parasite fed off it. She wanted to feel something other than emptiness. She wanted to forget.

Mia turned to face Rami's back and placed her hand on his shoulder. She left it there and felt his breathing quicken.

She stroked his back.

He turned to face her.

23

THE REAL ADDICTION

R AMI

Rami stood under the fixed circular shower head and enjoyed the warm water running from his head down to his toes. He followed the path of the water as he moved his arms, how it flowed and adapted, but still always continued towards its destination.

Maybe the shower water flowed straight into the river, and the longer he left it on, the sooner Dale would be pushed out to sea.

Less than ten hours ago he thought he was dead. He still worried an illness would catch up with him, but he felt okay, if anything he felt great, especially after making love to Mia.

He squirted some hotel shower gel onto his hand.

He wasn't stupid. For Mia, it was likely a drunken mistake, fuelled by the events of the last few days. It didn't mean things were repaired and back on. He rubbed the shower gel over his torso.

But...

But did it mean they weren't totally finished? They were like the water running over his body, taking different paths, but eventually ending up in the same place, flowing back to each other.

She surely wouldn't have had sex with him if she didn't feel *anything*? There must have been something in it and he was certain she had enjoyed herself. Maybe he could pitch trying a separation rather than a full-blown divorce. Maybe she would miss him after some time apart and would want to try again. He did find she had softened towards him during the last few days. It seemed the therapist was right, all they needed was a shared experience.

He sang 'Everybody's Free' by Rozalla.

Maybe he was deluded. He had been in the shower for at least half an hour, nervous about facing her, wondering what his opening line would be.

He had left Mia a glass of water on the bedside table. Her drinking worried him, and it didn't look like something she would be stopping anytime soon. The signs had been there for years, with her drinking half a bottle of wine most nights, but now she had easily doubled that. He knew addiction when he saw it.

He was going to do it. As soon as he re-entered the room he would pitch separation. Then he would wait for his clothes to dry and go to buy toothbrushes and toothpaste. Tuesday, a day notorious for being rubbish, even considered unlucky in Greece due to the Fall of Constantinople, was going to be one for a new beginning.

He washed the shower gel off his body and wondered if Lyn was okay. She seemed resilient, but with no phone he was suddenly disconnected from everything.

He wished Dale's body was in the ground where it couldn't move, rather than being shoved around by the current.

He dried himself and touched his jeans, T-shirt and jumper

on the bathroom radiator. Still too wet. He wrapped the towel around his body.

He placed his hand on the door handle and took a breath. Life had given him another chance, and even though he didn't deserve it, he would seize it. He opened the door and stepped into the bedroom. 'Mia, I know it doesn't—'

The room was empty. His eyes shot around.

Her clothes were no longer on the radiator.

Her car keys were gone from the desk.

The glass of water remained full on the bedside table.

Mia didn't know Lyn had chucked his phone in the river. Maybe she sent him a message to explain she had to leave.

He shook his head, and the stupidity out of his mind. Whatever she did was calculated, and as usual, inconsiderate of his feelings. She wasn't flowing towards him. She was clear ocean water and he was festival toilet sludge.

He sighed. If anyone had addiction issues, it was him, dependent on her, and using fleeting moments of kindness in her selfish behaviour as a reason to stay hooked. The cruel lows meant the highs were even more absorbing.

With his clothes still wet he was stuck. He sat on the bed, a lonely man, wearing nothing but a towel. He stared out of the window. The glimmer of hope he had about their marriage may as well have been floating out to sea with Dale.

24

WHEN IN DOUBT, GET OUT

Mia

Mia sat in The Pantry Restaurant on the third floor of Jarrolds Department Store in Norwich city centre, watching her phone screen. The heavily bearded Paulo Beavis, CEO of a chatbot-led therapy start-up, presented his business via Zoom.

She glanced at the smaller box with her face in it, worried she looked a state, but the eye drops and make-up had masked her three hours of disrupted sleep, and thanks to the magic of Zoom, Paulo couldn't smell her. She had worn her damp, stinking clothes to the department store and bought new ones, but she still felt grimy.

She nodded. 'Paulo, I'm not sure people will take to a therapist chatbot, even if the avatar is a cute dog.' She sipped her coffee, which was more of a mug of whisky with a dash of coffee for colouring.

Paulo stopped sharing his screen and grinned his big American grin, which somehow made his beard appear fluffier, like a cloud. 'That little doggy has the mind of professional therapists from psychoanalysis, behaviour therapy, cognitive, humanistic, and integrative. And as we grow, our pool of pros will only get bigger and even more specific.'

Mia smiled. 'Yeah. But it's a dog chatbot. It's a lot to ask people to put their mental health in its care. There are loads of app-based GPs who've struggled, and they still had the human touch.'

Paulo pointed at the screen. 'That's why I need you, Mia. To make that cute, empathetic little gender-neutral doggy something people are gonna want to engage with. And that little critter is more than a virtual therapist. It also leads the user to lessons, articles, everything. Like a dog brings you your slippers or the paper, this one fetches you anything you need for your emotional health. And people will know it's powered by therapists. We just need stronger products to offer a more rounded experience, build that trust, and a name.'

'I thought you had a name?' she chuckled.

'Not the app, although that could use a rethink; I mean the doggy. Can't name the damn thing. Chat GPT gave me a long list but nothing's sticking. I asked the kids and their ideas were so bad I almost grounded them.' He turned his camera to face two toddlers, a boy and a girl, playing in the corner of the large home office. The 6 a.m. Los Angeles sunrise teased through the windows. 'Look at the little idiots. Butter wouldn't melt, but not a brain cell between them.'

Mia laughed. 'Hi, Ernesto! Hi, Sylvia!'

The kids ignored her. Paulo shook his head and whispered to the screen. 'Both take after their mother.'

Mia smirked and sipped more whisky. 'Probably for the best.'

'You're not wrong.' Paulo smiled. 'We've tried so many names, but they all offend. Dom, gender-neutral, means stupid in the Netherlands. Cal apparently sounds similar to a Russian word for faeces. Cara sounds like "khara" in Arabic which means poop. There's a theme where a much-loved name in one country is a lump of excrement in another.' Paulo shook his head. 'The downside of a global society.' He laughed.

Mia grinned. 'Why not let the user name it?'

Paulo tilted his head.

Mia shrugged. 'We store user names and data so that bots can personalise messages all the time, so why not do the same for the dog? Whatever you call it, someone is going to find it offensive, boring, too kiddy, too grown-up, or that it reminds them of their dead granddad. So, put it in their hands, and we can block out rude names, so you don't get screenshots of Arsehound the Dog doing the rounds on social media.'

Paulo nodded and laughed. 'I'll check with my engineers how much of a butt-ache that could be, but I love it.'

'Butt-ache isn't a bad name for a dog, either.' She smiled.

'Butt-ache the bulldog.' He scratched his beard. 'See, it's that kind of thinking which is why you'll be one of the last the robots replace. So, what's it going to take?'

Mia smirked.

Mia had sat in the car facing their garage shutter since 4 p.m. That was twenty minutes ago. She wasn't sure what she would say to Rami. She had no excuse for fleeing the hotel room, but she woke up still drunk and full of regret. She had pretended to be asleep until he entered the bathroom, then fled under the cover of the running shower.

She held the garage shutter remote, but couldn't press it. She tossed it onto the passenger seat, needing a few more minutes to think.

The shutter rose, revealing Rami's shoes, then ankles and waist. This was all a bit dramatic. Then the shutter got stuck.

Her heart raced as Rami crouched under the shutter and approached the car. He was all puffed up.

She braced herself and opened the driver's window, ready for a lecture about feelings, but accepting she needed to take it.

His anger faded. 'Give me a minute to sort the shutter.'

She exhaled and watched him wrestle with the shutter until it fully opened. She drove in and parked the car, the shutter closing behind her.

Rami stood between her and the open door to the hallway.

She stepped out of the car. 'I'm sorry, Rami. I panicked, but that wasn't fair.'

'No, it was pretty terrible.' He folded his arms. 'And you should probably stop driving while drunk.'

Her blood boiled. 'Don't tell me what to do. I'm fine.'

Rami huffed. 'You reek of it.'

She offered him a thumbs up. 'I'll spray more perfume.' She barged past him and into the hallway.

'We both need help,' he said.

She turned to him. 'What?'

'There's grief counselling, at a community centre in Bungay. This isn't something we can get through in our heads.'

She scrunched her nose. 'You want to go and share what happened with a group?'

'No. But that environment could help. We might learn coping strategies. It might be good to go together. And while we're on that, I know you probably regret last night.'

Every second.

'But, I felt something.'

She definitely didn't. She smirked.

'What?' he asked.

'Nothing.'

He joined his hands together as though praying. 'And I don't know why I'm suggesting this, especially after the way you treated me this morning. But, why not, instead of a divorce, while we wait for this whole Dale thing to play out, we try a separation?'

His eyes carried a pathetic glimmer of hope. She felt both powerful and awful about extinguishing it. 'I'm sorry, Rami—'

He raised a hand, cutting her off. 'No, I know. I had to ask. Even though I knew the answer.'

She nodded. 'Look, I'm not interested in grief counselling and exploring myself with a group of sad-sacks. I don't see how it'll help me.'

He looked at the ground. 'Okay, well, I might go.'

'It's like you're horny for suffering.' She folded her arms. 'Just, no matter how emotional or overwhelmed you feel, don't give the tiniest hint about why you're grieving.'

'What do you think I'm going to do; confess? Come on, Mia.'

'I just... Why not, instead of constantly thinking about the accident, try to do something normal to move forward. It's like you're stuck at the bottom of a well, but you're enjoying the ambiance and don't want to climb out.' She stepped towards the stairs, but stopped. Having left the hotel without telling him, she felt she owed him this. 'Also, on moving forward, I'm not going to be staying here beyond tomorrow.'

'What?' He had the look of a child whose balloon was floating off into space.

'I think it's best we have a clean break. It's unfair on you for me to linger.'

'I don't mind.' His lack of self-esteem was remarkable, but that was partly on her.

'I do. And it's not fair if I have another lapse and we...' She knew she wouldn't have a lapse, but felt she had to protect his ego.

He nodded. 'Where will you go?'

'I'm moving to LA tomorrow.'

His face fell. 'LA!? Los Angeles?'

'Yeah. Sorry. Found a job that was too hard to turn down.' She wasn't sorry at all.

He nodded. 'Well, thanks for telling me this time.'

25

VICTIM OR PERPETRATOR

RAMI

Rami scrubbed the car boot mat, putting every sinew into it as he blasted a Spotify playlist entitled "Sadness" from his laptop. When he felt something, he wanted to feel all of it; soak in it. It was his way of processing.

He had listened to Boyz II Men's 'End of the Road' and East 17's 'Stay Another Day', and now Snow Patrol's 'You Could be Happy' pulled at his soul.

This morning, he had hope that Tuesday would be a good day. Instead it had lived up to its reputation as a day of misery.

He attacked a particularly rank yellowish-black fluid stain as the lyrics about regret rang in his ears.

He had already cleaned his study, throwing all the sheets in the bin. The carpet under his bed was covered in Dale's fluids and could easily have been mistaken for a Jackson Pollock painting. Rami had to cut the stained section out and had covered the hole with a fabric storage box.

He stared into the boot and sighed.

So, his kisses made women run away, and his genitals made them leave the country.

Mia was selfish. She told him she had handed in her notice at work, and was going to serve it remotely while on holiday in Los Angeles, until her work visa came through.

Her new employer was going to let her do unofficial work, and it had crossed Rami's mind to report her so she would have to come back, but he sighed those thoughts away. What good would it do? She didn't want him.

It was all so one-sided. The lyrics bashed at his brain.

He swallowed his misery.

He replayed the song, picked the tools up off the garage floor and put them in various drawers. He stared at Dale's helmet on a shelf. He held it and turned it in his hands. The padding was damp and stained with blood and whatever fluids had seeped out of Dale's head wound. Rami dropped the helmet and it clattered against the hard garage floor.

He gulped down the vomit that rose in his throat, closed the boot and picked up the helmet, needing to wash it and any traces of Dale's DNA away. But first, he wanted to return to the river to walk along it, just to make sure Dale's body hadn't surfaced or gotten caught anywhere.

The doorbell sounded, followed by a knock. The Lyn trademark.

'Mia!' Rami shouted through the open garage door to the hallway.

Mia shouted down the stairs. 'She texted requesting I not answer it.'

'Yeah!' Lyn shouted through the letterbox. 'I'd rather you answer, Rami.'

He huffed. 'Give me a second.' He wrapped the helmet in a dust sheet and placed it in a plastic box. Maybe it would be smart to keep the helmet in the garage a while. The fewer items of Dale's out in the world the better.

He covered the box with another dust sheet, turned the music off and exited the garage, locking the door behind him. He answered the front door.

Lyn's smile couldn't hide the pain on her face. 'That was longer than a second,' she joked. She seemed smaller than usual, and as though she had no energy left. For once she was dripping in misery, rather than jewellery, but still wore the dolphin earrings Dale had bought her. Mia and Rami were poison. Everything they touched became grey and lifeless.

Lyn held a gift-wrapped box.

'I wonder what that is?' Rami said sarcastically.

'Sorry for dashing your phone in the Ouse. But, this is the latest model, better than your old cack.' She handed the box over. 'I would've come earlier,' she raised her voice, clearly for Mia's purposes. 'But, I was exhausted from having to walk four hours and seventeen minutes back to the hotel last night.' She gazed beyond Rami, expecting some sort of response from Mia, but it never came. Her eyes settled back on Rami.

He shrugged. 'I'd invite you in, but I know the answer.'

She looked at the floor. 'Yeah. Was just heading to Jenny's anyway.'

Rami stared at the box in his hands. 'Thank you, Lyn.' He leaned in. 'And, about last night...'

She placed a hand on his shoulder and whispered. 'Don't. It's fine. Just, let's not tell Dale when I find him, 'cos he can be over-protective and might belt you.'

Rami smiled, concealing the dread for when she would learn Dale was gone for good. 'Deal.'

'Walk me to Jenny's?' Lyn asked.

He stepped outside, closing the door behind him, and they walked towards Jenny's house.

Lyn turned to him. 'I know it's not my place. But you'd do well to get in a different space to her.'

'I know,' he said. 'Won't be a problem from tomorrow onwards, though.'

Lyn's eyes widened. 'Very Mia to leg it.' She knocked on Jenny's door, triggering Ballula's bark. 'You just call me if you need to talk or anything, Rami. But don't let her manipulate you.'

'Thanks, Lyn.' She was a kind soul. She didn't deserve any of this pain they had dumped on her.

Jenny answered the door, her cheery demeanour seemingly on holiday.

Lyn raised her hand for a high five. 'Ready to find a sexy bastard?'

Jenny grabbed Lyn's hand and held it. She shifted her eyes to Rami then back to Lyn. 'Come in and sit down,' she said solemnly.

'You're chatting arse, Jenny!' Lyn barked, pacing in front of the basement sofa.

Jenny, holding an iPad, sat next to Rami, who awkwardly sipped his cup of tea, with the gift-wrapped box on his lap.

He had to look at the iPad again, and was confused as to whether to be relieved or petrified.

Jenny pointed to the screen. 'I'm sorry, Lyn, but it's all here, love.'

There were three different photos of Dale, all with different names.

'How?' Lyn asked, clenching her fists.

'Maybe you should sit back down,' Rami said, worried Lyn would turn into a mini hurricane and destroy everything in the room.

'I don't want to sit down!' she snapped, then looked momentarily apologetic. 'Sorry,' she softened. 'I just don't get it.'

Rami offered a sympathetic smile. He glanced at a map Jenny had placed on the wall, as though she had her own police station. Rather than pins representing key places and people, she had DnD figurines. For Dale, there was an elven knight stuck to Bungay, while Lyn was represented by a scantily clad female druid in Great Yarmouth.

Jenny pushed herself up on the sofa arm and sat on it. 'My pal took the details you gave and he dug into them. Dale has three identities. There's who you know, Dale Boswitch Ragnor...'

Rami would've never have guessed the B was for Boswitch.

'He's also known as Steve Loving, and Martin Müller.'

The moustache did give Dale a certain German quality.

Lyn collapsed onto the sofa and hyperventilated.

Jenny sat next to Lyn and held her hand. 'Purse your lips and breathe, as though you're whistling.' She guided Lyn through it, until she calmed down.

'Thanks,' Lyn said.

Rami sipped his tea, clueless as to what to do, and not sure what this meant, both in terms of the search for Dale, and for his guilt. Did it mean they had killed a bad person rather than a charity worker? Did that matter? Killing was killing. Sweat formed on his neck.

Jenny rubbed Lyn's back. 'There's also no registered charity called Band Together. Just a holding page and social media accounts with no activity. And none of his identities have an address in Bungay.'

'So what does it all mean?' Lyn asked. 'That he's a fraudster? Or that he was hiding his identity from someone? Like, was he someone who took a wrong turn and needed to find a way out? What do I do with this info?'

She looked to Rami for an answer. He sipped his tea again to buy himself a moment.

He sympathised with her attempt to see Dale as someone who was potentially in a tight spot, making him a victim rather than the perpetrator, much like he did with Mia. 'Maybe he was just trying to right wrongs that were forced upon him,' Rami said.

Jenny's eyes met Rami's and suggested otherwise. She pulled Lyn's hair off her tear-stained face. 'There's more, love, but I don't want to overwhelm you.'

Lyn closed her eyes and leaned her head back. 'Just hit me with it, J.'

Rami put the teacup to his lips, even though there was no tea left in it.

Jenny glanced at him, then back to Lyn. 'Dale has a wife.'

26

THE DREAMS WORTH CHASING

MIA

Mia searched boxes and bags in their messy loft. The space was congested with eight years of tat and faded sentiments.

She opened a plastic bag and took out an old George Foreman grill they had used once. It was like their marriage: an okay idea at the time, but not worth the maintenance. She placed it in an unmarked box and returned to the pile of boxes labelled, "Mia."

Rami, sitting on a dusty, overturned shelving unit, placed the dead man's helmet in a cardboard box. 'But, this changes everything. Are you sure you shouldn't stay a bit longer?'

Mia searched another box containing old university folders and books. 'What's going to change? There'll be more coverage, some awful tabloid headlines, probably some stuff about him being part of a criminal network or sex gang, but nothing that hits us.' She pushed the box to the left-hand side of the loft. 'These are for binning. I'm never going to revisit them.'

Rami nodded. 'We also need to walk the river together when it's lighter, to check the body hasn't surfaced.'

'That doesn't need both of us,' Mia said. 'You'll be fine.' She pointed to the box in front of Rami. 'Why are you bringing his crap up here?'

Rami took some duct tape and over-did sealing the box. 'Because the less stuff of his out in the world, the fewer things they can find.' He huffed. 'Do you not think you should stick around for Lyn? Despite her decking you, she needs you.'

Mia scoffed. 'We did Lyn a favour. If we didn't accidentally kill him she might have never figured out he was a sleaze and she could be in the middle of getting trafficked to Libya.'

Rami glared at her as though she had said something insensitive.

'What? It's true. Or she could've married the guy never knowing anything.' Mia wiped the dust off a plastic crate. 'I hope she plans on apologising to me soon.'

'I don't think we can justify killing a man—'

'*Accidentally*.' She glared at him.

Rami exhaled. 'We can't be sure he was a criminal. There are probably bigger issues in his life we don't know about. And who knows if he wasn't turning a corner with Lyn? Then we stepped in and...' He smacked his hands together.

Mia ignored him, opened the crate and stepped back, a pain in her throat. 'I told you to throw it all away.'

Rami joined her.

Mia opened a wooden chest within the crate, full of newborn baby clothes, stuffed toys, and wooden animal figurines.

He sighed. 'I couldn't do it.' He picked up an avocado teddy bear.

Mia had told him not to spend so much money on things until the baby was actually with them, but he couldn't help himself. He always acted on imagination rather than reality. She moved to the other side of the loft. 'She's dead, Rami.'

He placed the avocado back in the chest and closed the crate.

'For a while I used to come up and look at them. Found them comforting.'

Maybe his naive hopefulness wasn't all bad. 'Do what you want with them. I'm never stepping in here again anyway.' Her hand trembled. 'I also think we shouldn't talk for a week once I go. Just to help with the transition.'

His eyes widened. 'What about the whole dead body thing?'

Why couldn't she have a clean break? 'Okay, if there's a *serious* development in that. But otherwise, we need a cut-off. No small talk, just the task at hand. As horrid and cruel as it sounds, you'll thank me in the long run.'

He picked up an old frame: an oil painting of Norwich Station that his grandmother had painted. Mia had made him move her art up here, as she had wanted the house to have their personalities.

'Try not to live in the guilt,' she said. 'There's nothing you can do for him now. What happened has happened, and yes, it was awful. But, here we are. You can move on, with it being part of you, making sure to live better, or sit in it and have a gloomy life. At least make his death worth it.'

'Yeah. You're right.'

The doorbell sounded.

'For fuck's sake,' Mia said. At least Lyn didn't bang on the door as well this time.

'It's not her,' Rami said. 'Someone answered my tutoring ad, but they wanted to meet first, to make sure I'm not useless, I guess.' He shrugged.

'You sure you're up to it?' she asked.

'You told me to try to be normal.' He placed the painting on a box and descended the loft ladder until only his head was visible. 'Here's to trying.'

Peace at last. Mia picked up a box of crockery they had bought for when they had guests over. They never had guests over.

'Hello,' Rami's voice boomed. 'Thanks for coming over.'

Mia put the box down and approached the loft hatch. She crouched down and grabbed a ladder step to pull it up and shut Rami and his new victim out.

'I'm Rami, obviously, otherwise you've got the wrong house.'

The visitor laughed heartily.

Mia recognised that laugh.

'And I'm Wilfred, obviously, otherwise you're about to be burgled or murdered.'

Both men laughed.

Mia dropped the ladder.

Mia stood a few steps from the bottom of the stairs. Her entire body shook with a nervous, confused, angry energy.

She was tempted to return to the loft, but she had to know what the hell was going on.

Rami and Wilfred had been discussing writing for ten minutes, laughing constantly like two old friends.

Mia took a breath, descended the final steps and strode into the kitchen.

Rami was sitting in the armchair, while Wilfred, dressed like a man you could rent, in his shiny suit and silk shirt, leaned forward on the sofa. He grinned at her.

Rami pointed to Mia. 'Wilfred, meet Mia. My, erm...'

'Ex-wife,' Mia said.

Wilfred stood and extended his hand. 'An absolute pleasure. I'm Wilfred Throckmorton.'

She shook his hand and stared into his eyes, trying her best to say "fuck off" without uttering the words. The warm rush she used to get from his touch had evaporated. Not even a flicker. She released his cold, creepy hand, wishing she could rake her nails down his palm to his wrist and slit his radial artery.

Rami pointed to Wilfred. 'He works at the same company as you. I'm amazed you've never met.'

'Different departments,' Wilfred said, sitting back down.

'Soon to be different companies,' she replied, enjoying watching his grin fade. She stood behind the kitchen counter to give herself a barrier. She took a bottle of red wine and poured some into a glass. 'You decided to do something more creative?' she asked Wilfred.

He cleared his throat. 'Yes. I've always had a love for film, but I keep putting it off, then I saw your husband's – sorry – ex-husband's advertisement in the TV and Movie Store and took it as a sign.' He smiled.

Mia sipped her wine. 'It's great when you find your passion. In fact, Rami, you should show him some of your screenwriting books.'

'Great idea! Back in a moment.' Rami rushed out of the kitchen like an excited child, his footsteps hurrying up the stairs.

Mia approached Wilfred and whispered as aggressively as she could. 'Don't you dare.'

'Where are you going?' he asked, standing.

'America, to get away from him, and from you, so this little stunt hasn't really worked out, has it?' She downed her wine and returned to the counter to pour herself more. Rami's footsteps tapped on the floorboards above them.

Wilfred followed her. 'This just confirms something has happened.'

'Drop it, Wilfred.'

'But I have a keen interest in cinema.' He scratched his cheek.

'You've fallen asleep during every film we've ever watched, and you thought *Magic Mike* was a documentary about a magician,' she said. 'This is stalking.' Tears formed in her eyes. 'If you actually really care about me, you'll stop this.'

Sadness flashed across Wilfred's face.

Rami's footsteps moved through the room and down the stairs.

Wilfred rushed back to the sofa, plastering his fake grin back on.

Mia inhaled her tears. It wasn't simply his actions that hurt, but how quickly she had fallen out of love with him. The charming, open, collaborative man was showing himself to be pathetic, calculating and obsessive.

Rami held several books. 'I know you've not made a decision. But, I'd suggest reading one of these.' He placed the books on the sofa next to Wilfred. 'Just to understand the terminology used. Then a lot will make more sense as you get writing.' Rami opened the drawer under the sink and took a tote bag. 'Or, they'll put you off forever. Some can be overly prescriptive, but you should know the rules you'll be judged against. My personal favourites are *A Swim in a Pond in the Rain* and *Writing for Emotional Impact*, but see which resonates with you. If you decide this isn't for you, just drop them off or I can collect them.' He placed the books in the bag.

Wilfred smiled. 'You've already sold me on this with your passion, Rami.'

Mia's face fell. If he wasn't doing this to get closer to her, then what was he trying?

Rami beamed.

Wilfred stared past Rami and directly at her. 'When you really care about something, you should do everything for it. I've recently found myself with more free time, so I think I should dedicate it to pursuing my dream more ferociously.'

'That's a very admirable outlook,' Rami said.

Mia swallowed the lump in her throat.

27

HOME IS WHERE THE HATE IS

RAMI

Rami, energised by his chat with Wilfred, pressed Jenny's doorbell as the cold night air swirled around him. He loved this cul-de-sac, but it created a wind trap, allowing it to blast him from all directions.

He pressed the doorbell again. Perhaps Jenny couldn't hear it over Lyn's crying and Ballula's barking.

What a twenty-four hours. He would be thrilled if absolutely nothing else happened until he was fifty. He didn't even want any post.

What did getting a new student so soon after such a heinous deed say about the world and how it moved? Was it the universe's way of trying to convince him that he was unlucky with the Dale incident? Was he being rewarded for disposing of a terrible man? Or, was it simply proof the world moved on because business is business?

With Mia about to leave the continent, he didn't really know what to do with himself beyond the tutoring. So much of the last couple of years had been around trying to salvage his marriage, to show her they should be together. Now, he was going to be in an empty house that was a constant reminder of the biggest failing of his life.

Jenny opened the door, sighing and shaking her head. She leaned into Rami and whispered. 'I don't know what to do. I can't ask her to leave while she's like this, but Iris is looking at me like I've shat... dumped in her Crocs. Come in.'

Rami offered her a sympathetic smile. 'I'd take her, but she and Mia still aren't talking.'

Jenny waved him in and shut the door behind him.

He removed his shoes as Jenny passed him and stood in the living room doorway. Rami followed.

It was like the saddest scene from a rom-com. Lyn was sitting on the sofa, crying, wrapped in a blanket with her feet in a foot spa. Ballula jumped and barked around her. All that was missing was a tub of ice cream.

Rami took a breath. 'Lyn, do you want—'

'No!' she yelled and continued wailing.

Rami shrugged at Jenny, who raised an eyebrow and led him into their pristine kitchen where Iris sat at a white counter, watching *MasterChef* on the iPad with noise-cancelling head-phones over her ears. She shook her head at Jenny and Rami then took a bite out of a biscuit, the crumbs dropping onto the counter.

Jenny closed the kitchen door behind them and leaned on it. 'I will give Mia four hundred pounds if she comes here, apolo-gises, and takes her back.'

Rami smiled.

'Seriously,' Jenny said. 'If Iris doesn't get her foot spa back in an hour, I'm toast.'

Iris ignored them. She took another bite of the biscuit, more crumbs falling. It seemed deliberate.

Jenny stared at the crumbs.

Rami sat at the counter with Iris and addressed Jenny. 'If you can survive the night, she can come back to ours tomorrow. Mia's moving out.' He gazed at the terrazzo floor tiles, wondering if he needed to gut his entire house to remove all traces of Mia.

'Good for you,' Jenny said.

'Wow.' Rami met her gaze, surprised at her bluntness.

'What? She's a sulky twat... sod... person,' Jenny said. 'It's like she's had an argument with her smile and is giving it the silent treatment.'

Rami nodded. 'I guess I appreciate that, Jenny.'

Iris pointed to her bottle of juice, offering Rami some. More crumbs fell from the biscuit.

Rami raised a thankful hand. He turned to Jenny. 'I still remember when you wanted to get money to plant more flowers in the communal grass beds and she didn't want us to contribute.'

'Exactly. Allergic to colours and happiness. And she protested to them building an old people's home nearby because of extra traffic.'

'Maybe I'll realise I'm lucky at some point.' He sighed. 'Doesn't feel that way yet.'

Ballula scratched and barked from the other side of the kitchen door. Rami stood up and opened it, allowing a burst of Lyn's crying to enter with the dog. Rami closed the door behind Ballula and stroked her.

Jenny picked Ballula up and kissed her. 'Sorry, love. You'll get extra treats later.' She put Ballula down, who ran through the dog door and into the tidy, AstroTurfed garden, lined with plant pots and illuminated by uplights in the stone tiles. 'And Mia's never stroked Ballula. Tells you everything about a person the way they react to a dog. I've got a long list of things I dislike about Mia if you want me to go on.'

Rami chuckled. 'It's okay. Thanks.'

Jenny folded her arms. 'You'll definitely feel lucky at some point. My ex was a dick... idiot, but I didn't think it until I met Ms. Cheery over here.' She nodded to Iris who gave a thumbs up. 'Showed me what a relationship actually is.'

'Cheers, Jenny,' Rami said.

Iris chomped into another biscuit.

Jenny shook her head at the crumbs. 'A relationship is cleaning up after someone.'

Rami laughed. Jenny was honest, open, and more importantly herself, and her relationship shone because of it. Rami had been playing a part in Mia's miserable world, and it was joyless.

He didn't want to think about Mia anymore. 'Did you write your film outline?'

Jenny winced. 'Well... I kind of got distracted by the whole investigation thing.'

Rami nodded. 'Good, procrastinating like a true writer.'

'I'm calling it research,' she said.

Rami made a doubtful noise.

'I promise I'll get to it. It's in my head. I just needed to stir some things around.' She looked down. 'Yeah, even as I'm talking I know it's pointless excuses. I'm useless.' She opened the drawer under the sink and grabbed a cloth and antibacterial spray.

'You're not,' Rami assured her. 'But do it to move forward. And I suppose with Dale being dodgy, you don't need to work so hard to find him, so that'll free up time? Seems every mention is like a knock to Lyn.'

Jenny sprayed the counter and Iris' crumbs. 'That heartbroken woman deserves closure. Even though he's a rotten piece of... not knowing will eat at her. Plus, with her face all over the news, who knows who else is going to come forward from the fella's life. She's going to have the worst time, so I'll do everything I can to find him. In some ways, I hope the bugger's dead.'

She wiped the crumbs away and shook her head at Iris who smiled. She turned back to Rami. 'But don't worry. I'll get you the outline.'

Rami swallowed, wondering if he would ever be able to stop worrying.

28

WE ALL NEED A TRAVEL COMPANION

Mia

Mia, wearing her long-haul flight-ready tracksuit, looked out of her bedroom window at the cul-de-sac one last time. The final time.

The orange slither of November sunrise emerged against the dark blue night and peeked over the city. She would never forget today. Wednesday the 8th of November: the day she started again.

She scanned the street, worried Wilfred would be watching her room. Had she caused this toxicity in him? She had mistreated him, but thought she was doing what was best to help him move on. What was worse: being in a relationship with him and sharing the secret, or making him this dreadful wreck of a human desperate for answers? Maybe this was just who he was deep down and events had extracted his true nature.

She shuddered, entered the ensuite bathroom one last time and checked she had everything. She opened the mirrored cabinet where the medication that got her through her marriage would remain: sleeping pills, and aspirin for the endless Rami-induced headaches.

She exited the ensuite, grabbed her handbag, checked she had her passport and wallet, then left the empty bedroom, refusing to look back. She wouldn't miss it.

Rami waited at the bottom of the stairs. She had heard him shuffling about for a while, probably worried she would leave without saying goodbye again.

Her entire life was in the hallway by the front door. Two suitcases and thirteen boxes. 'I'll sort the delivery in the coming weeks, once I have a place,' she said.

'That's fine. Take your time,' he said. 'Have you called Lyn?'

Mia shook her head and caught herself in the mirror. The cut had slightly healed, but her pride had a long way to go. 'No point. New life, new friends, fewer headaches.' Her phone sounded. 'That'll be the taxi.'

Rami nodded.

Mia grabbed the handle of one of her suitcases and opened the door. She nodded to a painting, bubble-wrapped on top of the boxes. 'If you need to move anything, be careful with my Rothko print.'

'Will do.'

Mia wheeled her suitcase and crossed the threshold for the last time. She hoped the heavy feelings and agitation would remain within the bricks. 'Oh, and I've sorted the early cancellation fee for the car lease. You'll just need to drop it off next week. I doubted you wanted to keep it.'

'Yeah. I think I'm going to get back into cycling.' Rami followed her with the other suitcase, but instead of rolling it he carried it, probably trying to appear masculine.

The driver took the suitcase from Mia and placed it in the boot, then the one from Rami.

Mia opened the car's back door, then turned to Rami. She had imagined him and Wilfred chatting, becoming friends. What if Wilfred revealed the affair? He had nothing to gain from it, but he had been behaving so pathetically that she wouldn't put it past him. She needed Rami on her side, just in case there were any developments with the body.

She took Rami's hand and he looked surprised. 'What I said, about not talking. I didn't mean it.'

'Really?' His eyes lit up.

'Let's keep in touch,' she said. 'I want to know how things go for you, and it's exciting you have a new student.'

He nodded, barely containing his smile. 'Thank you.'

'It's all going to be fine, okay? We did good,' she said.

Rami grimaced.

She hugged him. 'Yeah... you know what I mean.'

He squeezed her, a bit too tightly for her liking. She pulled back from him, avoiding his teary gaze.

'Good luck,' he said. 'Make sure to get up and walk around on the flight to avoid blood clots, and it's common to become dehydrated, so drink plenty of water and not too much alcohol—'

'I'm thirty-five years old, Rami.'

He raised an apologetic hand. 'And I need to stop acting like a worried husband.'

She forced a smile. 'Take care.' She entered the car and closed the door.

The driver accelerated away.

Mia kept her gaze forward, but knew Rami would be staring at the car and waving.

Mia, sitting in her Virgin Atlantic business class pod, reached into her handbag and took her phone out, ready to turn it off. Just eleven hours until a new beginning.

She checked her WhatsApp messages. There was one from Wilfred:

I hope you have a safe flight xxx

A week ago she would've read that as sweet and loving. Now it read as sinister and something designed to make her feel powerless. She half-expected him to turn up on the flight, or that while airborne, a flight attendant would pull off their face revealing they had been Wilfred under a mask the entire time. She shuddered. It was another lingering influence of Rami's to think of awful worst-case filmic scenarios.

A message from Rami came through:

Have a safe flight. Message me when you land

She turned her phone off.

She scanned the in-flight entertainment, but had no desire to watch any films, knowing Wilfred would soon be discussing writing with Rami.

Music could get lost, too. There was enough noise in her mind, and she would rather eat her own ears than put on a podcast. There was one for everything, even types of linen and its applications.

She spotted the air steward, with his beaming smile and contractually obligated eagerness to please. She raised her hand to call him over.

He approached, an air of faux friendliness around him. 'How can I help you, Madam?'

'Can I get an orange juice, please?'

'Of course, Madam.' He left to get it.

Madam...

She could be anything she wanted to be now. Maybe she would change her name and forget anything ever happened in the UK. It was like when she first went to university in Warwick. She had told herself she would shed her sixth form reputation and be less of a drunk and less angry. Then on the first night, she had twelve shots of Aftershock and punched a lamppost. This would be different.

A thud drew her attention.

It was just someone dropping their carry-on luggage.

Having the body in their house had heightened her stress response to every sound. Her mind was too alert to sleep.

She scratched the back of her hand and shuffled in her seat. She crossed her legs and noticed a bump forming on her left shin, pushing against her tracksuit bottoms.

It grew and grew.

She panicked and rubbed it, and her body boiled.

She pulled her tracksuit bottoms up, and her shin bone poked out.

She stifled a scream and closed her eyes. She was imagining it. It would go away. The dead man was out of her life. None of this was real.

She took deep breaths, opened her eyes, and her leg was back to normal.

The air steward brought over her glass of orange juice.

'Thanks,' she said, exhausted. 'And, actually, could I get a glass of champagne, please?'

He looked at her quizzically and nodded. 'Of course.'

'Helps me fly,' she said with a half-smile, underlining her status as the one to be served, not judged.

Paulo had told her he was getting an executive car to pick her up from LAX. What a dream. Luxury treatment all the way to her hotel bed.

The air steward brought the champagne over.

'Thanks,' Mia said, knocking it straight back. 'Another please.' It tasted like peace.

She rubbed her shin, checking it over and over.

'Madam? Madam...'

Mia's eyes blurred into focus and she snorted.

A banging sound shook her and she knocked her funny bone against a wall. She groaned, finding her bearings. She was in a small white room.

Slowly she realised it was the airplane toilet.

'Madam? Madam! We've arrived.'

She was sat on the toilet, her knickers and tracksuit bottoms around her ankles.

'Fuck,' she muttered. 'Sorry!'

She pulled her knickers and tracksuit bottoms up, then closed the toilet lid and flushed it.

She washed her hands and avoided the mirror. She unlocked the door and opened it.

'Sorry. Bad stomach,' she slurred, noticing a dribble of vomit on her top.

The air steward's professional expression faded as he took in her appearance. 'Do you need assistance?'

'I'm fine.' She returned to her seat, grabbed her handbag and stumbled back past the air steward.

'Have a wonderful stay,' he said.

'Whatever.'

She staggered through immigration and to baggage claim.

She stopped in front of the conveyor belt and closed her eyes to steady everything. When she opened them, the cling-film-wrapped corpse travelled around the conveyor belt. She retched and rubbed her throbbing head.

She sat on the trolley until her bag arrived, struggling to get it off the conveyor belt and dropping it onto the floor.

She rejected an offer of help and wrestled it onto the trolley. Her body dripped with sweat.

She ignored the judgemental glances from those around her.

She couldn't wait to get into her taxi and sleep. There would be absolutely no small talk with the driver.

She wheeled the trolley through arrivals, thankful to have something to steady herself. She scanned the crowd through her blurry eyes to find her name on a board.

Her heart sank as she spotted Paulo Beavis holding a sign with Mia's name on. He stood next to his family. The grin in his big beard faded into a look of concern. Paulo's wife gave him a look that told Mia exactly how she felt about what she was seeing.

Paulo stepped in front of his two children to greet Mia, and possibly to shield them. 'I promised you an executive car,' he said, opening his arms.

He hugged Mia and she felt deep shame.

She whispered in his ear. 'I need to drink to fly. I have an awful phobia.'

He patted her on the back and chuckled. 'It's fine. I was going to suggest lunch, but let's get you to the hotel instead.'

'Thank you.' She wanted to die.

29

____

A FULL-TIME JOB

RAMI

Rami sat in the back of Lyn's Lexus, while Jenny was in the front passenger seat. They entered Tuckswood, the one and only place Rami had been mugged in his life.

It was the kind of neighbourhood people visited if they had hit rock bottom, but wanted to dig around to see if there was anything underneath those rocks.

Rami watched an Instagram video on his phone of a woman that looked like Brexit in human form. She seemed to have a phobia of dentists and her aggressive gesturing next to a skip suggested low approachability. 'I'm Steve Loving's wife. That bitch on your news don't know nothing; she's just after sympathy. Steve's a loving dad and husband, even if he does love a drink or two. If you see him, message us, not the slag.'

'See what a twat she is!?' Lyn said.

'She's got a unique charm about her,' Rami replied.

Lyn's scrunched-up face remained focused on the road.

Rami checked his phone. Mia hadn't replied to his text, asking her if she had landed. He knew she had from the flight

208

tracker. Perhaps she was insincere about staying in touch. Another olive branch covered in thorns.

Jenny placed a hand on Lyn's shoulder. 'It's important you let me ask the questions to start with, as we build a rapport with her.'

Lyn slapped the steering wheel. 'I don't want a *rapport*. I've got so many abusive messages because of her! People calling me a home wrecker, a slapper, and a cock sorceress, though I think the last is meant to be a compliment? Doesn't feel like one.'

Jenny removed her hand. 'The police will have seen the video and have likely already taken a statement. So, just let me approach and start things off.'

'Fine,' Lyn said.

Rami had been on his way to walk along the river, but Jenny and Lyn saw him as he left the house. They roped him in to whatever this was. At least he would remain close to the investigation.

Lyn pulled into the Asda car park and found a space. She took a breath and rubbed one of her dolphin earrings.

'You ready, Lyn?' Jenny asked.

'Let's do it,' Lyn replied.

They all got out of the car.

Rami looked around the car park, expecting locals to be shooting up or throwing empty beer cans at each other's heads. 'The things she said were in the heat of the moment,' he told Lyn. 'Maybe she's actually regretful and reasonable. These videos always make things look worse.'

Lyn shot Rami a doubtful glance.

Jenny approached the door and turned to Lyn. 'Calm and collected.'

Lyn nodded and they entered the cafe. The air was heavy with misery. A few of the lights flickered, and the sandwiches looked as though they had been chucked onto the shelves rather than organised. There was a "Caution Slippery Surface" sign over a massive coffee spillage that nobody had cared to clean up.

Rami noticed Jenny's unease at the mess. He shook his head. 'This is what I imagine a cafe would look like in purgatory.'

'Don't.' Jenny laughed. 'It's making me itchy.'

Dale's wife stood behind the counter and handed a customer their coffee and greying sausage roll. She caught a glimpse of Lyn and stared at her.

Jenny approached the counter. 'Hi, Trinity.'

'What do you want?' she replied. She also wore dolphin earrings.

'My name's Jenny, this is Rami, and she's—'

Trinity turned her nose up at Lyn. 'The slag my fella was porkin'.' She looked Lyn up and down and shook her head. 'Those earrings look shit on you.'

Jenny held Lyn's hand, as Lyn took deep breaths.

Trinity leaned on the counter. 'He was with me on Thursday before he went missing. Was probably headed to yours to tell you to fold your flaps in for good. You've done something to him.'

Rami raised a hand in peace. 'Let's maybe go easy on—'

'Wanker!' Lyn lunged over the counter and punched Trinity on the nose.

DI Amini and DS Opoku sat on Rami's sofa below the empty space where the Rothko print once hung. DI Amini reeked of a horny teenager's amount of aftershave, while DS Opoku finished writing Lyn's statement in her notebook.

Lyn was slumped in the armchair, an ice pack on her lip, and rage in her eyes.

Rami leaned against the kitchen counter, wondering what to

do with himself, and concerned his house was becoming a hub for Norfolk crime.

DI Amini huffed. 'Lyn, this is the opposite of what we asked you to do. Please, just let us do our job.'

Lyn sat up. 'And what job have you done since the last time we spoke, huh?'

Rami poured himself a glass of water from the filter jug. His hand stung from a scratch he had earned trying to restrain the warring widows.

DI Amini rubbed his eyebrows. 'It's not been easy with the constant harassment we've been getting thanks to your social media posts. I've been called useless, been spat at, we've had endless prank calls to the station, and idiots think it's funny to film their mates nicking my hat.'

Lyn smirked then looked down. 'Well, people are turning on me now, so...'

DS Opoku nodded. 'Yes, when the press get something to latch onto it can be overwhelming. I'd suggest you avoid the news.'

Lyn shrugged. 'And what happened to the CCTV? To the phone signal?'

DS Opoku tapped her shoes against the wooden floor. 'I'm afraid we can't tell you more about the investigation. We have information, which we'll release when appropriate.'

Lyn stared at the officers. 'Because I'm still a suspect?'

Rami noticed her nails digging into the ice pack. 'Lyn,' he said calmly, but she ignored him.

DS Opoku bit her lip.

Lyn slammed the ice pack off the floor, startling the officers. 'What more do you need from me? It was my bloody birthday. You've got when he last called me, and you know where I was.' She took her phone out, got up and squeezed herself between the officers, showing them her screen. 'Look, my calls to him. All through the damn night 'cos he was late. And then a shitload to

Mia. And look, photos, from the night until ten when I got too sad, stopped the party and buggered off home.'

Rami moved out from behind the kitchen counter and picked up the ice pack. 'I can confirm she did try to call Mia many times, but we were in the middle of an argument, so Mia didn't answer.'

'Is Mia here?' DI Amini asked, a bit too excitedly.

'No.' Rami folded his arms.

DI Amini stood up. 'Well, we appreciate your cooperation, Lyn, but until he turns up in some capacity, we can't close any avenue of suspicion, because we can't place anyone in relation to him.'

She huffed. 'You're a very repetitive man.'

DI Amini's shoulders fell. 'Because it seems you need to hear things repeatedly.'

Lyn glared at him.

DS Opoku raised an apologetic hand on behalf of her colleague. 'We're doing everything we can,' she told Lyn, then stood up.

'Yeah...' Lyn replied, slumping onto the cushions.

DI Amini turned to Rami. 'Thanks for your time.'

'No problem,' he said, wishing to never see them again.

DI Amini turned to Lyn. 'And count yourself lucky that Trinity doesn't want to press charges.'

Lyn scoffed. 'Was it your work that drew out his bloody skeletons, or mine?'

DS Opoku placed her notepad in her bag. 'You have to trust the process. And now we have the support of the Missing Persons Unit, who are advising us.'

DI Amini took his hat off and spun it in his hands. 'And please stop pulling others into this, Lyn. That Jenny is an inter-fering pest who doesn't know anything. We've spoken to the person who's been giving her information, and we'll be sure to have words with Jenny, too.'

Lyn huffed, stood up and walked over to the fridge. 'Bye then.'

DI Amini shook his head.

'I'll show you out,' Rami said.

He walked them to the front door and opened it. 'Hopefully, we can stop meeting like this.'

DS Opoku nodded. 'We'll be in touch if we need anything else.' She stepped outside.

DI Amini looked past Rami to Lyn. 'And we should have this wrapped up soon if you let us do our job. Then you can look forward to the holidays.' He turned to Rami and gestured to the boxes. 'You moving?'

'It's Mia's stuff,' he said.

DI Amini nodded. 'Where's she going?' he asked.

Rami gestured to the open door, not caring to get into it. 'Let us know if you need anything else.'

DI Amini left and Rami closed the door. He muttered, 'Arsehole.'

Rami returned to the kitchen, where Lyn sat on the sofa eating Rami's blueberries.

He opened the French doors to the garden, letting Jenny limp back in from her hiding place between the shed and brick wall.

Jenny rubbed her hands and touched the radiator. 'That Amini's a pillock. They're just nervous because you're making them look bad and forcing them to do some work. But, we should let things settle because of you belting Trinity. Let the news do its thing and see what comes next.'

Rami offered Lyn the ice pack and she took it back gratefully, dabbing her lip.

She sniffed. 'I don't even know why I'm looking for him. What am I gonna get from finding him? He's scum.'

Jenny sat next to Lyn. 'It's normal: you want to face him. You want some kind of closure.'

Lyn nodded. 'What I want is to chin him and boot him down a long flight of stairs.' She put the blueberries down on a sofa cushion, ripped her dolphin earrings off and threw them at the kitchen wall. 'Every time I see anyone wearing dolphin earrings I'll think he's bonked them. Wanker!' She took slow breaths. 'I need a shower.' She stood. 'Reckon I'll stay here tonight, Rami, if that's okay?' She walked upstairs before he could answer.

Rami shrugged at Jenny. 'Make yourself at home, Lyn.'

Jenny chuckled.

He picked the packet of blueberries up and returned it to the fridge, then picked up the earrings. 'Might not be bad having her here for the night. Even though this place felt empty with Mia in it, at least she was in it, you know? Now there's no sound. No Mia turning the tap on. No Mia's footsteps on the stairs. And no Mia frustratedly tutting from another room.' He dumped the earrings into the bin.

Jenny got up and limped to the kitchen counter. 'It'll pass, Rami.'

He nodded and joined her. 'Yeah, I know. I think.'

'I guarantee it.' She leaned in. 'But, there's something I didn't want to say in front of Lyn.'

Rami swallowed. 'What is it?'

'Trinity mentioned Thursday, the night he vanished. And if he was with her before driving to Lyn's party, if he was even heading there, then he wasn't driving out of Bungay.'

Rami's breath caught in his throat. He coughed.

Jenny showed Rami a map on her phone. 'He'd have been taking the A47 if he was leaving Tuckswood.'

'But we can't be sure,' Rami said.

'No, we can't. I need to find out more, but don't tell Lyn. I'm going to try to see Trinity again, to make sure she's not bullshi... telling porkies.' Jenny put her phone in her pocket.

Hopefully Trinity was as stubborn as she looked. 'But, the

police likely know the same thing and will be looking,' Rami pointed out.

Jenny raised an eyebrow. 'Just because they might have information, doesn't mean they're doing anything with it.'

Rami wished she would drop it. 'Okay, but be careful.'

'I will. I'm staying quiet for a few days, and my mate needs to be wary now. Plus, I need to put more time in with Iris before she kills me. She's worried now that the fella's a wrong 'un that this could get a bit dangerous, and she has a point.'

Rami nodded. He had to call Mia.

30

HEAD IN THE SAND

Mia sat on her towel on Venice Beach, which had more litter on it than was acceptable. Her peaceful Thursday morning of trying to re-energise herself in the sun was broken by Rami's panicked voice.

She had missed five of his calls yesterday, as she had passed out as soon as Paulo dropped her at the hotel.

'It's fine, Rami.' She placed the phone between her shoulder and ear, squirted more suncream onto her hand, then rubbed it on her arms. 'What's Jenny going to find? We avoided CCTV on the way to Belaugh, and if she sees the car on any camera, it'll be coming into Norwich from the B1150.'

'Yeah, but we told her we hit a deer on the A140 from Cromer.'

Someone walked past Mia, a bit too close, dropping some more litter. 'Which is really nearby, so no issue. Honestly, calm down,' she said, watching a couple surf. Maybe she could try surfing at some point in her new life.

'Sorry for panicking,' he said. 'I guess walking up the river is bringing back the fear. Seen nothing so far, though. So, either he's made it out to sea, or he's found a spot to relax on the riverbed.'

'It'll be okay, Rami.' She would love just one day. One day with no mention of the body. 'And if you're worried about Jenny, then think of a way to distract her. Maybe kill her dog.'

'Wow,' Rami replied. 'I hope you're joking.'

She felt no guilt about saying it. 'It's an awful dog. Looks like a dust buster.' She rubbed lotion on her feet, shins, then thighs. She placed the bottle on the sand.

A bloody, broken shin bone poked out of the sand.

Mia screamed.

'What? Is it a shark?' Rami asked, fear in his voice.

Mia closed her eyes and steadied her breathing. It wasn't real.

Rami continued worrying. 'Mia? Do you need me to call someone? Mia?'

She opened her eyes and the bone was gone. 'It's nothing, Rami. Sorry. It was just a dead pigeon.' She raised her arm to onlookers to gesture that everything was fine. 'And why would you assume shark? I'm on the sand.'

'Dunno. Panicked. And I read that Venice is known as the shark tooth capital of the world, because plenty of species of shark have made it their home? Even the prehistoric megalodon.'

She huffed. 'Well, thank you for ruining the sea.'

He chuckled. 'Shame about the pigeon, though.'

'Yeah,' she replied, focusing her eyes on her towel.

'Looks like you helped me to calm down and I did the opposite for you,' Rami said.

'Yep. But it's fine. The more normal things we do, the sooner the balance will tip back in our favour.'

'Yeah,' he replied.

'Speaking of normal, when's your session with that Wilfred guy?'

'Tonight. I've got a bit more river left, then Lyn needs me to go to her flat with her in case she breaks down when she opens the door. Wilfred will be round at eight.'

'Great. And... just be careful about how much of your life you share with Wilfred. You can be a bit too open sometimes.' She lay back on her beach towel and closed her eyes.

'My plan is to get him sharing his story, not to dig into mine,' Rami replied.

Mia swallowed, worried about how much Wilfred might feel like sharing. 'Yeah. Have fun.'

'Anyway, I'd better go. Need to fully focus,' he said.

'Wait,' Mia said. 'Do you ever, see... him?'

'Who?' Rami asked.

'Who do you think? *Him*...'

Rami lowered his voice. 'Oh. Well, with Jenny knocking on the door every hour, Dale's bodily fluids in every crack in the house, and Lyn's endless tears ringing in my ears, I pretty much live with him.' He let out a long breath. 'Can't all just slip away to LA.'

She smiled. 'I'm sorry. If it helps, LA is mostly litter. I think they just put the sand on top of it.'

Rami laughed then cleared his throat. 'I thought I saw him floating by one of the pillars on the bridge by King's Lynn, but it was just a sack.' He huffed. 'Look, I know you like to chop things off and move on, but life doesn't work like that with the big stuff. There's residue, you know? It might be why you're seeing him. Lingering emotions you need to process. But, you're in LA, so if grief counselling isn't your thing, you could probably find some sort of humming therapy, foot massage therapy, or talking to donkeys therapy. Or join the other middle-class clichés searching for themselves in a goblet of ayahuasca.'

'I'm not that much of a prick,' she said.

He paused for longer than was acceptable. 'Anyway. My hands are getting cold so I need to put them back in my pocket. I guess all this divorce stuff will start moving next week?' he asked.

She swallowed. 'I need to get settled here for a few days first. Is that okay?'

'Yeah.' He sounded thrilled.

'And tell me how your lesson with Wilfred goes. Really pleased for you.' She couldn't relax until she knew what Wilfred was up to.

'Thanks. I'll message you as soon as he leaves. Bye.'

'Bye.' She hung up, picked up the sun lotion and applied some to her neck and face. She stared at the waves, scared she would imagine the man again.

31

PLANTING SEEDS IN POISONED SOIL

RAMI

What struck Rami the most about Lyn's huge detached house wasn't its close proximity to Sheringham's beaches, or how much money she had made from her Instagram videos, but what a shambolic mess it was. Other than the filming set in the corner of the open-plan living room for her guitar videos, the rest of the place looked like she had invited Cocaine Bear over for tea.

Lyn collected unwashed plates from the kitchen counter and placed them in the dishwasher. 'It's not normally this dirty, I just...' She sighed.

'Don't worry,' he replied, picking up an armchair that had been tipped over. 'Cleaning wouldn't have been at the top of my list either.' The 4.30 p.m. November sunset filled the room through the French doors, giving the filth a romantic glow.

He moved to the sofa and spotted a framed collage of photos on the wall, many featuring Mia. She and Lyn looked happy. Over the last few months, Rami found himself looking at photos of himself and Mia on his phone, and noted how there was a smile on her face, but her eyes were dulled.

He picked up a few dresses from the floor and placed them in a neat pile on the side of the sofa.

'Oh, God,' Lyn said.

'What?' Rami asked, approaching her.

Lyn's energy-drained face stared at a pair of yellow men's Calvin Klein boxer shorts. Like the ones Dale was wearing when Rami and Mia ran him over. Maybe having the same underwear made cheating easier? There was no chance of accidentally leaving the wrong thing in the wrong home.

'Please, I can't touch them,' Lyn said.

Rami wondered how many more low points he could experience. 'Okay.' He opened a few drawers until he found some tongs.

'No, don't use them,' she said.

'I'll wash them after.'

'I don't want anything of mine touching anything to do with him.'

Did she expect him to re-tile the kitchen?

She cried. 'Maybe we can package them up and send them to his latest girlfriend.'

Rami swallowed. 'I'm sorry, Lyn.' He wasn't sure whether to hug her or not, so he put the tongs away. 'At least you know now, rather than a few years into a relationship.'

Last night, another woman associated with Dale had appeared on the news, claiming to be his girlfriend of two years. So, not only did he have his wife Trinity and two young children, there was also a twenty-two-year-old trainee nurse from Thetford.

Lyn nodded. 'I just... bollocks to it all.' She dragged herself into the bathroom. As soon as she closed the door, Rami grabbed the tongs, gripped Dale's boxer shorts, and threw them in the bin.

He put the tongs back in the drawer as Lyn's cries rose in volume from behind the bathroom door.

Rami gazed around the room; another lifeless shell thanks to a broken heart. Dale being awful helped him manage the guilt, but in some ways Lyn might have been better off living a lie. She would be happier than she was right now.

He opened the drawer, took out the tongs and washed them, then put them back. He put the kettle on, then looked through the cupboards for any teabags, finding a glass jar loaded with peppermint tea.

He made a mug of tea for Lyn and placed it outside the bathroom door. 'I've left you some tea, Lyn. I can clear up and you just do what you need, alright?'

She offered an acknowledging groan through the tears.

Rami cleaned the house and Lyn remained in the bathroom, apart from the two seconds when she took her cup of tea.

He had changed her bedsheets, towels, and anything that may have come into contact with Dale. He put a high-temperature wash on as he hoovered and mopped the floor, then hung everything from the washing machine on a heated clothes rack. He cleaned the mirrors, thinking there were far too many.

He wished he felt this ready to give his own home a deep clean, but he didn't want to remove every trace of Mia just yet.

Exhausted, Rami knocked on the bathroom door. 'I'm done, Lyn. Call me if you need anything.' He put his shoes on and picked up three tied-up bin bags. He opened the oak front door, ready to return to his lonely shell. He noticed a brick on the driveway that was obviously intended for the door. Probably local scumbags who had decided that Lyn was a homewrecker.

The bathroom door clicked open. 'Thanks, Rami.'

He dropped the bin bags and grabbed the brick, tossing it into a hedge before she could see it.

Lyn appeared in the doorway, her face worn from crying. 'You've been a legend.'

'No problem,' he replied. 'I hope things get easier.' He knew they wouldn't.

She walked up to him and hugged him. 'Bless you, Rami.'

'Like I said, just call,' he reminded her.

'I'm not turning my phone on,' Lyn said. 'The comments are too much.' She released the hug.

'It'll pass. It's just idiots wanting to create a story.'

'Still hurts.' She wiped her nose on her blouse.

'The press just want a target, and it doesn't help that you're attractive, while Trinity looks like she does her make-up while running on a treadmill.'

Lyn smiled. 'She does, doesn't she?'

Rami nodded sympathetically. 'Goes with the image of making her a victim. It'll calm down. See you later.'

'See ya.' She closed the door.

Rami dumped the rubbish bags in the wheelie bins. He heard a screeching akin to an orca crying for its baby and felt the pain in his bones.

He turned back and knocked on the door.

Lyn answered, her eyes puffed up. 'You forget something?'

'Go and put on whatever makes you feel comfortable. You're coming with me,' he said.

'I definitely would've preferred the pub,' Lyn said, looking around the gorily decorated escape room.

Rami pulled on the handcuffs that attached him to the radiator, hoping this would be the only time he was ever cuffed. 'We can go to the pub once we escape becoming the cannibal's supper.'

Lyn touched the blood-stained radio and pulled a cassette out. She grinned. 'Even terrible people have great taste.' She showed Rami the cassette, 'Hello' by Lionel Richie. 'Not sure about cassette though. Someone needs to introduce this cannibal to Spotify.'

He smiled. 'At least the soundtrack to our deaths won't be creepy at all.'

'Maybe he'll recreate the video, but instead of clay, he'll use our intestines to sculpt the face of the person he loves.'

'Don't be sexist. The cannibal isn't necessarily a man.' Rami cast a glance at the desk. 'Maybe there's something in the desk drawers.'

Lyn pulled a blood-stained armchair over, stopping underneath a vent. 'Solved it.' She stood on the armchair.

'What about me?'

Lyn shrugged. 'I'll nip to the shop, buy some bolt cutters and be right back.'

Rami laughed as Lyn pulled on the vent. 'Maybe there's something we can use up here.'

The speaker in the corner, with a camera above it, crackled and a smarmy, nasal voice came through. 'The vent is not part of the game, and please don't stand on the furniture.'

Rami tutted at Lyn. 'Naughty, naughty.'

Lyn faced the camera. 'Well, maybe don't have a vent if the point is escape.' She shook her head and searched the desk drawers.

The speaker crackled into life again. 'The vent is so that you have adequate ventilation.'

Lyn, amused, looked at Rami. 'Bit of sass on them, hey?'

'I think you've made an impression.' Rami searched around the floor, finding nothing but blood stains. It all felt a bit real, being handcuffed in front of a crime scene. He shook the thoughts away. He had become better at that since Dale was gone, and even more so since they had learned that he was terrible. It worried Rami that he might be able to forget about Dale one day. He didn't deserve to.

Lyn pulled the drawers out of the desk to search behind them.

'Great idea,' Rami said.

The speaker crackled. 'Please do not remove the desk drawers.'

'I'll put them back,' Lyn said.

'This is your final warning.'

Lyn stuck her middle finger up and waved it around.

The speaker crackled. 'That is impolite.'

'You've not seen impolite yet,' she replied.

Rami looked towards the camera. 'Trust me, you don't want to see that.' He nodded to the washing basket full of bloody clothes. 'What about in there?'

Lyn grimaced, grabbed a pair of bloody Marigolds from the desk and pulled them on. 'You're lucky being the one chained up.' She walked over to the washing basket and tossed clothes out of it. Blood-stained underwear, followed by a jacket, then a police vest. 'The cuffs!' she said victoriously, searching the police vest pockets and finding a key.

'Amazing,' Rami said.

Lyn approached with the key and smiled. 'What's it worth?'

'Oh, come on!'

She laughed. 'Do you feel really helpless?'

Rami sighed. 'Incredibly.'

Lyn placed the key just out of Rami's reach. 'Go on.' She stood and watched. 'It's good to have a little stretch. Your posture's a disgrace.'

Determined, he stretched for the key, just out of reach. Just a little more. The radiator came loose, breaking off a section of the wooden wall.

Rami and Lyn exchanged a guilty look. Rami retreated to the wall and pushed the radiator back, trying his best to slot it into place. 'Nothing to see here.'

Lyn stifled her laughter and picked up the key. She unlocked

Rami from the handcuffs. 'Stop causing trouble, Rami. You'll upset our overlord.'

He stood up and they high-fived. He shook off his limbs. 'Right, let's find a way out.'

Rami tapped the wooden faux-cabin walls.

Lyn eyed up a poster of Elvis. She tried to pull it off the wall, but it seemed strongly stuck down. 'Maybe there's a safe or something behind here.'

The speaker crackled. 'Please do not peel the poster off the wall. It's hard to peel, because it's not meant to be peeled.'

Rami bit his lip, containing his laughter.

Lyn scoffed. 'You're a proper buzzkill, mate. Is this an escape room or a museum?' She turned to Rami. 'Shall we just sit here 'til he comes back to munch us?'

Rami stared at a mounted human head on the wall with antlers fixed to it.

Lyn approached. 'What you reckon, Rami?' She placed a hand on one of the antlers.

The voice crackled. 'Before you think it, the antlers are not levers to a secret room.'

'How do we know you're not working with the cannibal, trying to throw us off the right answers?' Lyn countered.

Rami smiled. 'Yeah. We can't be sure that you're not one of the challenges. The cannibal might be paying you off.'

Lyn nodded. 'Or he's offered you dinner. Which bit of us have you got your eyes on?'

The speaker crackled. 'My role is supervisory and to protect the health and safety of guests, and the integrity of the game. You are currently compromising the latter.'

'I'm just looking for clues,' she said.

The speaker crackled. 'We have plenty of clues that don't require destruction. If you're struggling, I'd be happy to offer you a hint.'

Lyn looked at Rami, mischief in her eyes.

He smirked and nodded.

Lyn yanked on the antlers. The head came off the wall, tearing some wallpaper off with it.

Rami and Lyn sat at a table in the corner of The Edith Cavell pub, still laughing.

'Kicked out and banned not even ten minutes in. Must be a record,' Rami said.

'What a bloody jobsworth.' Lyn sipped from her glass of wine. 'Thank you, though. Was better than moping at home.'

'It was fun,' Rami said. 'Did you know the first escape room was opened in Japan in 2007?'

'I did, actually.' She smiled.

'Really?'

'I had a quick read when you said we were going. And I found that there's one in Greece that's an entire house and takes three hours to complete.'

'Wow.' He made a mental note of that.

'Might see if some of my girlfriends wanna go for a weekend away. We can try to get booted out of that.'

Rami laughed. 'Where have your girlfriends been during all... you know?'

Lyn shrugged. 'Not many live this way. Gyal Pal's in London, and while everyone calls or messages, there's not much they can do for someone who's missing, right? Especially now he's a dickhead. They message to check on me, but that's dwindling.'

'Still. You need your support network.' It was sad how life moved so fast. It reminded him of when his nan died. One day, everyone was checking in, then as the days passed, the check-ins became less frequent and the loneliness grew.

'Doesn't help that I punched my closest supporter in the face,' Lyn added.

Rami nodded.

Silence hung between them and Lyn scanned the room. 'Do you think people are looking at me?'

'Arrogant. They could be looking at me,' Rami said, trying to lighten the mood.

She folded her arms and smiled. 'Because of the news, you tit.'

He smiled back. 'No. Honestly. You're fine.'

She played with her bracelet. 'What are you up to tonight? Do you want to go for some food? I think it'd be good to just… not go home yet, and to exist again, outside of the news and all this… shit.'

Shit he had caused. 'I'd love to, but I have a new writing student coming over at eight.'

'Oh,' Lyn said, staring into her drink. 'That's great, though.' She took a breath. 'You must think I'm a nutter.'

'Why?'

'Throwing myself into it with Dale after only a few months, like some desperate bint latching onto anything that smiles at her. Mia always warned me to take my time, feel things out, and she was right.'

Rami shook his head. 'No. Your approach is wonderful, Lyn. So many people are scared. They tip-toe. They keep others at arm's length and there's all this nonsense with dating games. But you, you've no barriers, immediately. You're yourself.'

'Only way I know how to be. Hasn't worked so far.' She rested her chin on her hand.

He held her gaze. 'My first girlfriend, right at the start, told me about how her previous relationship went wrong, so she wanted to be cautious. That turned into a year of everything being done on her terms. She wasn't *in* a relationship, she *had* one, and it was just a thing for her to pick up and put down when she wanted. And obviously that ended terribly, because there was always a barrier, a fear. I'd much rather be like you, dive in heart first. Sure, it hurts twice as much when it goes wrong, but it also gives you something honest and wonderful if it doesn't. No regrets.'

'I have quite a few regrets about Dale,' she said.

'I think this is quite a unique situation.'

She placed her hand on his. 'Thank you, Rami.'

He didn't know what to do with it, so didn't move.

She let go and took her phone out. 'I've got another fact for you.'

'Amazing; go on.'

'So, our cannibal's one true love, Lionel Richie, has a room in his mansion, and it's full of taxidermy versions of himself through the years.'

'I'm not that stupid.' Rami raised an eyebrow.

'It's a shrine to himself. Calls it the Lionel Shrinel and the floor is vinyl. I swear on my brother's life.'

Rami laughed. 'Really?'

'100 per cent true. On. My. Brother's. Existence.' She sipped her drink to underline her point.

Rami took his phone from his pocket. 'I have to text my cousin. He's a true Lionel lover.' He sent the message.

Lyn cracked up.

Rami stared at her. He kind of knew, but wanted to humour her. At least he would keep telling himself that. 'You bastard. And you just swore on your brother's life.'

'Yeah, but he's a tit.' Lyn smirked. 'You had it coming. But, true facts are he did nearly become a priest, and was a wicked tennis player. Not as interesting.'

'I can't believe you tricked me.' He laughed and wondered how he would cope in the lonely house after his session with Wilfred. Spending the afternoon and early evening with Lyn had helped him to forget about his looming divorce and having to get used to the void in his home. 'Why don't you come back to the house and stay a while longer?'

She looked confused.

'Your huge house is empty, and I know that's not easy, because Mia's been gone barely a day and my house is miserable. Might just be good to have life around us, you know? Someone moving, existing.'

Lyn nodded. 'I do hate being at home. Makes me think about all the plans we had together. Wonder what plans he had with that twenty-two-year-old nurse and Trinity?'

'As harsh as it sounds, you're free of him now,' Rami said. 'The offer's there. You could bring your filming equipment and use the living room. Not as fancy as your place with our French doors facing a weed-filled garden, but...'

'It's a great idea. Thanks, Rami.'

Rami, his laptop closed, sat at the kitchen counter with Wilfred, discussing Wilfred's story. Lyn was outside picking weeds in the cold night, as she had told Rami that she wanted the background of her videos to look less like Shrek's pubes. Rami had been tempted to tell her that Shrek had brown eyebrows, and therefore likely brown pubic hair, but then realised he was probably the only person on earth who would care.

Wilfred was dressed for something far more formal than tutoring, and sat rigidly, as though he was conscious of how every movement made him appear. Rami admired the confidence he must have had to be so thoughtful in how he presented himself. Rami was used to wearing whatever was clean and comfortable, and very much wanted to fade into the background.

Rami sipped his water. 'If you want to write about that heartbreak, be sure you're ready to face it. Some writers find exploring the raw emotion of an event helps them to create something more powerful, while others find it too painful to get so personal. If you're not there yet, don't be scared to park it for a few years.'

Wilfred made notes on his iPad with his Apple pencil. 'Well, I was a bit stuck with it, but oddly, when I was here and saw you still lived with your ex-wife, it opened up a new avenue for the story. What was that like?'

Rami shrugged. 'She wasn't here long enough for that to really be a thing. She asked for the divorce last Thursday, and a week later, she's gone.

'Was it coming for a while?' Wilfred asked, making notes. 'You don't have to tell me anything, obviously.'

'No, no, it's fine. It's good research, right?' Mia had warned him not to open up, but she didn't understand his line of work. Talking was an integral part of progress and understanding humanity. 'She'd probably say it was coming, but for me, I thought we'd get through it.'

'Not too dissimilar to my experience.' Wilfred lightly tapped his Apple pencil against his cheek. 'My wife told me the day before our anniversary.'

Rami winced.

'Yes, exactly,' Wilfred said.

'Mia told me in the car. We were driving to Lyn's party, then we got into an argument, and that was it. She said the word and boom. Job done. I guess there's never a good time, is there? Two minutes later I'm crying in a service station toilet and having to face the awkward car journey home.'

Wilfred chuckled. 'And you were fine with living in the same place?'

Rami shrugged. 'I couldn't exactly kick her out, and I had nowhere to go.'

'What about a hotel, or family?' Wilfred asked.

Rami loved his curiosity, trying to understand a character's thought process and what they would do in a specific situation. 'I've got no immediate family nearby. My dad vanished when I was young, and my mum's been in the ground for over a decade.'

Wilfred looked confused, almost cross.

'What?' Rami asked.

'Nothing. That's just unfortunate,' Wilfred said. 'I'm sorry about your mother. And father, obviously.'

Rami scratched his cheek. 'Everyone's dealing with something. And being completely honest, I thought if Mia was still here, if we were still close to each other, that she might regret her decision. Or at least think it was made in the heat of the moment.'

Wilfred nodded and made a note. 'I like that – staying in the person's life in the hope it might repair things. That desperation.' Wilfred raised a palm. 'Sorry, that sounded like an insult.'

'No need to apologise. It *was* desperate, and a bit pathetic.' Rami sighed. He took Wilfred's empty glass and poured him more water.

'I think it's actually romantic,' Wilfred said.

'I guess it's a matter of perspective, right?' Rami replied, handing Wilfred the glass filled with water.

'Thanks. Can I ask you something a bit more personal?'

Rami shrugged. 'I think we're past being cagey. Just don't base this character on me.'

Wilfred laughed. 'I'll call him Rambo.'

Rami smiled. 'Only if you give me the actual Rambo's body and great hair. Ask away.'

Wilfred nodded. 'Do you think Mia was being unfaithful? Only because, I think my wife was cheating on me.'

Rami considered moments where he had suspicions. The clothes not being in her wardrobe, but even before then. There was a time she was meant to come home from a work trip in London, but messaged him at 10 p.m. to say she had to stay another night. Surely she would have known she needed to stay during work hours? 'There was a minute or two I replay in my mind,' Rami said. 'But, I asked her outright and she said no. I know that doesn't mean much, but what does dwelling in those doubts do? She said something that stuck with me, which was, and I'm probably misquoting here, but she said something like, "You'll always have questions, but get to a point where you no longer care about the answers." It makes a lot of sense.'

Wilfred nodded. 'In theory.'

'Yeah. But it kind of hammers home that it's up to me how I deal with it. Dwell and be miserable, bitter and resentful, or try to take control of my life. She's not sat there worrying about me and she's not going to fix my emotions. It's on me to sort myself out.'

Wilfred stared at him a moment. 'Interesting.'

Rami scratched his neck. He trusted Wilfred, and maybe having another broken-hearted man's perspective could help. 'And, it's weird, but since she left we've been closer. She's actually sending me messages and asking how these sessions are going. Never cared before. Maybe...' He sighed.

'Relationships are strange,' Wilfred said, a more serious look in his eyes. 'You never know what might happen.'

'Yeah,' Rami replied, feeling a pinch of hope. 'Anyway, it's time to do a writing exercise.' He opened his laptop and turned it to face Wilfred, showing him a slide with instructions. 'Any questions, I'm right here.'

Wilfred studied the slide. 'Perfect.'

Rami watched Wilfred scribble notes, and then he glanced at Lyn, tipping a bucket full of weeds into the garden bin.

The house had been dead for so long, even with him and Mia in it. Now the house was alive with conversation, activity, and energy. Rami saw hope for a future, even though it saddened him that Mia wasn't a part of it.

32

THE MEANING OF LIFE

Mia

Mia, having barely slept, sat in the circle of fellow grievers on the beach by Santa Monica Pier. Was the beautiful backdrop helpful, providing hope to people? Or, did it highlight how shit their lives all were?

She had wanted to avoid a group, but yesterday was torture. After speaking to Rami, she was on the bus, and she screamed as she imagined the man being hit. Everyone had turned to look at her, and she immediately got off, needing to sit on a bench with her eyes closed to steady her breathing. Then she tried an online therapist, but closed her laptop as soon as their face had popped up on the screen.

She had thought going for a walk would help, which apparently nobody did outside of Venice Beach. She had spotted a man who looked like the one they had accidentally run over, and he was urinating by a bus stop, leather trousers around his ankles. Another figment of her imagination.

After that, she had returned to the hotel and decided not to leave. She had tried another online therapist, but when their face turned into the dead man's, she slammed the laptop shut and stayed in bed for the rest of the day with her eyes closed. Things were so bad that she looked forward to hearing from Rami.

Today, she was trying group therapy. It had shocked her to see what there were groups for. There was an adult adoptee group, one on how to befriend yourself, and one for people who couldn't say no. She had also seen several on miscarriages she couldn't read more about.

She had found grief groups with names such as Don't be a Grief Thief, and The Art of Grief, and Good Mourning, but opted for the straight forward, Grief Group.

The session leader, in a far too formal dress, had long blonde hair, perfect white teeth, and a body you could only get through a payment plan. It was as though somebody had typed "beach-perfect wealthy grief counsellor" into an AI generator and birthed her through a 3D printer.

Mia felt cheap in her shorts and vest. She could sense her mother tutting at her appearance from across the ocean.

Other attendees included a woman with too much dirt in her fingernails, a man who looked like he had chased the dragon, caught it and now kept it as a pet, and an old man who had spent so much time in the sun that he had become a sun-dried tomato.

Part of Mia had hoped to come across a celebrity, as she had heard a lot of Hollywood actors attended groups, but they were probably at the ones for addiction issues.

The group leader moved a chair to the side. 'Hopeful Friday to you all,' she said. 'Everyone get a little closer. We're a little lighter this week.' She smiled at Mia. 'We have a new joiner today. If you're happy to, would you like to introduce yourself?'

Mia nodded. 'Hi everyone, I'm Sophie.'

'Nice to meet you, Sophie,' the sun-dried tomato said.

The others waved and the group leader smiled. 'I like to start every session by sharing my grief, just to warm us up. I'm Shauna, and I lost my younger brother, Kyle, six years ago. I used to pick him up from work, because it was in Watts and not the safest place. But, one night I was tired, and I wanted to stay home and play a video game. I told him to get the bus, and next thing I know my mom calls crying, telling me Kyle's been mauled by a couple of dogs. So...' She exhaled. 'That's me.'

Mia shuddered. This was far heavier than she had expected.

The dragon chaser raised his hand. 'What game?'

'Excuse me?' Shauna asked.

'What video game?' the man repeated. 'I meant to ask last session.'

'*Final Fantasy 16*, but that's not really—'

'Great game,' he replied.

Shauna nodded and forced a smile. 'Moving on. Sophie, would you like to share anything?'

'No. I'm... I'm here to observe.' Although, what would listening to others do?

The one with dirty nails raised her hand. 'I'll go. I was thinking about my cat—'

'Actually, I'm ready,' Mia said.

Shauna raised a palm towards her, but Mia steamrolled on and the woman with dirty nails accepted defeat.

'I recently lost my husband, and I keep seeing him everywhere,' Mia said and massaged her forehead. 'And I don't know what to do.'

Shauna leaned forward. 'It's actually normal to see someone, or hear them and feel their presence after death.'

Mia huffed. 'But, it's not him. It's bits of him. He didn't die in... the best circumstances. So I'm seeing bloody and broken parts of his body.'

'Cool,' the high man said.

'No,' Mia said. 'It's not cool. Are you even in the right group?'

Shauna remained calm. 'Let's not diminish others, Sophie.

But, Saed, seeing broken and bloody parts of a loved one's body is not something we want to celebrate.'

'It is if they've been cheatin' on you,' the filthy-nailed woman said.

Saed laughed.

Shauna turned back to Mia. 'Sometimes I cope by talking to my dead brother, saying the things I would have liked to say to him. If you're comfortable, is there anything you'd like to say to your husband?'

Mia nodded, and a heat rose through her chest. She thought for a moment. 'I'd say. Why me? Why did you have to come into my life? Why couldn't you have been anywhere else that night?' She was so used to holding back, but she felt herself able to let go.

The others looked confused.

'I wish we'd never met.' Mia's throat ached and she found herself thinking less of the dead man, and more of Wilfred. 'Death has taught me how selfish you are... were, and how you weren't the person I fell in love with.'

Shauna's eyes widened, shocked. Saed grinned.

Tears formed in Mia's eyes. 'I'm not sad about you dying. I'm not. I'm sad about what your death represents, because now I see the truth about who you really are... were. That my mother might actually be right in the way she lives her life. And that's a horrible thought.' She took a breath and her hands trembled. 'When you died, I learned that happiness, optimism, and love are all just illusions, and people are packed full of secrets and lies they mask, deceiving each other to make themselves feel like they fit somewhere in this shit world. Life is something to tolerate however we see fit, until our hearts have had enough of beating.'

The sun-dried tomato offered Mia a tissue.

'Thank you,' she said. She never realised how much she hated her life. She had not been living for herself at all. Her job;

she never wanted that. It was because her mother pushed her, saying women needed stability. Mia had wanted to be a pianist, but Andrea squashed that as foolish. She believed creatives were selfish children who never grew up.

And Wilfred, she knew now he was just an escape. Mia's soul was trapped in a sad norm, and he was a break from it. She took a breath and stood up. 'Good luck to you all.' She left.

～

Mia lay on the bed in her hotel room, fully dressed, on the phone to Rami. It was 10 p.m. now, and 6 a.m. in Norwich. 'I've been in the exact same position for four hours,' she said.

'Get out and see stuff. You've got the Getty Museum, the Griffith Observatory. Just go somewhere,' he said.

She rolled onto her side. 'I can't be bothered. It's actually too sunny here. Exhaustingly sunny. It's like the sun is trying to blind everyone to how depressing it all is. At least England presents itself in all its gloom.' She huffed. 'Plus, Paulo has me meeting investors in a few weeks, so I'll prep a presentation for that. How's your new student?' She swallowed her anger at the thought of Wilfred.

'He's good. He asks a lot of questions. He's writing about a divorce, so it oddly feels very similar to therapy,' Rami said.

'Is that good for you?' She sat up against the headboard.

'What?' he asked.

'Digging into all that with a stranger. You're still vulnerable. Maybe it's not the best idea.' She got up and closed the curtains, then got back into bed. She put the phone on loudspeaker and placed it next to her as she stared at the ceiling.

'It's my job,' Rami replied. 'And it's fine.'

She bit her lip. 'Yeah. I just... It's just I worry about you is all.'

He didn't say anything.

'And...' she said, then stopped herself.

238

'And?' he asked.

'I, erm... I spoke to some people from my old work. Wilfred once got reported for stalking another employee, and some people have said he's a compulsive liar. I don't know how that affects you, but, I don't know if massaging his ego in regards to his failed marriage will be a good thing.' She winced, wishing she hadn't said anything.

'Oh,' Rami said. 'Thanks. I'll be mindful of that.'

She looked at her trembling left hand. 'Anyway, I'm going to shower.'

'Okay. Chat soon,' he said. 'And thanks. I worry about you too.'

She hung up. She opened her laptop, to a presentation of Paulo's start-up: Compassion Companion. Dreadful, cringe-inducing name. She had to think of an alternative.

The silence killed her. She closed the laptop and ordered an Uber to a beach bar.

33

A BITTER TASTING MENU

RAMI

Rami walked jauntily along the pretty bar and restaurant lined St. Benedict's Street. Christmas was on the horizon, well, twenty-five days away, but the festive street lights had fully committed.

Three weeks had passed and had been by Rami's definition, normal. Sure, guilt still attacked him, but he had better coping strategies, such as repeating to himself that Dale was a scumbag, and that it was an accident. Yes, he had caused a lot of pain, but there was an argument that Dale was causing more pain while alive and may have continued to do so.

God, he sounded like Mia.

The paranoia was still there, though. As long as there was no body, there was no murder. But as long as he didn't know where the body was, there was no peace.

During the last three weeks he had walked along the river five times, checking for any signs of Dale. If the corpse was going to resurface it would have by now. How long would it be before Rami was convinced that Dale would not be found? It had been thirty days since they hit him. In six months? A year?

Likely never. There would never be a day when Rami would feel free.

He sighed as he approached Benedicts restaurant.

Mia and Rami had messaged each other a lot over the last three weeks, and he got the sense she might have missed him. She didn't always pick up his calls, still doing things on her terms, but her terms didn't seem as cruel as they had been. She was interested in him and asked questions, rather than ending messages with no sense of continuing a conversation.

Lyn had fit into the house perfectly. Rami had helped her to film some videos to get back to normality, and she cried less frequently. Although, certain moments in films would trigger her, like when Marley died at the end of *Marley and Me*, or when Miguel sang to Mama Coco in *Coco*. Her gentle soul was a much needed presence, even if it added to his guilt.

Jenny had made progress with her story, but thankfully not with her investigation. She had told Rami that she had reached out to Trinity a couple of times, but had been rudely dismissed. As a result, Jenny had stepped back from searching, to avoid trouble from the police this close to the birth of her child. It was a welcome relief.

Rami had been a bit more careful about sharing with Wilfred after what Mia had said about him being accused of stalking. During their six sessions since, Rami had tried to work him out, and Wilfred did seem to be a good man. Rami didn't like judging people based on other people's opinions, so he had accepted Wilfred's kind invitation to dinner tonight. He hadn't told Mia, as he knew she wouldn't approve.

Rami had wanted to bring Mia to Benedicts in the past. Reviews suggested they were very considerate of intolerances, but his offers had been rejected.

Rami straightened his blazer. It was the first time he had worn one in years, but he loved how Wilfred's clothes projected power. He wanted to see if dressing up would boost his own confidence. He pushed the door open into the cosily lit, stripped-back open area, with unadorned windows looking out onto the street. The staff wore blacksmith-style aprons, and everyone seemed happy.

Rami spied Wilfred sat in the corner. He was dressed like he owned the place and was easily the most formal thing in the restaurant.

Wilfred grinned on seeing Rami and stood, a bottle of red wine in his hand. 'Welcome! The guest of honour!' He gestured to the table.

The waiting staff smiled, as though they knew Wilfred well.

After five courses of the tasting menu, which included a delicious potato dish that had a potato foam so light it could've floated away, Wilfred poured himself more wine, his second bottle, and nodded at Rami. 'You sure you don't want any? It's delicious.'

Rami shook his head. 'Thanks. Honestly, I live off water and the occasional herbal tea. Less pressure on my weak gut, especially if I'm trying new things. And I find I need my inhibitions so I don't slip into old habits.'

Wilfred nodded. 'I admire your discipline.' He placed his big hand on Rami's shoulder and squeezed it. 'And I owe you the biggest thank you of my life.'

Rami smiled. All he wanted was to have a positive impact on someone's life; to help them follow their dreams.

Wilfred's grip was a bit too tight, but thankfully he soon released it. 'You've awoken something in me, Rami. I love writing and everything to do with it.'

'That's great to hear,' he said. 'So, does that mean you've written some sample scenes?'

Wilfred laughed, his red-wine-stained teeth the sign of a

good night so far. 'One of the great things about writing that I love, Rami, is that thinking about writing is also writing.' His laugh filled the room.

The next course arrived: Norfolk crabmeat packed into a smooth, elastic pasta, with various fancy presentations of vegetables Rami had forgotten about as soon as the descriptions had left the waiter's mouth.

Wilfred took a huge forkful. 'I did, however, in my procrastination, come up with some film titles based on remakes, all starring me.'

Rami sprinkled sea salt over the dish. 'Okay, that wasn't the homework, but, still a creative exercise, so I'll let it slide. Plus, I like that you're dreaming big.'

Wilfred nodded, proud of himself. 'There's *Throckodile Dundee*, *Throcky*, or *Throcked Up*.'

Rami laughed. 'You could have *Attack the Throck*.'

Wilfred clicked, appreciating the suggestion. 'And *Lock, Throck, and Two Smoking Barrels*.'

'If you had a twin it could be *Throck, Throck, and Two Smoking Barrels*. Oh, what about *The Throcky Horror Picture Show*, or *School of Throck*?'

'Yes, Rami!' Wilfred clenched his fists victoriously.

One of the great things about life was that friendships could form at any point. It showed that fresh starts existed everywhere, and at any age. Unless someone was dead, of course.

Rami ate more and took a breath. 'I need to thank you, too, Wilfred. Things have been so rough, for a long time, but... while it'll be different, I can see a positive future, finally.'

Wilfred smiled. 'I'm glad we could help each other move on from our marriages of misfortune.'

Rami drank more water. 'Well, weirdly, things are actually good with Mia.'

Wilfred wiped his mouth with his napkin. 'In what sense?'

Rami felt light. 'We've been messaging loads, and I even

think she misses me. It's early on, obviously, and could just be her using me while she gets settled, but, it tells me that it's not totally final. She's not been pushing the divorce proceedings as much as I thought she would. And, I don't get the feeling I repulse her anymore.'

Wilfred folded his napkin over and over. 'And do you want a reconciliation?'

'I think so. Sure, she's been mean, miserable, manipulative, just all the bad m's, but she's actually confiding in me, showing she cares.' Maybe he would call Mia later and share how he felt. 'That's got to mean something. It's like the good Mia I first met is trying to come back and burst through the layers of bad Mia.'

Wilfred adjusted his watch strap. 'I don't know, Rami. I think holding on to these things is dangerous. If you're not comfortable being alone, let's get you on the apps, but you shouldn't be trying to go back. Not yet.'

Rami's shoulders slumped. 'I know it's probably a fantasy, but... maybe all she needed was distance to see that we have something worth working for.'

Wilfred's expression changed from jolly to angry. 'It's annoying that you're so much nicer than I thought you'd be.'

'Thanks,' Rami answered, then realised what an odd thing that was for Wilfred to say. 'What do you mean?'

Wilfred leaned back in his chair and stared at Rami. 'I don't care for writing. It's narcissistic, childish, and machine learning is slowly eradicating the need for it.'

Rami tensed, confused. 'Are you okay, Wilfred?'

Wilfred grabbed the bottle of wine and turned it in his hands. 'Whatever Mia is doing, she doesn't want you back.'

Rami swallowed his hurt, then chuckled nervously. 'This is you giving me tough love, right?'

Wilfred huffed. 'I was having an affair with Mia.'

The life drained from Rami's body, and the warm joy of a night out with a friend became hollow misery.

She had manipulated him again, and so had Wilfred.

'So, what is all this?' Rami asked, unsure what to do with his fork.

Wilfred's eyebrows narrowed. 'It had been going on a year and a half, and the night she said she wanted to divorce you, she called me from a petrol station, *elated*.'

Rami's throat tightened.

Wilfred pushed his chair back, putting more distance between them. 'She told me she was going to drop you home, show her face at Lyn's, then meet me at a hotel.'

Rami wanted to drive his fork into one of Wilfred's eyes; or maybe it would be better to dig it into his own chest to scoop his heart out. His breathing hastened.

Wilfred drank wine straight from the bottle. 'But, then she called, because you wouldn't let her leave. She said you threatened to kill yourself, and the next day that your mother was unwell. Your mother, who has been dead for quite a while.'

Rami's head throbbed. She had lied, constantly. Everything was a lie.

Wilfred held the bottle of wine more menacingly. 'Then she ended it. So, I want to understand, what changed in her? She lied about your mother, and about your suicidal tendencies, so what happened to make someone go from excited about a new chapter, to ending something magical so urgently and fleeing the country? I need to know, Rami.' Wilfred's eyes welled up.

Rami gripped the fork as tightly as he could. He stared at Wilfred and gritted his teeth. He tossed the fork onto his plate, stood up and dragged himself towards the restaurant exit.

'Rami, I need to know!' Wilfred yelled.

~

'She's pure evil,' Rami said, sat on the sofa, weeping into Lyn's shoulder, his blazer crumpled up on the kitchen tiles. 'The only reason she'd been chatting to me was to find out what he was up to. To make sure I was still on her leash in case she needed me.'

'I'm so sorry, Rami.' She stroked his back.

He pulled away. 'Did she ever mention anything to you?'

Lyn raised her palms. 'I swear. You'd think she would, but it just shows what a secretive nut she is. I actually thought about contacting her today. No chance.'

'Yeah...' He wanted to call her to scream at her, to call her every awful name running through his mind, but at the same time he never wanted to speak to her again. Part of him blamed himself. Maybe she was unfaithful because he wasn't a good enough husband. Maybe he had pushed her to be unfaithful.

His phone rang. It was Mia. Lyn grabbed the phone and silenced it. 'Full blanking needs to come into effect.'

He nodded. 'I'm blocking her on everything.' Was Wilfred the only one or were there others? His mind flipped through every moment of suspicion. Even her walking to the shops to buy some spinach had a hint of deception to it.

He was an idiot. Any time he had been suspicious he dismissed it, not allowing his mind to tip into catastrophe, because he feared the truth. He would never ignore his instincts again.

Lyn stood up. 'Follow me.'

'I quite like not moving,' Rami said. 'Maybe I won't move until the new year.'

'Shut it. Come on.' She walked into the hallway.

Rami stumbled after her.

Lyn stared at Mia's boxes of belongings, which were no closer to leaving the house. He had also taken that as a sign that she wasn't fully committed to leaving. Instead, it was more dominance. Another flag planted. She owned him.

Lyn pointed. 'What shall we trash?'

'What?'

'You need some fire, Rami. You can't just take it all and not give back. Take something of hers and smash the shit out of it. Trust me. I've chopped up someone's clothes, slashed tyres, and one bloke treated me so shitty that I poured his dad's ashes into his coffee.'

Rami stared at her. 'Wow. I was with you until the ashes.'

Lyn shrugged. 'Yeah, that was a bit harsh, but I don't regret it. Now say Mia's a dick.'

'Can't I just lie down on the cold floor and die?'

'Say it, Rami. You've got to release this shit.'

'Fine. Mia's a dick,' he said.

'Put something into it, mate,' Lyn requested.

'Mia's a dick!' She was such a dick.

'Now keep saying it!'

Rami repeated it, over and over, until the adrenaline pumped through him. 'I fucking hate her!'

'Exactly!' Lyn replied.

Rami grabbed Mia's bubble-wrapped Mark Rothko print and marched into the kitchen. He leaned it against the wall and ripped the bubble wrap off it.

'Oh, that horrible thing,' Lyn said.

'She loves it more than anything else. If any dust got near it, it was instantly wiped. She cherished it more than our wedding photos.'

Lyn raised an eyebrow. 'It's just a coloured square. What is wrong with her?'

Rami nodded. 'It's apparently about human emotion.' He clenched his fists.

Lyn scowled. 'Well, it's making me angry. Go to town on it.'

Rami stomped the frame, breaking it.

'Let it out, Rami!' Lyn patted his back.

He picked up the frame and whacked it against the kitchen counter edge, bending it. He chucked it onto the floor. 'Fuck colour theory!'

'Yes, Rami!' Lyn cheered.

He grabbed one of Mia's Japanese knives. She hadn't bothered to pack them, and he wasn't going to do it for her. He slashed at the canvas, over and over. Every rejection another slash. Every harsh insult another stomp. He reduced the canvas to shreds and the frame to splinters. It belonged in a gallery as a piece of modern art about the destructive power of a toxic marriage.

He took slow breaths and dropped the knife. He stared at the wreckage, his body exhausted from the emotional beating.

Lyn placed an arm around him and rested her head on his shoulder. 'You've got to promise yourself, no being stepped on anymore. You're better than that.'

He rested his head on hers and put his arm around her. They stood in sad comfort for a moment. 'I'd better go to bed. See you in the morning.' He stepped away from her.

She offered him a sympathetic smile. 'Just knock for me if you need anything.'

He dragged himself upstairs, uncertain of what in his marriage had actually been true.

34

SHAMBLES IN THE SAND

Mia

Mia stared out at the beach from the cafe table. She put her shades on, trying to block out the mid-morning sun, and turned her laptop to avoid the creeping glare.

She was done with the sun now, and with LA. Twenty-five days and she had realised the traffic was endless, and the main green spaces were golf courses. She was also fed up of being tormented whenever she got on a bus. A few days ago, a man holding a bag overflowing with bibles had aimed a lighter at her like a gun, and she had spoken to too many people with big dreams, living bleak realities. They all had blind optimism, like Rami, that everything would work out.

It had been three days and still no replies from him.

The last message was sent on November the 30th, and now it was the 3rd of December. The longest Rami had not replied to her was one day when they had started dating, because he was trying to be cool.

Had Wilfred said something? She didn't want to ask him.

249

Picturing Wilfred's face, or even imagining his voice, made her furious.

She sipped on her ginger kombucha. It tasted like sweat.

Maybe Rami was overwhelmed and had confessed? But, then she would be getting calls. There was no way he would take the fall for her. Maybe he had killed himself?

All signs pointed to Wilfred.

She clicked through the presentation on her laptop, making sure she was ready to deliver it to Paulo's investors in a few hours.

She Googled: "Missing man Norfolk." No results suggested Rami had been caught. Just headlines about more of the man's lovers coming forward, selling their sob stories.

She scanned the slides once more. She was proud of the new company name she had come up with, which Paulo loved. Good riddance to Compassion Companion, and hello Circle of Care, highlighting the overall rounded experience, helping people with whatever emotional need they had in a circle of trust. Not her best work, and it did sound a little culty, but it was better than suggesting a creepy companion.

Mia closed the laptop and called Rami again. It went straight to voicemail.

Three days was too long. Something was wrong and she had to find out what. She texted Wilfred:

Did you say something to Rami?

His reply was instant:

I'll tell you if you tell me what changed x

Everything spun and she put her head in her hands, trying to shut out the noise. Rami was such a drip that he might decide to confess out of hurt. She needed to talk him down.

She packed her things and walked along the beach trying to call him again and again. Heat pulsed within her and she walked faster to release the tension, her flip-flops fighting against the sand.

She left Rami multiple voicemails. In some she denied the affair, calling Wilfred a liar, then scolded herself for thinking that would work. In another voicemail, she played events down as a tiny blip, and blamed Rami becoming distant after Becca killed herself.

Her body shook and she dropped her phone on the sand, barely any strength left in her. So what if he was angry with her? There was no way he would confess. He had nothing to gain.

She stared at the sea, not sure if she felt guilty, or annoyed that she had been caught. Maybe it was guilt. She didn't want to hurt Rami this way. She wanted him out of her life, but not devastated. He was swept up in her hatred of her own existence.

A flash of the dead man, face down on the shore, wrapped in loose strips of cling film, invaded her mind.

She screamed, her breathing accelerating. She turned around and tripped over a blood-smothered motorcycle helmet. Pain shot through her toes.

She blinked and the motorcycle helmet became a rock.

An old man with a broken foot shook his head at her from a nearby bench. 'That ain't a soccer ball, lady.'

Mia got up and stumbled into a bar, wincing through the pain. She sat on a stool and closed her eyes, box breathing until the rush calmed.

~

BANG! BANG! BANG!

Mia stirred, squinting through a gin glaze.

She was back in her room, fully clothed, lying on the carpet next to her bed, one flip-flop on, the other in the bin. Her body ached. She wasn't sure if she was hungover or still drunk, but the nausea didn't care.

A muffled voice sounded from the other side of the door. 'I can't open the door, sir,' said someone who worked in the hotel.

'I'm concerned for her welfare,' Paulo's muffled voice replied.

Mia's chest tightened. 'I'm coming.' She stood groggily. 'Just need a moment.'

She looked in the mirror at the mess before her, quickly patted her hair down and drank some water. She had a whisky stain on her dress and a cut on her right elbow.

The meeting.

'I'm so sorry,' she said, opening the door. 'How late am I?'

Paulo stood there with a paper bag of groceries. His frown suggested annoyance, but his eyes drooped with sympathy. 'It's ten at night, Mia. You gonna invite me in?'

She nodded and stood aside, feeling as embarrassed as when she got disciplined at university for stealing a catering trolley when drunk. She had wheeled it two miles to her halls of resi-dence and denied any involvement, so they made her watch the CCTV evidence.

Paulo turned to the concierge. 'We're good.'

The concierge looked at Mia.

'It's fine,' she said.

The concierge nodded. 'Call reception if you need anything.'

Paulo entered and grimaced at the waft. 'Jesus, Mia.' He opened the curtains and a window.

He placed the bag of groceries on the desk and sat on the chair.

Mia sat on the bed. 'I've had a lot going on back home with the divorce.'

He reached into the bag and took out a carton of orange juice. He opened it and handed it to Mia. 'You embarrassed me, Mia.'

She hung her head. 'I know. I don't have an excuse. I'm just. I don't know.' Everything hurt and felt disconnected.

Paulo took more items out of the bag. Some fruit, more juices, and some painkillers. 'I've been in your shoes, Mia, and they're not comfortable.'

She nodded.

He cleared his throat. 'I want to work with you, but not until you're right.'

She clasped her hands together. 'I promise I won't drink again. I will do anything and this isn't the norm. Please.' She shuffled on the bed.

He scratched his beard and stared at her. 'Look, I can square things with the investors. Even though Jerry is going to make crappy jokes and be an ass. What I can't square is putting an addict into this job, in a new country, with none of her network here.'

'I'm not an addict,' she protested. 'I'm just dealing with—'

'You get yourself back home, around people, and get into AA. I'll be checking in regularly once I'm a little less pissed off. Then we can discuss something in future and us sponsoring that visa.' He stood up.

'You can't fire me.' Mia stood up.

Paulo stopped at the door. 'Technically, you don't work for me yet. So, I'm not firing you. I'm looking out for you.'

Mia folded her arms. 'It won't look good for a mental health company if I tell the press I've been working for you illegally, and that you're now discarding me because I'm struggling personally and missed a meeting.'

Sadness washed over Paulo. 'Mia, what do you expect me to say to that?'

'Say we carry on as planned,' she replied.

He turned the door handle. 'I know it's not you talking, and that's the problem. I went through the exact same motions, pushed my family and my ex-wife away. What you need to realise is it's not your fault, but it is up to you grab it and wrestle with whatever it is stirring this up. I'll be waiting.'

She grabbed his arm. 'Please, Paulo. I've not been unemployed for ten years.' She didn't know how to be out of work. She imagined her mother's judging tut that was a punch to all self-esteem.

Paulo placed his hand on Mia's. 'I'll be checking in with you, and you know how to reach me. You can live with this.' He opened the door and left.

The click of the door closing was like a switch, turning her career off. A career she had spent years building, even though it was one she didn't want.

She slumped back on her bed and took long breaths. She gazed around the room. No sign of her handbag or laptop. At least she had her phone and purse, and her passport was on her desk.

She drained the rest of the orange juice in one, then reached for another, but the nausea hit her harder. She ran into the bathroom and threw up.

No.

She checked her period tracker app.

Fuck.

35

LET ME START BY SAYING...

RAMI

Rami finished scrubbing Lyn's breakfast plate while she was upstairs. The mechanical task of making her a boiled egg on a bed of spinach, with a drizzle of olive oil, had helped over the last few days. He needed more processes and habits to distract him from Mia's deception.

He sat at the kitchen counter and crunched into a celery stick covered in hummus. The living room area was ready for filming, with Lyn's electric guitar at the foot of the sofa. He was thankful for Lyn bringing energy into the house and compassion into his life.

If there was one good thing to come of all this misery, it was her.

He gazed into the hallway, where Mia's boxes used to be, glad they were gone. He had given them all to the Saint Henriette Hospice charity shop in Bungay, and the old woman was thrilled. She said it was more donations than she would get some entire months.

Rami had put more of his nan's paintings around the house, trying to move forward.

The last few days had been awful. He questioned every moment in their marriage. She had gone to therapy with him, knowing she was cheating. She had celebrated his last birthday with him, albeit without enthusiasm, knowing she had deceived him. Every single day was a lie.

How could she treat his emotions with such callousness?

Ignoring her calls and text messages had given him a taste of what it was like to be the one in control. He didn't like it, which confirmed just how rotten to the core Mia was.

Her barrage of voicemails yesterday revealed that Wilfred had told her he had confessed to their affair. He had listened to them multiple times, analysing her tone and word choice, and had concluded that nothing was genuine.

Rami huffed and sprinkled sea salt onto the hummus.

Lyn came downstairs in a low-cut, black thigh-split dress. Rami tried not to stare and shuffled in his seat.

She chuckled. 'Was gonna ask how I look but I think I'm alright.'

He gazed at his celery. 'Yeah... I, erm... I have nothing.'

Lyn smiled. 'You've got a very expressive way about you. You'd be shit at hiding anything.'

He became increasingly self-conscious.

Lyn switched the ring light and Sony camera on, extended the tripod, and sat down on the sofa. 'Can you help me check the framing?'

Rami nodded, stood up and approached the camera, looking at the display screen. 'You are very much the centre of this mini universe.'

'Great.' She leaned forward and picked up her electric guitar.

Rami swallowed. He had found Lyn increasingly attractive over the last few days and would beat himself up about it. He deserved misery. Being attracted to someone made him no better than Mia, especially as he had murdered that someone's dodgy boyfriend.

Lyn crossed her legs, revealing her snake tattoo. 'Any requests, Rami?'

He struggled to think on the spot. 'Erm, what about something by East 17?'

Lyn scrunched her nose. 'No offence to East 17, but try again babe.'

Rami chuckled. 'Okay, I think it's about time you moved back to your house,' he joked.

She smiled. 'Get over it.' Her eyes widened. 'I got one. Press record please.'

Rami pressed record and watched, unsure of what to do with his arms.

Lyn started playing, and Rami tried to work out what it was.

He stifled his laughter as he realised she was playing an electric guitar cover of 'Hello' by Lionel Richie. She smiled at the camera, but he knew it was for him. There was a real intimacy about the framing, how she looked at the lens as she played the song.

He was pulled into a different world. A happy one. He regretted how harshly he had judged her in the past, always viewing her as Mia's annoying friend, rather than the good one out of the two.

This was a departure from the heavier musical content on her page. Rami had been through her entire back catalogue recently, as he lay alone in bed.

She finished and paused a moment. 'Cut.' She grinned and leaned her guitar against the side of the sofa.

Rami stopped the recording. 'That was incredible.' He rushed to the kitchen counter, poured her a glass of water, picked up his plate with the remaining two celery sticks and handed them to her on the sofa.

'Thanks.' She took the water and a celery stick.

He sat next to her, half a metre of sofa between them. 'I owe you an apology, Lyn.'

Her eyes met his, confused. 'For what?'

He didn't want to ruin the lovely morning, but he needed to be open, to live in a way that was completely the opposite to Mia. 'I've not been very nice about you in the past. I've judged you unfairly, when really, I've had no right to judge you at all.'

She put the glass of water down, giving nothing away.

'You're brilliant, Lyn. You're you, with no bullshit, no fakeness—'

'Apart from these.' She grabbed her breasts. 'And a few bits and pieces around my gob.'

He chuckled and gazed at the patch of sofa cushion between them. 'Yeah, I've made jokes about those, too. Sorry.'

She shrugged. 'Don't worry. I've been judged forever.'

'That doesn't make it okay. I'm lucky you've been around, even if it is in the weirdest circumstances, and even though you have no respect for East 17. I'm really sorry.' Something in his brain had changed. He even found her powerfully offensive zesty perfume comforting.

She smiled. 'I kind of get a kick out of proving people wrong. It'd be boring if everyone just thought I was amazing straight away. No challenge.'

'I wouldn't worry about that,' he replied.

She glared at him. 'Doughnut. What kind of things did you think?'

He swallowed. 'Really? The apology not cutting it?'

She chuckled. 'I'm just curious.'

He took a breath. 'I... once said... that it's great you're doing your bit to clean the oceans by sticking most of the dumped plastic into your face.' He hung his head, praying she wouldn't punch him.

She laughed. 'I like that one.'

He sighed. 'It isn't even factually correct, as the materials used for plastic surgery are different to the plastics that end up in the ocean.'

She smiled at him.

'I'm an arsehole,' he said.

'Yeah. But everyone's got an arsehole moment in them. Main thing is to not let the moment last a lifetime. And I've not exactly been fair about you either. Always thought you weren't good enough for Mia. Turns out it's the other way around.' She crunched into the celery and grimaced. 'Really? Salt on this?'

'I won't be shamed,' Rami said.

Lyn drank some water. 'People are always unfair, judging, assuming, not really knowing who someone is, or what they're up against. Way of the world, I guess. Just gotta shut the shit out and keep the good ones close.' She leaned back on the sofa cushion. 'Can I ask you something?'

'You've never asked to ask me something, so I assume it's about either the miscarriage or Becca?'

'Becca. I wasn't fair about that, because you know that saying, "There's no smoke without fire," and all that bollocks. But, what actually happened? The she-Satan mentioned some stuff, but it was probably what suited her.'

Rami swallowed. Talking about it made him question every detail, and his mind would over-analyse the smallest moments, gestures, the way he had said anything and how it would have been interpreted. He took a big breath. 'Well, Becca was a high-achieving kid, from a family of arseholes. But, she didn't actually get accepted onto the course, because her sample script was offensive. Like, discriminatory drivel. But, the university's auto-mated system, instead of sending the rejection email, acciden-tally sent her an offer of a place on a Friday, so she celebrated all weekend, then the university tried to correct their error on the Monday. But, God help the person who tries to tell rich parents their kid isn't ready, especially when the parents are a lawyer and an MP.'

Lyn winced. 'Oof.'

'Oof, indeed. So, she joined the course with less of a chip and more of a potato farm on her shoulder. And she had this block, where she couldn't take feedback. A trait likely handed down. I tried. I wrote her gentle feedback about the xenophobic crap she was writing, but she'd reject it saying it was her art and that her parents liked it. The same, dominating, micro-managing parents who were rumoured to have chosen what she wore to university. Her home life seemed very high-pressure and low love.' Rami choked up.

Lyn didn't take her eyes off him.

'So, when it came to her final script I drew the short straw and was her first marker. The script remained the entitled anti-immigration nonsense Nigel Farage and Suella Braverman would get off to. Obviously not together, because... racism.' He shook his head, knowing he shouldn't be making light of anything. 'I failed the script, and I was pretty harsh in my feed-back.' He sighed. 'The day the results came out, a year, four months and two days ago...'

Lyn shuffled over and put an arm around his shoulder.

'She killed herself. Afterwards her parents accused me of bullying her and driving her to suicide. Nobody questioned the parenting in the situation, or anything else that might have been going on in her life. The sympathy for the MP got them a local election win too.'

Lyn shook her head.

Rami pulled at his eyebrow hair. 'I adored that job. After years struggling I had finally found the thing I loved doing. The hearing cleared me of any wrongdoing, but the university were cowards.'

Lyn squeezed his shoulder.

He wiped his eyes on his sleeve. 'Obviously, I feel horrible, and I should've found other ways to help her. But was I a bully? A constant toxic presence pushing her to the brink of taking her own life? No. For that you need to look closer to home.'

Lyn removed her arm. 'It's not your—'

'It is, Lyn. Partially. If I'd said nothing, if I hadn't failed her, maybe she'd still be here today.' He shook his head. 'I know my part in it. I could've just let it go rather than pushing the point. And, I'll have to live with what I did forever.'

That and Dale. Whose life would he destroy next?

Lyn picked up the glass of water and offered him some. He drank, then handed it back and she placed it on the floor.

Rami cleared his throat. 'I appreciate that "There's no smoke without fire," makes sense as a saying. But, it's an easy way to discredit someone. I was the final drop of lighter fluid on that blaze. Her parents were the rest of the bottle.'

Lyn took his right hand and rubbed it. 'I'm so sorry, Rami. I'll tell my Insta Lynstas to never vote for the twat MP.'

Rami chuckled. 'Please, don't make me laugh. It's too depressing to laugh about.' His brain felt heavy.

'Thanks for telling me, Rami. I should've asked you sooner.' She smiled.

It felt like a boulder covered in spikes had been lifted from his back. He wasn't sure why he hated talking about it. It had made him distant from Mia and pulled him within himself.

They sat in silence a moment and Lyn let go of his hand. 'Don't think I'll ever use "There's no smoke without fire" again.'

He exhaled. 'I also don't like, "There's no use crying over spilt milk." It's basically saying suppress your emotions.' He shook his head. 'That's why so many people are messed up today. As kids they're told not to cry.'

'Yeah, that's terrible. I'm not a fan of "Money can't buy happiness." I get it, but I grew up with sod all in a council estate, and I promise you, having money is bloody great, and I'm very happy I get to go abroad for holidays instead of the yearly camping trip to Clacton-on-Sea.'

Rami laughed. 'I used to go to Lebanon as a kid and I'd complain about it.'

'You're one of the lucky ones,' Lyn said.

'Yeah. Until my mum sent me on a camping trip with the scouts, but out there, the scouts are future army. So, it was all making a mile-long path of stones, and sharing a tent with fifteen guys and a scorpion. Not the best introduction to camping, especially for a London city boy who'd run when he saw an ant.'

Lyn laughed and rested her head on his shoulders. 'What was the scariest thing you saw out there?'

'One of the other scouts wiping his arse with a leaf.'

Lyn groaned. 'I meant insects!'

'There could've been one on the leaf.' Rami put an arm around her. He wasn't sure if he should, but he wanted to.

She placed a hand on his thigh. 'Thanks for suggesting I stay here. I've loved it.'

'Loved as in you want it to end?' Rami asked, worried.

'Nah, but, can't stay here forever, can I?' she replied.

He couldn't see a reason why not. He had no other plans. 'There's another common saying, but I do like it.'

'What's that?' she said.

'Everything happens for a reason.' He stroked her arm, his heart racing.

Lyn lifted her head, gazed into his eyes and smiled. 'Yeah, it's a good one, that.' She kissed him.

His entire body tingled.

He pulled back. 'I'm slightly traumatised by the Queen of Misery and questioning everything. Is this a test of some kind or a pity kiss? I really don't want a pity kiss.'

Lyn straddled him and placed his hands on her waist. 'Don't ruin the moment, you daft twat.' She kissed him again.

~

Bloody. Hell.

Rami lay in the main bedroom queen-sized bed staring at the ceiling, Lyn wrapped in his arms. Sure, the performance anxiety Mia had cursed him with had made it a bumpy ride, but Lyn didn't make him feel bad about it.

She kissed his cheek. 'I know we're both vulnerable. But I like this.'

'Me too.' He expected to feel guilt, but he didn't. The regret about killing Dale was there, because he had taken a life, but the guilt was overpowered by joy.

He stroked Lyn's hair behind her ears. 'Why don't we just dive in, heart first, and if we realise we're just two wounded souls latching onto something, then we can be honest with each other.'

Lyn kissed him.

Rami stuck a calendar to his fridge and couldn't stop smiling. They had spent the last eighteen days getting to know each other; and each day had been amazing. The joyous energy could have had something to do with Christmas shining in every corner of Norwich, and the only dampener was that Rami had wasted so much time clinging onto a rotten marriage. He never believed he could meet anyone other than Mia, and that fear had kept him trapped. Mia had made him feel not only unlovable, but also barely likeable.

Rami marked events down with a green pen, wanting to preserve memories and plan future ones. On Wednesday the 6th of December they had been to London to watch *Wicked The Musical* with Gyal Pal, whose name Rami still refused to say out loud. They had done a ghost walk in Cambridge on the 10th of December, and even tried axe throwing on the 17th, which reminded Rami of the advice from the therapist. If he had gone axe throwing with Mia, he probably wouldn't be alive today. He drew an axe into the relevant box on the calendar.

Lyn had returned to her home for a couple of days and would arrive for dinner in an hour. Rami couldn't wait. He had spent so much time being careful around Mia, worried about saying something that might trigger her anger, or make her think less of him. Being with Lyn was the opposite. He could say anything, and it would be taken in the right spirit – a desire to engage and share. It was amazing to feel... liked.

He made an olive oil and lemon dressing to go with the spinach he was going to steam. He enjoyed East 17 playing from his laptop, as Lyn would likely turn it off as soon as she arrived.

The number of Dale's lovers had settled. There was Lyn, Trinity, the twenty-two-year-old nurse, a pensioner he was probably trying to weasel some inheritance out of, and a zookeeper from Lowestoft.

There had been no more news from the police, and Jenny remained quiet on the investigation front.

Paranoia still occasionally crept in. Sometimes it would hit him hard, like yesterday, when he decided to return to Belaugh. He wanted to check if the motorcycle was visible through the water during daylight, but the river was gloriously murky. He must have stared at it for over an hour, watching the water move, seeing if it would reveal his secret. He worried that in the summer, when people were more active around the water, that somebody would discover the motorbike. At one point, he even got on his hands and knees, his eyes millimetres from the surface. He considered returning with a sack of bricks to dump on top of the vehicle to further tip the odds in his favour.

Between bouts of paranoia, he did find himself able to be more present. While Lyn was a constant reminder of his deed, he was learning to live with it.

He questioned whether he loved her, or if he was just caught up in everything and reaching for something. He wasn't even sure what being in love felt like anymore. With Mia, it felt like he was in service, just trying to please. This felt balanced. He said heart first, and right now, his heart was leaning towards love. If she got scared and ran off, then it wasn't meant to be. He was done with caution, with apprehension, with regret. He was going to be one hundred per cent Rami and take what came.

He realised that deep down everyone was weird. And now it wasn't about hiding that weirdness, but rather, finding someone whose peculiarities were compatible with his.

He sprinkled sea salt over the haddock and placed it in the oven, then draped a cloth over the dinner table. He was ready.

The doorbell rang. Maybe she was early, as excited as him to be together.

He walked as lightly as he had in ages towards the door. He opened it. His heart clenched and his face dropped.

'Hi, Rami,' Mia said.

36

NEVER GONNA GIVE YOU UP

Mia

Mia expected Rami to react to the news by inviting her in, but he stood in the doorway as though he were a security guard. She could easily push past him, but decided to cede him his territory.

'Did you not hear me?' Mia said.

Rami shrugged. 'Well, congratulations to you and Wilfred. I hope the baby gets his sense of humour.'

Rami tried to shut the door, but Mia stuck her foot between the door and frame. 'It's yours, Rami. Me and Wilfred always used protection to stop anything like this exposing our affair. Even the last time we did it after I asked for the divorce.'

Rami's face, a mix of anger and hurt, peeked through the gap between the door and frame. 'What do you expect me to do? Welcome you back in? Get back together? Believe you?'

She chuckled. 'I don't want anything to do with you. But, you're the father, so you should probably be involved.'

He gazed down at the wooden floor, and she looked past

him, noticing her boxes were no longer in the hallway. 'Where's my stuff?'

'In the hands of anyone who shops at the Saint Henriette Hospice charity shop in Bungay.'

'What?' Mia tried to push the door open but failed.

Rami wouldn't budge. 'You should hurry. See what you can get your hands on. But you won't find your precious Rothko. That's been reimagined and is currently on display at the local dump.' He nudged her foot out of the way with his and slammed the door shut.

Mia stepped back. 'You can't just toss away someone's belongings!' she shouted at the door.

'But you can toss away someone's feelings?' he replied, his voice breaking.

Mia took deep breaths and gazed out at the cul-de-sac, wondering if she should boot the door down. Her hands shook, the tremors more frequent since she had stopped drinking. She had considered not telling Rami about the pregnancy, but there were still loose ends.

She turned back to the door and spoke more calmly. 'Listen, I'm sorry about the whole Wilfred thing. And, when you're ready, we can come to an arrangement about the baby, should it make it.' She swallowed, petrified of the past repeating. For the last year and a half the loss had dragged her down, but now it was motivation to avoid alcohol, and more importantly, avoid prison.

Rami didn't reply, but Mia knew he was there as she hadn't heard him drag his feet away.

She checked that nobody was around, then placed her head next to the door. 'I know it's a lot, but I had to tell you. And, we have something to protect, so it's important you tell me what you and Wilfred spoke about. He's up to something.'

Rami sighed from the other side of the door and Mia was sure she heard him crying.

'Go away, Mia,' he said.

37

KEEP ON MOVING

RAMI

Rami sat opposite Lyn at the dinner table. He had barely touched his spinach and the slightly burned haddock. The news had sucked the excitement out of the evening.

Rami had imagined what seeing Mia again would be like, and in each scenario he had pictured himself in control, able to be dismissive of her without care. But, when he saw her at the door, the exhaustion and burden in her eyes, hurt knocked any pre-planned sentences out of his mind. He didn't want to feel hurt. Hurt meant he still cared.

She must have been lying, manipulating him.

Lyn sipped her wine. 'You okay?' She had a glow about her; a glow of hope.

'Yeah,' he said, smiling, noticing a flicker of doubt on her face.

He shook his head. He had promised heart first, no nonsense. 'No. I'm not okay, Lyn.'

'What's up?' Her face wore worry.

'Bloody Cersei Lannister's back,' he exhaled.

'Oh God, what does that short-legged Lucifer want?' Lyn got up and walked around to Rami.

'She said she's pregnant.' He hung his head. 'I don't really believe her. But, what if it's true? I can't abandon a kid. I always swore I'd be nothing like my dad.'

Lyn sat on his lap and put her arms around his neck. 'Then don't be like him.'

'What about?' He gestured between the two of them. 'Do you really want to be part of this mess?'

She kissed him. 'We can figure it out. You can share custody, and that kid will need you to counter Mia's personality. Plus, I can be a positive influence.'

He smiled. 'How do you make even the worst things seem manageable?'

She shrugged. 'Just amazing like that.'

Rami stroked her hand. 'You are. You honestly... you make everything warm. You're so kind, you do everything with passion. You're inspiring.'

She grinned. 'Slow down, Rami, sounds like you might love me.'

His heart raced and his neck tensed. He smiled at her and nodded.

Her eyes welled up. 'Well say the fucking words you plank.'

'I love you.' He truly meant it.

She kissed him and he relaxed. 'I love you, too.' She pulled back and wiped her eyes. 'These have been the weirdest weeks of my life.'

She didn't even know the weirdest part of it. Dale's broken corpse flashed in Rami's mind, but he blocked him out.

Lyn held Rami's hand and rubbed her thumb over the back of it. She seemed nervous. 'I was thinking, do you fancy staying at mine for a couple of weeks?'

'Yeah, sure. I'd love that.'

'It can be a trial, right? To move in together properly.' She bit her lip.

He hugged her tightly, hoping squeezing her would release Mia from his mind. Lyn's body was warm and comforting. He had always viewed her as broken and desperate, but realised she was the least broken person he had ever met.

She stood up and took his hand. 'Come on.'

'We've still got food, it'll—'

She released his hand and folded her arms.

He nodded. 'It'll be completely fine.'

She led him towards the stairs.

The doorbell rang.

Lyn huffed. 'If it's her, can I hit her?'

Rami nodded. 'I'm not one to condone violence, but yeah. Just make it count.'

Lyn chuckled and answered the door.

It was Jenny, her serious face countered by her Christmas jumper of a dragon wearing a Father Christmas hat and breathing presents rather than fire. 'I've got news.'

38

ONE TEAM, ONE NIGHTMARE

Mia

Mia sat on her mother's sofa watching the Saturday morning news. Rami had texted Mia about it last night, but she hadn't seen his messages until this morning.

She turned the volume up.

A gormless, skinny, stoned teen in a T-shirt and gloves stood on the riverbank of the Bure, chatting to a news presenter who was wrapped in winter clothing.

Mia's stomach turned and she was suddenly desperate for a drink. She fought the urges, and was glad she had made Andrea throw all the alcohol out of the house.

The teen and the presenter stood in front of the dead man's cordoned-off motorcycle. 'A few of us was having some tinnies in Ryan's dad's boat. While I was taking a slash I looked out the window and saw some weird lookin' fella staring at the water, for ages. At one point he was on his knees like he were tryin' to kiss it. Thought he must be hiding something.'

'And what did the man look like?' the presenter asked.

Mia's blood boiled.

The teen put his hands in his pockets. 'Can't say. He had a hat and snood on and was pretty far. Bit wiry. Bit like a nonce.'

The presenter cleared their throat. 'And you retrieved the motorcycle alone?'

Mia stared at the screen, absorbing every detail, breathing slowly, and cursing Rami.

The teen rubbed his nose. 'Nah. Got my uncle, Wes, and his winch down. I was gonna dry the bike out and keep it, but I looked in the box on the back and under the McD's wrapper and first aid kit there was another compartment.'

Mia's eyes widened.

The teen continued. 'Found some wallets and a wedding ring. I recognised the names on the IDs in the wallet from the news of that dead fella.'

'*Missing*,' the presenter corrected. 'Missing man.'

The teen scratched inside his ear. 'Yeah, come on. He's proper dead. So, I called the police and gave them the wallets and the ring. There was no cash in them, or weed. Just the IDs, promise.' He looked sheepish.

The television turned off and Mia turned to Andrea, holding the remote control.

Andrea limped away, towards the front door. 'You have a visitor.'

Mia dragged her feet to the door, trying to calm herself so she wouldn't scream at Rami. He stood in the entrance looking haunted, his beanie nearly covering his eyes.

Andrea waited by the stairs, listening to the conversation.

'Can we go somewhere for a chat?' Rami asked Mia.

'Yes,' she replied.

Andrea approached the doorway and glared at Rami. 'I hope you work harder to keep your next partner, if anyone is idiotic enough to have you.'

'Mum...' Mia warned.

Rami sighed. 'Go fuck yourself, Andrea.'

'It's Mrs. Russo,' she corrected.

He stuck his middle finger up at her and walked away.

~

'Why couldn't you just leave it?' Mia huffed, struggling to face him.

She and Rami sat on a bench in Cambridge's Jesus Green park, in front of the empty, frost-covered skate park. The wind felt chillier and the skeletal trees more overbearing.

'I had to check. What if in the summer some people decide to picnic there and they find it? I was going to go back and dump a load of bags of bricks in the water to cover the bike. We can't outrun this. Everything we've done is like an unexploded bomb.'

Mia zoned out, scanning the area and considering which swear word to call him. Behind them were the fence and trees separating them from the currently out-of-use lido, and ahead was grass, trees, and the path. Aside from a couple of dog walkers and two middle-aged women heading towards the tennis courts, this area was Mia and Rami's.

Mia rubbed her gloved hands together. 'They're going to be looking for you now.'

'I was well covered on the bicycle. 'I'm more worried about this.' He showed her his phone. It was a split-screen image on the *Eastern Daily Press* website from the night they dumped the motorcycle. Each half of the image was of the same frame, but at different times. The left side showed a fox in the foreground, and Rami's blurry figure on the motorcycle. It was such poor quality that it was impossible to work out it wasn't the dead man. 'Guess it's a good thing I wore the helmet and his clothes.'

The image on the right was taken twenty minutes later. Their car was caught, but again, the low-quality night capture made Mia a blur, and the cracked windscreen was hardly visible. It was clear it was a Toyota Corolla, but thankfully the side-on shot didn't show the license plate, the damaged side of the bumper or broken headlight.

'It's all over the news,' Rami said. 'Taken from a local's doorbell camera. They're asking if anyone who was in Belaugh the night he vanished has any information, and for the driver to come forward, in case they saw something. It's a witness appeal.'

Mia studied the photo again, and could barely make out the blurry Rocky Balboa bobblehead on the dashboard. 'Okay, so the driver isn't a suspect,' she pointed out.

'No. But could become one. And now it looks likely it's something more sinister than a fraudster or sex fiend running off. So, they may look a bit harder.' Rami huffed and put his phone away. He pulled his hat over his eyes. 'It's never going to end. And Jenny's convinced that Dale took the A47 out of Norwich. The only thing stopping her searching is that Dale's dodgy wife won't speak to her.'

'Fucking Jenny!' Mia clenched her fists. 'Busybody prick.'

Rami re-emerged from under his hat. 'If the search goes onto the A47 and far enough along it, she might connect our car and us to it.'

'So, you keep her close to see what she's doing. Try to throw her off somehow,' Mia said.

He exhaled. 'I just want it to go away.' He put his head in his hands.

The chilly wind blew against them.

'Me too,' she replied, watching the women headed to the tennis courts stretch by a bench. That's what she wanted, to go back to a life where she could make plans with people.

'About the baby...' Rami said.

'I'm keeping it,' Mia stated.

Rami nodded. 'I wasn't suggesting... I was going to say that if it is mine – because I *will* be getting a paternity test – then I want to be part of its life.'

'Honestly, Rami, if you want a paternity test, go for it. But it's your child, as much as I wish it wasn't. I don't need you involved. I'll be very happy to raise the kid on my own, but it's yours.'

He sighed. 'Yeah. Suppose you've nothing to gain from this.'

'Exactly.' She shuffled. 'It's about our child, not us. So, we need to work out custody rights when we go through the divorce.' Despite Rami's annoying qualities, she couldn't deny that he would be a dedicated father.

He nodded. 'Yeah. If you still haven't, I'd be happy to file the petition, especially in light of the Wilfred revelation,' he said.

She half-smiled, tempted to say something to knock his newfound confidence, but she decided to let him have his boost. 'I'll do it,' Mia said.

Rami stood up. 'Okay, but get on with it. And I will be mentioning the adultery, and fighting for everything I can get.'

She knew that as soon as the process began his bullishness would fade. 'Do whatever makes you feel powerful, Rami.'

'We don't all crave power.' Rami put his hands in his pockets. 'I'll keep you updated about Jenny. I was talking to Lyn, and the most important thing is that our child is loved.'

'What has Lyn got to do with anything?' Mia asked.

'We're... together,' Rami said, gazing at the grass.

Mia chuckled. 'You and Lyn? As in Lyn for the win, Lyn? Lyn, as deep as a puddle, Lyn?' She laughed.

Rami tutted. 'She's the best person I've ever met.'

'She's a head case, Rami, with the same pattern for everyone. Let me guess: it's refreshingly intense at the moment, with excitement, openness without boundaries, and jumping into everything, just being free. She's probably already said she loves you.'

Rami wiped his nose on his coat sleeve and didn't answer.

'It'll fade,' Mia said bluntly. 'I know things were shit with us, but that's no reason to become more of a fantasist. She'll be bored of you within two months; probably sooner. She'll become distant, then you'll get insecure and start acting weird, then your great romance will be in the river along with the corpse. So many of her panicked exes would find me on social media and message me, asking if they'd done anything to upset her. She creates needy wrecks.'

'Is that when you stepped in and shagged them?' Rami asked.

'Fuck off,' she replied.

'Good chat.' He stood up. 'The baby comes first, but we're not okay.' He walked away.

Mia huffed. The cruelty of her infidelity wasn't lost on her. She called after him. 'I am sorry, Rami. I can't turn back time, but I mean it.'

Rami turned, hurt etched on his face. 'Sorry because you got caught?'

Mia stood and approached him. 'Because there were better ways to handle being in a dying marriage.'

Rami swallowed. He poked his trainer toes against the gravel. 'It's just... nobody deserves...' He choked up.

'I'm a piece of shit,' she said. 'I know. And you might not believe me, but I didn't want to hurt you. I've made shit choice after shit choice, and it's because I'm not happy. I'm sorry you got caught up in my shit.'

Rami blinked his tears in.

Mia never wanted another relationship. She wanted no say in another man's emotional wellbeing.

She gazed at the empty skate park behind Rami and imagined the dead man's body sliding down the ramp, his bloody head wound streaking the timber. Her eyes widened.

'What's wrong?' Rami asked.

'I'm still seeing visions of him.' She winced and looked away from the skate park. 'I don't know what to do.'

Rami huffed and looked momentarily sympathetic. 'I'm here for the baby, not to be your emotional crutch.'

He trudged away.

39

SURPLUS TO REQUIREMENTS

RAMI

Rami lifted his rucksack and laptop bag into the boot of Lyn's car, which was parked outside his house.

He scanned the cul-de-sac, which he loved to look at during the night. It was always calming under the moonlight, if the clouds weren't blocking the moon.

Jenny's house was decorated for an alternative Christmas, and Jenny, in her slippers and colourful robe, was in what looked like a tense conversation with the police.

A life-sized model of a sorcerer in a Father Christmas-style cloak and hat towered over DI Amini, who pointed aggressively at Jenny.

DS Opoku stood next to a stuffed, snarling ogre dressed in elf greens.

Lyn exited Rami's house and closed the front door, drawing his attention away from Jenny. She spotted Rami's rucksack in the car boot and smiled. 'That all your clothes for two weeks?'

He shrugged. 'I don't care for style. I only wear clothes to avoid offending people with my nudity.'

'Don't do it on my account.' She smiled and closed the boot. 'Come on then, roomie.' She kissed him, got into the front seat and turned the engine on.

Rami took his house in. Could he really move? He had always seen his life playing out here, with Mia, as a family.

He would miss the connection to his nan, but she would be pleased for him whatever he did, as long as he was happy. While the house held memories of her, the most important ones were in his mind, and in how he lived every day. The way he huffed whenever the weather changed was exactly what she did. His need to hoover every three days had her regimented living stamped all over it, and she would be equally worried and proud by the amount of salt he put on his food. The memories weren't in the walls; they were in his veins, in his actions. Plus, the pain of Mia's deeds still lingered. With the baby, Mia would be in his life, and they had to share their secret, but at least at Lyn's house he didn't have to think about Mia every time he stepped through the front door. The best way to move on was to move out. Then hopefully the hurt would pass.

Rami approached the passenger door and opened it, concerned with what Mia had said. What if this incredible feeling with Lyn was just momentary? Their relationship did feel special, but was he tricking himself again? He had managed to deceive himself into thinking he and Mia could salvage what was awful, so was something similar happening here? Was it his grief, or fear of being alone messing with him? His chest ached.

He pushed Mia's miserable words away, certain she was being manipulative. Lyn was an honest soul with no agenda. Everything between them so far suggested this was a unique relationship.

DI Amini and DS Opoku drove away in their police car, waving at Lyn and Rami.

Lyn smiled as she waved, but muttered under her breath, 'Wankers.'

Rami chuckled and entered the car. The heat from the air-con comforted him.

Jenny limped towards them.

Rami opened the passenger window. 'Was that a friendly visit?' He smiled.

'A good old-fashioned slap on the wrist for trying to talk to Trinity. Can I?' She gestured to the back seat. 'I can feel icicles forming on my nipples.'

'Get in,' Lyn said.

She entered and Rami closed his window.

'Oh, that heat feels lovely.' Jenny shuffled to the middle of the back seat. Her face was between Lyn's and Rami's. 'Thanks to them my investigator mate's stopped talking to me.'

'Sorry,' Rami said, dancing inside.

Jenny scoffed. 'I even offered Trinity cash for a five-minute chat, but she spat at me. That woman is pure-bred awfulness.'

The dancing became a full-on rave.

'But, I did find something,' Jenny said.

The police shut the rave down.

Lyn waved a hand, refusing. 'Jen, babe, I appreciate every-thing you've put into this, but I'm kind of done.'

Rami held Lyn's hand.

Lyn angled herself to get closer to Jenny. 'You've been my hero. But I want to move on. If he's dead, I'm sad for his kids, but I'm fine. And, if he's alive, there's no way I'm chatting to him again. I've got closure, and that's the knowledge that he was a tit. So...' She shrugged. 'I don't want to be pulled into this anymore. It's bad enough with the shit I got off the press, online, and from randoms in the street.'

Rami stroked her hand.

Jenny squeezed Lyn's shoulder. 'I'm sorry for all you've had to deal with, Lyn.'

She smiled. 'The new year's coming, and I'm already on a fresh start.' She looked at Rami, then back at Jenny. 'I'm taking him to Turkey in January to get away. And you and Iris have got the baby to think about. Let the police do it their slow, useless way, and we can all get on with looking forward to next year.'

'I get it,' Jenny said. 'I admire your positivity.' She leaned back.

Rami took deep breaths, trying not to think about the something Jenny had found.

He turned to Lyn. 'You sure you don't want to know?'

Lyn shrugged. 'Don't care, really. What's it going to do?'

'Maybe one day you will care,' he said.

Jenny raised a hand. 'This isn't definitive, but it could point to something.'

Lyn huffed. 'Fine. Not like it'll matter. But, seeing as you put the work in, J.'

Jenny leaned forward again. 'So, DS Silly Sausage and DI Idiot Man...' She took a breath. 'I can't wait until my kid's old enough so I can swear again. Anyway, they're convinced that Dale went from Trinity's to another lover who hasn't come forward – one in Belaugh, thanks to where they found the motorcycle. They think this mystery lover did something. But, that's fancy thinking. The last image they have of Dale on his bike before the doorbell camera footage in Belaugh is at the BP petrol garage in Plumstead, so they assume he's turned off the A47 and onto the A1270.'

Rami nodded. 'Okay. Why does that seem wrong?'

'Because, Lyn, you told me that he was on his way to you after he called. And if you're him, living a lie, would you want any suspicion? He'd be doing exactly what he said, to keep up appearances, because in all these stories that have come out, none of the women suspected him of being a wrong 'un. Everyone was tricked, because he was very good at what he was doing.'

Lyn took a breath. 'Tosser.'

Rami squeezed her hand. 'It's okay.'

Jenny raised a finger. 'Now, that bloody A47, Yarmouth Road, there's sod-all in cameras, despite my appeals to the council for years, but, what was found with his motorcycle? A McD's burger wrapper. I popped my head into the one off the A47, flashed the manager my dodgy CID badge.' She chuckled. 'I got it made years ago when the police rejected me, just to get close to some investigations. There's a shady fella who runs a falafel van near Anglia Square who can get anything. Anyway. I flashed the badge, mentioned the case, scared the shit out...' She blinked. 'Put the fear in him, and got him to show me the CCTV.'

The tension in Rami's head was close to making his skull cave in.

Jenny smiled. 'Our fella was there, chomping down a burger, on his way to Lyn's, a good hour before this stuff in Belaugh. So, I think something has happened along that road.'

Rami nodded. 'He could've got a call and turned back.'

Lyn stared ahead, not reacting.

'Yeah, he could have,' Jenny said. 'And something could have happened on the way up the road, but I'll be sure to find out before the police do and humiliate them. Show Amini he needs to work harder, not just find the easiest way out of something.' Jenny squeezed Lyn's shoulder. 'Sorry to bring it up again.'

'It's fine,' Lyn said, but her eyes welled up. 'Him being missing doesn't get me. It's the fact I didn't see what an arse flake he was.'

Rami rubbed her hand. 'We've all fallen for bad people. It doesn't mean there's something wrong with you.'

Lyn smiled at Rami.

Jenny shuffled towards the car door. 'I'll leave you to it. Plus, I need to go and pretend that Iris' couscous salad tastes of something other than sand.'

'Thanks, J,' Lyn said.

Rami opened his door. 'I'll help you to your house, Jenny.'

'You're a good 'un, Rami Harami,' she replied.

Rami exited the car and opened Jenny's door, helping her out of the car and to her house. 'Look, it feels weird saying this, Jenny, because you're doing an amazing thing, but, maybe you should leave it. Even though Lyn says she doesn't care, I know it bugs her.'

Jenny tightened her robe. 'I know, and I'm sorry. But, if there's a murderer, do you really want them out there?' She grabbed her key from her robe pocket.

Hard to argue. 'You're right. Just, maybe tell me how it's going and I can break things to her in gentler ways.' He looked at the car, where Lyn was turned away.

Jenny nodded. 'Fair point. Can't imagine what it's like inside her head right now.'

Rami scratched his cheek. 'At some point she'll be fine and she'll look at the fact that in this rubbish she gained a friend in you.'

Jenny smiled. 'Hopefully. You still on for Christmas shopping tomorrow to chat through my story outline?'

'Can't wait,' he replied.

'Until tomorrow.' She entered her house and closed the door.

Rami dragged his feet back to the car. He opened the door and Lyn was crying, but with a smile on her face.

'Is this a situation?' Rami asked.

Lyn beamed at him. 'That Lionel Richie video, the electric guitar cover. It went viral and he's only gone and seen it. His people have contacted my agent! She just emailed.'

'That's incredible!' Rami said.

Lyn's grin shone. 'Still a lot to sort through, but it sounds pretty solid. He's offered for me to join him on the European leg of his tour. Three months from the middle of Jan! Says he wants to throw a few stylistic curveballs into his set.'

'Amazing!' Rami said. He had never seen her this excited.

'And don't worry about the holiday to Turkey. We can reschedule that. April?'

'Let's see,' Lyn said, elated. 'Who knows what might come after it.'

'Of course,' Rami smiled. 'I'm so happy for you. We'll make things work around this.'

Lyn drove them out of Norwich and towards her home in Sheringham. She spent most of the time talking to her agent, then had Rami play her Lionel Richie's greatest hits.

As Lyn swayed her head along to 'Stuck on You', Rami watched the dark frosty fields blur past the window. Three months apart was a long time. 'Hey,' he said. 'I could come with you on tour? Not like I'm that busy.'

Lyn nodded. 'Yeah, but I'll be moving around so fast and practising, we won't have much time to spend doing stuff. I don't think you'd like it.'

'But, we'd be together.' That's what mattered.

'Let's go through the dates when we're home,' she replied. 'Maybe you come for a few. I've got to be social, and if you're there I'll be worried you're bored or lonely, so I won't be fully present, you know?'

He swallowed. 'Yeah, we'll make it work.' He stared at the empty fields as Mia's words about Lyn getting bored of him attacked. 'It's such a great opportunity for you.'

She screamed her excitement. 'This could be life-changing, Rami! Life changing!'

He tried to silence Mia's voice, but it grew louder.

40

REUNITED AND IT FEELS AWFUL

MIA

Mia wrapped her scarf around her face, then pulled her hood up, leaving only her eyes to feel the night's chilly wind. She pulled her gloves tighter.

She couldn't risk being spotted walking through the cul-de-sac, so she walked along the quiet roads behind the houses. She moved into the middle of the street, hoping to avoid any doorbell cameras.

The street was mostly quiet, with the odd bleak Christmas gesture: if it wasn't a dangling piece of tinsel on a withering plant, it was a semi-deflated snowman, or some barely functioning fairy lights.

Mia reached the weed-covered alley on Ranworth Road and quietly crept along to where another alley passed the backs of the gardens in her cul-de-sac. She found her house and crouched, sneaking along as she counted gardens, arriving at Jenny's wooden fence. She had expected to see some tacky decorations, but it seemed Jenny had front-loaded those.

She thought she saw someone at the end of the alley, but it

must have been her imagination. 'Fuck,' she muttered, hoping nobody would be out.

She scanned the upstairs windows of the surrounding houses, checking for activity. It was wonderfully quiet.

Even in the frost, sweat smothered her. This was a terrible idea, but still better than sitting back and waiting. Rami was too passive.

Mia reached into her pocket and took out a handful of soft dog treats that she had shoved waxy blocks of rat poison into. She peered through a crack in the fence, eyeing sections of Jenny's tidy AstroTurfed garden.

Jenny only had herself to blame. If she had kept her nose out of Mia's business, Mia wouldn't need to distract her.

Mia reached over the fence and moved along it, dropping the toxic treats.

She checked her pockets, found a loose piece of rat poison and chucked that over the fence. Good riddance to an annoying dog. She didn't tell Rami as he would've definitely stopped her. For some weird reason he was fond of Jenny and her creature.

She wiped her gloves against her trousers and turned to leave, but a large figure in a puffer jacket with their hood up stood at the end of the path, blocking it. Judging by their size, they were male.

She wanted to turn and run, but her legs froze.

The man didn't move. Maybe she was imagining the dead man again. She closed her eyes and took a couple of slow breaths.

She opened her eyes, but the man was still there.

He pulled his hood down, allowing the moonlight to shine on him.

Wilfred.

Mia's body shuddered. She steadied herself and marched towards him.

He wore a smug expression, and he didn't step aside.

'Move, Wilfred,' she said. 'Follow me again and I'll call the police.' She hoped that would remind him who had the power here.

He stepped aside.

She hurried past him.

'I know what you did,' he said.

'Whatever.' She continued into the middle of the road, feeling more secure.

'I saw Throcky in the photo on the news. I know, Mia.'

She stopped and turned around. 'I don't know what you're talking about.'

Wilfred approached her and checked the houses around them. He whispered, 'The night it all changed. We spoke around nine-fifty, while you were at the BP station in Acle. You said you were going to drive Rami home, then go to Lyn's and come to me. But then your car is in Belaugh around ten past eleven. Why?'

Mia tasted acid and blinked away any emotion that tried to escape through her eyes. She had to hold her position. 'I think your mind is playing tricks on you, Wilfred.'

Wilfred reached for her hand, but she pulled it away.

He pointed at her. 'Then you called me around midnight saying you couldn't come to the hotel, blaming Rami being sad, then you blamed it on his mum having cancer, even though she's been dead over a decade. I know what you did.'

Mia scanned the area, worried to be in the vicinity of her dog-destroying crime. 'You're obviously creating fantasies to deal with our break-up, but there's no substance here, Wilfred. Please, I'm concerned about you. This isn't healthy.' She walked away.

'Okay,' he said. 'Maybe I'll just tell the police what I know, like a good Norfolk citizen trying to help with the search for the poor, missing man. Then, they can decide whether I'm deluded or not. Maybe they can investigate Acle, start connecting the car to the two places. Maybe they'll call you for a chat and you can tell them they're imagining things.'

Mia stopped and clenched her fists.

'I only want to talk,' Wilfred said.

Mia sat on Wilfred's sofa, holding a cup of tea, not entirely convinced he hadn't laced it with something. She positioned herself so she could quickly leave should she feel any more threatened.

His knee was about a centimetre from hers.

Her skin itched.

He smiled, excited. 'I get it now. You were scared to tell me, because of how bad it is, but I can handle it. We can deal with this secret together.'

There was a time when Wilfred saying that would have been her dream, but now that she knew him, at his core, those words were like handcuffs. 'I wanted to tell you, Wilfred, that day by the lake. But then you were so happy, because you'd told Samira the truth. You had this lightness, and I couldn't take that away from you with another secret.'

He took her hand.

She wanted to pull it away, but needed to figure out how to handle this. How to handle him.

He pressed her hand to his cheek. 'But, that lightness was because of you. You are the lightness in me, Mia. Now, we can finally be together. And, to be quite honest, judging by the news reports, that man was a champion fiend, swinging it around in every village he passed through.'

Mia gently pulled her hand away. 'Wilfred, it's not that simple. This whole thing has wrecked my mind. And Rami's involved, too.'

Wilfred waved his hand around dismissively. 'I can handle

Rami; he's a pussycat. In another life he would've made a good low status friend.'

Mia placed her cup of tea on the table and stood. 'I need time, Wilfred. This is a lot.'

'Okay,' he said. 'You can have time.'

'Thank you,' she said, desperate to get out of his house.

'You can have time, here.' Wilfred's face darkened.

'What?' Mia's chest tightened. She could grab the hot tea and throw it in his face.

'You will live here now.' He smirked. 'And if you refuse, I'll tell the police.' He leaned back. 'You think I'm being cruel, but you've been through a big thing. As you say, your mind isn't right, but I can help you come out of the other side.'

He was a full-on psychopath.

He patted the sofa cushion next to him. 'Rami had me watch *The Shawshank Redemption*. And it's like when Morgan Freeman says that Andy Dufresne crawled through a river of shit and came out clean on the other side. I will pull you out of that river of shit.'

Mia backed towards the door. 'This is blackmail, Wilfred.' She pulled the handle, but the door was locked. Her body numbed and she walked towards the living room window and opened it. 'You're sick.'

He held up his phone. 'You sure you want to leave?'

Mia stopped. 'Wilfred...'

He placed his phone down on his thigh. 'I suggest you sit, and in time, I promise, we'll be back to being the greatest double act there ever was.'

Mia stared at Wilfred. He had taken everything Mia had hoped for about love, put it in a tin, shaken it around, and then shat on it.

41

THE PROTECTOR

RAMI

Rami and Jenny walked on the upper level of the Chantry Place shopping centre. It was busy, but not so busy as to make Christmas Eve feel overwhelming.

Fairy lights and tinsel snaked around every handrail and doorframe. A reindeer sled made out of blinking lights was next to the massive Christmas tree standing in the middle of the shopping centre, rising through its three floors.

Charity workers dressed as Father Christmas threw fake snow around, dancing and singing. All that was missing was Cliff Richard belting out 'Mistletoe and Wine'.

Jenny stopped and leaned on the railings. 'Sorry,' she said. 'Just need a minute.' She rubbed her knee. 'Wish bionic limbs would hurry up and become mainstream.'

Rami smiled. 'We're not in a rush.'

'You're right about it not being too rammed,' Jenny said.

'See. You let everyone go in the weeks leading up to it, pressured by ads and discounts. They all fight, push, make Christmas very un-Christmassy, and then on Christmas Eve, it's just panicked partners and the smarter ones among us picking up the pieces.' He gestured to the shops. 'Obviously stock's an issue, but there's so much out there we'll always find something.'

Jenny puffed her cheeks out and exhaled. 'It'd help if I knew what to get Iris,' she said. 'Impossible to buy for her. Got her a scarf last year, and she smiled, but in her eyes I saw a flash of divorce. Maybe I'll get something for Ballula, instead. She's been a bit poorly.'

'Oh no, is she okay?' Rami asked.

'Probably ate something she shouldn't have. Hopefully it passes quickly.' She huffed.

'Maybe she needs more belly rubs,' Rami said.

Jenny smiled. 'Well, she'll get her wish as I'll be home more. I've had enough.'

'Enough of what?' Rami asked, hopeful.

Jenny picked up some fake snow and chucked it from the upper level onto a group of shady teens below, then hid. 'I popped my head into some places on Yarmouth Road, flashing my fake badge. They've all sent me CCTV footage from the night Dale disappeared.'

Rami massaged his neck, trying to steady the shakes.

'I started looking through it, but then I just stopped,' she said.

'How come?' Rami scratched his chest.

'The guy's a wrong 'un, right?'

'One of the wrongest wrong 'uns ever to have wronged,' he replied.

'In my mind, he's been killed. No two ways. But, whoever did it isn't some crazed serial killer. They're most likely a rejected lover, partner of someone he fiddled about with, or someone he defrauded. And – it's hard to say this, but maybe the world is better off without that man in it slinging hurt every which way.'

Rami nodded. 'That sounds so much harsher at Christmas time, Jenny.'

Jenny threw some fake snow in the air and let it drift down on them. 'There's doing right by the book, then there's knowing what's right in the situation. I'll leave it to PC Prat and Detective Dopey to fumble their way through it. But, it was also what you said in your feedback about my story outline. About obsession.'

'The consequences of being obsessed not coming through enough?' he asked.

Jenny limped on and Rami followed. 'Exactly. And I'll sort that out, but what about in my life? I've been obsessed with finding out what happened. I said it was to help Lyn, but it's actually for me, and it's totally selfish. To get one up on the police for rejecting me, and...' She choked up.

'You okay?' He took a crumpled tissue out of his pocket. 'I promise it's not used; it's just old.'

Jenny took it and nodded appreciation. 'Fifteen years ago, I was in a hit-and-run with my sister. I got the bad leg, she got the body bag.'

Rami gasped. 'Oh, shit. I'm sorry.'

Jenny shrugged. 'I've never accepted that the police gave it their all. It's why I wanted to become a copper. To be better and to care about cases as if I were the one feeling the pain of them.' She took a long breath. 'So, I've doubled down on this to prove I can be better than they were.'

Rami flicked fake snow off his shoulder. 'From what I've seen you're way better than them.'

She raised a palm. 'I know it's an unhealthy way to be trying to make up for it. So, I thought about stuff. What if me limping about and bugging people winds Iris up? She's got the patience of a saint, but I've been testing it. And what if the police get so sick of me investigating that they charge me with interfering? Having those two dimwits at my door is not something I want on a regular basis. And what if I bring danger to my home and pain to others? The fella was dodgy, and could've kept dodgier company.' Her shoulders slumped, as though she were losing her sense of purpose.

'And you've got the baby coming,' Rami said.

'Exactly. Maybe it's all this Christmas bollocks... stuff. But, I feel like I should be looking towards life, instead of poking around in death. DS Useless and DI Imbecile can do their thing. I'm done.' She linked arms with Rami.

His heart felt full. He could live and let go of fear. 'Well, with more time to write I can't wait to read your script. You're ready to start it with the outline notes in mind.' He stopped to glance into the window of Pandora, the jewellery shop. He stared at a tiny passport charm dangling from the bracelet in the window.

Jenny chuckled. 'Ah, jewellery. The easy gift when you've not got a clue. Unless you're married to Iris who hates everything.'

Rami smiled. 'No. It's not that. I got Mia the passport charm when we moved from London to Norwich as a joke, because she always complained it was too far.'

Jenny smirked. 'Sign of a good joke, having to explain it.'

Rami chuckled. He bought the charm with his first teaching payment. At the time Mia loved the gift. He exhaled his feelings of regret. 'I'm getting Lyn a record player.'

'Sounds like you know her well.' Jenny patted his shoulder.

'I think so.' He looked away from the charms, trying to shake Mia out of his mind.

Jenny poked his arm. 'Puke the burden out, Rami. Otherwise you'll get stomach cramps.'

He was grateful to have grown closer to Jenny through this bizarre time. Her approach to life made her so easy to connect with. 'I guess I'm a bit scared. Since Lyn's had this tour come in, I've dropped down on her list of concerns. I'm worried she might think this is just a temporary thing.' Mia had stabbed her cruel words into his brain. He found himself analysing everything Lyn did or said with a suspicion that she was about to dump him.

'Can't live in fear, Rami. Follow where the feelings take you, or you'll live half a life. Unless the feelings lead to something illegal, of course.' She fixed him with a faux stern look.

He smiled. 'Thanks, Jenny. I was going to ask if you thought it was weird that we were considering moving in with each other so soon – should all go well – but I guess I know the answer.'

Jenny nodded. 'Weird is holding back because of outside views. And she's lovely. Fifty million times better than that frowning cow.'

'That's the mother of my child you're talking about,' he said with a smirk.

'Well, I hope the kid turns out like you. And I hope mine turns out like the sperm donor: a Mediterranean artist.'

Rami laughed, soaking in the warm glow of the Christmas lights and the sense of freedom.

They continued walking through the shopping centre and out of the exit, passing under Christmas trees in the shape of arches, made entirely out of lights. Rami's steps were lighter and everything seemed... good. Sure, he was anxious about Lyn, but this time of year provided hope. He pushed his paranoia away.

They walked towards St. Giles Street, through the festive town centre, passing students in Christmas fancy dress doing the walk of shame.

They approached Richer Sounds.

Jenny let go of Rami's arm. 'I'm really glad I hired you, you know?'

'Me too, the money's been a godsend,' he replied.

Jenny laughed. 'Right, you're fired.'

Rami smiled. 'You're a hero, Jenny. And a great friend.' He hugged her. It felt strange that so many good things had come from running Dale over.

She patted him on the back. 'Alright, that's enough, you sap. Go get the gift that'll get you laid.'

Rami's phone rang. 'It's Mia.'

'Just reject it,' Jenny said.

'It could be about the baby.' He answered the phone, and Mia's crying set alarm bells off.

~

Rami, frustrated, and Mia, crying her eyes out, walked up and down Mia's mum's Japanese-style garden. Andrea probably knew nothing about Japanese style, but it was all for show to distract from her miserable soul.

Rami shook his head. 'How do I know you're not just trying to get something out of me?'

'What would I have to gain and what do you even have to give?' Mia stared at him with a hatred reserved for canvassing politicians. 'He knows, Rami. He fucking knows.'

Rami shrugged. 'Well, he won't say anything because he doesn't want to lose you, so... enjoy.' Rami walked towards his shopping bags by the sliding doors to the kitchen. Andrea hovered inside like a grumpy ghost.

'He's imprisoning me, Rami,' she pleaded.

He turned to her. She looked so small and pathetic. Her confident aura shattered. 'A couple of hours a day in the yard looks good on you.' He picked up his shopping bags, regretting his cold words, but wanting to show her how hurt he still was.

Mia walked towards him, her hands clasped, desperate. 'He dropped me here and is picking me up at six. He's forced me to put Find My on everything. He basically owns me.' She cleared her throat and trembled.

Rami thought his well of sympathy had dried up, been filled with concrete and boarded over, but seeing her like this nudged the part of him that felt protective. It reminded him of the times their marriage was at its strongest, which was when Mia was vulnerable and needed rescuing. Like when she was struggling with her misogynistic boss at work, or when her aunt died, or when she had Covid. When she felt good about things, their marriage was terrible. Despite the cruelty, Rami took it as a sign that deep down, Mia found safety in him.

His shoulders slumped and he sighed. 'Just call his bluff.'

Mia stared at him, fear in her eyes. 'You want to risk that? If he can't have me he has nothing to lose.'

'Inflating your sense of importance.' He raised an apologetic hand.

'What about our baby?' she asked. 'Wilfred has this knowledge. Whether he cashes it in today or tomorrow, he has it. Then, our baby will be taken away. And if he's forcing himself into my life, he's in our baby's as well. And...' She closed her eyes.

'And what?' Rami asked, worried he already knew what she would say.

'I told him that... the baby was... to keep him on my side.'

'You...' Rami squeezed his eyes shut, his body tense. He didn't want that manipulative bastard anywhere near his child, let alone thinking he was the actual father.

Mia stepped closer. 'I'm sorry. I panicked.'

Rami stared at the grey sky. 'So, you had an affair with a psycho, and now you've basically handed my child to him. Do you want to give him my house, too?'

'I was desperate.' Mia wiped her face with her hands, then spoke quietly. 'I think there's a way to solve it.'

'So solve it.' Rami glanced into the kitchen and saw Andrea shake her head and leave the room. Probably off to sacrifice a virgin.

Mia took breaths to calm herself. 'It needs both of us. As well as Wilfred, there's the body, still undiscovered, but with people looking harder and getting closer. You're right. We will never outrun this. We have two guns pointing as us, and even if Jenny has stopped she might get curious again. Please, Rami. I need your help. We need your help.' She looked to her belly.

They hadn't even made it to the twelve-week scan.

But, it still hit him how much he wanted this baby. He remembered the scan where he first saw Sarah's spine. He couldn't wait to see that spine in the world, to touch it and to hold her. He welled up. This was a second chance, to see his child grow, to witness their first little toothless smile and see their personality develop. To cut their delicate little fingernails to stop them scratching themselves, and give them baths. He and Mia were robbed of the little things and more with Sarah, only able to experience them in their imaginations.

They had to protect what was there. Their baby hadn't had an affair. It hadn't mowed anyone down. It hadn't lied or hurt people. It was innocent in this world.

Rami looked at Mia's teary face. 'How?'

Mia nodded, appreciative. 'You're not going to like it, but unless you have any other ideas, I think it's the only way.'

42

THE MOST HUMANE WAY TO KILL
A DEER

MIA

Mia, sitting in the passenger seat of Wilfred's Tesla Roadster, gripped her handbag as Wilfred pulled into Rami's garage. He sang along to Mariah Carey's inappropriately upbeat, 'All I Want for Christmas is You,' which played on the radio.

Mia was exhausted from how much she had been shaking. The tension was in every joint and every movement. Any time Wilfred moved, she flinched.

She pressed the remote button on her keys to close the stuttering garage shutter.

Wilfred turned the engine off.

He smiled. 'We should get a little Throcky for this car, and I'll get you on the insurance once things have settled.'

She forced a smile. 'A Throcky would be great.'

'I know.' He grinned. 'That's why I already got one.' He took a Rocky Balboa bobblehead from his blazer pocket, reached out and stuck it on the dashboard in front of her.

She wanted to rip it off and jam it into his mouth, then

298

stamp on it until it destroyed his teeth and ripped through his throat.

Wilfred grinned. 'I'm so glad you're coming around to this idea. I guarantee, things will feel as they used to soon. Especially with our little Throcksickle.' He touched her belly.

Mia shuddered. She had convinced him that by some miracle they had conceived, even while using protection. He took it as a sign of his potency. 'We're so lucky.' She wished she could vomit lava all over him.

'I can't wait to sing "Throck-a-Bye Baby" to it.' He smirked.

Mia half-smiled.

Wilfred frowned. 'I expected more for that.' He opened the door. 'Right, where's this box of baby stuff?'

'In the loft,' she said, exiting the car and hoping her plan would work. She had told Rami that her side of the plan was to play along with Wilfred a little longer, while gathering evidence to get him charged with false imprisonment. It was the only way Rami would agree to his part. However, if she could go through with her real plan, Wilfred and his car would be at the bottom of the river in what looked like a suicide. With his broken marriage and Mia's rejection, it would add up. The obsessive messages he had sent which shook her soul now presented an opportunity.

She had bought sleeping pills from the pharmacy earlier to poison Wilfred with an overdose, but he had checked her handbag as soon as he picked her up and tossed them away, demanding she use natural remedies while pregnant. Now, her only hope was that the medicine she had left in the ensuite bathroom was still there. She could sneak it back in her underwear to use later. It was the only way to be free of him. He had too much control with what he knew. Mia thought about his children for a moment, but they'd be better off without this awful man in their lives. His wife would likely be suspected, which would also help.

She unlocked the door connecting the garage to the hallway.

She glanced into the kitchen and living room area. Rami had removed every trace of her. What if he had removed the medication from the cabinet? He wouldn't. There was no point. It's not as if medicine was a reminder of her.

Wilfred followed. 'I don't see why we need to collect old baby things when we can just buy new ones.'

'They have sentimental value, and I want to get them before Rami sells them,' Mia replied.

Wilfred shrugged. 'Lead the way.'

Mia dragged her feet upstairs. Although her mother was religious, Mia had avoided putting too much belief in things she couldn't control, but she found herself quietly praying that this would work. 'The crate is at the back of the loft unless Rami moved it.' She reached for the loft hatch.

'I've got it.' He opened it. 'Don't over-exert yourself.' He pulled the ladder down.

'Thanks.' She forced a smile. 'While you get it I'm going to use the toilet.' She turned around.

'Wait,' he said.

Mia steeled herself and turned back to him.

'A kiss first.'

Mia froze as his lips met hers. He groaned his approval, while she tried not to retch. It was as though she had never been kissed before, but rather than being excited and her heart fluttering, she was terrified. His lips were like a cold net and his tongue a rusty chain.

He finally pulled away.

She entered her old bedroom and trembled towards the ensuite.

'Your phone and handbag.' He followed and held his hand out.

Mia passed everything over and huffed. 'You want to watch me piss as well?' she said defiantly.

He raised an accepting hand. 'Not really the kind of thing that gets me rocking, or Throck—'

She entered the bathroom and slammed the door to cut him off. She locked it, then washed her mouth out in the sink, trying to remove every trace of him. She sat on the closed toilet lid and took slow breaths, trying to calm herself. She relived their affair, regretting every minute of it. Moments of absolute joy were drowned in the gloom of his controlling, obsessive personality.

How did she not see shades of the psycho within? It was because of Rami. Had he not sucked the life out of her like some kind of happiness vampire, then maybe she wouldn't have blindly thrown herself towards Wilfred. Her marriage, and hatred for the path her life was on, had left her a shell, desperate to escape. If it wasn't Wilfred, she would've fallen in love with the postman or maybe even a cousin.

She stood up and steadied herself. She stared at the mirrored cabinet doors.

She opened them.

Empty.

Fuck.

43

THERE'S ALWAYS A CHOICE

RAMI

Rami dragged himself into Lyn's house and placed his locked suitcase and bag of Christmas presents next to her sea of shoes. He removed his trainers, which had felt like slabs of concrete for the entire journey. His mind turned, trying to work out what to do.

Lyn approached him, wearing a green sleeveless midi dress. She became increasingly beautiful every time he looked at her, as the kind soul within shone through her already stunning appearance. 'Hello, gorgeous,' she said.

She wrapped her arms around him and his body felt light, before pain akin to being dropped stomach-first onto a bollard shot through him.

She kissed him.

He looked her up and down, 'Wow.'

'I look great, don't I?'

'I was commenting on the decorations.' Rami smiled, masking the pain in his heart.

She laughed. 'Muppet. Get this on.' She grabbed a Father

Christmas hat from the console table and placed it over his head.

He fought back tears. He didn't have to do it, but what other choice did he have?

'You okay?' she asked.

'Yeah, just tired.' He gazed over the decorations to distract himself. They were almost more impressive than the city centre Christmas lights. A huge Christmas tree dominated the corner, while an inflatable snowman guarded the sliding doors to the garden. There were full stockings everywhere and so much tinsel it was hard to see the wall. Enough for him to make a noose out of to end his miserable life.

He did not have to do it.

Maybe there was another option. If he told Lyn the truth about Dale, she might understand, want to be with him even more, and together they could find a solution. The search for Dale was getting closer, even with Jenny stopping her investigation, but it didn't mean the truth would be discovered. Rami could have it all, a relationship with Lyn, and raise his child, if he could just trust her and have faith the police would fail.

He cast his eye over the collage of photos that once had Mia in them. She had been relocated to her rightful home in the bin, and replaced with photos of Rami and Lyn from the last few weeks. They included: The pair of them outside the escape room after being kicked out, with their thumbs up. A photo of Rami asleep on the train to London as Lyn smiled and pointed at him. The two of them at Banham Zoo posing with the penguins. All memories of togetherness. Of two people who had hope of a future. Or, was he as replaceable as the photos that had been slid in and out of the frame over the years?

He took the wrapped presents out of his bag and placed them under the tree. There was a pile of gifts she had bought for him; way more than he deserved. She definitely cared about him, but how long would she care for? What if she started to get more tours? Would she realise it was a life that didn't suit a partner? Especially one who didn't have the independence to match hers?

She prepared the dinner table with crackers. Everything she had done for them showed effort, love, and care. 'Come on then,' she said. 'Let's get the party started.' She waved him over.

She was a magical human being. The love he felt growing between them must have been real, and diving in heart first was a wonderful way to live. Honesty over regret. But fear prodded his brain. His only reference points were his first girlfriend, who got bored of him, and Mia, who actively despised him.

He had made the selfish choice when they ran Dale over. This was a chance to put things right.

He walked over to Lyn, his body aching. 'Lyn, there's something I have to tell you.'

44

ALL I WANT FOR CHRISTMAS IS YOU DEAD

MIA

Wilfred carried the heavy plastic crate down the shaky loft ladder. Mia hoped he would fall, but he seemed to have the balance of a *Cirque du Soleil* artist.

'I take back my judgement, there's some rather snazzy baby goodies in here,' Wilfred said.

Mia's heart raced, unsure of what to do. This part of her plan was just as important as Rami's. Maybe she could search the other bathroom for medication, or the kitchen cabinets. Rami must have been on something to deal with being who he was.

Wilfred stared at Mia a moment, a flash of sympathy in his eyes. He placed the crate down on the carpet and took her handbag from the top of it. He handed it back to her, her phone inside it. 'Look, I'm sorry I made you feel like a prisoner. I don't want that. You can come and go as you please, as long as you have your location on, and as long as we agree times you'll be back. Just until I feel that reconnection.' He placed his palm against her heart, and she willed it to slow down. 'With time, your heart will feel more relaxed around me again. I promise. And you'll realise that everything I've done was right. You've been through something so gigantic that you don't have a full handle on your emotions, but trust me, we'll get there, together. Then the love will flow as it used to. Imagine what that first big hit of oxytocin returning is going to do for our little creation.' He smiled. 'Speaking of oxytocin, you know what helps release it?' He raised an eyebrow and touched her shoulder.

Mia shuddered, wishing the house would collapse on the pair of them. Every nerve was on fire and her head throbbed.

Wilfred cleared his throat and picked up the crate, straining. He stepped towards the top of the stairs and stopped. 'On the topic of sex. You should probably have an elective C-section. Samira went vaginal and for a while it was as though someone had closed down my favourite bistro.' He turned to walk down the stairs.

Mia screamed and lashed out, shoving him.

Wilfred's ankle buckled and he fell forward, his head smacking against the crate as it collided with a step. He tumbled down the stairs, the thud of the crate's contents clashing with the cracks of his bones.

He lay on the wooden floor, groaning through laboured breaths, his right ankle broken, and his left shoulder dislocated.

Mia's heart raced. She watched him squirm as blood trickled from his head wound. It reminded her of when she and Rami saw the body in the bushes.

'Mia...' Wilfred struggled to speak.

Shaking, she carefully walked down the stairs and stood over him. His arrogance buried beneath agony.

'Please, Mia. Everything... for you. And... cherub.' He reached for her with his left arm.

She pressed her boot into his ribs, and he groaned. She used to look at this man with the belief that they could spend the rest of their lives growing together and squeezing every ounce of joy from existence. She was excited for them to lift each other, to challenge each other, and to love each other.

She spat at him. 'The baby's not yours.'

Wilfred's eyes fluttered. 'Mia, please. Ambulance.'

His phone lay next to the wooden chest of baby items, a few feet from him.

Adrenaline pumped through Mia. She picked up his phone, turning it off.

He tried to push himself onto his left foot, but he fell and crashed head-first into the wall. 'Mia...' He closed his eyes, breathing heavily.

Everything she had been through since they killed Lyn's boyfriend weighed her down. She needed to finish the job. Rami would have no choice but to help her.

She dragged herself to the kitchen. She took her mobile phone out of her handbag, her trembling hands struggling to grip it. She opened the kitchen drawer, which contained various takeaway flyers and business cards.

She took DI Amini's card and dialled the number as she rushed past Wilfred, twitching on the floor.

'Mi... Mia...' he pleaded.

She marched upstairs to her old room and closed the door, hoping that when she opened it he'd be dead.

She glanced out of the window, where Jenny, weeping, loaded Ballula into the back of a pet ambulance. Jenny and Iris hastily entered the vehicle and it drove away.

Mia hoped Rami was holding up his end of the bargain. She prayed DI Amini would pick up.

He answered, the sound of a busy pub in the background. 'What?'

'Hi, DI Amini, it's Mia, Lyn's friend.'

'Who?' he answered.

'Lyn Fisher, the woman with the missing boyfriend. You came to our house and spoke to us a month ago about it.' She fell onto her old bed, staring at the ceiling.

'Oh, hello there! Of course I remember you. Merry Christmas, Mia! What are you up to?'

'Yeah. I think I know what happened to Dale.'

45

CRACKER FULL OF COAL

RAMI

'Bloody hell, Rami,' Lyn said, holding his hands over the kitchen breakfast bar. 'Your face screamed that it was something fatal.'

He smiled, his head boiling under the Father Christmas hat. 'Sorry, I didn't mean to sound so serious. But, I have been worried and we did say we'd be honest about everything. So, I didn't want to pretend.' He had been ready to tell her he and Mia had killed Dale, but the second she looked into his eyes the words retreated. He couldn't stand the thought of her looking at him any differently.

He was a coward.

'You don't have to be scared,' she said. 'Three months will whizz by, and I'll bring you out for some of the weekends. It'll be a piece of piss. What do you think's gonna happen? That I'll end up dating Lionel Richie?'

He laughed. 'Sorry; I know it's pathetic. My fear is that, as your career grows – because I know it will – I'll become something holding you back.'

It had sounded less pathetic in his head.

'If you keep fearing the worst you'll probably manifest it.' She walked around and sat on the breakfast bar, her legs either side of him. She pulled him in.

Rami nodded. 'You're right.' She deserved everything that this time of year was meant to offer. The hope, the joy, the kindness. Instead, she had Rami, the biggest lump of coal on earth. The actual biggest lump of coal weighed 15-tonnes and was Grade II listed in Bedwellty Park, Tredegar, but he was the biggest metaphorical lump of coal.

'There is something I wanted to talk to you about though,' she said.

'Oh?' Nobody ever said they wanted to talk about something unless it was bad. If it was positive, they would say they had great news, or something brilliant to share, or have a big grin on their face. Lyn's smile was gentle and sympathetic. The kind that preceded a punch to the heart.

She held his hands, another step towards a dumping. 'I've always been heart first, and that's been one botch job after another. So, for once, I want to use my head.'

Rami gazed at her hands, scared to look at her face. 'Okay.'

'And please don't think it's a bad thing.' She lifted his head to look into his eyes. 'I just think we should press pause on moving in together.'

He swallowed the lump of rejection wedged in his throat. 'How come?'

'With me touring, other things might come of it, so I don't know where the best place for me to live is even going to be. And you have the baby coming and will want to be near wherever they and Miss Muppet end up. While big things are still up in the air, we shouldn't be diving in so quick.'

He wanted to convince her that they could still press forward, but he knew where this was headed. 'That's sensible.'

Lyn kissed him, but it felt loaded with pity. 'If it's meant to be, everything will work out, and if it's not, we've had a banging time, haven't we?'

'The bangingest.' He forced a smile.

'Right, let's munch.' She hopped off the counter and approached the oven.

Maybe she was just being sensible, and everything would be amazing. It scratched at him though. It seemed she was getting her excuses in early, serving him a shit sandwich on a fancy plate.

One thing was for certain. Lyn didn't *need* him.

Rami glanced towards his locked suitcase.

Banging on the door woke Rami up, but Lyn, snoring, didn't flinch.

Rami removed the cashmere-covered goose down duvet and rolled out of the queen-sized bed. He put his clothes on and glanced at Lyn. He descended the stairs, each step bringing him closer to the reality of his deed. He answered the door.

DI Amini stood there in all his grumpy glory. DS Opoku rubbed the hangover out of her eyes.

'Merry bloody Christmas,' DI Amini said. 'Where is she?'

'She's sleeping,' Rami replied.

DS Opoku nodded. 'You should probably wake her up.' The stale wine scent flowed from her breath and up Rami's nostrils.

Rami plodded up the stairs, fighting the urge to cry.

He touched Lyn's shoulder and woke her up. The last time he would probably touch it.

She smiled at him groggily. 'Morning gorgeous.'

He bit his lip. 'The police are here.'

She sat up angrily. 'Tossers, here to ruin Christmas. I'll give them a piece of it.' She pulled on her robe and stomped downstairs.

Rami took one final look at the room. The arguing began downstairs. He received a WhatsApp message from Mia, set to disappear in twenty-four hours:

Kill your fear. You can do it.

In a different context that would have read as Mia being encouraging, from a place of love. He trudged downstairs.

'Piss off!' Lyn yelled at DI Amini and DS Opoku, who held a piece of paper Rami assumed was a warrant. Behind the duo was what looked like a forensics team.

'We've had new information concerning the disappearance of...' He glanced to Rami, frozen behind Lyn. 'We'll go with Dale, as you two knew him.'

46

SOLD DOWN THE RIVER

MIA

Mia sat in the interrogation room, on the opposite side of the desk to DI Amini. He asked the questions, while DS Opoku consulted notes on a laptop.

Mia had expected to be nervous, but she had never felt calmer.

She ran through her story. 'I should've suspected it sooner. She's always had a temper, but I always thought it was for show, you know? I never thought she would act upon it.'

DI Amini nodded. 'So what happened to make you suspect she had something to do with Dale's disappearance?'

Mia swallowed. 'I went over to her house to apologise for everything. For being a shit friend. And to tell her I didn't care that she was dating Rami.'

DS Opoku lifted her head from the laptop. 'Just for the record, your husband, Rami?'

'Soon to be ex-husband,' Mia said.

DI Amini shuffled in his seat.

Creep.

Mia noticed Wilfred's blood under her fingernail and placed her hand on her thigh. 'After we had a drink, I went to the loo and noticed through a crack in the basement door that a motorcycle helmet was on the floor. Obviously, it could've been hers for riding on the motorcycle with him. It could've been his that he just left there, but I had this nagging feeling, because her behaviour had been so *off*, recently.'

'How do you mean?' DI Amini asked.

'Well, there were the erratic voice notes she sent me on the night of the party, which you've heard. Her punching me in the head when I told her to calm down. Her punching that woman – Trinity, was it?'

DI Amini nodded.

'And her saying that he was travelling from Bungay to her party, which proved to be false. On the surface, with that man's lying lifestyle, it was totally plausible that he'd tell her that. But, it could also be her trying to keep eyes looking elsewhere. Plus, she kept interfering with your investigation, even when I told her not to. She created a circus with her Instagram followers, and then involved that busybody, Jenny.'

DI Amini huffed. 'She's been warned.'

'Jenny's the worst.' Mia placed a hand on her heart. 'I've known Lyn for seventeen years, and I'd never seen her get physically violent, but it seemed to become a common theme. So, when she went to the kitchen to get another bottle of wine, I snuck into the basement and had a look, and that's when I saw the helmet was scratched and the stains that could have been blood.' Mia forced tears out.

'Do you need a tissue?' DI Amini asked.

Mia shook her head. 'Sorry. It's just hard to think of my Lyn in this way. I just want her to get the help she needs to get right in the head.'

DI Amini drank from his mug of tea. 'And your soon to be ex-husband. Do you think he has any involvement in this?'

'Rami?' She shook her head. 'He's not got it in him. She was probably using him to suggest things with her and Dale weren't that serious. Poor fool probably thought there was something real there.'

DI Amini turned to DS Opoku. 'Any other questions?'

DS Opoku thought a moment. 'Not from me, for now. Although I'm still struggling to connect Lyn to the motorcycle being spotted in Belaugh village.'

DI Amini waved a dismissive hand. 'We have the helmet. We have a motive, means, and it seems an opportunity. I think we should be able to wrap this up.'

Mia shrugged. 'Glad you two are on it.' She sniffed her fake tears in.

47

GOOD ENOUGH FOR ONE THING

RAMI

Rami sat in the back of the police car bawling his eyes out. He had come so close to telling the truth in the interrogation room, but he had to do what was right for the baby.

He gazed out at the empty Christmas Day Norwich streets as an officer drove him home.

To save himself and his baby, he had to sacrifice Lyn. He had wanted to tell her about Dale, but it was fanciful. He was banking on poor odds. He would need the investigation to keep failing, and for Lyn to want to be with him upon hearing the truth, and to be okay with Mia's part in it. It would give her the power forever. If she fell out of love with him, she could use it. It was too big a risk.

Lyn deserved so much better. He had lobbed a grenade at her wonderful future. Her only interaction with Lionel Richie would likely be when one of her cellmates screeched 'Dancing on the Ceiling' through the cellblock.

Rami deserved to die. Horribly.

He peered at a house in full Christmas swing. A loving

family inside. He doubted anyone in that household had built their happiness on a murder.

Nothing bound Lyn to him other than a whirlwind romance. Emotions changed and faded. People changed and lost interest. If Rami had learned anything, it was that love had a shelf-life. What didn't have a shelf-life and was stronger than love? Fear.

He and Mia were bound by fear. Fear of losing their child, and fear their secret would be discovered. Fear of prison. Mia needed him, and it was in that need and fear that he found hope. Hope that they had a future, because thanks to what they did, she would need him forever.

From fear, a reconciliation could grow.

He received another disappearing message from Mia:

I'm at home. You'd best have done it.

The police car pulled into the cul-de-sac and stopped outside Rami's house. 'Here you go,' the officer said. 'If we have any more questions we'll be in touch.'

'Thanks,' Rami replied. 'Merry Christmas,' he said with no enthusiasm.

He exited the car and dragged his feet towards his house. He stood at the door holding his key and cried.

He re-read Mia's messages. She was terrified, but there was no sense of a team in her messages, just her exerting control. He was desperate for a hug, but doubted she would give him one.

He gazed at Jenny's house with the alternative Christmas scene, where he had witnessed so much love. Every inch from the decorations, the personality, the honesty between Jenny and Iris and her desire to do good screamed love and life. Their child would grow up in the most beautiful atmosphere imaginable, because everything came from love.

He stared back at his door, bland, soulless, nothing. His body trembled. When it came to their struggling marriage, Mia had opted to kill it. When they hit Dale, he let her and fear push him to continue on death's path, killing any closure for those connected to him, disrupting their lives. Now Lyn, her life was dead, all so Rami and Mia had freedom to raise their baby in a house of death.

He pictured Lyn crying as the police took her away, all because of him. This person, who poured love into everything and was rewarded in her career, poisoned because he acted out of fear.

He recalled Jenny's words: "Can't live in fear, Rami. Follow where the feelings take you, or you'll live half a life."

There was a difference between caring for someone and being stuck with them. There would be no reconciliation with Mia. She would never love him, and he knew it. He was afraid to accept it, because he put so much into their marriage and was scared to start over. But, Jenny had shown him he could have genuine friendships, and Lyn had shown him he was loveable and could be an equal in a relationship. While the bonds were born out of a dark deed, they were real.

Mia chose fear at every juncture. It's why she ended up in the wrong marriage. Fear would dominate her until she learned to be happy in her own company.

This choice was the worst for the baby. Mia had called Rami a fantasist, and he was being one now, imagining them being a happy family, when the reality was a miserable atmosphere built on animosity and secrecy.

His heart raced and fear tried to make him put the key in his door, to continue on this path, but he slammed the key down on the doorstep and marched towards Jenny's house.

Every muscle trembled, as though waking up from the numbness. He buzzed Jenny's door.

She answered, exhausted and holding a poorly looking Ballula. 'Rami,' she said, surprised. 'Thought you were at Lyn's.'

The words were on the tip of his tongue.

'Rami!' He looked back to his house. Mia stood in the doorway.

Her warning look and voice rammed the confession back down his throat. He turned to Jenny while taking a few steps back. 'There was a change of plans, but I'm heading back there later. Just wanted to wish you a Merry Christmas.'

Jenny nodded. 'Not the merriest.' She kissed Ballula. 'Some fucker, and I won't be correcting that swear word, poisoned this little ballerina.'

Rami's face dropped. 'What?' He knew exactly who.

His marriage, Dale, Lyn, Ballula. This was a pattern that wouldn't end. Who was next? And would their child ever be more than a moment away from more death?

Rami turned to Mia, and on noticing his facial expression hers shifted to rage. She hurriedly put her shoes on.

Rami pleaded with Jenny. 'Watch the CCTV, please.'

'Rami!' Mia rushed towards them.

'What's going on?' Jenny asked, keeping an eye on Mia advancing.

'We killed Dale... and... and now we've framed Lyn, and Mia poisoned Ballula.' The catharsis was so intense he dropped to his knees and the tears flowed. He barely felt Mia smacking his head and pulling his hair.

She kicked him. 'You fucking worthless piece of shit! You've ruined my life.'

Rami smiled, his body lighter and his heart finally unclenching.

Through his blurry eyes, he noticed Jenny place Ballula down, step forward and punch Mia.

4 MONTHS LATER

48

FREE AS A BIRD

Rami sat on his bed in his cell in HMP Norwich, keeping to himself, as he had done every day. It was all so slow. He wasn't sure if being alone with his thoughts was a good thing. At least not this much.

He stared at the phone attached to the faded yellow wall, which somehow had more personality than the home he had shared with Mia. He had put Jenny and Lyn on his friends and family list, but neither had picked up his calls, and his apologetic messages didn't persuade them to call back. Being here made him realise he had no friends. He had spent so much time throwing everything into his decaying marriage that he had neglected his life. He wouldn't do that again.

He understood why Lyn wouldn't want to talk to him. When she learned the truth she released a scathing video, but it made Rami smile. It was another example of her putting her emotions into everything and feeling the world. He was glad he hadn't destroyed her approach to life and he knew she would be okay.

Part of him fantasised that when he got out in five years, maybe she would agree to meet with him.

What hurt the most with Jenny was how she looked at him when he was handcuffed. After opening up about her sister dying, Rami must have represented all the awfulness she had ever felt, and she probably saw the driver in him.

Rami lay back on his bed. Every day, during the most mundane activities, such as showering, or folding his socks, Mia's voice would attack him, reminding him of how he ruined her life.

He counted himself lucky. The day he confessed, Jenny pinned Mia down and called the police. When they arrived, they found Wilfred, barely alive, in his Tesla's boot. Another example of Mia choosing death. It was a miracle he survived.

Mia was fortunate to only get seven years in prison. Rather than dangerous driving, it was deemed careless, and her five years bumped up to seven because of the cover up and GBH to Wilfred. Her defence was that Wilfred was abusing her, and when his wife came forward and backed up Mia's claims that Wilfred was an abuser, the judges adopted a more sympathetic approach.

Rami didn't know where Wilfred was now, and he didn't care.

Had Rami made the right decision? He was sure he had, but then he would think of the baby, and how he wouldn't get to cut her little fingernails until he had served his sentence.

Mia was going to have eighteen months with her in the mother and baby unit in Peterborough, then the baby would live with Andrea. Rami would rather she were raised by a stray cat, but knowing he could get out earlier on good behaviour to save his daughter from Andrea's dreadful personality motivated him.

Noise outside his cell stirred him and he shot up on his bed. It was nothing. He was never sure if he would become a target for saying the wrong thing, or just for how he looked. But, this was where he deserved to be. It was better than living a lie, condemning more people, and raising a child in misery. The awful present was necessary to be able to start again and have a hopeful future.

Mia had likened him to a dog, calling him loyal, but he preferred to latch onto a different quality, that dogs were full of love. For the rest of his life, he would make decisions out of love, not fear.

Rami's mind drifted to Dale. His body had surfaced in The Wash, an inlet of the North Sea. Three more lovers had come forward, and Rami regularly replayed that night in the field.

He closed his eyes, tired of thinking.

Someone tapped on his cell door. 'Rami, need you to come with me.'

Startled, he wondered what he had done. Scenes from TV shows and films where an inmate was led to a beating played in his mind, but he shook those away. Love before fear.

'Rami. One more knock and I'm coming in,' the guard said more firmly.

Fear had love in a chokehold. 'I'm coming.' Rami stood, his hands sweaty. He opened the door.

The guard nodded, his expression giving nothing away. 'Warden wants to see you.'

Rami couldn't hide his confusion, but he didn't feel he had the right to ask what it was about. 'Okay...'

The guard handcuffed him and led him along the block. Rami received a few curious glances from other inmates. He tried to avoid eye contact in case it was taken as an act of aggression.

The guard opened a door for him. 'Don't know what you've done, but he seemed pretty pissed off.'

Rami's heartbeat shook his body. 'I —'

'I don't want to know,' the guard said and overtook him.

Rami desperately tried to stay positive, but fear washed over everything. He could barely see where he was going and his legs were weak.

The guard held another door open and Rami entered a larger room than expected.

The visitation room.

The guard laughed and Rami's heart could have burst.

'Alright, Rami Harami.' Jenny stood by a table, grinning, Ballula on top of it, and Iris sitting down holding their baby girl.

The guard unlocked Rami's handcuffs. 'Your reaction was priceless. I won't let you forget that for as long as you're here.'

'Cheers, Errol!' Jenny beamed. 'Well worth you fleecing me for twenty pounds.'

Rami laughed, almost hysterically. He rushed up to Jenny and let the tears flow in the warmth of a much needed hug.

GET A SHORT STORY FOR FREE

As a thank you for buying this book, I'm offering a free follow-up short story. It's a few months after the story ends, with Wilfred still pining for Mia, and her finding help from an unlikely source.

To get your copy, all you have to do is join my VIP Crew. It won't cost you a penny - ever.

Head on over to https://www.mark-boutros.com/vip-crew and claim your copy!

If you enjoyed what you read, please consider leaving a review. It really helps indie authors gain visibility. If you didn't enjoy it, then just pretend you didn't read it and move on.

I wish you well.

ACKNOWLEDGMENTS

I've loved writing this, and there are a lot of people who helped me to make it what it is.

Firstly, a massive thank you to Pixie Britton, the wonderful author of the *Kill or Cure* series. Her early feedback telling me my characters were awful helped me to make them just a touch less awful. And Lauren, legendary book blogger over at www.readersenjoyauthorsdreams.com who gave me tips on my murder research and some brilliant notes.

Gytha Lodge, author of greats such as *She Lies in Wait* and *Killer in the Family* among many more deserves a huge thanks. Her advice got me an agent and pulled me out of my own head. She is a superb writer and average friend. Read her books if you haven't.

I'd also like to thank Adam Croft, best-selling crime author. He, again, had nothing to do with this book, but needs thanks to feel like he has a purpose. So, thanks. You're the best.

My agent, Rachel, has been amazing throughout. Her enthusiasm and notes made this a much better book. I promise I will make you money one day.

I owe a lot to Tom McDowell, a writer I aspire to be like and a friend who has been there since the start of my TV writing days. His advice, encouragement, and terrible jokes keep me going.

Nicola Hodgson did an early edit of this and is one of the best editors around. Constructive, no ego, thorough, and someone I will always go back to.

Thanks also to David Price for proofreading it and helping

me to spot my sloppy errors. He's a brilliant writer who needs to put his creativity out there.

A huge thanks goes to you, the readers. Thanks for coming on this journey of love vs fear. I hope you enjoyed it. If you didn't, don't tell me, so I can assume you did. Ignorance is important to a writer, and it's too late to change anything.

Thanks to my parents. They're wonderfully supportive, kind, and never put pressure on me to get a proper job.

And my final, biggest thanks goes to my wife, Cinthia. Her support is everything and she even read drafts of this while pregnant, and then while we figured out what to do with a newborn. She and our daughter are amazing, and I want to be clear to those who have asked, no, Mia is not based on Cinthia. Cinthia is a good human. Mia sadly is based on many of my charming qualities.

That's it for now. If you wanted to be thanked but weren't, then consider this your thanks. Thank you. Well done. You earned it. Wear it on your soul.

ABOUT THE AUTHOR

Mark Boutros is an International Emmy nominated screenwriter, hybrid author, story consultant and writing teacher. He loves writing, even though it is often painful.

His work has been broadcast on the BBC, Sky One, Sky Arts and more. He has also written more books you can see below.

He also runs a writing consultancy and school with brilliant BAFTA nominated writer, director, author, and performer, Nat Luurtsema. You can see more at www.workingwriters.co.uk

When he's not writing or teaching, he's coming up with excuses to avoid socialising.

You can find more at www.mark-boutros.com/book-library

Mark's other books:

Karl's Kingdom Book 1: The Four Walls

Karl's Kingdom Book 2: Rise of the Deathbringer

Karl's Kingdom Book 3: In Memory Of...

The Craft of Character: How to Create Deep and Engaging Characters Your Audience Will Never Forget

Creative Writing Exercises: Improve Your Craft Through Play

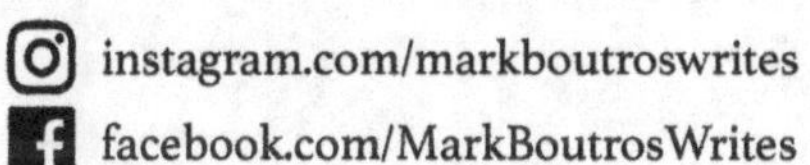

instagram.com/markboutroswrites

facebook.com/MarkBoutrosWrites